The moment the dragon's cry sounded was like a fragment separated from the line of Time itself. Kelida's heart crashed against her ribs, sickening her with the force of her fear. Cold to her bones, her muscles frozen, she watched helplessly as the dragon's wings cut back along its glittering, ebony sides, watched in horror as it touched the ground. The beast's massive head reared high. With terrifying speed, its forelegs shot out as though reaching for something.

Reaching for her! For Stormblade!

Stanach roared, a sound like a wordless curse, and dove between Kelida and the daggered claws. The dragon's huge wing caught him hard and swept him to the ground. He rolled instinctively, came up staggering, and fell to one knee. Fast as lightning's strike, the dragon's long neck whipped to the side. Teeth bared and dripping venom, eyes murderously bright, Darknight saw Stanach just as he fell.

"No!" Kelida screamed. "No! Stanach!"

The DRAGONLANCE® Saga

DragonLance Saga

H•E•R•O•E•S

Volume Two

STORMBLADE

Nancy Varian Berberick

Cover Art
LARRY ELMORE

DRAGONLANCE® *HEROES*

Volume Two

STORMBLADE

©Copyright 1988 TSR, Inc.
All Rights Reserved.

First Printing: August 1988
Printed in the United States of America.
Library of Congress Catalog Card Number: 88-50059

9 8

ISBN: 0-88038-596-9

TSR, Inc.
201 Sheridan Springs Road
Lake Geneva, WI
53147 U.S.A.

TSR Ltd.
120 Church End, Cherry Hinton
Cambridge CB1 3LB
United Kingdom

**To Cathy,
sometimes known as Rooney,
my *lyt chwaer*,
my little sister.**

As much as it may seem that we do, writers never work alone. After the last word of the tale is written, before the computer is set to transform all those ones and zeros into a story, one realizes that there are people to be thanked. It is the nicest part of writing a book.

Most especially I thank Bruce, my husband and my best friend, for teaching me how to read maps and elevations, for his understanding and for his patience during all those days and nights when he must surely have thought nothing remained of his wife but ten fingers madly dancing on a keyboard. I'm back! My brother, Mark Varian, gifted me with "Tyorl's Song." Thank you, Mark, it's been a delight working with you.

For long-distance aid and comfort through just about every phase of *Stormblade*, I thank Doug Clark. As Lavim Springtoe might say, you don't have to see a friend to know he's there. (The holders of phone company stocks in New Jersey and New Mexico likely thank us both!)

Too, I would like to thank Lt. Bill Wiggins of the Morris Police Academy in Morristown, New Jersey, for providing me with some very helpful publications about wildfires.

Aba"

Eastwall'

Solace

Que-sha

Xak Tsar

Haven

Qualinost

N

Pax Tharkas

Skull ap
(aman)

Thorbardin

of

•••••••••••••••••• Route of the refugees

— — — — — Route of Tyorl, Lavim and the rangers

Astinus's Note

Historians call the years between 348 AC and 352 AC the War of the Lance. The naming has become popular among the peoples of Krynn. It was a time when the gods strove against each other, Good against Evil. Takhisis lent her dragons, dark creatures of death and fire, to her war leaders and called those leaders Highlords. Paladine and Mishakal chose to dispense their aid and grace to those fighting against the dragonarmies and the Dark Queen in other ways. Paladine walked for a time with the kender Tasslehoff Burrfoot and his companions. He was known to them as Fizban. Mishakal gave her learning and lore to one of the kender's companions, a Plainswoman who understood the meaning of faith, and who restored that faith to many in Krynn.

But these are the larger events of that war. Others are referred to in history only by a line.

One such line intrigues many who study history. It is found in the record of the year 348 AC: "Nordmaar falls to the dragonarmy. The dwarves in Thorbardin forge a Kingsword and call it Stormblade."

There is only one other line that references the Kingsword, and it appears two years later: "Lord Verminaard's slaves escape from his mines at Pax Tharkas, aided by a group of companions, among whom are the kender Tasslehoff Burrfoot and the mage Fizban. Dwarven Kingsword located."

Between those two lines, and beyond them, lies a tale that may explain why, after carefully refraining from offering aid to those fighting against the Dark Queen, the dwarves of Thorbardin at last entered the War of the Lance.

How much of the tale is true history and how much embroidered legend, I am yet considering. Though much of it, I will say, has the ring of truth. For the rest, and that is only little, I offer this: In Thorbardin the dwarves say that legend is truth condensed, so that everyone—even a gully dwarf—can understand it.

PROLOGUE

As the bard hears, faint but clear, the elusive melody and secret harmonies of the song he was given his voice to sing, as the storyteller knows, deep within his bones, the words and silences of the tale he was born to tell, so the dwarf Isarn Hammerfell knew that Stormblade was the reason he had come to swordcrafting. The sword would be his masterblade and stood, almost seen, behind every blade he made, waiting patiently for its birth.

It waited for Isarn Hammerfell to consider himself worthy.

When this blade was forged, when it came from the fires and the cooling oils, to perfect balance and cold blue beauty, Isarn would offer it to his thane, to Hornfel of the Hylar.

If Hornfel judged it good, he would honor the mastersmith, as thanes have done for generations, by displaying the sword with masterblades generations old.

The blade once hung, Isarn would make no other sword. The forge at which he'd labored for so many years would become the forge of his apprentice and young kinsman, Stanach Hammerfell. Isarn would lay down his hammer, his tongs, all the tools which he had known and loved for so many years, and gently finish his days in honor.

Because the forging of this blade would be his finest work, the embodiment of his vision and matchless skill, Isarn used none but the purest steel, newly fired from hard, black wrought iron created by his own hand.

He went to the mines himself, though he was a mastersmith and need not have chosen his own ore. He knew, and none knew better, the look of perfect ore, the feel of it, the bitter smell of it. He stalked the dark, lantern-lit iron mines searching the broad veins for the ore he knew would be the purest. There it was mined under his supervision.

None saw him for many days after he returned to his smithy at Thorbardin. Deep within the mountain's heart he waited, designing Stormblade. Never once did he take ink to parchment, for the design was composed in his heart and in his soul. He knew what the sword would look like. His hands knew how it would feel. His ears already heard the song of hammer and anvil, fire and steam.

The ore was brought to him. All that remained was to find the right jewels for the sword's decoration. The hilting of the sword would be the task of Isarn's apprentice Stanach Hammerfell. It was the traditional sign of the master's trust in the one who would follow.

There are not only weapons crafters in Thorbardin, but jewelers, goldsmiths, and silversmiths as well. Isarn went among his companions, the masters of those crafts. From the master of the gemsmiths he received five flawless sapphires. Four were the color of the sky at twilight, and the fifth was the pure, deep blue of midnight and deeply starred. These would decorate the blade's grip. The finest gold was found for the blade's hilt, and a lustrous silver to chase it.

The sword conceived, it was now ready to be born. Isarn

Hammerfell, assisted by only his apprentice, began to create his masterwork.

Isarn and Stanach built the furnace fire themselves. They filled the two troughs, one for the water to cool the wrought iron, one for the oil to cool the steel. Stanach pumped the bellows with the slow, steady rhythm Isarn had taught him. Coaxing the fire, Stanach watched the orange light slide up the smooth stone walls of the forge. This was a task he had not been required to perform since the first, fumbling days of his apprenticeship. How familiar this task was now. Yet, how different!

None but he and his master Isarn would see Stormblade born, and Stanach knew that he would never again feel the magic of crafting so intensely until, years from now, he gave life to the unimaginable vision of his own masterblade.

Steel is made from the elements of the world. Dug first as ore, it is shaped through the agencies of fire and water into wrought iron. Stanach watched now as Isarn made the thick, dark iron. Each of his master's moves was careful and considered. Isarn, who had a thousand times before made his iron with the unthinking skill of one whose hands move almost without will, took each step of the making as carefully now as any apprentice first permitted to approach a forge.

Stanach watched his master as though seeing him perform the task for the first time. I will remember this, he thought. The forge fire pulled the sweat from him. He wiped his face with the back of his hand, his eyes on Isarn. Always, I will remember this.

And always, he thought as the ore came from the forge, he would remember the look in Isarn's eyes. It was the look of one who loved and saw nothing but the thing he loved.

They were silent while the iron cooled. Nothing needed to be said. Stanach had no questions. Isarn had nothing but the bond between his soul and the elements. When the iron was finally cool and hard, a rough black mass, Isarn placed it in a clay container, itself earthborn and still remembering the kiss of flame.

Stanach lifted the vessel, heavy with charcoal dust and iron, and placed it in the furnace exactly where his master directed. Sweat ran ceaselessly down his face now, soaking his thick black beard. His hair clung to his neck. He had long ago abandoned his loose forgeman's shirt for a leather apron. His thickly muscled arms gleamed with a golden reflection of flame.

The heat of the furnace sought to mimic that of the fires said to burn ceaselessly in Krynn's heart. In this terrible heat the charcoal dust combined with the surface of the wrought iron to create a hard, gleaming sheath: steel.

Stanach dragged a bucket of water from the farthest corner of the forge. Cool hours before, the water was now warm, as though it had been lying in the sun. He ladled a drink for Isarn, and then another for himself. In their parched throats it tasted like wine.

Stanach drew another ladle from the bucket and poured it over his head. It ran hot down his neck and back, and he felt suddenly sad. For the first time since they'd come into the forge, Stanach remembered that when Stormblade was finally more than a vision, he and Isarn would no longer work side by side.

Isarn, his master and his kinsman, was also his friend. A shadow of loneliness, like a cloud racing across the moons, touched Stanach's heart. He placed the empty bucket outside the smithy for the forge-boy to refill, then returned to the fire and the leaping shadows. He watched the old dwarf patiently waiting for the iron to become steel, faithfully waiting for the miracle Reorx had worked for his children since the first dwarven smith had set up a forge.

It is a miracle, Stanach thought. A bonding and a binding. A bond with the gods, a binding of elements. It was the first lesson Isarn had taught him. Trust the gods; know the elements; trust your skill. The crafting of the simplest blade is nothing less than worship. This worship Isarn had been perfecting for all his life.

The steel came thick from the fire, crimson as the red moon, glowing like the sun. Stanach, his eyes squinted tightly against the wild heat, brought the stock to the anvil. Isarn, his large hands gentle now, lifted the hammer. He was ready to begin the shaping of Stormblade.

Steel is not carved the way wood is, but drawn by being

placed upon the anvil and hammered until it has reached the proper length and taper. Though he had made countless swords before this one, though hammer and hand were one, each of Isarn's strokes was prudent. Every raise and drop of the hammer was a considered one. Yet, the considering was done quickly, based upon both knowledge and instinct. The steel could not be allowed to cool to the point where it was no longer malleable.

The hammer's anthem rang through Isarn's smithy, a joyous clamor which set Stanach's heart soaring. It was the Song of the Masterblade he heard, and he knew that Isarn's hammer and anvil had never sung like this before. They would not sing like this again until Stanach himself forged another masterblade.

There were no words to the song but those the master and apprentice heard in their souls. The song celebrated a blade which was long and slim, and Stanach knew by the look of the weapon alone that it would balance perfectly in Isarn's hand. The master shaped it with file and rasp, and the filings fell to the stone floor of his forge like silver dust.

Stanach came to think of the blade as a shaft of argent starlight.

The blade formed, it must now be returned to the fire again to be tempered. "This," Isarn Hammerfell told his apprentice, "is the blade's last journey into the fire, its last dance among the flames."

Stanach had heard the words before—so many times! Now, as he watched Isarn plunge the blade into the tempering fire, he heard them as if they were fresh and new.

Isarn performed the functions of this last heating and final quenching as carefully as all the functions before. Stanach had built the fire to exactly the right temperature, and now he checked the oil for proper coolness. Satisfied, he looked to his master and the sword.

In this final heating the blade was not a shaft of starlight, but a crimson extension of the sun, a blood-red arm of fire.

When Isarn finally plunged the blade into the oil, Stanach watched the sun-glow cool and fade. Red iron became silver steel, pure as snow, strong as the mountain itself. Isarn, his lungs filled with bitter steam, sweat glistening on his face and thick forgeman's arms, gently withdrew Stormblade from the trough.

He wiped the shimmering oil from the blade with a soft cloth, his strokes gentle caresses, and laid the sword upon the face of his anvil the way one would lay a newly born babe upon the breast of its mother.

Stanach watched the play of the forge fire's reflection in the pure steel, watched the orange light slide along the keen edge of the blade. Fascinated, his heart thudding hard against the cage of his ribs, he stepped between the fire and the anvil.

His shadow did not banish the light from the steel.

Stormblade, perfect in every detail, bore a heart of fire. That heart ran in a thin streak of crimson light within the cooling steel itself, and no shadow could dim it.

Eyes wide, old, gnarled hand shaking as though palsied, Isarn reached for the blade, then drew back his hand as though he could not, or would not, touch the steel.

"Do you see it?" he whispered. "Oh, lad, do you see it?"

Stanach had no words. He nodded dumbly and took a half step back from the steel. In that moment, as his eyes filled with the beauty of the as yet unhilted blade, the words of a fragment of poetry so ancient, so often quoted, and so little believed that it had become the street chant of children, whispered in his heart.

> Mountain dwarves know. These things a high
> king make:
> A Kingsword heart-touched by Reorx the Father.
> A soul formed to wisdom in the crucible of strife.
> The hammer which legendary Kharas keeps in
> the mists.

A Kingsword to wield, made for the king, carried by him through all the days of his reign, and finally buried with him. A soul made wise by the fires of strife: the flames of battle, aye, and experience and judgements made, decisions lived by. The Hammer of Kharas, long hidden and believed to be more than a myth by fewer dwarves each generation.

Yet, myth or truth, no bid for the high kingship of the mountain dwarves had been made successfully since the

Hammer of Kharas had been lost.

Stanach shivered, suddenly cold despite the sweat trickling down the sides of his face. He closed his eyes, breathed once deeply to still the shivering, and looked at the sword again.

The steel's crimson streak pulsed gently, as though it were indeed a heart touched by the hand of Reorx and brought to life. As he watched it, Stanach's own heart began to take on that newly born beat and rhythm.

Legend told that only a Kingsword breathed like that.

No Kingsword had been forged in Thorbardin in three hundred years. And yet now—

Stanach shook his head.

He knew the legends. What dwarf did not? There had been a line of high kings once. The last, Duncan, had reigned during the Dwarfgate Wars three hundred years ago. He'd had a champion and friend, "legendary Kharas" of the poem. It was told that Kharas, whose name meant "knight" in Solamnic, had crafted a war hammer at Reorx's forge. It was told that none fought with more skill than Kharas during the bloody and bitter time after the Cataclysm, when the invading armies of humans and hill dwarves led by the mysterious mage Fistandantilus had sought admittance to the mountain kingdoms and access to what they imagined were the riches of Pax Tharkas and Thorbardin.

Thorbardin had been successfully defended from the attackers, but more than Pax Tharkas had been lost. Dwarf had warred against dwarf. This, the greatest of all sins, enraged Reorx. In his fury, the god struck with the same hammer he once used to forge the world; the one, legend said, that had helped make Kharas's war hammer. He was not pleased to simply destroy the world that so filled him with anger. He unmade it.

In that unmaking, the face of the world, twisted and torn as it was by the Cataclysm, was changed yet again. The Plains of Dergoth became a seeping and haunted marsh, known now as the Plains of Death. When the god's hammer struck Zhaman, which had once stood tall and proud, the fortress of the mages collapsed and fell in upon itself, unleashing a great scorching storm of sand and stone.

It has been said that the ruins of that place, when first Kharas saw them, were shaped in the image of a huge and grinning skull. Now called Skullcap, it is a fitting grave-marker for the thousand who were slain as they killed their kin.

But the face of the world was not the only thing changed. Soon after the war, Duncan died. His sons greedily fought for the high king's throne before Duncan had even been buried. Kharas, grieving for his friend and king, watched their cynical fight for power and decided that none of them would rule.

He entombed Duncan in the magnificent burial tower now known as Duncan's Tomb. A place of mourning and magic, it hung magically suspended above the ancient dwarven burial place called the Valley of the Thanes.

He then hid his war hammer with the aid of magic and Reorx himself, and decreed that no dwarf would rule as high king in Thorbarin without it.

Legend or truth, Stanach reminded himself, no dwarf had been crowned high king since. The histories were filled with tales of dwarven suffering during times when a high king was needed to rule the people. Times like these, he thought, when rumors of war seeped in from the Outlands, accompanied by reports of dragons and the Dark Queen's rising.

Stanach wiped cold sweat from his forehead with a shaking hand. None could rule without the hammer, and none could rule without a Kingsword. Through the years, many had tried to have such a sword forged, some because they knew that it would be enough to rule Thorbardin as king regent, some because they hoped it would point the way to the Hammer of Kharas. Though these swords had been beautiful works of craftsmanship, none had ever been a Kingsword. Reorx had never touched the blades, never gave them the crimson heart of red-glowing steel. . . . Until now.

It was said among the smiths that the voice of every dwarven hammer striking an anvil's plate would be recalled for all time in Anvil's Echo, the huge, dwarf-built cavern connecting Northgate to the city of Thorbardin. If the legends were true, Stanach thought, the ringing of Isarn's hammer must be sounding the keynote and shaping the echoes of centuries of work into an eternal song in Anvil's Echo.

He shivered again. When he looked away from the god-touched steel, he saw that Isarn was weeping. He had crafted a Kingsword for his thane, for Hornfel of the Hylar.

CHAPTER 1

*Though in times past, in the years before the Cata-*clysm, it had been a city exactly like every other dwarven-built city. Thorbardin, the last of the once-great dwarven kingdoms, was now unique in Krynn. Built inside the mountain, in a cavern spanning twenty-two miles from north to south, fourteen from east to west, Thorbardin was both a great city and an almost unbreechable fortress. Southgate, with its fortifications and several secondary lines of defense, guarded the city at one end. The ruins of Northgate, destroyed during the Cataclysm and now only a slim, five-foot ledge above a valley one thousand feet below, warded the way to Thorbardin from the Plains of Death.

Here the mountain dwarves had lived for centuries

among their smithies and taverns, temples, shops and homes, and even parks and gardens. They grew their crops in the farming warrens deep below even the city itself, having abandoned the fields outside Southgate long ago, after the Dwarfgate Wars. Their light came from crystal shafts, sunk deep in the cavern's walls and ceiling, which guided the sun's light into their city and farms from the outside.

Though Thorbardin itself was called a city, it was composed of six smaller ones, one for each of the six thanedoms, or realms, which lay within the mountain. All but one bordered the edges of the dwarf-made body of water called the Urkhan Sea.

The sixth, and most beautiful, was the Life Tree of the Hylar. Shaped like a stalactite, it rose from the sea itself in twenty-eight levels. In this central city, approachable only by boat, the business of government was conducted. The council of Thanes sat there, presided over by its nominal leader, Hornfel. It was the only ruling body Thorbardin had possessed for three hundred years.

The politics and policies of six dwarven realms were woven there, tangled there, and sometimes fought for there with all the ferocity of a fierce and independent people. The dwarves watched vigilantly over their rights and freedoms and would not suffer them to be encroached upon.

Thorbardin was the ancient home of the mountain dwarves. All else, even their own lands outside the moutain, were the Outlands.

There were places below the great city of Thorbardin where none but the *derro* Theiwar mages went. These were the Deep Warrens, and they were far below even the dungeons and the farming warrens, beyond the wide, high delved cavern that cradled the city in the mountain's heart.

Magic was done in these places, and all of it was black.

Deep in the mysterious realms of the Theiwar lay the Chamber of the Black Moon. Torchlight, like transparent blood, splashed across the walls of the high-ceilinged cavern and vanished into the heights. Though upon first view the place seemed to be a wholly natural and virtually untouched cavern, the chamber was in truth the result of many years of skilled labor.

On the walls were gilded metal cressets shaped like tightly woven baskets. These cressets fit neatly into stone niches carved from the living rock of the walls. The walls themselves were smooth, the stone polished to display its natural colors in all their striated variety.

The floor at first appeared to be jagged stone. Upon closer inspection, it proved to be as smooth as polished wood. A thick layer of glass overlaid the contours of the stone. Poured as liquid fire from a vat, guided by the arts of magic, it had not settled in the depressions made by the natural rock, but formed as a clear, thick sheet an inch above the floor's highest point.

Despite the use of four centuries, no place could be found where the glass floor was damaged. It was said that the glass would never scratch, not even under the tip of the hardest diamond.

In the center of the floor, crafted by the same magic art, was a simple, round dais of solid black marble. Upon the dais, as though suspended in air, rested a thick-legged clear glass table. Behind that table was a deep seated chair, dressed in soft black velvet.

It was here that Realgar, thane of the Theiwar, studied his ancient magical tomes, worked his spells, and plotted murders.

This night, while Stanach and his master watched a crimson heart of fire beat in a sword made for Hornfel, Realgar did not plan a murder.

This night he planned a theft. The murder, he thought, smiling, would come later, when history would call Hornfel's death a traitor's execution.

A Kingsword had been forged for the Hylar.

The informer had used no such word as 'Kingsword.' He didn't seem to know what the strangely marked blade really was. He had simply been repeating tavern gossip carried by the bucket-lad who served at Isarn's forge.

"According to the lad, the sword was strangely marked," the informer said. "Red-scarred steel. Not the perfect blue-silver that usually comes from the master's forge."

No, Realgar thought now. Not the perfect blue-silver, but a steel blade with a heart of fire, as the legendary Duncan's was said to have.

But was this a Kingsword, made to invest a high king and then be entombed with him when he died? No dwarven smith had forged a Kingsword since Duncan's had been buried with him three hundred years before; since Kharas, Duncan's champion, had hidden his god-forged hammer and rendered the dwarves kingless until it could be found again.

But the gods were abroad now, ranging in the worldly plane, and would manifest their strivings, Good against Evil, in the war some said would soon rage across Krynn. Dragons, dark creatures of Takhisis, had been seen on the mountain and coursing the night sky. Realgar bared his teeth in a slow smile. This night a god may well have visited Thorbardin.

Had Reorx touched Isarn's forge fire? Had he transformed simple steel into a Kingsword?

Isarn must have thought so. Though the master himself had gone from the smithy in exhaustion to rest, he left his apprentice to hilt the blade and, according to the bucket-lad, charged the apprentice to stay all night with the sword.

If it were a Kingsword, Isarn Hammerfell would not leave it unattended, but would set a guard. Realgar's hand fisted. Aye, guard it well through the night and present it to their thane in the morning, newly forged and hilted. A mark of the god's favor.

A Kingsword would not make Hornfel high king. Nothing but the Hammer of Kharas would do that, and even Hornfel could not believe that the hammer could be found now. Too long lost, too secretly hidden, the hammer would never again invest a dwarven high king.

But a Kingsword, gleaming with the forge's light, could invest a king regent, and the thane invested would be Hornfel.

Many on the Council of Thanes would welcome Hornfel's investiture. If any could tame the quarrelsome council, it was the Hylar. True, even he would not be able to tame them often. Yet, even now, with only a hereditary right to head the council and no more rank than the other five thanes, he did so more frequently than any other. Far too often the Council of Thanes moved as Hornfel wished them to move. As king regent, Hornfel would rule the council. Though none would call him high king, he would rule Thorbardin.

Realgar hissed a curse. The desire for power had always sung in him, like the wash and sigh of his own blood through his veins. He had advanced to the thaneship of the Theiwar not by hereditary means, but along a wide path cut by murder, deceit, and dark magic. He hated the Hylar, son of ancient high kings, as naturally as he loathed sunlight.

Slowly, Realgar unclenched his fist. He moved his hand in a graceful gesture of magic and whispered the words of a summoning spell. A clutch of shadows pooled before the glass dais, became thicker, and took on a smoky substance.

"Aye, Thane," a voice whispered in the moment before the shadows had fully become form.

Realgar did not speak until the thief knelt before him, When he did, he spoke only briefly, gave the thief his charge, and dismissed him. Alone again, he turned to the planning of Hornfel's death.

Isarn might think it a sign of his god's favor that a Kingsword had been created at his forge. Realgar, who worshipped a dark and evil goddess, felt Takhisis's hand moving in the currents of the night. By morning, he would have the Kingsword and be king regent of the six dwarven realms.

Skarn was Realgar's thief, but not Realgar's man. He wiped the blood from his hands, thought about killing the apprentice where he lay unconscious on the stone floor of the smithy, and then saw the sword. Stanach was forgotten.

Newly hilted, straight and slim, its blade was the color of Solinari itself. The steel's heart was streaked with the sun's red light. It lay on the anvil's face where it had been when Stanach, bending over it to smooth some final work, had fallen to a blow from the hilt of Skarn's dagger.

Skarn's plan came fully formed. Realgar owed him a debt of vengeance. 'Master,' he called the thane, but had never thought of him as such. Skarn thought of him always as the one who had caused the death of his son.

A carelessness with magic, Realgar had said. It was no

apology, barely an explanation for why Tourm had died.

Though the *derro* were a race inclined to the dark arts, Realgar did not permit mages about him. He was too jealous of his own power. He did, from time to time, train as assistants those talented enough to learn the skills for simple spells. Magelings, he called them, and spoke the word always with a proud sneer.

Tourm had been one of these. He could have been more. With the proper training he could have gone into the Outlands, traveled to the Tower of High Sorcery, and taken his Test with the masters of the Black Robes. He would have passed that Test. The fire of magic had burned in his soul, the desire to dance with its flame was the thing by which his life had been ruled.

And Realgar had known that. He must have sensed the potential of Tourm's power. Sensing that potential, he recognized a threat. He'd asked Tourm—no, commanded him—to work a spell he knew his mageling had no skill to control. Realgar had watched him die screaming, while formless things of darkness and shadow, born in the Abyss, gnawed the flesh from his bones and tore the soul from his body. Tourm had worked the spell, it was true, but worked it at Realgar's command.

Tourm's was a death Skarn had been waiting many years to avenge. Now he'd found the path to vengeance.

Skarn lifted the sword from the anvil and smiled coldly. Realgar wanted this sword. The thief didn't know why, and he didn't care. He only knew that when the thane had spoken his orders, his desire for the blade lay naked in his eyes. More than desire, Skarn thought now. Realgar needed that sword.

There were secret ways out of Thorbardin, shadowed paths across the Outlands that even the border patrols didn't know. Skarn knew them. He left Stanach lying where he'd fallen. By the time Realgar knew that the Kingsword was not coming to him, Skarn was gone from Thorbardin.

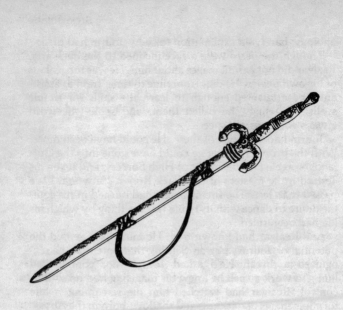

CHAPTER 2

A child woke, whimpering and sobbing, from the same nightmare that haunted most of the eight hundred humans trying to find peace in sleep: the nightmare of slavery. The stars, dancing silver lights in the black vault of the sky, watched as a woman rose wearily and lurched, still half asleep, toward the child. She was not the youngster's mother. She was a woman who had seen her own child die that same morning. In the two days since these people, once slaves in the mines of Pax Tharkas, had fled the mountains, five men, sick and old, and two children had died.

So far, Tanis Half-Elven thought. He stared into the flames of the dying campfire and toed a bundle of kindling closer. He was tired to his bones. Eight hundred people went only slowly through the narrow mountain passes between

Pax Tharkas and the South Road.

And the South Road was not a route to freedom. It was only a place to start.

A footstep, soft as the woman's whisper of comfort to the whimpering child, sounded behind Tanis. He turned, dropping his hand to his short sword, and then smiled an apology when he saw who stood behind him.

"Goldmoon," he whispered. "I've been wondering where you were."

She was lovely, the Plainswoman, and though her face was pale and lined with the same exhaustion Tanis felt, she radiated a kind of calm peace that touched the half-elf like a soothing hand. "I was looking for Tasslehoff."

"Find him?"

Goldmoon smiled. "No. Of course not. It was a good excuse to walk into the hills for a while."

"I wouldn't think anyone would be looking for an excuse to do what we've been doing for two days and will likely be doing for too many more."

She dropped gracefully to a seat beside Tanis. "Sometimes walking alone is what I need to help me think. Tanis, where are we going to take these people?"

Where, indeed. Tanis cocked his head. "There aren't many choices. Verminaard will have his draconians all over this mountain behind us soon—if he doesn't now. Tas blocked the gate well enough, but it won't hold. We've got to get these people out of here soon. We can't go back now. We have to go ahead."

"To where?"

"There's only one place that would hold them, Goldmoon, only one place that is anything like safe now."

"Thorbardin." Goldmoon shook her head. "The dwarves haven't taken any interest in the war these three years, though its been tearing Krynn to pieces. What makes you think they'll admit eight hundred refugees to Thorbardin now?"

Tanis tossed the kindling onto the fire and watched the flames lick the twigs and bark. "We'll reason with them."

"It's been tried."

"We'll plead."

Goldmoon sighed. "They hear no pleas, Tanis."

Tanis, his green eyes glittering dangerously, smiled with no humor. "Then we'll make them hear."

Eight hundred voices, he thought, cannot be ignored.

High on the eagle-haunted slopes outside Thorbardin, there was a series of narrow ledges which, though they could not be seen from the deep clefts and valleys far below, have been known to the dwarves for as long as Thorbardin has stood. It was impossible to climb to the ledges from the valley. The mountains forbade it. But from within the dwarven fortress there is a way to reach the ledges. Narrow paths led up from the Southgate wall, paths that only a mountain goat or a dwarf born in Thorbardin would use. A wild windsong howls along those paths. Summer or winter, the air is cold there and thin. Stanach Hammerfell always thought of these ledges as his own.

He climbed to them now, a filled flask tied to his belt. All day the forge fires had dragged sweat from him like blood; the steam of the cooling troughs sucked at his lungs until he wondered if he would ever breathe again. He needed the peace of the heights now; he needed a place to think.

Stanach propped his back against the eternal strength of the mountain stone. The first sip of the potent dwarven spirits warmed his belly. Far down in the valley, night settled to fill the deeps and clefts, covering the gold and brown leaf-strewn slopes with cold black velvet.

Only an hour ago, Stanach had learned that Stormblade had been found in the Outlands beyond Thorbardin. From the lands where dragons cut the sky on wide leather wings and armies fought while gods strove against each other, whispering rumor came of a young ranger who carried a sapphire-hilted sword. Two years after its theft the Kingsword was found, and Hornfel even now prepared to send men to fetch it home. It would be no easy thing. Hornfel feared that the Theiwar Realgar had also heard the rumor. The Hylar's men would have to be swift and on their guards. A Kingsword was something Realgar would kill to have.

There was never a time when Stanach looked into the

flames of his forge and did not remember the night
Stormblade had been born of ore, fire, and water. There
was never a time when he forgot that on the night the
Kingsword was born, it was stolen. That night, Isarn—his
master, his kinsman, and his friend—began a slow descent
into grief and madness. Stanach did not care about the danger. He wanted to bring Stormblade home.

He would be going, if going he were, with his kinsman
Kyan Red-axe. A border patroller, no one knew the Outlands as well as Kyan did. Or so Kyan said, and Stanach, for
the most part, believed him. Though he and Stanach were
of an age, Kyan had always seemed older. It was his experience, his look of being always on guard for dangers that
Stanach could only imagine, and the look of being able to
handle those dangers with ease, that made him so. Stanach
who never ventured outside Thorbardin, but stayed close to
his home and family, as most dwarves did, would willingly
place his life and safety in Kyan's hands.

Were Kyan not safety enough, Hornfel was sending the
mage Piper to accompany him. What, Stanach thought,
could possibly happen that Piper couldn't take care of? He'd
known the golden-haired human for all of the three years
that Piper had been at Thorbardin. Jordy, his name was,
though all in Thorbardin called him Piper. Named so by the
dwarven children for all the glad singing of his flute, lanky
Piper and Stanach were close friends. The mage's carefree
good spirits lightened the dark brooding that had become
Stanach's nature.

The best times were spent in the taverns of Thorbardin,
killing time and kegs of ale. The best times got better when
Kyan, in from the borders, joined them, trying to pass off
one outrageous story after another as Reorx's own truth.

Stanach wanted badly to accompany them. But he needed to find a way to convince Hornfel that he should be with
those sent to retrieve the sword.

He did not consider this easily. The thought of leaving the
mountain and separating himself from the pattern of well-
ordered days frightened him.

A son of wealthy Clan Hammerfell, his future was
assured. He was a fine craftsman in a respected trade. His

father had lately begun to speak of marriage contracts, and his mother's dinner conversation was now laced with references to one dwarf maid or another, subtle recommendations which both amused Stanach and intrigued him. Seventy-five was not a great many years for a dwarf to have attained. Stanach was young yet by his people's reckoning and not in any great hurry to take a wife and begin his family. But a family, too, is wealth and riches of a kind. That wealth cannot be inherited from a father's coffers.

"You earn it with trust," his mother had told him. "It's not a matter of filling cradles and watching children grow. It's a matter of giving the woman you wed, the children you sire, the friends you find, reasons to trust you. Then, though you go dressed in rags, you are wealthy."

Stanach rested his forehead on his drawn up knees. He was poorer than any ragged gully dwarf. He was a trust-breaker.

I should have guarded the sword better!

Aye, but he hadn't. The Kingsword had been stolen. Though Isarn did not blame his apprentice, there was no need to; Stanach blamed himself and paid the guilt-price every time he saw a forge fire.

A warrior Hornfel would send, and a mage. What need would there be to send the apprentice who had lost the sword in the first place?

Then Stanach smiled. His cousin Kyan Red-axe was a fine warrior; Piper, a powerful mage. But neither of the two had seen the sword, neither would know it but from its description. Stanach saw it every night in his sleep.

He raised his eyes to the jeweled sky, to the red star gleaming above the mountain's highest peak. Legend said this star was the gleam of Reorx's forge.

"I know I should have guarded it better," he told the god. "Father, if you give the wit-craft to convince Hornfel to allow me to accompany Kyan and Piper, I swear by Stormblade itself that I will ward it well and carry it home."

His prayer made, Stanach rose from the ledge and, framing the words of his request to the thane, returned to Thorbardin. Trust-breaker, he called himself. He couldn't live with the name any longer. With Reorx's help, he would find a way to go with his cousin and Piper into the Outlands and bring Stormblade home.

CHAPTER 3

Blood soaked the dust of the road. Four dwarves lay dead, and the only things moving were the wind plucking with cool fingers at their hair and beards, and a crow screaming in the hard blue sky.

Stanach had no thought for three of the dwarves but to be glad that they were dead. The fourth was Kyan Red-axe.

Stanach closed his eyes and bowed his head. Even the finest, most skilled warrior cannot always defend himself from a coward's attack. His kinsman Kyan Red-axe was dead of a crossbow bolt in the back.

A cairn, Stanach thought. He looked up at the crow. We have to build a cairn. For a dwarf to die, with no cairn or tomb to shelter his body was a traitor's death. Kyan Red-axe did not deserve that. Stanach's belly twisted sickly when he realized that this might be his kinsman's fate.

The breeze, light and cool, freshened and carried the fading scent of sulphur. Smoke, thick and rolling only a few moments before, thinned to curling tendrils now that the magic fire was gone. Stanach turned and looked for the mage. He saw him a little way off to the side of the road, leaning against the broad trunk of an oak. His red robes were the color of Kyan's blood.

Blood spilled for Stormblade.

"Piper, we can't leave him here."

Piper shook his head. "We can't stay. They'll be back. They're here for a reason, my friend. The only place this road goes to is Long Ridge or the sea. Realgar's men jumped us the minute we came out of the transport spell. They were waiting for us. We're in trouble, Stanach."

Stanach, his hand on Kyan's chest as though still reaching for a sign of life, looked closely at the mage. Like most humans, Piper seemed taller than anyone needed to be. His face white and drawn, his blue eyes dim. The mage was spent. He sweated in the cold air, and the sweat plastered his sun colored hair to his face and neck.

Piper had loosed two fire-spells, long arms of flame, the instant he and the two dwarves had come out of the transport spell. Realgar's guards had been waiting. Now, drained by the exertions of the transport and the fire spells, the mage would be no threat to anyone for at least a few hours, and certainly not to the four Theiwar guards still lurking somewhere nearby.

Stanach looked around. The dark line of the forest lay in the shadows to his right. Barren ground rose to stony hills on his left. Half as high as the trees, a tumbled pile of stone climbed to the sky at the brink of the woods.

The crow's hoarse cry seemed closer now.

Piper pushed away from the oak, passed through the shadows, and stood behind Stanach. "We have to leave him, my friend. I'm sorry. But we don't dare stay here any longer."

Stanach closed his eyes again. Kyan had a war-cry like summer thunder, like a madman's howl. He had a strong right arm and a warrior's heart, fierce and generous. He would have no eulogy and not even a hastily built cairn. But he would be remembered.

Stanach got slowly to his feet. He looked up at the sky. The sun had started its long slide down to the west and soon would be setting. He didn't want to be caught in the night. Theiwar did their best work in the dark.

"Piper, how far to Long Ridge?"

The mage shrugged. "Eight, maybe ten miles through the forest. Five by the road."

Stanach grunted. He picked up his sword, wet with Theiwar blood, and cleaned it as best he could on the grass by the roadside. He slid it into the scabbard across his back and slung his pack over his shoulder. "We'd better go. If that's an occupied town as you say, I don't imagine they'll be letting strangers in after dark, eh?"

"Likely not. And—" Piper stopped suddenly and pointed to the crest of the closest hill.

Dark as wolves, the four Theiwar, only recently fled, had returned. The shortest among them pointed down toward the edge of the trees.

Piper laid a light hand on his friend's shoulder. "And we'd better split up."

The four drifted slowly down the slope. Wolves circling. They'd been waiting for the mage's fire to vanish, waiting to return and finish the killing they'd started.

Stanach shook his head. "No. We stay together."

Piper's voice was shadowy and thin. "If we stay together you can be sure we'll die together." His fingers tightened on Stanach's shoulder. "One of us has to get to Long Ridge. Let's double our chances, eh? You head for the town. These woods aren't Qualinesti, but neither are you a woodsman, so don't wander, Stanach. It wouldn't take elven wards and magic to get you firmly lost in there.

"Keep to the shadows and the trees. Have the road always in sight and you'll find yourself in a farming valley before you know it. The town sits on the crest of the valley's northern slope. Find Stormblade, do what you have to do to get it. Then get out."

The dwarves began to put distance between themselves. They fanned out in a semi-circle, still moving slowly. The wind kicked up dust at their feet so that they seemed to be moving a hand's width above the stony ground. Stanach cocked an eye at his friend.

"And you?"

Piper's grin was slow and knowing. "I still have it in me for one more spell. Leave me to me, Stanach." One of the guards laughed, a high, howling sound. "And leave them to me, too. I'll lead them a fine chase and lose them fast. You just find the sword. I'll double back and meet you here in two or three days. We'll be back in Thorbardin before you know it."

"Aye," Stanach said wryly, "on the wings of another one of your transport spells, staggering and stumbling and looking for a place to vomit."

Piper shrugged. "It's better than walking."

Stanach agreed. "Wait then. But not forever. If I don't find the sword soon, we're going to have to track it together. Give me a five-day. If I'm not back—with the sword or without it—do what you think is best." He looked one last time at Kyan and at the blood in the road. "Luck, Piper."

"Aye, luck, Stanach. And if you're luckless, do what you have to do. Now go!"

Stanach scrambled for the shadows and the trees. Five yards into the wood, he heard voices raised in oaths to evil gods and turned to look back.

Like a wave of smoke, a thick black cloud funneled down from the sky. Rustling and a high, nervous chittering filled the air as a sweep of bats, day-blind and guided only by Piper's will, descended upon the slope of the near hill like a hundred small carrion crows.

Silently, Stanach blessed his friend for the time that spell purchased and headed north.

Stanach gagged on the thick stench of old burning. He'd heard reports of the war from Kyan and his fellows who walked the border patrol along the western edge of the dwarven holdings. He thought he knew, from their tales, what he might find here in the Outlands. He had never imagined the kind of destruction that lay before him now.

At one time, and not too long ago, the valley must have

been fertile. Now, he thought, the sparrows would starve before winter. As Piper had said, the town lay on the ridge's crest on the valley's northern end. Almost everything below that ridge lay in scorched ruin.

The light of the setting sun fell soft and purple across once-cultivated fields, showing wide black swaths where the flames had run down the length of the vale. Here and there, in scattered patches, small sections of the crops had gone untouched by the fire. These crops, unharvested, shimmered like narrow veins of gold. The fire-blackened willows along the banks of the river, which bisected the valley north to south, clawed the sky like the groping fingers of skeletons. As far as Stanach could see, farmhouses, barns, and small outbuildings lay collapsed, mere piles of rubble now.

A dragon had flown through here.

Laughter, rough and drunken, rose from the valley and echoed against the ridge. Looters, Stanach thought. The place had not been burned that long ago. It would take the dragonarmy soldiers weeks to finish stripping the farmhouses and the dead.

Only two weeks ago, Pax Tharkas in the Kharolis Mountains had been taken by the Highlord Verminaard. The forces of Takhisis had begun their assault on Abanasinia. The wisdom of Thorbardin had it that these humans, blind seekers after new gods, and the elves who had recently fled Qualinesti, had brought this war down on their own heads. They were living with the disaster they'd called upon themselves now. Or they were dead of it.

No business of mine, Stanach thought as he slid his sword from its scabbard and turned away. His business was to find a Kingsword, and at least two hours of walking lay between him and the town. If he didn't want to be caught in this wretched valley he'd have to hurry.

Still, he was happy to leave the place behind. The wind was picking up now and it mourned through the ruined fields sounding like newly made phantoms.

Breathing the dark scent of rich loam, Piper lay as silently as a ghost behind a tangled pile of uprooted trees. The

Theiwar guards were as noisy as a passing herd of cattle. Brown and brittle, the fallen leaves rustled beneath their feet, and twigs snapped and popped under their booted feet.

When he'd fled into the woods, Piper had regretted that he hadn't the strength for an invisibility spell. He grinned now as one guard with a wounded arm tripped over an oak's tangled roots. A blind and deaf mule could keep out of their way!

He listened for long moments as they went on, calling to each other and cursing the thick underbrush. Piper hoped they planned to hunt their dinner in these woods; they'd likely warn every rabbit, deer, and squirrel for miles around that there were dwarves about.

After a time, they angled north as Stanach had, keeping to the edge of the wood. Piper shook his head. At the rate these four were going, Stanach would be in and out of Long Ridge before the Theiwar penetrated the valley. Stanach, dwarf though he was, and as likely to make a racket as these four, had at least a two hour start on them. Piper sat up, peered around, and satisfied himself that he was alone.

Two hours head start, he thought, and not searching for a mage who had somehow managed to make himself invisible without a spell. Piper grinned and got to his feet, brushing off his red robes. He squinted up at the sky, brighter here in the shadows of the trees than it had seemed out on the road.

Another hour or so before the sun set. Enough time to tend to Kyan.

Piper approached the dead still lying in the road. Like black creatures of the night, a half-dozen carrion crows cursed at him before taking flight. One, perched on the shoulder of one of Realgar's guards, only found a better balance and cocked his head, eyeing the intruder with cool insolence. I see you, the crow seemed to be saying, and I'll see you again.

Piper shuddered and pitched a stone at the bird. The crow took flight, screaming. Piper bent to his work.

The mage dragged Realgar's three assassins off the road and far into the darkening woods. Like Stanach, he was only concerned about Kyan.

He would make a true cairn for Kyan Red-axe. He looked

again at the sun and judged that he would be commending the dwarf's spirit to Reorx as the sun turned the stone red with its last light.

Piper thought it was fitting.

"Aye," he said, speaking softly to the dead as he worked. "You'll not go untombed, Kyan, my friend. When word is brought back to Thorbardin that Kyan Red-axe is dead, a king regent will mourn for you."

As he worked, the mage also thought. Realgar's guards had ambushed them while he, Kyan, and Stanach were hardly more than a shimmering of the transport spell in the air. Are we that unlucky he wondered, or are they that lucky?

Piper dragged the last of the cairn stones into place and went to sit beside Kyan in the road. The sun was only a red glow and slanting golden shafts behind the western horizon. The road to the north lay in darkness.

Piper smoothed the dark leather jerkin over the breeched and bloodstained mail shirt that had failed to protect Kyan Red-axe from a crossbow bolt. Perhaps, he thought as he bent to lift his friend and bear him to the cairn he'd prepared, perhaps Realgar set guards on this road because he already has people in Long Ridge who are looking for Stormblade. They are either going to return this way, or Realgar looks to make certain that no other searcher gets into town.

He laid Kyan in the cairn, then carefully placed the covering stones over his body. As he knew it would, the sun's last crimson light glowed across the stones.

"Let it be a reflection of the light of the god's forge," he murmured. "Farewell Kyan Red-axe."

Without thinking, he moved his hand to the flute at his belt. While he'd been working, soft, sad notes had been playing in his mind. Piper shook his head. Kyan's dirge would have to go unsung for a while. The notes of the flute would carry far in the clear night air.

Night settled fast on the road, and Piper sat down in the grass, his back against Kyan's tomb. He watched the first early stars appear in the sky and marked the places where the two moons, the red and the silver, would soon rise. He would wait, as he'd promised Stanach.

Piper drew a long breath. Stanach's no warrior, he thought, and no mage. But he's sworn and ready to keep his oath no matter what he meets.

He wondered if he should try to catch up with Stanach but discarded the idea. No sense crossing paths in the dark. If Stanach found the Kingsword tonight, he'd be back tomorrow.

When you set a place to meet, Kyan once said, you either keep it or you spend a few days chasing down your friends while they wander around looking for you.

Kyan had often dispensed his border-lore over ales in Thorbardin's taverns. On one such tour of the city's drinking spots, he mentioned this bit of wisdom. Piper bowed his head. He'd hear no more such lore from Kyan Red-axe, no tales of his adventures. Kyan was dead in the Outlands.

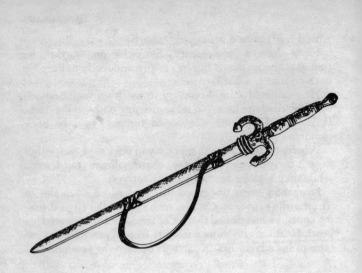

CHAPTER 4

The citizens of Long Ridge did not become seriously interested in questions of theology until the red dragon struck. The town supported the religion of the new gods, the religion of the ancient gods, and the more common religion of indifference. In Long Ridge, the High Seekers were not zealots, and the believers in the old gods, whom some called the true gods, were quiet enough about their creed. In some towns, the faithful of each party broke the heads of unbelievers. In Long Ridge, life had been too steady, too assured, too sweet for religious arguments.

Fed from the produce of the rich farms along the river valley and the game abounding in field and wood, Long Ridge proved the old dictum that a hungry man will fight, while a well fed man will smile contentedly and look toward his next meal. When Solace to the north of them was destroyed, the citizens of Long Ridge should have looked to the skies. They did not.

When he came, red-armored Verminaard, fresh from his easy victory over Solace, took Long Ridge in a day. He needed no flight of dragons, only one, his crimson Ember. He barely needed his troops of soldiers, still stinking of burned vallenwoods and death.

While his army poured into the town, Verminaard and the red dragon Ember fired the farms in the valley, dealing destruction and death with an iron-fisted hand. By the time the farms were reduced to burning wastelands, his troops had surrounded Long Ridge, moved in, and strangled the town like a torturer's band of soaked leather, drying and tightening around a helpless victim's throat.

The Highlord permitted his soldiers enough license to blunt the edge of their bloodlust. Then, with half the town destroyed and a good portion of the populace dead or marked for slavery in the mines at Pax Tharkas, Verminaard called a halt to the looting, raping, and killing. He set Carvath in command of the occupation with orders to squeeze out of the town and its citizens whatever wealth remained. A dark eyed, thin young human captain, Carvath reminded all who saw him of a wolverine, though some might have thought the comparison unfair to that foul-tempered, vicious animal.

Hideous draconians, drunken human soldiers, and even goblins owned the streets of Long Ridge now. They were brutal and savage victors who took what they wanted when they wanted it and did not hesitate to kill any who offered protest. They were like wolves feeding in a shepherdless fold.

While the elves cast the blame at the door of the humans, the dwarves, in their mountain fastness of Thorbardin, filled with bitter and ancient disdain, held both races accountable for sins of the past and the present. They would happily have blamed them for sins of the future as well.

In Long Ridge, people tried to survive the occupation of Highlord Verminaard's brutal army day by day. When the slaves in the mines of Pax Tharkas rebelled and fled the mountains, Verminaard turned his attention away from insignificant Long Ridge and left the town wholly in Carvath's hands.

In the dark cold nights of late autumn, the people of Long Ridge wondered if they should have taken their gods more seriously.

The tavern was called simply Tenny's and it was, in as much as it could be, a "free" tavern. That meant it was only occasionally visited by the draconian officers of the occupation and, by Carvath's orders, forbidden to the common soldiers. It was an open secret that Carvath's spies frequented the place, though their business most often had to do with things well outside the ken and concern of the town's citizens. It was for the sake of these that Carvath had granted the tavern free status.

Tyorl watched Hauk over the rim of his tankard of ale. Hauk was just the type of man Finn liked best for his rangers, for his Nightmare Company—young and bold, with a grudge against the dragonarmy in general, and with Verminaard specifically. Every man or elf in the company had lost friends or kin to Verminaard's draconians. Hauk's village had been wiped out by the savage warriors; his old father, his only kin, had been killed by them. Tyorl, though his own kin were safely fled to Qualinesti, had lost friends and a homeland. The two were typical of Finn's rangers.

Finn's men prowled the eastern borderlands between Qualinesti and the Kharolis Mountains for the pleasure of wreaking that vengence on isolated draconian patrols. Finn saw no reason not to take advantage of Tenny's status and had sent Hauk and Tyorl to find out what they could about Carvath's plans for patrol movements in the area.

Tonight, Tyorl had heard something to confirm the rumor of a troop movement into the foothills of the Kharolis Mountains. The Highlord would be moving not only troops, but a supply base as well. Verminaard, still furious over the loss of his eight hundred slaves and looking for a way to salve his wounded pride, wanted to take his war south and east. He wanted Thorbardin, and he wanted to take the dwarven kingdoms before winter.

The rangerlord would snarl when he learned of Vermi-naard's plans and most of the snarling would be in the direction of Thorbardin. Finn railed constantly against the dwarves who would happily let ranger companies scour the borders of Thorbardin but still held back from entering the war. Still, it would not stop him from doing his best to torment the Highlord's warriors.

But first things first. Hauk laid his sword on the table beside his horn-handled dagger. Firelight from the deep, broad hearth slid along the sword's golden hilt, with its silver chasing and five sapphires. The light warmed the coldly perfect facets of the jewels and illuminated the thin crimson streak which seemed to live in the heart of the steel blade. The four men drinking and playing at daggers at the next table had fallen silent.

Aye, the elf thought, trouble. He hoped he could get the both of them back to Finn in one piece. Tyorl crooked what he hoped was a diverting smile.

"That's a fine sword," the largest of the men drawled. He rubbed his fist along his jaw, scrubby with a week's growth of beard, and lifted his tankard in salute to the blade. Ale slopped over the tankard's rim, running down his fist and arm.

Recognizing the local, Hauk eyed the sword, his head cocked as though it had only now occurred to him that the blade was, indeed, a fine one. He nodded, his smile easy and open. "Aye. Fine enough to stand at wager, Kiv?"

Kiv glanced around the table. His three companions nodded, noses deep in their tankards, eyes tight with the look of men who wished to betray no interest in a matter for which they had, in fact, a great deal of interest. Those sapphires were worth a fortune! Kiv looked last at the elf, Tyorl.

The elf only shrugged. "It's his sword. I suppose that means he can wager it where he will."

Kiv grinned and wiped his hand, wet with ale, along the leg of leather breeches stiff with old grease. "So it is." He turned to Hauk. "Well then, pup, the target will be of my choosing. Miss or refuse it, and the sword is mine."

Hauk rested his hands lightly on the wide-planked table, still smiling with disarming innocence. None but the elf saw

41

the chill in Hauk's eyes.

With a sigh, Tyorl lifted his tankard and settled against the wall. He'd known Hauk for three years. Those three years had taught him that he could depend on Hauk to watch his back in battle, to put himself between Tyorl and a sword blade if he had to; they'd also taught him not to interfere in any matter when Hauk's eyes looked like ice.

He and Hauk had been playing at daggers the whole night for dinner and ale, and as yet they had not had to pay for a crumb or a round. It was a good thing, too. The last of their money had gone for lodging, and neither had so much as a bent steel coin. Hauk liked to boast that he could feed them by wit and dagger alone. He usually made good his boast, but Tyorl sensed they were playing another game now.

No one was offering food or drink as a wager. Kiv's belt pouch had jingled with steel coins at the night's start. Though considerably more drunk than he had been an hour ago, the big man still had enough sense to know that it was time to start recouping the night's losses if he wanted to eat tomorrow.

"The sword," Kiv rumbled, "against what?"

"You tell me."

Kiv leaned back in his chair. The wood creaked softly. He folded his hands comfortably over his belly and stared at the tavern's low, black-beamed ceiling. "Everything in my friends' pouches."

The three shifted uncomfortably. One made as though to protest. Kiv, his eyes still on the smoky beams, only gestured absently at the sword as though to call the man's attention to the gold and silver, the gems. The man subsided, a greedy light in his small dark eyes.

Hauk snorted. "How do I know there's anything left in those pouches?"

Kiv snapped his fingers, and the three dropped their pouches on the table. Neither Hauk nor Tyorl missed the full, heavy sound of coin ringing against coin.

The elf, his eyes sleepy and hooded, smiled again. The coins weren't worth a hundredth of the sword, but Hauk would not miss the target. On the far wall someone had painted a gray, vaguely man-like shape. A wine stain was its heart. All but five of the two dozen strikes at the target's heart were Hauk's.

Around them the rise and fall of a dozen conversations seemed to find a level and settle. At another table, four townsmen collected fresh tankards from the barmaid and hitched their chairs around for a better view. Other men shifted in their seats, picking up the scent of a grand wager.

Across the long common room, two dark-clothed dwarves leaned a little forward. Not enough to seem very interested, Tyorl noted. That in itself was interesting when he considered that the two had no attention to spare for anything but their own conversation until now.

The barmaid, her wooden tray now empty, left the table beside Tyorl. Weaving through the tables with a sure grace, straight-backed and slim, she deftly avoided the laughing snatches of the tavern's patrons. Her hair, the color of a sunset and catching the firelight like polished copper, hung in two thick braids over her shoulders. Pretty creature, Tyorl thought absently.

Kiv, glancing over his shoulder, settled deeper into his chair, made it groan, and closed his eyes. The target's the girl," he said softly.

Hauk feigned a look of bemusement and scratched his beard. "He means her tray, doesn't he, Tyorl?"

For a moment, Tyorl did not think Kiv meant the tray at all. He took a long, slow drink, and set the tankard down on the table. As though considering Hauk's question, he looked from the girl, halfway to the bar now, and back to Hauk's dagger on the table. Spilled ale gleamed on the blade.

"Of course he means the tray," Tyorl slipped his own dagger from its sheath. "Don't you, Kiv?"

Kiv never opened his eyes. He grinned, a cat's lazy, dangerous grin. "Of course. Her tray. Dead center or it's no hit."

The man who had objected to the wagering of his purse laughed nervously. "No points for hitting the wench?"

Firelight danced down the edge of Tyorl's dagger. Kiv opened his eyes, saw the blade, and shrugged. "None at all," he said pointedly.

The room was silent now but for the light sound of the girl's footfalls as she returned to the bar. None stirred or seemed to breathe, and she, knowing suddenly that she was the focus of attention, turned slowly, the wooden tray in her hand.

Hauk, his eyes hard as his sword's blue sapphires, closed his fingers over his dagger's grip. Tyorl almost heard him thinking: bad wager! But he wasn't going to back out of it.

Tyorl cursed silently. His own dagger still in his right hand, he snatched up a tankard with his left and flung it hard.

"Girl! Duck!"

Green eyes wide, the barmaid dropped and, as she did, she raised the tray over her head to deflect the tankard. Hauk's dagger cut the smoke-thick air, a flash of silver too swift for the eye to follow.

The girl screamed, someone raised a staggering, drunken cheer, and then the only sounds heard were the low thud of steel in wood and the barmaid's sobbing gasp. That gasp hung for a long moment in the air, then vanished under a rising wave of voices and the clatter of a chair falling to the floor as one of the townsmen at the next table ran to the girl. She had fainted.

The serving tray also lay on the floor, Hauk's dagger quivering in its exact center.

One of the dwarves at the far end of the tavern, one-eyed and narrow-faced, rose and left the common room. Cool, fresh air swept into the tavern; the blue haze of hearth smoke danced, then fell still as the door closed behind him.

Tyorl noticed the movement. His friend, face white above his short black beard, pushed himself to his feet and sheathed his sword. "Dead center, Kiv."

Kiv closed his eyes again, not turning to see. A slow flush mottled his face.

Tyorl swept the three money pouches from the table. "Go apologize to the girl, Hauk. Our friends will be leaving now."

Kiv shook his head. "I've got no place to go just yet."

"Find someplace." Tyorl ran his thumb along the hilt of his dagger. "You're done drinking and wagering for tonight, your pouches are empty."

Kiv looked from Tyorl's dagger to Hauk's hand where it

lay on the hilt of his scabbarded sword. The decision was taken from him as his companions rose.

"Come on," one said sourly. "You've lost us our coin, Kiv. Leave us our heads in one piece, eh?"

Kiv licked his lips and drew a careful breath. "I think we've been cheated. You interfered, elf."

"No," Tyorl said simply.

Sapphires gleamed between Hauk's fingers like cold blue eyes. Kiv moved forward but his companion's hand dropped hard on his shoulder and held him.

"Come on, Kiv. Give it up."

Tyorl smiled.

The big man shoved himself hard to his feet, kicked his chair out from behind him and left. Hauk loosened his grip on his sword and went across the room to retrieve his dagger.

The talking in the common room wavered and then rose. Tyorl settled back again against the wall. He couldn't wait to get out of Long Ridge.

The flat odor of spilled ale mingled with the sour reek of unwashed bar rags. Slumped behind the bar, Kelida clamped her back teeth hard and swallowed tightly. She closed her eyes and again saw the firelight streaming on the dagger's blade.

She heard a moan and knew the voice for hers. He'd nearly killed her! Outside in the common room, the hum of conversation had returned to normal. Tenny, the barman, snapped an order to the scrub boy. Ale splashed into a tankard from the keg by the door.

She'd worked at the tavern for only two weeks, but the first thing she'd learned was to keep out of a dagger's path. Tenny admired the sport and did not mind that his wall served as a target. Nor did he seem to mind that, a moment ago, his barmaid had been the target.

Consciousness was returning. Someone had sat her up, splashed her face with water. Now, footsteps sounded behind her. She turned. It was the dagger-throwing young man.

The blade was sheathed again. His hand was nowhere

near it. His face gray beneath its weathered tan, he dropped to a crouch beside her, and Kelida saw that he was perspiring heavily.

"I'm sorry," he said. His voice was deep, and when he tried to pitch it softly it broke a little.

"You gambled with my life," she accused.

He nodded, "I know."

When he held out his hand, big and rough with callouses, Kelida shrank back. He was like a bear, stocky, broad-chested, and black-bearded. Unlike a bear's, his eyes were blue. She kept her eyes on his, aware suddenly that he was between her and the door to the common room. He read anger in her face and sprang to his feet. When he stepped to one side, the path to the door was clear.

"I'm sorry," he said again.

Kelida stood, edging toward the door. "Just leave me alone!"

"It's over," he said. He smiled then, a self-deprecating twitch of his lips. "I was sorry the moment the dagger flew."

Before she thought, Kelida turned on him sharply, her hands fisted. "Would you be sorrier if I was dead?"

He didn't move. "But I did not intend to miss—"

"You gambled with my life!" Suddenly she blazed with outrage and fury. She flew at him, scratching and kicking. She raked his face with her nails. Before he captured both her wrists in one of his big hands, she saw blood spring from the scratches above his beard. He held her hands high and away from his face. She spat in his eye.

He wiped his face with the back of his free hand and drew his sword. In that moment, Kelida saw his blue eyes very clearly. He stopped and freed her hands at once.

"I'm sorry. I did gamble with your life." He balanced the sword across his two open hands and held it out as though making an offering. The sapphires on its grip captured what light there was in the dim storeroom and made the jewels look like twilight. As though it were the soul of the blade, or a blood stain, a slim crimson streak marked the blue-edged steel.

Kelida backed away, not understanding the gesture.

"Take it."

"I—no. No. I don't want it."

"It's mine to give." He smiled encouragingly. "It's what I wagered tonight. It's yours; rightly won when your life was gambled."

"You're drunk."

He cocked his head. "Drunk? Aye, a little, probably. But, drunk or sober, I'm giving you the sword."

When she made no move to accept the weapon he laid it on the floor at her feet. He unbuckled the plain leather scabbard at his hip and laid that beside the sword. Saying nothing more, he turned and left.

For a long time Kelida stared at the wealth of jewels, gold, and steel. Then, very carefully and as though it were a snake and not cold steel, she stepped around the sword and into the ale and smoke reek of the common room.

The young man was just walking out the door. The elf, his companion, leaned comfortably against the wall. He looked up from his tankard, gave her a long and considering look, and raised his drink in salute. Kelida avoided his eyes.

The townsmen at a table next to the elf rose to leave. Fresh air gusted into the tavern again as they left. The table did not remain empty long. A black-bearded dwarf claimed it. He tossed his pack down on the floor, unslung an old leather scabbard from his back and laid it near to hand. He signaled for a drink, and Kelida went back to work.

The one-eyed dwarf lurking outside the tavern had no rank and, worse, had no clan. The Theiwar were, above all, dwarves of Thorbardin, and so viewed a clan-reft dwarf as nothing less than a living ghost. He was a creature to be ignored, to be looked past as though he did not exist. No unnecessary word was ever spoken to him by Realgar's guards. In the normal course of social interaction, such a one did not exist. None knew what the clanless guard had done to deserve his fate, though many speculated.

Some said his mortal offense had been commited at the thane's behest. Some said he had acted on his own for the sake of the thane. Whatever the reason for his crime, Realgar kept him close.

The blood of mages ran in his veins and, though he was

47

not a fully trained mage himself, he was competent enough in the minor workings of magic to cast small spells and to act as Realgar's eyes and voice. Through his eye the thane saw; with his voice the thane spoke.

His name was Agus. Among the Theiwar he was known as the Gray Herald. It had been whispered that the Gray Herald could slit a man's throat and smile into his eyes while doing it.

In the dark shadows of the alley between the tavern and the stable, Agus now waited for Hauk. The opposite end of the garbage-strewn alley opened on the stable's paddocks and smithy. The Gray Herald's companion, Rhuel, waited there.

Across the street two dragonarmy soldiers, humans both, walked unsteadily in the direction of their barracks. Drunk, the Gray Herald thought, and no problem to me.

From the stable came the quick impatient thud of a horse kicking back against its stall. The dwarf felt the wood at his back shiver with the impact. A stableman cursed, and the horse whinnied high.

The tavern's door opened. Noise and light spilled into the street, then faded as the door closed. The Gray Herald stood away from the stable wall, his dagger in hand. Footsteps, hollow and slow, approached. Down the alley, Rhuel stepped from the shadows.

The Gray Herald drew a short breath and peered out into the street. Hauk, head down and thinking, walked away from the tavern in the direction that would bring him past the alley. The Gray Herald smiled and moved his right hand in a swift gesture. Magic sighed in the shadow of the alley.

Hauk stopped at the alley's mouth and cocked his head as though he'd heard his name called. He looked back the way he'd come and saw no one. The street was empty. All he heard now was the muffled sounds of laughter and conversation from the tavern. The Herald moved his hand again, the gesture more complicated now.

Though he believed he was continuing down the street, Hauk stepped into the alley and a sleep spell. The one-eyed dwarf doubted Hauk would even remember the long, slow fall before he hit the ground.

Kelida turned up the last chair and dropped the floor mop into a wooden bucket of dirt-scummed water. The tavern was quiet now but for the banging of pots in the kitchen and Tenny's grunts and curses as he hauled empty ale kegs out to the alley. With the back of her hand she brushed at the hair escaping in wisps from her braids. Her feet sore, her arms aching from carrying trays loaded with tankards, she was more tired tonight than she'd ever been. Not even during harvest time, with field after field of corn, wheat and hay to cut, stack and haul, had she ever felt as tired as this.

Her throat tightened. Unbidden, sharp tears pricked behind her eyes. There would be no harvest this year. None next year. Someone, in bitter humor, had said that the farms were plague-struck. A plague of dragons.

No, Kelida thought now, just one dragon. One had been enough. She would have nightmares about the day the red dragon struck for a long, long time.

She turned around at the sound of the front door opening. Some late-returning lodger, she thought, and looked to see who had entered. The elf, whose friend had wagered with her life at daggers, closed the door quietly behind him. Kelida bent to lift the bucket, and the elf crossed the room with three long strides and took it from her hand.

"Let me," he said. "Where does it go?"

Kelida gestured behind the long trestle that served as the bar. "Thank you." She stepped behind the trestle to finish wiping it down.

The elf left the bucket near the kitchen door and returned to the common room. He leaned his elbows on the bar and, saying nothing, watched Kelida work.

"The bar is closed," she told him, not taking her eyes from her wiping.

"I know. I'm not looking for a drink. I'm looking for Hauk."

"Who?"

"Hauk." Tyorl smiled a little and mimed throwing a dagger. "You met him earlier. Have you seen him?"

"No." Kelida scrubbed hard at a sticky wine stain.

"By the look of you, you don't care if you ever see him

again."

She glanced up at him then. His eyes, long and blue, danced with amusement. Where his friend had been stocky and muscular, this elf was tall and lean. Hauk had moved with the solid step of a bear. This one had a deer's grace. Kelida did not know how to judge his age. He might be young or old. One could not often tell with an elf.

"Tyorl," he said, as though she had asked his name.

Kelida nodded. "I haven't seen your friend since—since he left the tavern earlier tonight."

"He hasn't been back to claim the sword?"

"He gave it to me."

Tyorl shrugged. "Oh, yes. Hauk's apologies, when he's had too much to drink are always extravagant."

Kelida glanced at him quickly. She thought suddenly that the sword which she'd thought so fine and expensive, might more appropriately have come from an elflord's coffers.

"Was it yours? He said it was his to wager. But—"

"Oh, it's his, all right. He's the swordsman, lady, I'm the bowman. If I need anything else, I've my dagger." Tyorl smiled. "I taught him to play daggers and can still beat him. It's enough for me."

In spite of herself, Kelida smiled. "That sword would buy half the town."

"It would buy the town and two more like it. He hasn't been back at all?"

"No. I—I have the sword." She'd left it in the storeroom, but wrapped in old flour sacking and well hidden behind two tuns of old wine. The wine was Tenny's best, and no one dared draw from the barrels but he. He hadn't had reason to draw from them tonight. She'd thought about the sword and the riches represented by the gold and sapphires all night. Perhaps she could sell it and find a way out of Long Ridge, though she had no idea of where to go.

"Shall I get it for you?"

He frowned. "You'd just give it to me?"

"What will I do with it?"

"Sell it."

Kelida shook her head. "And then what?"

"I don't know. Get out of here."

"There's no place to go. My family—my family is dead. No one travels the roads alone. I certainly wouldn't if I had something worth stealing." She looked at him closely. "Besides, that's your friend's sword. Why do you want me to sell it?"

"I don't want you to sell it. I'm just surprised that *you* don't want to sell it. Just as well. Sooner or later he'll be back for it."

Kelida returned to her wiping. "I said he gave it to me."

Tyorl ndded. "Well, you deserve a certain amount of revenge upon our friend Hauk." He smiled and pushed away from the bar. "Don't give it over quite so easily, lady. Make him sweat a little for it, eh?"

Kelida said nothing, but watched as Tyorl left the common room and mounted the steps for the rooms above. She retrieved the sword, an awkward bundle in the old brown sacking, and took it to her cold, drafty attic room at the top of the tavern.

The room smelled of the stableyard which it overlooked and the sour, smoky reek from the tavern, to which she had almost become accustomed. The lodging was fully two thirds of her pay. Meals and a few coins were the other third.

Kelida sank down on the pile of straw and rough woolen blankets that served her as a bed. She unwrapped the sword, slid it a little way from the simple, undecorated scabbard, and watched gold and silver, sapphires and steel catch the faint light of the stars.

Hauk had wagered all this wealth on the skill of his hand! Was he mad or had he simply been drunk? His clothes, hunting leathers and tall boots, made her think of a ranger.

His voice, she decided, was better used to shouting the triumph of a hunting kill or roaring a challenge. It hadn't dropped to soft apology easily. Suddenly, she found herself looking forward to morning and Hauk's return for the sword.

Then she remembered that she was angry with him. A little revenge, the elf had said. Kelida smiled. She supposed she did deserve a little revenge.

CHAPTER 5

Che stones wore badges of blood, the marks of the passage of eight hundred people. The refugees stretched out in a long, straggling line, staggering, lurching, falling. Some who fell picked themselves up. Others lay, tasting red dust and shuddering with cold, until they were passed by or helped to their feet. If helped, they thanked their rescuers when they had breath to. If passed, they picked themselves up. If they did not, they were dead.

Women with children in tow, babes at their breast, followed their men. Hungry, always hungry, they looked restlessly to the sides of the ragged line for signs of something to eat. The plains were empty. Nothing grew here, and the game had long fled before the army of refugees.

Hungry. They were always hungry.

The hills rose before them, passed under bleeding feet, and rose again. These were the Hills of Blood, red as their name, heartless crests of bitter stone and choking dust. The water here was brackish, foul tasting. No one stopped to fill a water flask. No one lagged behind to quench a thirst as painful as hunger.

Few thought to wonder if Thorbardin would be their place of sanctuary. Few had the strength to wonder, and none had the strength to consider what would happen to them if the dwarves refused them shelter.

We will make them hear, Tanis had said.

That was enough for people who had no place else to go.

"Hold! Enough!" Gneiss's cry for order cut through Rance's outraged tirade like lightning through a thick summer night. The Great Hall was hung with tapestries, each vividly depicting a scene from dwarven history, each skillfully woven with shimmering, richly colored threads. The hangings did not serve to mute Gneiss's deep bellow. Gneiss tried to ignore the headache thundering behind his eyes.

The hangings had never muted the roar and the rage of the battles waged in this Court of Thanes. Gneiss did not know why they should now.

Torches in silver-chased cressets flickered, as though before a stormwind. Shadows ran up the guardian columns and mingled with the darkness of the vaulted ceiling. The six dwarves meeting in the Court of Thanes fell silent.

Hornfel, Hylar and the son of high kings, waited patiently for calm to settle. Realgar, dark-eyed, dark-souled *derro* mage and plotter of murders, watched Gneiss like a snake watching prey. Rance, his ally, of the murderous temper and mind-clouding furies, stood stiffly, waiting not for a place to speak, but for his rage to cool enough so that he could carry on his tirade. Tufa, combed his fingers through his red beard in a way carefully chosen not to offer insult, but neither to offer encouragement. He looked away first. The gully dwarf Bluph looked at nothing but the inside of his eyelids and snored gently, sleeping even through the thunder of Rance's outrage and the lightning strike of Gneiss' cry for silence.

Rance, the Daergar thane, clenched his fists, his jaw as hard as stone. He was not easily silenced. "By the god's forge, it is enough! Eight hundred?" His voiced dropped, dangerously low. "I say no. Are we to welcome every tramp and vagabond who makes his way to our gates? No." He snorted scornful dismissal. "Next thing you'll ask is that we issue invitations to hill dwarves."

All eyes turned to Gneiss, till now quiet. Gneiss did not smile, though he could have. He prided himself on his control. He glanced at Tufa, the Klar's thane and ruler of the only clan of hill dwarves now living in Thorbardin. Rance's arrogant, disdainful remark told. Tufa's brown eyes, normally mild and patient, hardened.

Here is one, Gneiss thought, just ready to fall into Hornfel's camp.

Hornfel knew it and smiled. Aye, Gneiss thought, hide your smile in your beard, my friend. You see that Tufa is yours now.

Gneiss sighed and drummed his fingers on the broad marble arm of his throne. Bluph of the Aghar would also cast his vote Hornfel's way. He always did so as long as he was awake. The gully dwarf was a pathetic and useless creature at almost any juncture, but Gneiss did not think that Hornfel was prepared to scorn any aid in his bid to grant refuge to outsiders. Even that of a casteless gully dwarf.

At this moment, Bluph was snoring and gurgling, his head pillowed blissfully on the stone arm of his throne. Bluph had been happily doing so throughout the unprecedented evening council and even during Rance's most thunderous roaring.

Gneiss still didn't know where he stood upon the issue of admitting eight hundred human refugees to Thorbardin. He, like Rance, had no desire to fill Thorbardin's halls with humans. He was not, at the last, surprised that the Hylar harbored a kindly feeling or two toward them. After all, Hornfel had kept that gangling, yellow-headed mage close to him for the last three years. Where was that odd fellow, Piper, now?

Realgar leaned against the arm of his rightful throne with the bored attitude of one who watches endlessly quarreling children. The Theiwar throne held several scrolls, the sword he habitually wore to council meetings (which some believed was more than ceremonial), and his light cloak. Gneiss shivered as Realgar, sensing eyes upon him, turned and smiled.

It was the bloodless smile of a snake stretching wide jaws as he basked in a warm fall of sunlight.

Caught by the snake's eyes, Gneiss did not look away. Shuddering, he had the sudden impression that Realgar had been eavesdropping on his thoughts. Dark magics and darker passions lurked like shadows in the *derro* mage's flat, black eyes. They seemed to display the fierce satisfaction of one who carefully lays a plan that cannot go awry.

What plan? A cold thread of fear wove through the Daewar's belly and he forced himself to look away. It was no secret that Realgar opposed Hornfel. None lived today who could rightfully take the empty throne of the high king. None ever would. But there was a rumor that a swordsmith had forged a true Kingsword, that it was intended for the Hylar, and that blood had already been shed in dispute over its possession.

Gneiss gave the whispers scarcely more credit than the idea that someone would one day find the Hammer of Kharas. But . . . if the rumor were true, Hornfel might preside as king regent. That was not a thing Realgar would ever tolerate. The Theiwar's passion for power ran as deep as his dark soul.

Aye, Hornfel, Gneiss thought, I don't know if there is a Kingsword. But I do know that you'd better watch that one's eyes carefully. They may someday be the gauge of how long you have to live.

Gneiss leaned forward. "I will tell you this: there are points to be considered on both sides. Aye, this war is no business of ours. We did not cause it, and we don't fight in it. What the humans and the elves have brought upon themselves, they must deal with themselves."

Rance drew a breath to speak. Gneiss fixed him with an icy stare and continued. "Yet, the Hylar is right. We can choose to ignore the war, but that won't make it vanish. And it draws closer.

"The scout's report has it that these refugees have only now set out from Pax Tharkas. They are eight hundred and they are weak. They are not clamoring at the gate yet. Retire the matter. Think about it. It is also time to start thinking about how we will defend Thorbardin when there are dragonarmies crossing the Plains of Death and not ragged war refugees."

Hornfel, silent till now, glanced at Gneiss. There was more Gneiss could say, but he chose to defer to the Hylar.

When he spoke, Hornfel's voice was low and even. "The Daewar is right. We have time. But it's marked by the sound of the footsteps approaching our gates. Think, my friends, and think well. Like it or not, we're going to need allies soon. Pax Tharkas has not fallen. It's still a dragonarmy stronghold. Verminaard is not dead. The slaves he kept in our ancient mines have been freed, but not by an army. If the scout's report is true, those eight hundred have been freed by a band of only nine adventurers."

Hornfel's eyes narrowed. Golden torchlight gleamed in the depths of his chestnut colored beard. "Those refugees, wanted or not, are heading for Thorbardin. Make no mistake . . . Verminaard knows it."

"Aye," Rance growled, "I don't doubt that he does. Why, then, do you want to welcome them?"

Gneiss heard stone and ice in the Hylar's voice when he replied. "Because, Rance, we are dwarves of Thorbardin and we make our own choices. Verminaard does not dictate where and when we offer our hospitality."

He rose abruptly and gestured toward Bluph, still snoring and muttering. "The first good suggestion I've heard from the Aghar all year. It's late and we are all tired. We'll meet again tomorrow."

Gneiss watched as Hornfel strode from the Court. It was traditionally his right as a Hylar thane to open and adjourn council meetings.

He rarely exercised the right, Gneiss thought wryly, but when he did, he did so with not so much as a by-your-leave. The Daewar rubbed the heel of his hand thoughtfully, as Rance and Realgar exchanged glances.

Realgar traveled the dark tunnels beneath the farming warrens with ease. He carried no torch, nor was he obliged to feel his way. He was Theiwar, who not only tolerated the dark, they craved it. Here in the absolute blackness of the tunnels, his perfect night vision guided him. Widely dilated pupils obscured the brown rims of his irises. A dim red glow the color of the stone for which Realgar was named burned steadily within the depths of his eyes. Anyone looking into those eyes would think of bottomless flame.

Though he had spent all of the day trying, Hornfel had not yet won the Council of Thanes to his thinking. But he was close. It was a schemer's ploy, Realgar thought scornfully, to invoke the sacred tradition of dwarven hospitality. It was a ploy that might work. Few, if any, of the council members actually wished to offer refuge—and certainly not hospitality—to eight hundred vagabonds. Yet, none would view kindly a challenge to their right to do so.

As he traveled deeper into the heart of the mountain beneath Thorbardin, Realgar's thoughts became darker, taking on the lightless aspect of the tunnels.

He was a powerful speaker, this Hylar who pretended to the regency. Given enough time, he might convince Gneiss to cast his vote with the other witlings who then would open Thorbardin's gates to the ragtag legions of humans who were fleeing a war of their own making.

Realgar's fists tightened at his side. In the midst of the rant and the rage of Rance's opposition, the Theiwar had felt, like a cold blue shadow on snow, the touch of the Gray Herald's mind. At that moment, he'd seen the Gray Herald standing against a mud-spattered stable wall in a rain-wet alleyway in Long Ridge.

They'd found the ranger. They'd not found the sword.

Rance's fury was a child's pouting when compared with what tore through Realgar in that moment. None knew and none saw. Not even Gneiss, so intently staring. But the Gray Herald had heard his curse.

Earlier, he'd tracked the ranger with the Kingsword. When they set to waylay him, he'd had it. Now, they didn't know where it was.

Realgar snarled. That other ranger, the elf, must have it!

Or . . . who? Kyan Red-axe was dead. Hornfel's pet mage and mad Isarn's apprentice were still near the town, but as yet knew nothing of Hauk and Stormblade. They were busy eluding Brek and his guards. The human must be secured, and the elf must be shadowed.

"Bring me this ranger," he had communicated to Agus, even as he smiled at Gneiss. "I'll know who has the sword within the hour."

At that moment the Gray Herald had laid his hands upon the head of the young man and spoke the words of a transport spell. Rhuel and Agus now waited with the ranger, Hauk, in the depths of Thorbardin.

The tunnel widened, its weeping walls swept back and up to a suddenly heightened ceiling. Realgar bared his teeth in a deadly smile as he entered a broad, roughly circular cavern. The place was as dark as the tunnel had been, its walls as rough and damp. Realgar crossed the floor, smoother here, and stood over the body of the unconscious ranger.

Hauk stirred. The Theiwar smiled and waved absently, dismissing his two guards.

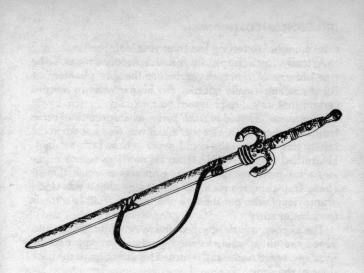

CHAPTER 6

In an alley, behind what had once been the most prosperous street of shops in Long Ridge, an old kender squinted against the wet night wind and brought his face closer to a locked door. The stink of burned wood filled the alley, and the kender sneezed once, then again. This shop was among the very few on the street still undamaged. The dragon had missed it, intentionally or not, and even the looting soldiers had not damaged it too much. The kender was having a difficult time with the lock.

Lavim Springtoe was absolutely not prepared to consider that he was getting too old to finesse even this simple lock. He was sixty, and that was not a great accumulation of years at all. Why, Lavim, like every kender, knew that Uncle Trapspringer had lived until well past seventy before he even admitted to feeling less than youthful.

Actually, Uncle Trapspringer had reputedly lived until the ripe old age of ninety-seven before the dire phantom of Rigar's Swamp finally got him. For his part, Lavim was not certain that any dire phantom had actually 'gotten' Uncle Trapspringer. That doubtful piece of information came from his father's cousin's aunt, and it was well known in the family that Aunt Evalia could never get the facts straight. Lavim had always heard—from his mother's sister's nephew, a far more reliable source who was a connection of Uncle Trapspringer's via a second cousin—that it was Uncle Trapspringer who got the dire phantom. Certainly it made for a better story.

The kender, a little stooped and very white-haired, surveyed the alley again, listened carefully for approaching footsteps, heard none, and returned his attention to the back door of the shop.

His eyes were not weak, his sight was simply impaired by the miserable pall of soot and smoke that had become what used to be air in Long Ridge. If his hands shook, Lavim was certain that they did not shake with age but with hunger. The place he sought entry to being a baker's shop, Lavim thought it likely that there would be something to eat lying about that no one was interested in. Afterwards, he would fix the lock so it locked even better.

He tossed his head, flipping his long white braid over his shoulder, and set to work again. All the fine lines of his wrinkled brown face deepened with his concentration. He leaned a little against the door, not so that his long, canted ear might be closer to the lock to hear the tumblers fall, but so that he could brace his shoulder for perfect balance.

It is said that eye level for a kender is door-lock height for the same reason a chipmunk has extra cheek space. A twist of the lock's horizontal bar brought the satisfying 'snick!' of a tumbler tumbling. A second twist, and then a third, and the lock was a lock no more. Obviously, Lavim thought as he stepped silently into the back of the baker shop, this lock was not meant to keep anyone out. In its own way it was an invitation.

A small loaf of brown bread lay on a table. Lavim pocketed it and thought how pleased the baker would be to discover that someone had saved his shop from the depredations of the mice that would surely have trooped through the place once they discovered food lying about. By removing three small honey cakes from a nearby shelf, Lavim rescued the baker from rats. He defended the hapless shopkeeper from ants when he filled a small pouch with sweet rolls, and considered his night's work done when he scooped four small muffins into his pocket, thereby saving the poor baker from an infestation of roaches.

Satisfied that the baker would return to his shop in the morning a happy man, Lavim Springtoe slipped back out the alley door, reset the improved lock, and headed for the tavern.

He wondered whether the tavern still stocked dwarf spirits. The current occupation—infestation, his father would have said—made the possibility highly unlikely. Few supplies were getting into Long Ridge these days, and those few were rapidly claimed and consumed by Verminaard's army. However, Lavim was a forward looking fellow. His father, who had possessed an endless store of kender common knowledge and passed most of it on to his son, liked to say than an empty pouch will never be filled unless you open it.

Lavim set out for the tavern chewing a large bite of honey cake and fortified with his father's optimism.

He was thirsty from all his work and good deeds, and a few hours still remained before the watch would cry curfew.

Stanach felt oppressed by the noise and heat of the tavern. The place smelled of wet wool and leather, sour wine and flat ale spilled long ago. But these were no worse than the odors in some of the taverns he and Kyan had frequented in Thorbardin. His sense of oppression was rooted in the overwhelming feeling that he was a stranger among strangers. Tenny's held more humans than Stanach had ever seen. Only a few of them, small groups here and there, seemed to know each other. Others stood shoulder by shoulder with fellow drinkers, yet seemed to stand alone.

The sound of their talking, the closeness of them, made Stanach wonder if there were enough air in the place for all to breathe.

We need more air in our lungs than you do, Piper would have said. The mage would have made the remark, Stanach thought, with a wry smile and a cocked head, if he were here to make it. Stanach didn't know where Piper was and he didn't even know whether the mage was still alive.

He smeared a ring of ale on the scarred table and scowled. Piper had survived. He was, after all, a mage. And a clever one, at that. He was also, Stanach realized, a stag surrounded by a pack of wolves. But a stag can break free and do serious harm to the pack. He held onto that thought and prayed that Piper had been able to lose Realgar's guards in the woods, as he had.

Stanach had come into Long Ridge at sunset last night, a cold wind at his back. He'd looked first for a place to lodge and then for a place to eat. He'd found both in Tenny's.

Food and a room were not all he'd found. Stormblade was, indeed, in Long Ridge. At least it had been last night.

Stanach tangled his fingers in his glossy black beard, tugging a little. When he'd come into the tavern last night, the place buzzed with the story of a ranger's grand wager: his sword against the money pouches of three companions.

A magnificent sword! Gold hilted and silver chased . . . five wonderful sapphires on the hilt . . .

A grand wager, Stanach thought. Aye, a grand wager. Though he'd looked for the ranger and the sword, even made discreet inquiries, he saw no sign of them last night. He had found no trace of Stormblade today either. The sword, and the ranger who had wagered it at a game of daggers, seemed to have vanished.

He was with an elf, one man had said last night. Stanach took a long pull on his tankard of ale and looked to the bar. The only elf he'd seen in the place, last night and tonight, was the tall, slim fellow talking now to the red-haired barmaid.

Stanach looked closely at him. He wore hunting leathers and high boots. A dagger was sheathed at his hip, a longbow and full quiver strapped across his back. He bore his weapons with casual ease. Stanach thought he had a look about him of one who had spent more time in the woods than in taverns. A hunter's look. Or a ranger's.

The barman called for the serving girl. His bellowing rose over the sound of men talking, the scrape of chairs, and the hiss and snap of the fire in the hearth. The call died in the man's throat. As though by command, the tavern fell silent. The door had opened and the dry, musty odor of reptile filled the room.

"Givrak," someone whispered, nearly choking on the name.

Stanach's first impulse was to close his eyes, to shut out the sight of what shoved through the silent crowd. When he was a child, Stanach had nightmares about things that looked like Givrak. He did not close his eyes, though, but looked. Every instinct warned him that this Givrak bore close and careful watching, if only so that one knew where to run when running became necessary.

Like the creatures of Stanach's evil dreams, Givrak was as big as a tall man, broad in the chest and shoulders, and had a reptile's head, flat and spine-crested. Wide, claw-tipped leathery wings were folded over his back. Though the things in his nightmares did not wear chain mail, Givrak did. Stanach, from where he sat at a corner table near the door, could not tell where the mail left off and the draconian's scaly hide began. His thickly muscled legs did not seem to be meant for walking, though Givrak, stalking the space before the bar, walked well enough on them. Worse, though, were his flat, black eyes.

Nothing like pity or mercy had ever moved in those eyes.

The draconian lifted his head. The light of the hearth fire and small lanterns glittered and danced along mail and skin.

The draconian moved slowly, like a snake rising from its coil. Stanach had not been in the town long, but two nights and a day were enough to know that in Long Ridge a draconian in foul temper did not often go victimless.

Everyone in the place held perfectly still. The barman's rag hung in his hand like a limp and dirty flag of surrender. Around the common room, men sat or stood in perfect silence. The place stank of fear. Stanach's sword lay across the table. He slid his hand closer to the hilt.

The barmaid, her face the color of whey, the freckles on

her cheeks standing out like fever blotches, drew a small, tight breath. Givrak turned at the sound.

The brutish draconian scented the girl's fear. His narrow, forked tongue flickered around lipless jaws. Stanach's fingers closed around his sword's grip.

His movements slow and easy, the elf stood away from the bar. His unstrung bow would be useless to him, but his right hand hovered near his dagger. Briefly, Stanach was aware of the elf's cool blue gaze as it judged him, quickly satisfied. The dwarf glanced at the girl. Her eyes were the color of emeralds and huge with fear.

It was then that the kender Lavim Springtoe sauntered into the tavern. Dressed in bright yellow leggings, soft brown boots, and a black, shapeless coat that fell nearly to his knees, he was old and wore his long white hair in a thick braid. A fine netting of wrinkles made his face look like that of an ancient pug-nosed child. He saw the draconian right away, but did not reach for the hoopak staff strapped across his back. Instead, he strode purposefully toward him, dusted his hands on his yellow leggings, and peered up at Givrak.

"There," he sighed. "Do you know I've been looking all over the town for you?"

Fearless as kender are, Stanach thought he saw the old one's breathing hitch just a little when Givrak turned toward him. But then, maybe not.

The draconian scowled, an expression as twisted and fearsome as any Stanach had ever seen. "For me, little thief?"

The kender did not flicker an eye at this gross insult, but grinned instead. His voice was smooth and surprisingly deep for one so small. "Yes, for you. There's someone looking for you, and he sent me to find you."

"Who?"

The kender shrugged. "I don't know who he is. He was wearing red armor and carrying a big helmet. You know, that helmet looked just like a dragon's head. It had horns and a mouthpiece that looked like fangs. Well, at least, I think it looked like a dragon—the helmet—I mean. I've never really seen a dragon except for that red one that flies over

every day. But then, it flies so high I can't really see its face
and—"

Givrak snarled. The kender sighed as though over the
impatience and ill manners of the draconian.

"Anyway, he said something about troop deployments,
or the Highlord, or something like that."

Givrak hissed. He, as well as anyone in the room, recognized the description of Carvath, the captain who commanded the occupation of Long Ridge. And if Carvath were
an invocation he could ignore, the mention of the Highlord
was not. None knew these days where Verminaard, still
smarting from the loss of eight hundred captive slaves,
would unleash his temper next. The draconian snarled
again, and turned, kicking a table on his way out, sending
tankards and goblets spinning to the floor. The door was
slammed with enough force to rattle the walls.

The tavern was silent for a moment longer. Then, a
groundswell of murmuring began which turned quickly into
a wave of voices, some frightened whispers, others angered.

The serving girl scurried around the bar to clean the mess.
Stanach scooped up a goblet and two tankards and handed
them to her. "Close, lass."

"Oh, aye," the girl said, her face still white. "I'm thinking
I've just spent all my luck for the year."

"You've made a good purchase with it, if you did."

The girl's smile of agreement was wobbly.

Stanach turned back to his table. The kender had claimed
a seat there. A runner for a dragonarmy captain, Stanach
thought, is not one I'd like to share a table with. He moved
to find another place when the kender waved him over. The
old one's eyes, green as spring's leaves, were bright with sup-
pressed amusement.

"Come on, join me. You're just the person I've been looking for."

Stanach eyed the kender carefully, checked the placement
of anything that was valuable to him, and resumed his seat.
He was curious.

"Me, kender? I thought it was Givrak you were looking
for."

The kender shrugged. "No, not really. Givrak, you say? Is

that his name? When I walked in and saw him, I figured it would be better for everyone if he had an appointment somewhere." He grinned. "They tell me I'm getting old, but I can still think young."

Stanach laughed. "You certainly can. Can you think far?"

The kender cocked his head. "What do you mean?"

"What happens when Givrak gets to that captain and finds out that it hasn't been sent for at all?"

"Oh." The wrinkles around the kender's long green eyes momentarily knit into a frown. But the smile was resilent. "I was hoping it would take Givrak at least a few hours to track him down and find that out."

"Aye, you hope. Perhaps you'd better talk fast, just in case. Why are you looking for me?"

"Well not you especially. Just a dwarf. My father used to say that if you're going to order dwarf spirits, check with a dwarf first. He'll tell you if it's worth drinking. Is there any spirits here, and is it worth drinking?"

Stanach eyed the little kender doubtfully. A good mug of dwarf spirits had been known to send brawny humans sliding for the floor. This kender, sapling thin and seemingly frail, did not look as though he could stand up to even one sip of the clear, potent drink.

Stanach shrugged. The question was moot. This tavern stocked nothing more than ale and pale elven wine. "Not a drop," he said. "You'll have to make do with wine or ale. What's your name, kender?"

"Lavim Springtoe." The kender extended his hand. Stanach, thinking of his father's ring on his finger, not to mention the copper rivets on the sleeve of his leather jerkin, did not accept Lavim's hand, but smiled instead.

"Stanach Hammerfell of Thorbardin. I'll stand you a drink of whatever you want, Lavim Springtoe, and we'll wish for dwarf spirits instead."

It had to be good enough. Lavim offered to go for the drinks, but Stanach shook his head. By the look of him, this Lavim Springtoe had been around long enough to have acquired the skill to filch the teeth out of a dragon's head. Let him pass once through the common room and the owners of missing money pouches, daggers, pocket knives, wrist braces, and Reorx only knew what else, would shortly be eager to hang him by his long white braid from the nearest roof beam.

Stanach went himself for the drinks. When he stepped up to the bar, the elf nodded to him, an acknowledgement of what had briefly passed between them when Givrak had turned on the serving girl. Stanach returned the nod. Now was not the time, here was not the place, but he knew that when he could approach the elf on the subject of Stormblade, he would stand a good chance of having his questions heard, if not answered.

Stanach was grateful for the chance that had brought the draconian Givrak into the tavern.

Lavim Springtoe peered into the quickly approaching bottom of his fourth mug of ale and deftly but absently relieved a passing townsman of his belt pouch. He was thinking hard, barely knew that he'd captured the purse, and was rather surprised when Stanach stuck his large, scarred hand almost under his nose.

"Give it over," the dwarf said firmly.

Lavim raised an eyebrow. "Give what over? Oh, this?"

"Aye, that."

Lavim held up the soft leather pouch and looked at it as though he did not quite understand how he came to be holding it. "Careless of the fellow to have lost it." Lavim hefted the pouch. It was heavy with coins. They clinked comfortably when he tossed the purse from one hand to another.

Stanach caught the pouch in midair. He turned, tapped the townsman on the shoulder and offered the purse.

The man grabbed the pouch swiftly from Stanach's hand. He would have raised a protest but saw something forbidding in the dwarf's expression and only offered a grudging thanks. Stanach nodded curtly and returned his attention to his mug of ale.

He's not thinking about the ale, Lavim decided, he's watching that elf at the bar for some reason.

The least perceptive kender can smell a secret when he is within a mile of its holder. Lavim Springtoe watched Stanach as carefully as the dwarf listened to the bits and pieces of conversation drifting around him.

Though Stanach had willingly stood for all the kender wanted to drink, sometimes signaling the barmaid, sometimes going himself for the refills, he listened to Lavim's chatter only absently, and only absently answered. Lavim fell silent watching the firelight smoldering in the smoky amethyst ring on Stanach's finger and flashing from the small silver hoop he wore in his left ear.

Nothing about Stanach seemed to settle into a firm impression. The ring made Lavim think of someone who wore wealth casually; the silver hoop conjured images of highwaymen and bandits. The dwarf's bearded face seemed at first to be settled into a fierce and forbidding expression. There were moments, however, when he wasn't remembering to look fierce, when the vulnerability of youth softened eyes black as coal and strangely flecked with blue.

This Stanach, Lavim thought, is quieter now than he'd been at first, like a tightly shuttered house. Closed things, locked things, were Lavim's favorite challenge.

Lavim leaned forward, elbows on the table, and began, by what he considered subtle means, to delve for the secret. He started with Stanach's sword. Scabbarded in old, well-oiled leather, the sword's hilt was simple, undecorated. The place where the guard met the hilt was not smoothly joined, though Lavim could see that this was the weapon's only fault.

"I see," Lavim said as though he'd just noticed, "that you don't carry an axe for a weapon."

Stanach nodded.

"I only mention it because I'm not sure I've ever seen a dwarf without his axe."

"Most of us prefer axes."

"But you carry a sword. It's a kind of a beat-up old thing, isn't it? Not, of course, that it isn't a good blade. I'm sure it is, but I just wondered."

"It's old."

"Was it your father's, maybe?"

Stanach looked up then, his eyes sharp and cautious. "It's mine." Then, as though aware of the abruptness of the answer, he smiled a little. "I made it."

"You're a swordsmith! Of course, I should have known by your hands. The skin's all scarred and pitted. From the forge, right?"

"That's right."

"Have you made a lot? Does it take long to make a sword? You've made daggers, too, I'll bet, and lots of other things. Did you ever make an axe's blade? They say that a dwarven blade is the best you can find and—"

Stanach laughed aloud, genuinely amused. Let a kender get in one question and you cannot possibly live long enough to answer the thousands of others that follow! "Whoa, now easy, Lavim Springtoe. Yes, I've made a lot of swords. This one I made first. The blade is good, the balance maybe not so good, but I'm used to it. And yes, daggers, too, and axe heads."

Lavim glanced again at the dwarf's hands, folded now around his empty mug. Though some of the scars were silvered with age, others were more recent. One, a long burn along his right thumb, still looked raw. No camping fire's burn, that.

It is as if he left his forge only yesterday, Lavim thought. But Thorbardin was hundreds of miles away. Still, here he is. By the look of him, he is one of the Hylar, one of the ruling clan at Thorbardin. Those, Lavim knew, left the mountains about as happily as a fish leaves water.

Long Ridge lay squarely under Verminaard's heel. Ember, the Highlord's red dragon, made daily passes over the town. Those people who had not been killed in the battle for the town were only barely surviving here. Why would anyone, except himself, of course, come to Long Ridge? Lavim's curiosity was like a spark in tinder.

What would bring a dwarf out from the safety of Thorbardin to this forsaken place?

There was no time to ask. From outside, the sound of a commotion, and finally a roar of fury silenced the tavern.

"Givrak!" Stanach snatched the kender's arm and jerked him to his feet. "Go to ground, Lavim. He's back, and I've no doubt it's you he's looking for."

Lavim only shrugged. "Maybe." His green eyes danced with mischief as he sat down. "I knew a draconian once who could never remember what it was he was looking for. It irritated him to no end, as you can imagine. He would turn purple after a while, so strictly speaking perhaps he wasn't a draconian—"

"If you don't go, you won't be drinking your ale, but leaking it like a sieve, kender. There must be a back way out, behind the bar. Go, now, go."

"But—"

"Go!" Stanach shoved the kender halfway across the room toward the bar.

Lavim stumbled, righted himself, and looked back over his shoulder. Who can understand a dwarf? Moody one minute, companionable in the next, then, all of a sudden and for no reason at all, like thunder and lightning! He made for the door behind the bar. Not because he was afraid of Givrak—the capacity for fear was not in him—but because the matter seemed so important to Stanach.

Dwarves, he thought, always tend to be a little touchy. Its all those hundreds of years in the mountains by themselves.

He flashed a grin at the serving girl. A tall elf, his blue eyes alight with amusement, grabbed Lavim's arm and hustled him through the doorway and into a storeroom.

"Go, kender," he whispered, "and don't stop running till you're out of town!"

Lavim wasn't going to run anywhere. He'd slip out the back, since it seemed to matter to everyone that he did, but he wasn't going to forget about Stanach. The kender pocketed a bung-starter, a small flask of wine, and several other interesting objects and slipped out the back door into the alley just as Givrak entered through the front and roared something about a "god-cursed, lying kender" who'd lived too long for his own, or anyone else's, good.

CHAPTER 7

The draconian Givrak was troubled with just enough intelligence to permit him to carry out his orders and, occasionally, to plan a simple strategy. Having received few orders this day, he turned a considerable portion of his slim intellect to the problem of avenging himself on the kender who had the night before cost him a venomous reprimand from Carvath for disturbing his sleep.

Givrak was of the opinion that the kender's hide would make a fine ornament for a stable door.

The draconian had two squads of soldiers under his command. These he roused at dawn with orders to set up barricades at the three roads leading from the town and then to accompany him on a search of Long Ridge. Givrak was certain that he'd find the kender before nightfall.

As he stalked the streets of Long Ridge, Givrak's anger became unholy anticipation. He was going to be enjoying himself soon. He knew a dozen ways to kill a kender and, even when he employed the quickest of these methods, the screaming did not stop before two days had passed.

The morning's cold wind up from the valley did nothing to freshen the sooty air of Long Ridge. It seemed to Kelida, walking out beyond the town proper, that the gray air could never be clear again. She stumbled, tugged at the sword smacking against her leg, and tried to settle the scabbard belt more comfortably around her waist. Sighing impatiently, she wondered how anyone could wear something this cumbersome and still manage to walk.

She'd tried carrying it and found it too awkward. Each step she took had sent the sword either sliding from its scabbard or digging painfully into her arms. Stupid thing! She'd be glad to be rid of it. She stopped at the broad road's first bend and tugged at the scabbard belt again. Her skirt twisted and bunched at the waist, and her blouse caught on the buckle and ripped.

Stupid sword! She didn't want it and she wasn't going to keep it. All it had given her was bruised legs and torn clothes. Well, Tyorl was just going to take the thing back. There had been no sign of his mad friend Hauk since the night he'd given her the miserable thing. Wherever he was, he wasn't interested in his wretched sword.

Or me, she thought miserably. Not that he ever really had been. He'd been drunk when he'd given her the sword. Likely he'd wandered off someplace and run afoul of dragonarmy soldiers. Then, probably, he would be wishing that he had his sword!

Kelida shivered, partly from cold and partly from the thought that Hauk might truly have had a need for his sword. She looked around. The road dropped beyond the bend to begin a long, steep descent into the valley. From where she stood, Kelida could not see the valley. Neither could she see the barricade set up by Carvath's soldiers, but she knew it was there. Like those at each of the three roads leading into Long Ridge, it had been set up at dawn. For some reason, it had been declared that no one would leave Long Ridge today. Some luckless person had fallen under the attention of the occupation.

Kelida wanted to see neither the farm where she had once lived nor the soldiers who had ravaged that valley.

What I want to see, she thought, *is Tyorl!*

He'd left a message for her with Tenny that he was looking for her. He was leaving Long Ridge and wanted to speak with her outside the town before he left. Kelida had felt a little sad when she'd gotten the message. If the elf was leaving, it must surely mean that he didn't expect to find his friend Hauk here in Long Ridge. If she would have welcomed a chance to work a little vengeance on the young man, she also would have welcomed the opportunity to hear his bear's growl of a voice again.

Kelida unbuckled the sword belt and let the weapon fall to the ashy dust in the road. The wind carried a rough curse and grating laughter from the direction of the barricade. Kelida would go no farther. She took a seat on a boulder's flat top, drew up her knees, rested her chin on her forearms, and stared at the black, scarred fields across the road.

The dragon's fire had been capricious here on the outskirts of the town. East of the road was black desolation. The western verge, however, defended by the broad, golden width of the dirt road, still showed sign of life. The thicket of slim silver birches that crowned the ridge was almost untouched. Sedge, its plumes the rusty gold of autumn, drooped at the roadside. White dead-nettle had scattered its blossoms in tiny petals around its roots, as though presaging winter's snow. Even the yellow toad-flax showed here and there.

"Well, fine," she whispered to the sword lying in the road, "I'm here. Where is he?"

His hunting leathers were the color of shade and birch. Kelida started and gasped when all of a sudden Tyorl stepped out of the shadows.

"Right here, Kelida." He smiled and cocked a thumb at the sword. "What's that doing here?"

Kelida let go the breath she had caught. "Where else should it be? If you're leaving, you'll want to take it with you."

"He gave it to you."

Exasperating elf! "I don't want it anymore. I never did want it. What would I do with it? I can't sell it; I can't wield it; I can't even carry the thing! Won't you please just take it, go wherever it is you're going, and leave me alone?"

Tyorl cast a quick look down the road toward the barricade and motioned her to silence. "Be easy, Kelida. I'm going, and that's what I wanted to talk to you about." He gestured toward the birch thicket. "Come here. I don't want to say this in front of half the dragonarmy."

She hesitated, then made a quick decision to do as he asked. The smile had vanished from his eyes, his voice was low and tense. Kelida picked up the sword and let him draw her into the shadows of the trees.

"Listen," he whispered, "and listen well. I don't know where Hauk is. I don't know what's happened to him, but I know he's not in this town anymore." He paused. "You know we're rangers."

Kelida nodded.

"Aye, and our lord is a man called Finn. He and our band are waiting for our return. I can't stay here any longer."

"You're just going to forget him?"

Anger flashed in the elf's eyes. Too late, Kelida realized that her question had been close to an insult.

"No, Kelida. I'm not going to stop looking. There's a lot of ground between here and the foothills. I'll look for Hauk every step of the way. But I have to get back to Finn." He gestured to the sword in her hands. "Please keep it. It may be that Hauk will come back here, looking for the sword and me. Will you tell him where I've gone?"

"But—"

Tyorl's fingers closed with a strong grip on her wrist. "Kelida, it's time for me to leave Long Ridge. Hauk and I managed to convince those who have an interest in such things that we are hunters. If I stay any longer, someone will surely notice that I haven't been doing much hunting. Their next guess is going to be that I'm a ranger."

Fear skittered up Kelida's spine. She asked the question before she realized it wouldn't be wise to know the answer.

"Where are you going?"

Tyorl hesitated only briefly. "Qualinesti's south border. Finn has work for us there. I'm sorry you brought the sword all the way out here. I wish I could carry it back for you, but I can't delay any longer."

"What about the barricade?"

"What about it? Finn would have my skin if I couldn't slip past a couple of half-drunk dragonarmy scum." He took the sword from her and ran his palm down the length of the shabby old scabbard. Cold sunlight glinted on the sapphires, making them gleam like ice. "He won this at daggers."

"I'm not surprised." Kelida smiled. "He has a good aim."

Tyorl chuckled. "Aye, he does at that. Keep it for him?"

The wind seemed to grow colder. Kelida thought of the mountains south of Qualinesti, wet and bleak in winter. She thought of Hauk and wondered where he was, why he had abandoned so valuable a sword, and as good a friend as Tyorl.

Then she wondered, where she had not before, if Hauk had simply slipped off in the night, deserting the ranger band. She stole a quick look at Tyorl.

No, the elf would never consider it. Kelida shivered and took the sword. How awkward it was! "I'll keep it." She hesitated for only the space of a breath, then rose on tiptoe and lightly kissed his cheek. "Good luck to you."

"Aye, well, we'll both need some luck, eh?" He smiled. "Thank you."

He took her arm and walked her back to the road. Because she was fumbling with the sword belt, Kelida didn't know that their way was blocked until she felt the elf's grip tighten. She looked up.

Three soldiers, a human, and two draconians, stood across the path to the road. One of the soldiers grinned, showing gapped yellow teeth. "A sweet good-bye," he drawled. His eyes flicked over Tyorl dismissively and fastened on Kelida, lingering.

Kelida's stomach twisted weakly.

Lavim Springtoe ran like a rabbit who knows he is too

fast for the hound, reveling in speed and the chase. Head down and laughing, he led the four draconians up one street, down another, through a tavern, and out the back door. Roaring and cursing in pursuit, they sounded like animated junkpiles, their swords crashing against their armor as they ran.

He ducked down a sooty alley. Nimbly leaping a fence, he gleefully shouted vile taunts to the four who, weighed down with armor and weapons, struggled furiously to climb. Before the first draconian dropped to the ground, the kender squeezed between a clammy brick wall and a garbage keg. He was only a little out of breath.

Lavim let the first one past. It was the second he was most interested in. He was Givrak and Lavim was certain that he would be by in a minute.

When Givrak lumbered by, sword out and gleaming in the watery morning light, Lavim's hoopak shot out between the draconian's legs and sent him sprawling into the first pursuer. The third, coming too fast to stop, piled into the other two, and the fourth only missed them by throwing himself against the opposite wall.

Lavim hooted with laughter and scrambled over the garbage keg and the three tangled draconians. He darted between the legs of the fourth and headed for the street. He dashed around the wide skirts of a woman, ducked under the long legs of a horse, and tore across the road. Behind him the draconians' curses told him that they'd untangled themselves and were yet in pursuit.

Lavim knew the streets and byways of Long Ridge as only a kender or a street urchin could. He made for a warehouse, half-burned in the taking of the town, snatching up stones and loose cobbles from the street as he ran. He'd not had this much fun since he'd run, two yards all the way, ahead of an avalanche of snow and stones down a mountainside in Khur. (The two yards was his estimation. Ish, the gnome who was with him at the time, claimed that the distance was closer to a quarter mile, that the avalanche was no avalanche at all but a little slide of snow, and that all of this did not take place on a mountainside, but on a gently sloping hill.)

The warehouse was huge, half a block long and wider than any building in the town. Once every kind of trade goods had been stored here: flour, wheat, corn, even bales of snowy wool. Of all the things stored here at the time of the fire, only ashes remained.

Lavim darted into the roofless building. Splashing through dark, ashy puddles from a recent rain, he made for the stairs at the back of the first floor. Givrak and his soldiers pounded behind him, bellowing curses and threats, scattering people like chickens before a gale.

The stink of burning permeated the building. The old kender paused at the bottom of the stairs. Leaning against a fire-thinned wall to catch his breath, he squinted up. There was still a second floor—or part of one. It jutted out from the stair wall like a barn's loft, black edged and splintered, covering only half the width of the building. From that perch he would be able to fire, with perfect impunity, the stones he'd collected.

Sucking in huge gulps of air still tainted with the acrid smell of burned wool and grain, Lavim eyed the stairs. He decided that a light-footed kender would be able to negotiate them and he started up. He moved swiftly on the theory that a soft, quick step would stress the already creaking stairs less than a heavy, cautious one. With half the steps negotiated, his left foot on an upper step, his right on the one below, the lower tread groaned and then collapsed with a splintering snap.

Lavim moved fast. He threw himself against the wall and grabbed for purchase above. There was none. Like a collapsing house of cards, the steps above fell away from the second floor. Lavim yelped, dove, and caught the splintery edge of the floor.

His hands clinging to the crumbling wood, the rest of him dangling over the two story drop at full arm extension, Lavim thought it might be better for him now if kender possessed wings.

He almost lost his hold when a hard, sharp bark of laughter sounded from far below on the first floor. Givrak, his reptilian eyes glittering balefully in the gray light, his thin, snakey tongue flickering, laughed up at the kender.

All his life, Lavim had never been able to resist a sure target. He twisted and spat down between his elbows. Though his aim had been a source of pride in his youth, it had lately been known to fail. It did not fail him now. He hit Givrak squarely between the eyes. The draconian's shriek of fury echoed around the empty warehouse.

Lavim flinched away from the silver flight of a dagger and elbowed himself higher. He wrapped one hand around a charred, wobbly post. He pulled, felt the post give a little, and dropped his hand back to the floor.

Givrak laughed, a grim, cold sound. "Give it up, ratling! There's no place to run, and I would like to discuss something with you."

Lavim twisted again, got a knee up, and then slid back. The weakened boards of the second floor groaned.

Metal crashed against wood. The draconian was abandoning his armor. Lavim, whose curiosity could not be quenched were he about to drop into the shadowy horror of the Abyss, peered down again. Givrak's armor was a pile of red metal on the floor, his short sword was clamped between long, fanged jaws. His wings, wide stretches of bone and claw-tipped leather, unfolded with crude, jerking motions. The other three stepped back, grinning. They scented an ending.

They're gliding wings, Lavim reminded himself, and draconians can't really fly. Everyone knows that . . .

Givrak couldn't fly. However, he had thick, powerfully muscled legs and could leap higher than even Lavim would have imagined. On the first leap, the draconian's long clawed hand raked and missed the shakey post to which Lavim clung.

On the second, black wings thrusting powerfully down, Givrak caught the splintered edge of the floor with one hand and shifted his sword from jaws to free hand.

The kender moved fast then, brought both knees up tight to his chest and twisted, throwing himself up onto the groaning floor. Givrak, laughing horribly, easily hefted himself onto the floor.

The rabbit was no longer certain that he could outrun the hound.

Lavim snatched his dagger from its belt sheath and slashed wildly. The blade did little damage to the draconian's tough, scaled arm. Lavim shifted his grip and tore the blade down and across Givrak's left wing, ducked beneath the roaring beast's huge arm, and brought the blade ripping up through the leather of the creature's right wing. A huge, clawed hand came down on Lavim's wrist and twisted cruelly. The kender's dagger fell from nerveless fingers.

Lavim, with the persistence of his kind, drove his knee into Givrak's belly. When the draconian doubled, howling, Lavim brought his other knee up hard as he could under the creature's jaw. Teeth clashed, Givrak's head whipped back. Lavim jerked his wrist free, retrieved his dagger, and bolted.

There was no place to run.

What used to be walls here were now only fire blackened beams and posts and lowering sky. A hauling strut jutted out from the side of the building, a black finger pointing to the hills. Below were the cold, hard cobbles of the streets of Long Ridge. Lavim stopped and turned. The draconian, limping and wings torn, lumbered toward him, murder in his black reptilian eyes.

Kender do not think often, but when they do, they think fast. Lavim Springtoe waited just long enough for Givrak to get up a a little speed, and then he ran for the sky.

Stanach had been looking for the elf since dawn with no luck. The kender was another matter. Stanach heard word of *him* everywhere.

The cooper, the blacksmith, and the candlemaker all had complaints. The cooper wanted his small adze back. The blacksmith vowed to turn Lavim over to Carvath's authority if he did not have his stamp and chisel in his shop by noon. The candlemaker only cursed his own foul luck to have survived the army's incursions only to see his few remaining goods carried off by a plague of kenders.

Stanach did not try to explain to the man that one kender hardly constitutes a plague. Semantics, in the matter of kenders, often depend upon which side of the counter one stands behind.

Still searching for Tyorl, the dwarf crossed Lavim's trail

at the butcher's shop, the tanner's, and the potter's. A boy had seen the kender dashing through the alley across the street from a tavern. From there, he heard that Lavim had indeed been in the tavern, but only briefly. He'd been chased by draconian soldiers.

Givrak! It could be no one else. Stanach thought about Tyorl and the sword. The chances were looking slimmer every hour that the elf would know where the sword was. But he was Stanach's only clue. If this clue proved fruitless, he'd have to start looking somewhere else soon or get back to Piper.

The kender could likely take care of himself. Kenders usually could. Aye, Stanach thought then, but if he's caught? He didn't want to think about what would happen to Lavim if the draconian caught him.

"Damn kender!" he muttered. He supposed he could look for the kender and the elf at the same time.

The next thing Stanach heard was that Lavim, white braid flying and legs pumping for all he was worth, had headed for a burned out warehouse in the middle of the block, the draconians still in pursuit. Reluctantly Stanach checked the release of his sword and headed for the warehouse.

He approached the warehouse's blackened skeleton from the opposite side of the street. A catbird's laughter, or a kender's, rang mockingly from above.

Stanach looked up in time to see a draconian plunge from the unwalled second floor of the warehouse, arms and legs whirling. The creature spread his wings, now useless, dagger-slashed leather, and screamed. Had the drop been steeper, Stanach would have been able to hear the wind whistling through those slashes. As it was, he only heard the thud of the draconian hitting the ground, the scrape and crack of scales and bones on cobbles. And Lavim's catbird cackling.

Stanach drew his sword and crossed the street. He kicked the draconian over. It was Givrak.

Stanach shuddered. Even as he recognized the draconian, Givrak's carcass turned to stone. His heart lurching hard, Stanach backed quickly away from the thing. He'd heard tales of what happened to the bodies of dead draconians, but had only half believed those tales till now.

Lavim leaned out over the edge of the building. "Stanach! Good to see you again! Is he dead? He forgot about those holes in his wings. The little details, my father used to say, are very important sooner or later and—Yo! Stanach! Look out!"

Givrak's three companions, having heard their fellow's scream, had bolted out the door opposite Stanach. Without a pause, they leaped over their fallen comrade, whose stony corpse was now turning to dust, and charged the dwarf.

After the manner of a good swordcrafter, Stanach's knowledge of the weapon did not stop at knowing how to make one. He was no warrior; he hadn't a fighter's instincts. But he had an intimate knowledge of the weapon and in his hand a blade was a deadly thing. He lopped the sword arm off his first attacker and left him howling on his knees in the street. He noticed that, wounded, the thing did not become stone.

Stanach did not waste time wondering why. He backed the other two against the warehouse, his sword a silver flash in the air. He wielded the blade double-handed as though it were an axe. Every move his two opponents tried to make was blocked by singing steel. A good many spans shorter than his attackers, Stanach stood naturally under their guard and pressed that advantage every time he could. One of the draconians stumbled, and in that moment between balance lost and balance recovered, Stanach raised his sword to strike.

Stanach's sword high, his guard clear, the draconian's companion lunged from the left and would have neatly skewered the dwarf had a fist-sized stone not caught him hard at the unprotected base of his neck and dropped him like a felled ox.

"Stanach! Don't let your sword get caught in 'em! The body will hold the blade till they turn to—behind you! Duck!"

Stanach did, and a blade whistled in the air an inch above his head. Another rock flew and missed. Stanach scrambled to his feet and turned only barely in time to deflect and arrest the downward thrust of a draconian's sword with his own. The draconian hissed. Teeth bared and dripping in long jaws, thin red tongue flicking, he threw all of his weight against Stanach's defense.

Stanach's blade moved back. Its razored edge was only a finger's width from the dwarf's neck. His hand, wet with cold sweat, slipped on the sword's grip. His attacker had the advantage of size and bore down on Stanach's blade with his own, all his weight behind. A bleak understanding shivered through the dwarf: he would not go down until he'd torn his muscles from his bones. Grimly, Stanach put his back into a last push.

A wild cackling sounded from above, Lavim's laughter. Another of his deadly missiles flew true and hit Stanach's opponent in the eye.

The next flew foul. A sharp edged stone caught Stanach on the right elbow, numbing his arm to the wrist. His sword flew from his useless hand.

His heart thundering painfully against the cage of his ribs, Stanach spun and dropped to his knees on the cobbles, groping for his weapon, sure that he would feel the fatal plunge of steel between his shoulders before he reached it. He cursed the kender's aim and gasped a prayer to Reorx all in one breath. At the same instant Lavim, shouted a hasty apology and fired another rock from above.

The draconian roared, staggering now under a rain of stones and cobbles. Lavim whooped. "Get 'im, Stanach! No! Don't! There's more of 'em coming! Run, Stanach! Run!"

Steel-soled boots rang against the cobbles like thunder roaring. Four more draconians rounded the corner at the top of the street. Stanach snatched up his sword in his left hand, scrambled to his feet, and waved up to Lavim.

"Get down here, kender!"

Lavim would have liked to, but he didn't see how that was possible. Wings, he thought, kender really do need wings! He crawled out onto the hauling strut and clutched at the beam with both hands. He dropped to his full length, peered down at Stanach below and yelled, "Catch!"

The best Stanach could do was break the kender's fall.

They went down in a tangle of arms and legs, cobbles biting into backs and knees. Stanach hauled Lavim to his feet, hoping that most of the kender's bones were still intact. Hanging onto Lavim's arm, Stanach ran faster than he'd ever run before.

Tyorl stepped in front of Kelida.

The soldier's eyes narrowed. He closed his fingers around the hilt of his sword.

"Aye," the soldier said, his fingers tapping a restless pattern against the hilt. "A sweet good-bye. You weren't leaving, were you, elf?"

The draconian laughed, a short, hard bark. "I think he was, Harig. What you saw must have been the wench's farewell kiss."

Tyorl's hand itched for a sword. Kelida looked up, her eyes wide. Her breathing harsh with fear. The pulse in her neck leaped.

"I'd wager she'd forget the elf fast enough after he's dead, Harig. Think you could take him?"

"The elf?" Harig snorted. "My blade's tasted elf blood before. Thin and old, but it will do."

Tyorl grabbed Kelida's shoulder and spun her aside, snatching Hauk's sword. As he did, Harig drew his sword, too. The draconian and the other human stood away. Neither made a move to intervene, but their eyes were red and hungry.

Harig bared broken, yellowed teeth in a grin. "What say you, elf? Is she worth a little blood?"

The breeze strengthened and moaned around the top of the ridge. The stench of burning and death gusted up from the valley. Along the hilt of Hauk's sword, sapphires winked and danced in jeweled pattern to a silent song of light.

Tyorl took an easy, loose stand and leveled his sword as though he were not the defender but the challenger. "All your blood," he said, his voice low and cold as only an elf's can be, "would not begin to measure the worth."

Tyorl saw Harig's intent to strike in his muddy brown eyes. Hauk's blade rose high and fell hard. The two soldiers howled and Kelida screamed. Harig was dead before he ever moved.

Tyorl moved fast. He grabbed Kelida's wrist and pulled her close. Again he leveled his blade in challenge, this time at the two remaining guards. "I can deal the same death to you if you want it."

The soldiers, swords drawn, flanked him. The draconians hissed, a sound that reminded Tyorl of snakes rising to strike. As they closed in, he prayed to gods too long neglected that his boast was true.

The cobbled streets of Long Ridge left behind, Stanach and Lavim made good speed. So did the pursuing draconians. The kender's head was down, his small legs pumping. Three belt pouches made of leather, two of cloth, bounced and swung wildly as he ran. Lavim wheezed now like an old bellows and wasted no breath in laughing aloud, though Stanach could still see the laughter in his shining green eyes. Lavim ran for the sheer pleasure of hearing the draconians' furious cursing.

When one of their pusuers lost his footing in a mud puddle, tangling two others and sending searing curses through the street, Lavim slowed to watch them thrashing and trying to sort themselves out. Stanach grabbed the kender's arm and, ducking down an alley, dragged Lavim after him. Lavim sprang over cracked barrels stinking of sour wine. Stanach didn't and only scrambled up out of the mud as the draconians entered the alley roaring. Stanach ran.

Stanach's heart crashed against his ribs. His legs began to weigh as heavily as lead and the stitch in his side threatened to drop him with every step.

As they approached the last bend before the road wound out of the town to begin its steep descent into the valley, a woman screamed, high and terrified. Neither the dwarf nor the kender could have slowed if he'd wanted to. They were at the bend in the road before the echoes of the woman's scream had finished rolling down into the valley. Lavim snatched Stanach's arm, dragged him to a halt, and pointed.

Stanach cursed. The elf he'd been searching for all morning was battling for his life against two dragonarmy soldiers. Blood streamed from his right shoulder and his face.

In the road, the serving girl from the tavern scrambled for rocks. She threw what she found at the draconians. Though her aim was good, her missiles gave the elf no help at all, but rebounded harmlessly from the mail of his opponents. What was she doing in the company of the elf, anyway?

Backed to the rocky edge of the ridge, the elf wielded his sword double-handed and with considerable skill. But Stanach knew that skill was not going to win out over numbers and a cliff's edge. The elf could not possibly hold his ground against the two draconians. If he didn't miss a step and plunge to his death over the ridge, he'd die on a draconian's blade.

Lavim, on the theory that anyone fighting a draconian could be none but a friend, bellowed an enthusiastic battle cry and threw himself headfirst at one of the embattled elf's attackers. The soldier and kender went down in the road.

Stanach moved more cautiously and with considered intent. He had not, as Lavim had, fogotten their pursuit. At any moment, four more draconians were going to round the bend. A kender, a girl, a bleeding elf, and a winded dwarf were not going to be proof against six of Carvath's creatures. Two dead draconians turning to dust in the road, however, might stop the other four long enough to make escape a slim possibility.

There was nothing Stanach wanted more at this moment than to be away from Long Ridge. He ducked in under the draconian's guard and thrust hard and up, killing the creature and dragging his sword free just as the elf fell to his knees, his blade rattling to the ground.

Stanach reached to return the sword. He found the elf's hand on the grip before his own. He looked down then and, for a long moment, he stopped breathing.

Crimson light streaked through the blood on the steel.

Great Reorx, he thought numbly. This is it! Stormblade!

Then, Tyorl was up and Stormblade was gone, lifted high in the elf's hand and out of Stanach's reach.

In the road, Lavim had snatched a rock from the girl and brought it down hard on his fallen opponent's skull. Bone cracked, the soldier screamed, and Lavim bashed again for good measure.

The elf was breathing hard. Stanach eyed him doubtfully. He was bleeding from a shoulder wound, his eyes were dull, almost unfocused. If you fall here, Stanach thought coldly, I will have what I've been searching for, my friend, and I will thank you for it. Oh, I will thank you for it!

The elf did not fall. He lifted his chin, wiped blood from his face, and, by an effort of will, focused on Stanach. "I am all right."

Stanach snorted. "But can you run?"

The elf barely flinched. "Run? If I have to."

Stanach pointed back toward the town. As he'd feared, the four draconians were rounding the bend. "You have to," he said grimly.

Aye, he thought, you have to. You and Stormblade have to run with me, my friend.

They ran.

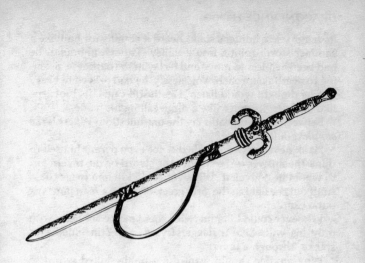

CHAPTER 8

There was no light at all. There had been none since he became aware of being in this place. Hauk didn't know how long ago that was. He was neither bound nor chained, yet he could not move. He lay on damp stone and cold seeped into him, twining around his bones with a fever's grip.

It seemed as if he had never been warm. His memories were all of a bone-deep terror, dying—and a question, endlessly repeated.

Where is the sapphire-hilted sword?

He had died twice since finding himself here. His first death was swift and agonizing, with cold steel in his belly and his blood rushing out of him. The second time, he lay in the eternal dark and felt death's slow approach. He'd sensed its remorseless hunter's stalk, heard it coming for him like a summer storm rolling into a valley. Though unbound, he had been helpless to move and he lay in the darkness, listening to death's approach. Voicelessly, he had prayed to every god he thought would listen. Death still came, its footsteps like thunder, its voice like a dirge calling his name.

Between his two deaths lay the one question: *Where is the sapphire-hilted sword?*

Hauk never answered. He did not even permit himself to think the answer or remember the sword or the tavern girl to whom he'd given it. Whoever could kill him twice could snuff out the light in the girl's green eyes like a man pinching out a candle.

Whoever could kill him twice could pierce her heart with only his will. Like a dagger flying, silver in blue-hazed smoke, through a tavern.

Why anyone should want the sapphire-hilted sword so badly, he did not know.

So, he existed in a wasteland of waiting and terror. He did not know when he slept or when he was awake. The darkness bred nightmares and the same evil dreams that haunted him sleeping haunted him waking.

Yet now, in the wasteland, Hauk slowly became aware that he was not alone. A change in the feel of the air around him brought the sense that something or someone moved, though only slightly, nearby.

Someone breathed in the darkness. Harsh gasping echoed around him, and by this he knew that the place he was in had walls. A voice muttered and whispered. Fear crawled through Hauk and settled, cold and heavy, in his belly.

This was not the merciless voice that had asked about the sword. That voice had been hard, as sharply edged as steel. This voice was different: thinner, broken.

Or was that his own muttering, his own whispering?

Light exploded in the darkness, sending shadows leaping up the walls and arrows of fire into his eyes. Hauk roared in pain. He had no ability to turn his head, none even to close his eyes. The light was quickly doused.

The fire-edged image of a dwarf, crouched on the floor by

his feet, lantern held high, burned behind Hauk's aching eyes.

"Who . . . ?" he moaned. No answer came but a sharply drawn breath and the soft scuffing of booted feet on stone.

"Who are you!" A sob. A low, tormented growl. Silence. Hauk was alone again in the wasteland.

CHAPTER 9

The cold wind pursued them to the very bounds of the forest and only softened once they stepped under the forest's eaves. Stanach shivered as the cool touch of superstition's fingers danced up his spine. Never did he think he would come into Qualinesti and it did not help that he was only a quarter-day's journey into Elvenwood. At the forest's edge, or at its heart, Stanach was certain that the place would feel the same: posted, warded, guarded.

All his life Stanach had heard tales of travelers who had wandered into Qualinesti. Those tales were never told by the travelers themselves. No one who entered uninvited ever came out of Elvenwood. Were it not for Stormblade and his promise to return it, Stanach would have made his farewells at the edge of the forest and taken his chances with the draconians. But his oath had been sworn by the sword's name, and his promise given to Hornfel, his thane.

He, Lavim, and Kelida had entered the wood following Tyorl. The elf was limping and slow, but none argued when he assured them that no draconian would follow them into fabled Qualinesti.

Though he offered no argument, Stanach was not happy to be heading west into the forest when Piper would be waiting for him in the southeastern hills. It had been two days since he left the mage to fend for himself in the hills south of Long Ridge. Had Piper escaped their pursuers? Four against one were bad odds.

Still, he thought as he shouldered through a thicket of thorny underbrush, we had no choice. One of us had to get to Long Ridge. Someone had to find the sword.

Stanach's heart sank. Ground creepers tangled with fallen branches. Thickets and underbrush swept across the ground as though they'd been commanded to confuse the path. He was following Stormblade blindly into Elvenwood and he felt like an intruder in the forest.

But someone had to find the sword, someone had to give meaning to Kyan Red-axe's death. He would follow Stormblade, find a way to claim it, and trust in Piper to be at the meeting place.

Kelida had carried Stormblade ever since they'd come into the forest. Tyorl had offered to carry it and been refused. Stanach didn't know why she had insisted on wearing the sword. The blade jolted against her leg with almost every step she took. He would not have wanted to nurse those kind of bruises.

The dwarf wondered how she had come by the sword. It didn't matter, in the end, how Kelida had acquired Stormblade; it only mattered now that he find a way to bring it back to Thorbardin.

He didn't know how he was going to do that. While it was true that he would not have scrupled to steal Stormblade, it was also true that he wouldn't take the risk of stealing from an elf in Qualinesti. Stanach didn't know what the girl and the elf were to each other, but he sensed at once that stealing from Kelida would be the same as stealing from Tyorl.

The elf was wounded, but not so badly that he wouldn't track the thief of so valuable a weapon through a forest he had known from childhood and which Stanach knew not at all. What run Stanach might make through the woods with Stormblade could only end with him dead of an arrow in the neck and the Kingsword lost again.

No, he thought grimly, let the girl carry it for a while longer, until I figure out what to say and what to do.

So, though he shivered with cold in the sunless forest, Stanach followed Tyorl. He'd come too close now to see Stormblade vanish into dark and deep Elvenwood.

Lavim, trotting along beside Tyorl, looked up, his green eyes bright. "Not too many ghosts, are there?"

Tyorl smiled at that, a crooked lifting of his lips. "Have you been expecting ghosts, kenderkin?"

"And phantoms and specters, although I think they might be the same thing. You hear all kinds of stories about this place. That's pretty odd, don't you think? I mean, they say that there's no way out of here once you get in, then they tell all these stories about things with no hearts, no souls, maybe even no heads! How could they know about—"

"Lavim, shut up," Stanach warned. Lavim turned and, seeing Stanach's dark scowl, snapped his mouth shut.

Kelida, who had maintained a grim silence during their flight from Long Ridge, kept pace with the others despite the awkward burden of Stormblade. She said nothing, but shadows moved like nightmares across her white face. Stanach caught her elbow and steadied her.

"Tell me, then, Tyorl," he muttered, "is the place haunted or do you simply hope to frighten us?"

Tyorl stopped and turned, his eyes sleepy and hooded. "No more haunted than anyplace else in Krynn."

Lavim, with a shrug in Kelida's direction, trotted off the path. He wondered what bothered Kelida and hoped he'd remember to ask her about it later. In any case, this was Elvenwood, and with any luck, though Tyorl's answer had been vague, the place would be haunted. Lavim peered into thickets and the deep, black shadows wondering what form the haunting would take. Things, from the kender's point of view, were beginning to look up.

After another hour of walking, when the crimson moon had set and the silver one was only a dim and ghostly glow behind lowering clouds, Tyorl stopped at last in an oak-sheltered glade. When Lavim volunteered to take the night's first watch none argued.

Tyorl limped to the stream to clean the cuts on his face and the long, shallow gash in his shoulder. Stanach gathered wood and laid the night's fire. Lavim had hunted while he explored and returned with two fat grouse. Kelida fell asleep before the birds were plucked.

The damp, cold wind danced with the flames and set the bare branches above clacking together and groaning. Stanach poked at the fire and eyed the clouding sky.

"It'll rain before morning." he said. Tyorl agreed. An owl swooped low just out of the fire's light, a shadow and a clap of wings. A fox barked beyond the stream. Near a small stand of silver birch, Lavim paced his watch. Neither Stanach nor Tyorl expected that the kender would hold his post long and both sat awake in unspoken accord.

Tyorl leaned back against a log, stretching his legs out beside the fire. His belly full, the fire warm, he settled almost peacefully. He looked at Stanach, his smile lazy and knowing as he ran his thumb along the edge of his jaw.

"Say it, dwarf."

Stanach looked up from the fire, startled. "What do you want me to say?"

"Whatever it is you've been about to say all evening. Whatever it is you want to say every time you look at Kelida's sword. It's a fine blade and you're likely wondering about how she came to have it." Tyorl nodded in Kelida's direction. She slept with one hand pillowing her head, the other on the sword. "You've no doubt figured out that she's not a good hand with the thing."

"How *did* she come by it?"

"Is that the question?"

"One of them," Stanach said drily.

"Fair, I suppose. It was a gift."

"Who gave it to her?"

"Why does it matter?"

Stanach watched the fire leap and curl around the hickory and oak logs. Tyorl's challenge was mild enough. Still, it needed answering. He tangled his fingers in his black beard, tugging thoughtfully. He remembered Piper's warning: *Do what you have to do to get the sword.* He sighed.

"It matters more than you know." The dwarf gestured toward the sword beneath Kelida's hand. "It's called Stormblade."

Old brown leaves skittered across the clearing, scrabbling against the rocks at the stream's edge and whispering in the underbrush. For a moment, the light of the red moon escaped the covering clouds, turning the shadows purple. Tyorl leaned forward.

"Nice name. How do you know that?"

"I didn't just make it up, if that's what you think. Near the place where the hilt joins the steel is the mark of the smith who forged it: a hammer bisected by a sword. Isarn Hammerfell of Thorbardin made the blade, and he named it. There's a rough spot on the hilt where the chasing hasn't been smoothed. Check, if you doubt me."

"I've seen both. You still haven't answered me, friend Stanach. How does it matter who gave Kelida the sword?"

"Good blood has been shed for Stormblade. And bad. Four that I know of have died trying to claim it. One, a dwarf called Kyan Red-axe, was killed two days ago. He was my kinsman."

Tyorl settled back against the log. Suddenly, he remembered the two dwarves in Tenny's and how they had watched the daggerplay with marked interest.

Neither Hauk nor the dwarves had been seen in Long Ridge since that night. There had been no reason to connect the dwarves to Hauk's disappearance. Until now. "Go on." he said.

Stanach heard the edge in his voice and tried not to react to it. This one would want the whole story and Stanach knew that he had come too far in the telling to start amending the tale now.

"I'm no storycrafter, Tyorl, but here's the tale. The sword was made in Thorbardin and stolen two years ago. My thane, Hornfel, and another, Realgar, have been searching for it since. Not long ago, word came that Stormblade had been seen. A ranger carried it and he was last known to be in Long Ridge."

"It's only a sword, Stanach." Tyorl snorted. "People kill with a sword, not for one."

"This one they kill for. It's a Kingsword. None can rule the dwarves without one. With one?" Stanach shrugged. "Thorbardin is controlled by the dwarf who holds Stormblade."

"A good reason to want it—yourself."

He's an Outlander, Stanach reminded himself, and too ignorant to know what he's saying. The dwarf tried patiently to explain. "It would do me no good at all. I'm a swordcrafter, nothing more. I don't have the armies backing me that Realgar has. I'd mount a pretty shabby revolution without a soldier or two at my back, eh?"

Tyorl shrugged. "I'll wager your Hornfel has a soldier or two."

"He does."

"Do you serve him?"

"He's my thane," Stanach said simply. "I helped make the sword for him. I was there when—when Reorx touched the steel." He stared for a long moment at his hands, tracking the scars on his palms. "He hasn't done that in three hundred years, Tyorl. No sword is a Kingsword without the god's touch. I was—I was supposed to guard the sword. I turned my back for only a moment . . . "

"And you lost it."

Stanach said nothing until the elf urged him to continue.

It was a strange story. Tyorl followed the paths of dwarven politics with some difficulty, but he had no difficulty understanding that for Stanach, and for the two thanes who sought the sword, Stormblade was more than a beautiful piece of craftsmanship. It was a talisman that would unite Thorbardin's factioned Council of Thanes.

Tyorl listened carefully, wondering as he did if the dwarves knew that Verminaard was even now laying plans to bring dragonarmy troops into the eastern foothills of the Kharolis Mountains. The Highlord had a hungry eye for Thorbardin.

His gods were elven gods, silver Paladine and the forest lord, the bard-king Astra. But Tyorl, watching the shadows pooled beneath the trees, sliding across brown carpets of oak leaves, recognized a pattern that only Takhisis the Queen of Darkness could weave. He moved closer to the fire, suddenly chilled.

"If you know the sword," Stanach said, "you've seen the red streak in the steel. It's the mark of the god's forge, the refection of Reorx's own fire. I saw it come red from the fire and, when the steel cooled, I saw the god's mark. This is a Kingsword, and the thane who has Stormblade will rule in Thorbardin as king regent. There's been no one thane to rule the dwarf-realms in three hundred years.

"It's a hard thing to be kingless. Something will always be . . . missing, longed for but never found. We know that we will never have a high king again. The Hammer of Kharas is made up of legends and hopes; it's not about to be found again. But, Stormblade will give us a king regent, a steward to hold the throne in the place of the high king who will never be.

"If Realgar becomes that king regent, the dwarves of Thorbardin are lost to slavery. He is *derro*, a mage and a worshipper of Takhisis. Thorbardin will be hers and will have fallen without a fight. He will do anything to capture Stormblade, and he's killed for far less than this."

A log, light and laced with gray ash, slid from the fire. Stanach toed it back into place. "In the end I suppose it doesn't matter how Kelida got the sword."

"It matters, dwarf." Tyorl sat forward, his blue eyes as hard as the blade of his dagger glinting in the firelight.

Stanach sat perfectly still, his eyes on the steel. "Aye, then? How?"

"It matters because she had it as a gift from a friend of mine. The ranger you mentioned. He's been missing these two days past. Would you know anything about that? Two dwarves, one of them was missing an eye, were in Tenny's the night Hauk disappeared—were they, by any chance, friends of yours?"

Stanach went cold to his bones. Realgar's agents had been in Long Ridge! "No friends of mine. I left Thorbardin with

Kyan Red-axe and a human mage called Piper. Kyan is dead. Piper is waiting for me in the hills. I went to Long Ridge alone."

"I'm wondering if you're lying."

"Wonder all you want," Stanach snapped. He remembered Kyan and the heartless scream of crows in the sky. "Those two in Long Ridge were no friends of mine. More likely, they were part of Realgar's pack. I'd wager that at least one of them is a mage. No doubt they waylaid your friend and didn't find the sword because he'd already given it to the girl.

"And if those two *were* mages, Tyorl, they could have had him to Thorbardin before you even thought to miss him. If he's not dead, Realgar has him. Me, I'd rather be dead. Know it: he's using every means to discover where the Kingsword is now."

It's likely, Stanach thought, the ranger *is* dead. He would not live two days if he had to depend upon Realgar's mercy. But Hauk must have kept his silence to the end. He saw the same thought in the sudden darkening of the elf's eyes.

"Aye, you know it." Stanach whispered.

Tyorl shook his head and looked up. "I only believe we've lost our watch. The kender is gone."

You don't doubt me, the dwarf thought. If you do, you're not going to take the chance that someone who will kill for Stormblade is following us now, following the girl.

Stanach nodded toward the birches, ghostly gray in the darkness. "I'll keep the fire. You get some sleep."

Tyorl shook his head. "The kender is *your* friend. It strikes me as convenient that he's gone and left you to take the watch . . . and maybe the sword, too."

"Me?" Stanach snorted. "Where would I go with it? Aye, back to Thorbardin if I could. I suppose I could kill you where you sleep. But you know better than that. I'd never get out of this forest before I died of old age." Stanach's smile held no humor. "Lavim said it: 'who enters Elvenwood doesn't get out without an elf to show him the way.' Go to sleep. I'm willing to wait for morning to talk about it again."

Tyorl, who had trusted the dwarf in Long Ridge, did not trust him now. He did, however, trust the forest. He didn't know what Stanach might do if he didn't have to fear Qualinesti. Though Stanach's assurances had been smooth and easily given, Tyorl wondered if they had also been true.

Kelida curled up tightly against the chill and damp seeping into her bones from the hard ground. She'd overheard enough of the tale Stanach had told Tyorl to know the sword that had bruised her legs, the one that now lay under her hand, was no ordinary blade.

Their voices, though pitched low, had wakened her. Then, she was glad enough to be awake. Her sleep had been foul with nightmares of fire and death.

She hadn't intended to eavesdrop, but when she heard the sword mentioned, heard it named, she could not help herself.

Hauk! Was he dead? Was he a prisoner of this Realgar?

Kelida squeezed her eyes shut. She remembered his hands, large and calloused, as he placed the sword—Stormblade!—at her feet. She remembered his smile and the way his voice broke when he offered his apology. What had happened to him?

If he's not dead, Realgar has him. Me, I'd rather be dead.

Tyorl slept nearby. Across the fire from her, Stanach sat his watch. Firelight gilded the silver earring he wore and gleamed red in the depths of his thick black beard. When he reached for a stout branch to toss onto the fire, Kelida sat up. He said nothing, only nodded. Kelida tucked a straggling wisp of her hair behind her ear and handed him another branch.

He took the wood and thanked her. She was surprised that his voice, often a deep, rumbling growl when he spoke to Tyorl, could be so soft. Kelida offered him a tentative smile. Though he did not return it, his dark eyes lost some of their grimness.

Encouraged, she went to sit beside him. She did not share his log, but sat on the ground, her back braced against it. She did not take her eyes from the hot dance of the flames.

Fire, thick and hot as the flames of a hundred torches, poured from the dragon's maw. Kelida screamed as the fire found the tinder-dry thatching of the farmhouse's roof. The

*house exploded around her brother and her mother. For a
long, horrible moment, Kelida saw her mother's face, and
her brother's. The boy was shrieking, the tears on his face
were the color of blood, reflecting the flames. Her mother,
hunched over the boy as though her own body might protect him from the heat, wore strangely mingled looks of des-
peration and resignation.*

*Then there was nothing to see but two small human
torches in a house made of fire.*

Kelida took no warmth from the campfire. A small, tame
reminder of her family's deaths, it only set her shivering.

"Stanach, where is Lavim?"

Stanach shrugged. "Out on kender-business. Who
knows? Likely he'll be back before dawn." Looking for
ghosts, he thought. He did not say this aloud.

"Have we thanked you for saving our lives?" she asked
quietly.

He didn't answer at once, but held perfectly still as
though asking himself the question. "No," he said at last.

"I'm sorry. We should have before now. Thank you. If it
wasn't for you and Lavim, Tyorl would be dead now, and
I—" She faltered, hearing whispers from her nightmares in
the hiss and sigh of the flames.

Stanach shook his head. "Don't think about it. It never
happened. Tell me, how did you come to be at the barricade
with Tyorl?"

"I was saying good-bye. He was leaving Long Ridge."

"Ah?"

Kelida saw the speculation in his eyes and blushed. "No,
it's not what you think. I—I've only known him for a day or
two. When Hauk gave me the sword, and then couldn't be
found, I wanted to give it back to Tyorl. He wouldn't take
it. He said Hauk might come back for it."

Stanach smiled. He saw the way of it now. The girl wasn't
interested in Tyorl at all. She was, however, interested in
this missing ranger, Hauk. He heard it in her voice and saw
it in the way she looked back at Stormblade. The sword
could have been hilted with lead, the sapphires could have
been no more than rocks from the stream's bed. It was
Hauk's sword and that was all that mattered to Kelida.

What mattered to Tyorl, however, was something else. He had an interest in the girl. Aye, that elf's eyes could be hard as Stormblade's jewels, but never when he looked at Kelida, never when he spoke of her. This would be something to consider.

"Kelida," he said, "won't your family be wondering where you are?"

"My father, my mother, and Mival, my little brother—" Kelida drew a steadying breath. "They're dead. We had a farm in the valley. It—the dragon came and—"

Stanach looked away, out beyond the fire and into the still and silent forest. The wind sounded like the echoes of looters' howls. Suddenly, he felt like one who, from idle curiosity, stares at a stranger's raw, open wound. "Hush, Kelida," he said gently, "hush. I've seen the valley."

Her sigh was ragged. "I have no one to miss me."

She was a pretty creature by human standards. Stanach looked at her out of the corner of his eyes. How old was she? Maybe twenty. It was hard to tell. Tall and russet haired, the farmers' sons in Long Ridge had likely been drawn to her green eyes like moths to a candle. Here in the dark forest, however, hers were not the eyes of a woman, they were the eyes of a lost child, large and frightened and staring at a world gone suddenly mad.

Twenty years! Stanach, who at twenty had been but a child, and who had never been able to understand how someone who had lived so short a span of years could be considered an adult, saw only a child in Kelida.

A child who had no one. For humans there is the family and all others outside the family were often only strangers. There is no clan, no large and deep well of strength and understanding to draw upon when a parent, a brother, a child dies. Stanach tried to imagine what that emptiness must be like, but could not. Once in a great while, for great crimes or sins against the clan, a dwarf would be declared outlaw, clan-reft. Such unfortunates were shunned by all and pitied by some. Kelida's condition was not the same. For her it was as though her whole clan, parents, brothers, children, cousins, aunts, uncles, all who shared her name, were dead.

Stanach shuddered. It was not to be imagined. He poked at the fire again and watched the small eruption of sparks dance into the night. The fire's light slid over Stormblade's gold hilt, colored the silver chasing to orange, and danced down the blue path of sapphires.

Stanach tugged at his beard. Aye, the ranger meant something to her.

"This fellow Hauk, have you known him long?"

"No. Only long enough for him to give me the sword." Kelida smiled shyly. "It's a foolish story." The smile died at once. Her green eyes grew dark and sad. "He's dead, isn't he? I heard what you said to Tyorl."

Stanach almost told her that Hauk was, indeed, dead. How could he still be alive? Then the dwarf realized, if she thought Hauk *were* alive and still Realgar's prisoner, a prisoner gallantly refusing to tell Realgar where the sword is in order to protect the girl he gave it to, she'd give him the sword. But only if he could convince her that by doing so, she'd have a chance to prevent Hauk's death. It shouldn't be hard to make her believe that if Realgar got the sword, Hauk would certainly die. The Theiwar couldn't leave him alive to give warning to anyone who might prevent his takeover of Thorbardin.

Oh, yes, she'd give him the sword. The chances were slim that she could save Hauk's life, but Stanach knew she would take those chances. She'd carried Stormblade into the forest, slept with it under her hand. It was Hauk's sword and she wouldn't let anyone else so much as hold it . . . unless she thought it would save Hauk's life.

He glanced at Kelida. Her arms clasping her drawn up legs, head pillowed on her knees, she was asleep where she sat. Just a ragged human girl, he thought, fallen in love with a ranger—though likely she doesn't know it yet.

Stanach touched her shoulder lightly to wake her. He returned her questioning smile with a nod. "Go sleep more comfortably, Kelida. The morning comes soon enough."

She returned to her cold bed and the sword. Stanach spent the rest of the watch carefully working out the details of his plan and ignoring the gnawing of his restless conscience.

"Do what you have to do," Piper had said.

He wondered where Piper was now, if he was safe, if he was waiting by the tumble of rocks that looked so much like a cairn. Four against one. Aye, but four against one mage. It would make a difference.

Do what you have to do.

Well, Piper, he thought, I am.

CHAPTER 10

Lavim returned to his companions as the wet gray dawn lighted the sky. Cold and shivering, the kender sighed and wished that he'd found some dwarf spirits in Long Ridge. His flask knocked hollowly against his hip. "White Disaster," some called the potent dwarven drink. Lavim had always considered the stuff the next best thing to a warm hearth.

Sometimes better, he thought, shoving his hands into the deep pockets of his shapeless, old coat and hunching against the icy drizzle. He'd found no ghosts, no specters, and no phantoms—with or without heads. For a forest hedged about with rumor and fear, Qualinesti was a singularly dull place. The campsite, however, promised to be more interesting.

Tyorl glowered at Stanach across the fire. Kelida, her green eyes sharp, her jaw stubbornly set, looked at no one.

Something's roused her, Lavim thought. The kender, careful of his cold-stiffened knees, dropped down before the fire. He held his hands as close to the flames as he dared and cocked an eye at Stanach. "What's going on?"

"Stubbornness," Stanach growled. "Simple-minded, damned, elven stubbornness." He tossed a bark chip into the fire and looked up at Tyorl, his black eyes hard and mocking. "Tell me, then, elf, are you going to take the chance that your friend Hauk is *not* Realgar's captive? Are you going to abandon him for his sword? Aye, well, I suppose you'd live well on what you could sell it for."

Tyorl leveled his icy stare at the dwarf. "I'll tell you what I'm not going to do: I'm not going to hand Hauk's sword over to you on the strength of a pretty tale. Where the sword goes, I go."

Lavim pricked up his ears. "Where are we going?"

No one answered.

"Fine then," Stanach said to Tyorl. "Come along. I think you believe me, elf. If you don't, there will be Piper to confirm my tale." Stanach laughed bitterly. "I suppose you'll grant that, if I'm lying, he could not have made up the same lies without my prompting, eh? Aye, come along. Ask him before I ever say a word. But, if you're coming, you'd best make up your mind soon. Piper won't stay around much longer before he decides I'm dead. Then, I'll be walking to Thorbardin," Stanach smiled grimly. "I suppose you will be, too."

"Who's Piper?" Lavim's face was a mass of wrinkles and a puzzled frown. "Why would he decide you're dead? We're going to Thorbardin? I've never been there, Stanach. I can't think of a better place to find some really good dwarf spirits, either." He glanced at the elf. "Is Kelida going, too?"

"No," Tyorl said.

Kelida, silent till then, looked up and spoke quietly. "Yes, I am."

Tyorl moved to protest. Kelida overrode him.

"I'm going with the sword. I can't go back to Long Ridge now. I would never find my way and—" She stopped, her eyes bright and almost fierce. "And—and the sword is mine. You've said it yourself. If Hauk is still alive, he's—what he's going through is to protect me. It was convenient for you to say the sword was mine when you thought he might be coming back for it, when you thought I could tell him where you'd gone. Then, the sword was mine. Well, it still is, and it seems that I'm the only one with any right to say where the sword goes."

"Hauk?" Lavim looked from one to the other of them. He should have stayed in camp, he decided. Clearly he'd missed something last night. "What sword?" His eyes widened as he saw Stormblade lying across Kelida's knees. "Oh. Are you talking about that sword?"

Stanach dropped his forge-scarred hand onto the kender's shoulder. "Easy, old one, save your questions for later." He nodded to Kelida. "Are you coming?"

"Yes, I am—"

"Aye," Tyorl drawled. "Do you know what you're getting yourself into?"

"Something worse than what I've already been through?"

Tyorl had no answer. It didn't matter, though. Instinct had warned him last night to keep silent on the matter of Finn. Now, he was glad that he had. Finn's rangers were waiting outside Qualinesti. Tyorl was certain that Finn would pick up their trail and find them before Stanach found the mage, Piper. He would lay the whole matter before the rangerlord: sword, tale, and his news that Verminaard was moving a supply base into the foothills of the Kharolis Mountains. Finn would decide what must be done.

"Very well, Kelida," he said. "You'll need warmer clothes." He held up a hand to forestall Stanach's protest. "I know a place where we can scavenge something for her. It's on the way."

Stanach tossed another chip into the fire. "Where?"

"Where?" echoed Lavim, all the more confused.

"Qualinost."

The sun broke from behind lowering, slate-colored clouds and its sweet, warm columns of light shafted down on the city. Four slim spires of the purest white stone rose from the corners of Qualinost at perfect map points: north, south, east, and west. Gleaming silver veins twined in almost-pattern through the snowy stone of the towers. Running out from the northern tower, high above the city, a seemingly frail arch leaped and connected with the southern spire. It was the same with the other towers, and so the city was bounded.

In the very center of the elven city, alive with light more vibrant than the sun's, rose the elegant Tower of the Sun. Sheathed in gleaming gold, the tower had been for years uncounted the home of the Speaker of the Suns. It, like all of Qualinost, was empty now that the speaker had taken his people, his children, into exile.

The elven city of Qualinost had been built by dwarves, from the design of elves, in a time when friendship, not today's brooding, sullen antipathy, graced the dealings between the two races. Tyorl entered the city of his birth with a heart torn between joy and sorrow.

Joy, he thought, because I never thought to see you again; sorrow that I should find you the vacant and empty-eyed corpse of a place once beautiful, now only coldly lovely.

The chill wind of late autumn moaned through the deserted city, sobbing around the eaves of buildings once brimming with life. It rattled through the last golden leaves of the countless aspens lining the streets. Once the sound had been rippling laughter, now it was a weak and weary dirge.

Beneath the wind, Tyorl heard the voices of memory. His father's quiet laughter, his sister's song. Where were they now?

Flown into exile with the rest of their people. Tyorl wondered if he would ever see them again. He shook his head as though to shake off the memories and the questions.

The houses and shops and all the buildings of Qualinost were made of quartz the color of dawn's light. These, too, were empty now, their windows dark, their doorways filled with shadows and the echoes of memories only Tyorl noticed. Broad paths of shimmering crushed stone marked the streets and avenues of Qualinost. All along these glittering paths were black fire-rings and piles of gray ashes, like dirty thumb marks on the streets of Qualinost.

Kelida, shivering and silent beside Stanach, leaned against an aspen's thick, gray trunk. The city was not ravaged, only empty, but she felt here the same sense of despair she had felt when she looked at the blackened, skeletal beams and posts of her own home.

Stanach, who counted his mountain home among the riches of his life, recognized Tyorl's sorrow. He looked from Tyorl to Kelida, he homeless, she clanless, and Stanach shivered.

It was Lavim who finally broke the silence. There was nothing in his deep, merry voice to tell any that he sensed the elf's sorrow or the dwarf's pity. He sidled up beside Tyorl and pointed to the nearest pile of ashes.

"Tyorl, what are those? They look like the remains of watch-fires, but there's too many of 'em to be that."

Tyorl glanced down at the kender. "They were not watch-fires, kenderkin. I wasn't here to see it, but I'm told that the people burned most of what they couldn't carry with them into exile. Those are the marks of funeral pyres, and the funeral was for a way of life."

Lavim tucked his blue-knuckled, freezing hands beneath his arms. "What a shame, Tyorl. Burning is the worst, if you ask me. Whatever it was, I would have hidden it, or carried it in my pouches, or sold it to a gnome vendor. Burning is such a waste. Now, you have to start all over again."

"It would never be the same. It has changed."

He might have said 'it has vanished' or 'it has died.'

Stanach shook his head. "All who live change," he said quietly. "Even, it seems, elves."

Tyorl's blue eyes, soft only a moment ago with his sadness, iced over and grew hard. "No, dwarf. We have known no change for too many long centuries. The only change an elf knows is death."

Stanach snorted impatiently, already regretting his fumbling attempt at comfort. "Then you're dead already, Tyorl, and wasting good air that others could be breathing. Your city, your way of life has changed. Perhaps we should consider you not an elf but a ghost, eh?"

Tyorl drew a breath to answer, then turned back to the silent city. "Perhaps."

Lavim watched as Tyorl led Kelida away. His long eyes narrowed, and he absently twirled the end of his thick white braid around a finger. "Stanach," he said, "if the elves burned everything before they left here, what's Tyorl going to find for Kelida to wear?"

Stanach shrugged. "I don't know. Ever since we got within a mile of this place, that damn elf has been more ghost than anything else. Maybe he'll spirit up something for her." Stanach started down the road. "Let's go, Lavim. The sooner we get out of here, the easier I'll be."

Lavim fell in beside the dwarf. He still didn't know half of what was going on. Kelida's sword, some missing ranger, and a couple of dwarven thanes all figured into it somehow. And who was Piper?

A small wooden stag, frozen by the woodcarver's art into a graceful leap, lay caught in a tangled nest of silver necklaces and golden earrings. A child's toy amid a mother's jewelry. Stanach reached for the oak stag and freed it as gently as though it lived. He turned it over idly and then smiled. Carved in the belly of the stag with deft strokes that might have been only the careful feathering of the beast's fur, was a stylized anvil bisected by a dwarven F rune. A dwarf's craft.

Stanach put the stag carefully aside and looked around the room. The place was a shambles.

Beautifully wrought tapestries, woven floor coverings, and soft pillows, whose designs were picked out in bright silk thread, lay scattered about the room as though thrown down in desperate haste. A tall wardrobe, elegantly painted with a delicate, stylized hunting scene, lay where it had fallen during someone's frantic preparations for exile.

Lavim staggered into the room, his arms loaded with a pile of mismatched clothing. "Here you go, Stanach. Tyorl says to look through these for Kelida."

"Aye, and where is she?"

"Taking a wash. She insisted, and Tyorl didn't argue. Said it would give him some time to look for gear." Lavim dumped the clothes on the floor and dropped down among them, happily rumaging through cloaks and hunting costumes, boots and blouses. "I guess they didn't burn *every-thing* before they left, did they?

"You know, Stanach, this place must've been really nice not so long ago. Its too bad the elves decided to leave. Me, I'd make those draconians drag me out of a place like this before I'd leave."

Fear, like shadows, hung in the air. It clung to the lovely buildings, lurked in the darkness of the apple garths and pear groves. Fear and sorrow walked the streets and laughed darkly at each dying aspen.

Stanach shook his head. Fear was nothing a kender could understand, and there was no sense wasting time trying to explain it.

The dwarf crossed the room and dropped cross-legged onto the icy marble floor. Curbing his impatience to be out of this sad room, this sad house, and the whole deserted city, he sorted through the clothing before Lavim could find a way to stuff the half of it into his pouches. The kender's pockets and pouches were bulging already. His middle looked too thick for one Stanach knew to be sapling-thin. If the search through the deserted homes and shops of Qualinost had been painful for Tyorl and uncomfortable for Kelida and Stanach, it had been a kender's dream for Lavim.

Stanach rescued a thick cloak from Lavim's interest. The color of pine boughs and lined with gray rabbit fur, it had been made for someone about Kelida's height and size. Next, he found a pair of hard-soled doeskin boots. The boots felt too heavy for their look. He peered into the interior of one and pinched an edge. The soft, supple leather was two layers thick and lined between with goose down.

"These look like they'll probably fit her."

Lavim picked up first one boot and then the other. "Nice stuff, Stanach. Kelida's going to be warmer than all of us."

"She's been colder than all of us this far. It's about time her luck turned. Why don't you take those to her and then go see if you can find Tyorl and hurry him up. And, Lavim—"

The kender turned, his arms full of cloak and boots. "Yes?"

"Knock before you go in, empty out your pouches before

you find Tyorl, and don't take anything else on your way."

Lavim's wrinkled face was all innocence.

Stanach's expression was firm. "And don't bother spinning any of your tales about how you came by the stuff—just get rid of it."

"But, Stanach—"

"I mean it, Lavim. That damn ghost of an elf is touchy enough. By the look of him, you'd think he was giving away his mother's best gowns."

"Maybe he is," Lavim said thoughtfully. His eyes, in their webbing of wrinkles, looked unaccountably wise. "Well, not gowns, because Kelida's probably going to be wearing breeches and not a gown, but maybe Tyorl used to know the person this stuff belongs to."

Maybe he did, Stanach thought. He didn't think on it further and did not regret his sour remark. It was a fine defense against the silent sorrow drifting around the room like old dust.

"Go on, Lavim."

Alone, Stanach swept the clothing into a pile against the wall and sat, elbows on drawn up knees, to wait in moody silence for his companions to join him.

He'd done what he had to do. It hadn't taken much to direct Kelida or Tyorl into believing that Hauk might still be alive. Kelida had even made the crucial connection herself: if Hauk was alive, he was protecting her.

On the walk through the forest, Kelida had told the dwarf the story of how Hauk had given her the sword. Even as she described her fear of Hauk in the storeroom, her voice told him that she had been moved by his apology.

Stanach was certain now that any doubt Tyorl might again raise about the wisdom of taking Stormblade to Piper would be countered by the girl. Kelida was convinced that the half-drunk ranger who had given her the sword was even now, like some paladin, protecting her from the *derro* mage who would kill to get Stormblade.

Maybe Hauk had been protecting her—while he lived. However, he was surely dead now.

Stanach closed his eyes.

Once Stanach found Piper, Stormblade would be magically returned to Thorbardin, and in Hornfel's hand, before Kelida or Tyorl had a chance to know it was gone. All Stanach had to do was keep the girl's hope alive, play on her dreams a little longer. And how did the foolish dreams of a simple barmaid weigh in the balance against the certainty of having one rule—Hornfel's rule—in Thorbardin?

They weighed not at all, Stanach told himself. Not at all.

A light, thin fingered hand touched his shoulder. Stanach looked up to see Kelida standing before him.

"Stanach? Are you all right?"

She'd contrived to wash somehow. In her borrowed clothes, a hunting costume of bark-gray wool and soft doeskin boots, the green cloak around her shoulders, she looked like a wood sprite. Stormblade was scabbarded around her waist.

Stanach scrambled to his feet. "Aye, fine."

"I thought I heard—"

"I'm fine," he snapped. He jerked his chin at the Kingsword. "You still insist on carrying it?"

Fire leaped in Kelida's eyes. "I've carried it this far."

"Aye, and tripped over it every second step. This isn't Long Ridge. If you carry a sword, people just naturally assume you can use it. You'd better know how, or you'll find yourself dead before you can untangle your feet and haul it out. Let me carry it. Or if that doesn't suit you, give it over to your friend the elf."

Kelida shook her head. "For now, the sword is still mine."

Stanach sighed. "The sword will be the death of you if you don't at least learn how to carry it." He jerked his thumb at the scabbard. "Buckle that lower and let your hip take the weight."

Kelida adjusted the sword belt. The drag of Stormblde's weight on her hip felt strange, but less awkward. She looked up at Stanach and smiled. "Now what?"

"Now, go find yourself a dagger. You won't be able to defend yourself with the sword."

Suddenly, he was angry with Kelida for no reason, angry with himself for every reason, and lonely behind the walls of his duplicity. Stanach turned away and stalked across the room to a window. He looked down into a courtyard; it was

---

111

better than looking at the shadows of hurt in Kelida's eyes.

Aspen leaves, like brittle golden coins, skittered and whirled before a damp wind. Their dry rattling was the only sound to be heard in this sad, deserted city. Ghosts wandered all over silent Qualinost. Ghosts and memories.

Or the whispers of his conscience.

Thirty feet long, its head as thick and wide as a big horse, its powerfully muscled legs longer than two tall men, the black dragon might have been a huge piece of the night as it separated itself from the cover of the clouds and dove low over the ridges of eastern Qualinesti. A cloud bank shredded under the wind of its passing. Solinari had long since set, but Lunitari's blood-red light ran along the metallic scales of its hide, leaped from its claws and dagger-sharp fangs in crimson points, and turned its long, narrow eyes, normally pale as frost, to fire. Sevristh was its secret and sacred name in dragon speech. It permitted itself to be called Darknight.

The dragon caught the wind under its wings and glided down toward the pine-forested, stony ridges that formed the border between Qualinesti and the dwarven mountains. A hater of light, its vision was superb when the sun had flown west. Though it did not fear the cold light of the moons, it saw more clearly when, as on this night, they were hidden behind thick, dark clouds.

The black dragon observed the lands below as a man might who stands over a well constructed map table. Dropping still lower, it swept over the high forests east of Crystal Lake and out across the low hills bordering the Plains of Dergoth, which the dwarves call the Plains of Death.

Darknight flew as Lord Verminaard's emissary to Realgar of Thorbardin. It would soon be addressing the dwarf as Highlord, if he accepted Verminaard's offers. He undoubtably would accept. The dwarf was known to be canny, ambitious, bold, and a little mad. He had the soul of a Highlord, a soul only a little less arrogant than that of a dragon. He waited for it now to arrive from Pax Tharkas. Sevristh would serve a new Highlord.

At least for a time. Verminaard's gifts all had teeth. Even

as he prepared to welcome Realgar as a Highlord, ruthless Verminaard already had plans afoot to move supply bases and troops in the mountains. With their strength to back him, he would depose the Theiwar and claim conquered Thorbardin as his eastern stronghold. Sevristh knew all this, and more.

The wind was a cold, fierce opponent who challenged the black dragon to dare its willful currents and invisible waves. Laughing as it flew over the marshes, Darknight skimmed the cloud-heavy sky, diving and rolling, thrusting with wings as wide as a ship's sail, and climbing, climbing until it burst through the thick, icy boundary of the clouds and came to the stars above ancient Thorbardin.

Aye, the dragon thought, all Verminaard's gifts had teeth and mine are sharp indeed!

"Let him do the work," the Highlord had said, "and give him whatever help he needs to do it. When the Council of Thanes is safely fallen, get rid of him."

For nothing but the pleasure of arcane exercise, Darknight cast a spell of fear and blackness. Tonight, in the dark and secret comfort of its den in the caverns below the cities of Thorbardin, it would lull itself to sleep with thoughts of small marshland creatures dying of a stopped heart and an overwhelming terror they could not have understood.

CHAPTER 11

The cold night wind cut through the valley, sighing in the boughs of the pines, turning the day's rain to slick ice on the shoulders of the mountain. Somewhere within the stone of the mountain itself lay Thorbardin.

Women with babes on their hips, men whose eyes were almost empty of hope, the refugees stood at the mountain's feet, searching the shoulders and flanks of the peaks for a sight of great Southgate. Some thought they saw it, shimmering in the night. Others turned away, too tired to look any longer.

A child's laughter rose high in the night air. It was hard to keep the children quiet. Only exhaustion would do that, and the journey of the past day had been a slow one. It was as though the eight hundred were reluctant now to approach the gates of the dwarven fortress, afraid to learn that their hopes had been in vain, that they had fled Verminaard's mines and the horrors of slavery only to be turned away from Thorbardin, the only hope of sanctuary they knew.

Fires sprang up in the valley, dim lights like small, hesitant stars. The smoke of wood, then of cooking, drifted through the air, settling like a gray pall over the river.

It would be a night of waiting and praying. It would not be a night for sleeping as the refugees sent their representatives, the half-elf Tanis and the Plainswoman Goldmoon, to lay their plea before Thorbardin's Council of Thanes.

There were many things Hornfel loved about his people. He admired their skills at crafting, found joy in their soul-deep loyalty to kin and clan, and appreciated their courage as warriors. He valued their hard-headed stubbornness and common sense. He loved their independence.

It was that independence that made it not an insult, but a kind of tribute, when the grizzled Daewar warrior, a member of the Guard of Watch on Soughtgate's ramparts, only turned for a moment to nod greeting to the two thanes in the rose light of dawn, then returned to his watch.

They are not awed by those above their station, Hornfel thought. They trust their thanes because we are their kin. None bows or kneels to kin.

He glanced at his companion whose eyes were sharper on the guards than Hornfel's. At this hour, Gneiss's Daewar made up the Guard of Watch, and Hornfel knew his friend well enough to know that he wanted his warriors to keep their watch with the best military precision. When the time came that Thorbardin entered the war, these Daewar would be the spearhead of the dwarven army. Gneiss was fiercely proud of his warriors.

Hornfel listened to the ring of mail and steel, the scuff of boots on stone, the barked order of the watch captain, and looked again at Gneiss, gone to lean against the breast-high wall overlooking the valley far below.

Cold wind raced around the ramparts. Born in the mountains, which shouldered proudly against the sky, the wind smelled of frost-touched pine forests and already freezing lakes, winter's icy promise. A thousand feet below lay the broad sweep of a string of alpine meadows. Dressed now in the rusty brown of autumn grasses, gilded with the new rising sun, the meadow held some of the richest soil in the Kharolis Mountains. This valley had lain fallow for generations. The cities in Thorbardin fed themselves from the produce of the farming warrens deep inside the mountain.

"See, Gneiss," Hornfel said, tracing the valley's borders with a sweep of his hand. "Eight hundred could farm this valley and manage to keep out of their own way and ours."

Gneiss snorted. "Are you on about that again?"

"I'm on about it still, my friend. We can't defer the issue any longer. You yourself brought me the word that the refugees have been challenged by the border patrols. How long do you think the border guards can hold back eight hundred hungry and frightened people? They are peacefully awaiting the word of the council. They won't wait long."

"Aye, blackmail, is it?" Gneiss turned away from the wall, his fist clenched, his eyes flashing with sudden anger. "Admit them or face them across a battlefield?" He cocked a thumb at the valley. "That meadow will be covered with snow soon, and the snow will be red with human blood, Hornfel. The council will not be forced."

Hornfel chose his next words carefully. "You've made up your mind about the matter? You think as Realgar and Rance do?"

"I think my own thoughts," Gneiss growled. The wind tugged at his silver-shot brown beard. His back still to the wall, to the valley and the idea of humans settling so near to Thorbardin, he watched his guards pace their watch. His expression, narrow-eyed and hard, gave Hornfel no clue to the thoughts that the Daewar claimed were not Realgar's, but his own.

"*Tell* me what you think, Gneiss. I've gone too long guessing, and none of my guesses seem to be right ones."

Gneiss, his eyes still on his guards, shook his head. "I think that my warriors are going to die in lands far from these mountains where we were born. I think they're going to die in a war that is no business of theirs."

The old argument! Hornfel had tired of it months ago, knew no better defense against it than the one he had already presented in countless council meetings. Still, he didn't speak until he'd mastered his impatience.

"It is our business now. Gneiss, there are eight hundred refugees at our very gate. A moment ago, you offered to water these meadows with their blood. *They are not our enemies.* Our enemy is Verminaard, he who's driven the elves from Qualinesti and walks the ramparts of Pax Tharkas. Verminaard enslaved these people. He'd like to do the same to us.

"When he controls the Kharolis Mountains, Gneiss, he controls the whole north and east of the continent. If you don't think he wants Thorbardin now, you are not the military leader I think you are."

It was a mark of his regard for Hornfel that Gneiss kept his clenched fists at his side. "Your words are hard, Hornfel," he said coldly.

"Aye, they're hard. The times are hard, Gneiss. If we don't choose soon, Verminaard will decide for us. I don't think we could live with his choice."

Gneiss smiled without mirth. "Gallows humor doesn't suit you."

"And a gallows wouldn't suit you."

The Daewar looked at him sharply. "Hanging is a traitor's death."

"Do you think Realgar would consider you anything else if he ruled in Thorbardin?"

"Realgar? Verminaard's creature? That is a harsh accusation."

Hornfel shrugged. "Only a suspicion, my friend."

Gneiss looked around him, at the mountains and the meadows, at the far reaches of sky, as though he suddenly understood something that he should have comprehended sooner. When he looked back to Hornfel his eyes held both anger and admiration.

"There is a Kingsword."

Hornfel nodded. "There is."

"What are you saying? You can't just make one of these, Hornfel! You—by Reorx!—you can't just trot down to the smith and order one up!"

Hornfel smiled wearily. "I know it. Isarn meant to make nothing more than a masterblade. But Reorx touched his hand to steel that night, and he made a Kingsword. You've heard the rumors —you must have. It's been stolen, Gneiss."

"Then why—?"

"I know where it is. So does Realgar." Hornfel briefly told him the tale of the sword's theft and finding. "Realgar wants Stormblade as much as I do. Reorx defend us, I hope he's no closer to having it than I am. Verminaard's creature or not, Realgar is dangerous."

Gneiss's hand dropped to the dagger at his side. "He'll be stopped."

"No. Not unless you want to fire Thorbardin with revolution."

Gneiss understood Hornfel's warning at once. The Council of Thanes was badly divided on the issue of the war and the issue of the refugees. Both, at times, seemed to be the same thing. Emotions, mainly anger, ran high. If Realgar died now, by fair means or foul, his realm would rise in war. Aye, then it wouldn't matter who had the Kingsword. The fire gleaming in its steel heart would be nothing more than a symbol of bloody revolution. The halls of Thorbardin would ring with the cries of dwarves killed by dwarves, as it had not done since the Dwarfgate Wars three hundred years ago.

"Tonight I will drink to his good heath," Gneiss growled, "and pray that he dies in his sleep before dawn."

Hornfel laughed. "Gneiss the Cautious!" He sobered. "It's time to stop being cautious; it's time to welcome those eight hundred refugees. Verminaard or Realgar, we are going to need them as allies."

"Humans? They won't all be like your fey mage Jordy."

"No one is like Piper. He is clever and he is staunch. I am surprised your deep-seeing eyes do not see that. It wouldn't matter if the refugees all had the sensibilities of gully dwarves. We need allies now."

Gneiss was silent for a long moment. When he finally spoke, Hornfel knew that if the Daewar had not come yet to a decision, he was very close. "Call a council meeting for tonight, Hornfel. I'll give you my thinking then." He started back toward the gatehouse and, when Hornfel moved to join him, he shook his head. "No, stay a while. You like the air out here. Stay and look down into your meadows and try to imagine what they will look like filled with humans. Then, listen for the sound of their voices in Southgate, my friend. They can't winter out there and will have to be sheltered in the mountain.

"Eight hundred." Gneiss snorted. "There won't be air enough in Thorbardin for a dwarf to breathe."

Hornfel watched the Daewar leave and turned back to the valley. An eagle sailed the wind far out over the meadows, the sun gold on its back. He would not try to second-guess Gneiss. It couldn't be done. He thought of his 'fey mage Jordy' and wondered where the mage was now, and if he, Kyan Red-axe, and Isarn's apprentice, Stanach, were still alive.

It had been four days since Piper had transported himself and his two companions to Long Ridge. Would it take four days to find the Kingsword? Aye, and longer if the ranger who had been said to be carrying it had left the town before they arrived.

They might all three be dead. Or not. They might have found the sword. Or not. The only thing he knew for certain was that Realgar didn't have it. The fact that he, Hornfel, still lived was the proof of that.

Though Hornfel had never seen Stormblade, he longed for the sword as though it had been his, cherished for many long years before it was stolen. He wanted to touch the steel, feel the bridge to rulers hundreds of years dead. Stormblade was his heritage, a Hylar sword made for the Hylar thane who would rule in Thorbardin as his eldfathers before him had ruled.

The wind from the mountains skirled high, as though it were an echo of one of Piper's war songs, or one of his tavern songs. Hornfel turned away from the valley.

"Young Jordy," he said, "if you're living still, I pray you're bringing the sword back."

If you are not, he thought as he returned a guard's nod and entered the gatehouse, then we'd all better watch our backs. If Realgar finds the Kingsword, it will only be a matter of time before war, revolution, or tyranny falls on Thorbardin.

The dwarf Brek put the tall pile of rock and stone between his back and the crimson light of the hated sun. Between this huge, nature-crafted cairn and the smaller, man-built one, lay the darkest pool of shadow. Here Agus, called the Gray Herald, communed with their thane. Brek closed his eyes against the growing light and hoped that Realgar would soon call them home.

He and his patrol had seen five dawns in the Outlands, cursing the day and longing for the deep warrens beneath Thorbardin. Mica and Chert, sleeping now as best they could in the shadows, had stood well against the rigors of the sun's bitter light. However, Wulfen, who was known as "the Merciless," was not quite right in his head. Brek was surprised that Hornfel's pet mage had survived under Wulfen's guard.

Brek bared his teeth in a feral grin. The ambush had worked well. They'd taken Piper as the moons set. He was returning from the nearby forest, a rabbit in hand for his breakfast. Even a mage must give way to a set crossbow at his back and swords gleaming before his eyes.

Brek hoped that Realgar wouldn't want the mage in a healthy condition. Wulfen, it seemed, had wreaked a full measure of vengeance upon the mage for the wound he took in the battle four days ago. Brek listened to the dawn wind as it rustled through grasses dead of frost. That wind sounded like the dry whispering voice of the Gray Herald. Brek shuddered.

It was not the doings of magic that made him shudder. Though he was no mage, Brek had been in the *derro* thane's service long enough to become, if not comfortable, at least familiar with the workings of magic. No, it was the clan-reft Gray Herald himself who stirred the hair on the back of his neck.

Shadow separated from shadow between the giant cairn and the Herald came to the edge of the comforting darkness. He threw back the hood of his dark cloak. A cold, baleful light flickered in the mageling's black eye; darkness filled the socket where his left eye had been. His face, normally mobile with strange, dark thoughts, was as still as a carved mask. Watching the Gray Herald the way one would watch a starving wolf, Brek put his back closer to the pile of stone.

"The thane will speak with you," the Herald whispered. Agus lifted his head. Like the reflection of distant storms, light flared high and then died in his eye. When he spoke again, it was not with his own rough, growling voice. As though Realgar stood beside him, Brek heard the thane's vibrant, steady voice.

You have the mage.

The dwarf moistened his lips nervously, drew a breath to speak and found he had to draw yet another breath before he could answer. The Gray Herald, the voice of Realgar, waited.

"Aye, Thane, we have him living still."

The sword?

Brek swallowed dryly. "He doesn't have it, Thane. We took him before dawn. Wulfen has been questioning him. The mage says nothing." Brek glanced at the small cairn, recently built. A fire ring and the little bones of past meals lay near the cairn. "But, he was waiting here, and seems to have been since we first did battle with him and killed Kyan Red-axe."

The Gray Herald sighed as though he'd heard something his companion had not. But, it was Realgar, many miles distant, who spoke, and it was the fire of the thane's anger Brek saw now flaring in the Herald's one eye.

The apprentice? The third one?

"There is no sign of him." Brek spoke quickly now. "The mage was waiting for someone. I think he was waiting for this apprentice, this Stanach Hammerfell. He'll have the sword, Thane. At least, he will have word of it."

Aye? Well, maybe he will. Wait for him. If he has the sword, kill him and take it. He's only one.

The thane's voice turned bitter, scornful.

It's likely you can manage that. If he doesn't have the sword, the Herald will bring him here to me. It may be that he will be better at providing the answers this god's-cursed ranger refuses to give.

"And if he has no word?"

Brek shuddered again, for now the thane spoke to Agus alone and it seemed that the Gray Herald spoke to himself, as the mad are said to do.

Yes, Herald, yes. The task of making an end to him will be yours, as it always is. Go. Amuse yourself with Hornfel's pet mage. Arrange it so that he's no trouble to us.

When he laughed, the Gray Herald's hands twitched as though they wound the ends of a garrote.

Piper saw fire behind his eyes, red and glowing as the mark of the Kingsword was said to be, crimson as the blood for which dead Kyan's axe had been named. He saw the light of the rising sun through eyes tightly closed against the overwhelming agony of broken hands.

The Theiwar spoke together in the shadows between Kyan's barrow and the giant's cairn. Piper heard the words as they echoed between the two piles of stone and knew that they would soon come to kill him.

Then, he thought, they'll sit here comfortably between the cairns and wait for Stanach and the sword. He'll be here today with the sword or without.

The words of a healing spell flickered in his mind like promises just out of reach. He had no means to enact the spell: Wulfen had broken his hands before he did anything else to him. Without the patterned dance of gestures, the spell was useless. Wulfen was not stupid. He'd swiftly removed any chance Piper might have had for arcane defense. The only thing of magic left to him was the old wooden flute still hanging at his belt.

They saw no harm in a flute long known to amuse children. They were wrong, and they were right. The flute's magic was a powerful force and could call up several spells. Some required precise fingerplay, some none at all. These were the most difficult spells, for they depended wholly on the timing of Piper's breathing. Yet, it all was useless to a mage whose fingers were ruined, who could barely draw a breath.

"Hornfel's pet mage," these Theiwar called him. It was not a naming Jordy resented, though he, as most of the dwarves in Thorbardin, thought of himself as Piper. He was the thane's man, bone and blood, and to be called Hornfel's was no disgrace at all.

There was blood in Piper's lungs. He heard it bubbling, swishing with every agonized breath he managed to draw. When he coughed, as he did now, small flecks of it stained his lips and then the cold hard ground. His thoughts, fragmented and scattered, drifted along the currents of pain. As though he could not bear to think on this moment, this place, this pain, Piper's thoughts drifted to other places.

Hornfel's pet mage. Aye. Piper had arrived at Thorbardin suddenly, and as bedraggled as a hound, three years ago. The storms had been raging that night: a wild summer battle in the sky, full of roaring thunder and blinding lightning. Piper still did not remember much about his arrival, though he'd heard the tale often enough.

A member of the Guard of Watch at Southgate had nearly tripped over the mage. Sodden and barely breathing, he lay huddled in the lee of the breast-high wall where only the watch himself had stood a moment earlier.

"Like storm-leavings at the water's edge," the guard had said later, enthusiastically quenching his thirst with his fellows in the guard house. "I tell you, I thought that boy was dead." That said, he drank deeply, his eyes thoughtful. "Maybe he was and magicked himself back to life. You don't ever know about a mage."

Piper hadn't been dead, though he had been as close to being dead as he thought he would ever like to come. Until now.

Piper swallowed only a little and tried not to breathe at all. He began to drag his broken right hand, inch by inch, down to his side.

They hadn't quite known what to do with him in Thorbardin. The captain of the Guard voiced the suspicion that the mage might well have been sent to spy out Thorbardin's defenses, and so saying, found the solution to the problem of the mage on the doorstep.

There are prison cells deep and dark in Thorbardin, and Piper woke in one of them, shackled and wondering whether he had miscast a spell seriously enough to transport himself into the Abyss.

He'd only wanted to go to Haven, and that was no long leap from the Forest of Wayreth. No long leap in magic.

He'd known he was yet in the mortal plane when he discovered that his jailors outside his cell were dwarves. The dwarf who brought him his rations of warm water and dry bread was uncommunicative, answering his questions with a grunt or not at all. Though he once brought the mage warmer blankets against the cold and damp, the dwarf guard never said a word more and was careful that Piper's hands were never free.

Always, he thought, his eyes still shut against the pain, his hand growing strangely numb as he dragged it toward the flute, always they know about a mage's hands.

After two days, Piper was brought before the Council of Thanes. Still bound and shackled for fear that he would try to defend himself with magic, or charm the council into believing him innocent of the charge of spying, Piper told his story of a transport spell gone awry to the six thanes in their great council chamber.

They wrangled long over the issue, as they were accustomed to do over almost any matter. "Spy!" some cried. Others had their doubts about that charge, but were not inclined to be understanding or absolve the mage of the sin of trespassing in the dwarven holdings. Dragons flew the skies of Krynn openly now, and armies were massing for war in the Outlands. If they could not be certain that Piper was innocent of the charge of spying, the Council of Thanes would happily consign him to the dungeons and iron shackles for the rest of his life, thereby settling the matter to everyone's satisfaction except Piper's.

Only one of the thanes had even considered the matter of Piper's freedom. That one was Hornfel, and he argued hard for the sake of the young human whose disarming innocence and genuine goodwill, coupled with the tale of miscast magic, moved him. Hornfel pledged his own word as bond for the mage and so pledging, bought Piper's freedom.

Piper, his hand wholly numb now, knew he'd touched the flute when he felt it roll against his side. He listened to the wash of his own blood in his lungs and seemed to hear

Hornfel's bemused sigh again.

"I usually judge a man aright the first time. But know this, young Jordy: you are the keeper of my word now. See that you keep it well."

Jordy had thought then that he'd have no trouble keeping Hornfel's pledge. He instinctively liked the dwarf and owed him his freedom. He was also fascinated by Thorbardin, where few humans had come before now. Jordy spoke impulsively and never regretted that he did.

"We'll trade pledges, sir," Jordy had said gravely to the dwarf who had saved him from the endless cold and darkness of Thorbardin's dungeons, "I'm in your debt and, if you'll have me, in your service."

In those two years, the young man was called by some Jordy, by others Hornfel's pet mage. Then, the children who ran in Thorbardin's streets and great gardens, delighted by the blond giant's music, began to call him Piper. The mage had found his by-name, a thane and lord to serve, and, though he wasn't looking for one, a home.

Piper, sweating in the cold dawn, marshalled all his strength and, with his forearm, nudged the flute carefully out and away from his side. It lay near his shoulder now. Bracing his feet against the hard ground, he did a slow, painful bend and grasped the scooped lip of the instrument in his teeth.

One of the Theiwar laughed, a sound like wind howling around barrows. Piper straightened. When he did, a broken rib moved in his lung, tearing and tearing. Blood leaked into the place where air should have been. He had no breath left for the complicated spells now. He had no time left either.

A spell, he thought, swift and sure to get me out of here!

A transport spell. Not to take him far, he hadn't the strength for that, but just to hide him well in the forest where they would have to search for him. It was likely not all of them will search, he thought as he slowly, painfully filled his lungs with air. However, Stanach might hear them and be warned long before he sees them.

Piper closed his eyes and thought of a glade he knew deep in the woods, near the borders of Elvenwood. These Theiwar would search long and far before they ventured too close to haunted Qualinesti.

Three notes he needed, all low and sounding like wind when it sweeps through the grass. Three words of magic. The words he had and the breath he found.

For a timeless space Piper felt no pain, no need to breathe. All sense of being drained away, like the tide dragging away from a shore, as Piper rode the music.

CHAPTER 12

THE MID-MORNING SUN SHONE THIN AND BRIGHT, OFFER-
ing little warmth. Its light arrowed down between the eaves
of the tallest trees, rebounding like gleaming silver darts
from the last shivering brown and red leaves of the underbrush. A cold breeze carried the rich scent of damp earth
and moldering leaves through the forest. Little more than a
deer trail, the path often seemed invisible to Kelida, like
something Tyorl followed more by instinct than sight.

Tyorl moved first down the narrow, shadow-dappled
path; Stanach next; Kelida behind him. Lavim followed last
and only occasionally. Like an old dog in new territory, the
kender ranged the forest on either side of the trail. No thicket, glade, beck, or stone outcropping of the slightest interest
was left uninvestigated. Though Lavim had long before

given up trying to call these fascinating landmarks to his companions' attention, he kept up a running commentary in a voice that still seemed too deep to Kelida for one of his small stature, but one that clearly spoke of the kender's pleasure in his surroundings and the sunny day.

"Damn good thing we're not trying to get through this wretched forest without anyone knowing," Stanach muttered.

Kelida smiled. Tyorl had made a similar comment moments before. For her part, she enjoyed the kender's delight. His cries of discovery ran like a tuneless, rhymeless trailsong through what would have been a silent journey were it left to Tyorl to provide conversation. Stanach was not to be looked to for anything but dour silence.

Her eyes on Stanach's broad-shouldered back, neatly bisected by his scabbarded sword, Kelida thought about his bad-tempered suggestion that she learn how to use the slim dagger she now carried.

When he'd snapped the warning to her in the sad, deserted chamber in Qualinost, Kelida's first reactions had been anger, then hurt. Her second had been to find a dagger. She had not, however, given Hauk's sword over to Stanach or into Tyorl's keeping. Since she'd adjusted the scabbard, Stormblade rode easier on her hip and leg, though it still dragged, and the sword belt caused her borrowed hunting leathers to chafe and rub at her skin.

She had set her sights on the modest goal of learning to use the dagger Lavim helped her find before they'd left Qualinost. Stanach, though he'd volunteered the suggestion that she find a blade, hadn't volunteered to teach her how to use it. According to what Stanach had said over the dawn campfire, they would soon be near the place where he expected to meet his friend Piper. Then, Thorbardin would be only a shaky breath and a transport spell away.

Tyorl had looked thoughtful at the news and made no comment. Remembering the look in his eyes, Kelida wondered now whether the elf was beginning to doubt Stanach's tale. Which part of it, she wondered, the part about the sword or the part about the mage?

Kelida shook her head and stepped over a downed sapling

in the trail. Stanach, a little ahead, looked back, his dark eyes moving, as they always did, to Stormblade's richly decorated hilt.

No, she thought, the tale is true. There was a light in his eyes when he looked at Stormblade, and it wasn't the cold light of avarice. He looked at the sword the way Kelida imagined someone would view a holy relic.

Whatever Tyorl thought, Kelida knew that Stanach's tale was not one spun to help him steal a valuable sword. He called it a Kingsword, Stormblade, or masterblade. He spoke of king regents and legends become truth. Behind his words, behind the tale, Kelida saw Hauk, somehow more shy and gentle than he seemed, and with his silence defending her from the wrath of a cruel *derro* mage who would kill to retrieve Stormblade.

From their first night in Qualinesti, Kelida had instinctively liked the dwarf. She remembered their conversation before the dying campfire. When she'd attempted to tell him about the destruction of her home, the deaths of her parents and her brother, he'd gently whispered "Hush, girl, hush."

So deep in her thinking was she that she did not see the tangle of thick gray roots snaking across the path. Her foot caught, she gasped, and fell hard to her knees. Up ahead Tyorl stopped and turned, but it was Stanach who came back for her. He grasped her elbows and lifted her easily to her feet.

"Are you hurt?"

Kelida shook her head. "No, I'm fine. I'm sorry." She apologized before she could even decide whether or not she needed to.

"You'd be sorrier if you'd broken an ankle." Stanach softened the warning with a smile, barely seen before it was lost in the depths of his black beard. "Our part is to watch the ground, Kelida. Tyorl will watch the forest."

Kelida looked after him when he turned and continued up the path. Silent as a cat rounding a corner, Lavim came up beside her.

"You all right?" Startled, Kelida gasped. "Lavim! Where did you come from?" The kender grinned and jerked his head.

"Back down the trail. Dwarves: I dunno. Strange fellows. They brew a good drink, though. Me, if I had all the dwarf spirits I could drink, I'd be the happiest person around. Swords, and kings who aren't kings—I don't know about that business. The dwarf spirits're why I'm going to Thorbardin. Can you imagine? All the dwarf spirits you could want, and made by the people who know how to do it! I figure I won't be cold all winter!"

Kelida hid a smile. No one had invited the kender along, but no one seemed inclined to try to banish him either.

"Stanach's right, though, you should watch the ground. I don't think you're used to walking in the woods, are you?"

"No, I'm not. I'll manage though." Her eyes on the faint trail, Kelida set out again, hurrying her pace to catch up with Stanach and Tyorl. Lavim fell in beside her.

"I only look up at the sky when I'm sleeping," he said. "Or when a dragon flies by. That's my secret."

"Good advice," she murmured.

The kender shrugged, ducked off to the side to make certain there wasn't anything of interest behind a broad-trunked oak, and rejoined her. "That Stanach's a moody fellow. Have you noticed that?"

"I have."

"He used to be a swordcrafter, did you know that? You should look at his hands sometime. They're scarred all over with little burns. That's from the forge fires."

Lavim warmed to this receptive audience and grinned, remembering Givrak in the tavern and the draconian patrols in the warehouse. "Stanach, he's nice enough when he's not being moody, but he has this strange knack for annoying people. He could really get into trouble one of these days if he's not careful." Lavim's eyes were suddenly wise, or so he imagined. "This mage, Piper —I figure it'll be a good thing when Stanach finally catches up with him. Somebody's got to keep him out of trouble. I figure that's what this Piper fellow does. You know, kind of keeps an eye on him?"

Kelida remembered the four draconians that had precipitated their flight from Long Ridge. "What did he do to get the draconians so mad?"

"Oh, you can't ever tell about a draconian. They're not like us, you know. They're mean as a way of life. Stanach aggravated a bunch of them outside an old, burned warehouse." Lavim paused, looked thoughtful, and then shrugged. "Maybe it had something to do with the four who were chasing me, or the one who fell out the window . . . I dunno. Like I said, you can't tell about 'em."

The kender's chatter was like a warm summer breeze. "I'll tell you," he said, cocking an eye at the girl, "the only thing meaner than a draconian is a minotaur—and even that bears thinking about. Ever see a minotaur, Kelida? They're, well, kind of strange looking. Big fellows! They have fur all over them. Not long fur, you see, but short. Like a bull's." Lavim frowned, then grinned. "And no sense of humor at all! If you ever see one try to remember not to—well, um, suggest that his mother was a cow."

Kelida's eyes widened. "Why would I suggest that?"

"Oh, it would be a natural mistake." Lavim's green eyes twinkled. "They kind of remind you of cows or bulls. They have real thick faces and horns and a disposition that definitely makes you think of a bad-tempered bull. I was around the Blood Sea last year, just passing through Mithas—" His laughter, deep-throated and merry, rang out suddenly. "That's when I learned that I might be old, but I can still run! No, they really don't like it if you talk too much about cows. I don't think there's a minotaur alive who knows what a joke is."

Kelida, smiling, trudged along beside Lavim, trying to follow the winding paths of a tale about three minotaurs, a gnome named Ish, and a bale of hay offered as dinner, for some reason Lavim never made clear.

As the track of the story became more confused and obscured with exaggeration and hyperbole, Kelida contented herself with watching the ground and trying to present the appearance that she was, indeed, listening to the kender. After a time, she remembered Stanach's insistence that she learn to use her dagger. She dropped her hand to the sheath at her hip. It was empty, the dagger gone.

"Lavim!"

Lavim looked around and up. "What?"

"My dagger—it's gone!"

"Oh, have one of mine." He slipped a bone-handled dagger from his belt and held it out to her. "I found it back on the trail, but, of course, I already have six or seven. Here."

It was obviously the one she was missing.

Kelida snatched the dagger and sheathed it awkwardly. "Just where did you find it?"

Lavim scratched his head in puzzlement. "I don't remember, but I knew it would come in handy."

Skillfully, he veered away from a mossy outcropping. "I heard Stanach tell you that you should learn. He was a little testy about the matter, but he's right. I could teach you."

"Would you?"

"Sure, Kelida, I'd be happy to." Lavim peered up the trail. Stanach and Tyorl stood waiting. When he winked, Kelida thought he looked like a disreputable old conspirator. "In my youth I was a sort of champion of Kendertown. Well, actually, second place. Sort of. Second place is really quite impressive, especially if there are at least two contestants, don't you think? Oops! Better catch up!"

Kelida smiled. She trailed after Lavim, her hand on the dagger's hilt, and reminded herself to check to see what else of hers the old kender might have 'found.'

The warm boulder felt good at Kelida's back. Here, on the high ground, the sun of the morning and early afternoon had dried the dampness from the grass and heated the rocks. The tree line was, temporarily, below them. The rock-strewn hill rose like a small island from the forest. This, Kelida knew from questioning Stanach as they'd climbed the hill, was not part of the foothills.

"Just a bump in the ground," the dwarf had said, his dark eyes on the tall, blue peaks to the south. "The real hills are farther east."

Kelida rubbed her aching legs. 'Real hills.' As though this were a meadow! The outcropping against which she leaned was as comfortable as the bricks her mother used to heat in winter to warm cold feet. A cloud's shadow slipped across the ground, and Kelida closed her eyes. The memory of her mother touched an empty, aching place within her. As though it had fled into that empty place, all the warmth seemed to bleed out of the day. Behind her eyes, she saw fire and death and a wide-winged dragon dropping from the sky.

To her left and a little below where she sat ran a laughing stream, cold from its passage through the earth. The sound of splashing and then an impatient snarl that could only have been Stanach's cut through Kelida's dark memories. She looked around.

Lavim, who had gone to fill their flasks at the stream, leaped up the slope and around the rocks bulging from the earth's thin skin with all the unconcerned skill of a mountain goat. The kender dropped down beside her.

"I did not!" he shouted over his shoulder, his eyes filled with impish green light. He passed Keldia her flask and unstoppered his own to drink deeply. "Stanach fell in the stream. The way he tells it, you'd think I pushed him!"

"Did you?"

"Not me! He slipped on a mossy rock. Look at him. Now, at least, he's got something to snap and snarl about."

Kelida peered over her shoulder. Stanach, wet to the knees, stalked up the slope like a grudge-holding hunter. He saw Kelida sitting with Lavim, so he veered away to join Tyorl. Kelida watched him take a seat on the ground near the elf. Each sat silently, not sharing his thoughts. When she turned back to the old kender, she saw her dagger again in Lavim's possession.

Lavim grinned and held up his hand, the dagger point balanced on his palm. "Look what I found again."

"Lavim, give it back."

The kender pulled back his hand and snapped his wrist. The blade now balanced on his other palm. "I thought you wanted me to teach you how to use it."

"I do, but—"

"Well, then?"

Kelida smiled. "All right. But, I don't think I need to know juggler's tricks."

"Oh, I dunno. It'd be easy to teach you some really simple tricks. I'm a really good juggler. Well, I s'pose it's not polite to say that myself, but I am and—" He shrugged when Kelida frowned impatiently. "All right. How about this?"

The kender jerked his wrist again, brought the weapon hilt-first to his right hand, and sent the dagger flying from his grip with a swift and subtle movement.

Kelida looked around quickly but saw no sign of the dagger. "Where is it?"

Lavim gestured toward a scrubby growth of naked brush. "There, getting us some supper." The kender scrambled to his feet, trotted across the stony ground, and reached into the brush. When he turned, he had a large gray-furred rabbit by the hind legs. The creature stirred weakly and then fell still. The slim, little dagger had pierced it cleanly through the heart. Lavim returned, tossed the rabbit down, and resumed his seat.

"That's one Tyorl won't have to waste a draw on later. A dagger is for stabbing and throwing, Kelida," he said, his tone serious now. Clearly, he was enjoying his role as weapons instructor. "Those are about the only things you can do with a knife. Well, besides cutting meat and picking locks, maybe."

He eyed her consideringly and then nodded. "You've got a good throwing arm. I saw that in the road outside Long Ridge. If those soldiers hadn't been wearing mail, you'd have taken 'em down with those stones you were pegging at 'em. Of course, you should have been aiming at their heads. You were probably too distracted to think about that. Here, take the knife."

The rabbit's blood steamed on the blade in the cool air. Kelida took the hilt between two fingers.

"No, no, not that way. Here, like this." Lavim laid the hilt along her palm, closed her fingers over the bone handle. "There, grip it like—I dunno, like you're shaking hands with it, but not too tight. There, pleased to meet 'cha."

The dagger's hilt was cold in her hand. Blood tapped against the hem of her cloak. Kelida shuddered. Dark and creeping, she felt nausea rolling around in her stomach.

"Now," Lavim said, "throw it. Throw overhand, just like you'd peg a rock, only a dagger's lighter so you have to get a higher arc on it. Go ahead, try to hit that old stump over there."

The blackened remains of a lightning-struck ash jutted up from a low scoop in the ground about five yards to the north. Kelida judged the distance, took a sighting, and threw. The blade wobbled a little, made the distance, and fell among the stump's gnarled roots.

"Not too bad. You got where you wanted to go, but you have to really put your arm into it." Lavim retrieved the dagger. "Try again."

She did, and this time the dagger's blade grazed the rough bark. On the third try, the dagger struck hard into the wood and stayed, quivering.

"There! You've got it now." Lavim fetched the dagger again and dropped down beside his student. "Now, throwing is fine when you have the room for it, and when you're more interested in hitting your target than keeping the dagger. The other thing a dagger is for is stabbing."

Kelida shivered again. She closed her eyes and drew a long, steadying breath.

Lavim tugged at her sleeve. "Kelida, are you listening?"

Kelida nodded dumbly.

"All right, then. Stabbing is funny stuff. Well, not funny, really, but strange. Don't stab down if you're in close. All you'll do is hit bone and make someone mad. You sure won't disable him. Stab up from below. That way you stand a really good chance of hitting something important like a liver or kidney. Got it?"

"I—I think so."

Lavim looked at her again. "You look a little green, Kelida, you feeling all right?"

Kelida swallowed against rising nausea. "I'm fine."

"You sure? Maybe we should talk about stabbing later? Why don't you try a few throws again?"

Kelida tried. Her first throw was off by a finger's width, her second hit the mark.

"One more." Lavim encouraged, "You're getting the feel of it." Kelida threw again and missed the stump by a yard.

Brown sedge and dead grass were thick around the stump. Kelida searched for a moment, but did not find the dagger. Beyond the stump, the hill dropped down toward the woods. Just before the dark line of the trees' shadows, she saw sun glinting off steel, the dagger's blade. Kelida started down the hill.

The low ground in the shadow of the hill was wet and marshy. Her boots squelched in the puddles and slopped in the mud. Kelida retrieved the dagger quickly. When she turned to start back up the hill, something fluttering in the close underbrush of the forest caught her eye. Frowning, Kelida took a few steps toward the thickets.

She pushed through the thorny scrub brush and stopped. The underbrush framed a small sward of late green grass. A young man lay there, his right arm twisted in an impossible angle beneath him, his swollen, broken left hand outflung as though appealing for mercy. From where she stood, Kelida could not tell if he breathed.

She raised a hand to her mouth and caught a finger between her teeth so that she wouldn't scream. Long blond hair trailed in a thin rivulet of water, mud-fouled and plastered to the side of his face. Encrusted with blood at the edges and angry red along the trough, a blade's deep cut scored that face from a swollen, bruised eye to just beneath his jaw. Great rusty splashes of blood stained his red robes; some were brown and old, some crimson and still spreading. Kelida drew a short, choppy breath.

"Lavim!" she cried. "Tyorl! Stanach!"

The young man moaned and opened his eyes. Once, they might have been as blue as a summer sky. Now, they were muddy and dull with pain.

"Lady," he whispered. He gasped and squeezed his eyes tightly shut, then ran his tongue around blood-stained lips and tried again. "Lady, will you help me?"

Stanach, his hands cold and shaking, dropped to his knees. His palm on Piper's chest, he felt for the rise and fall of life as he had when he crouched in the dusty road beside Kyan Red-axe five days ago. Piper still lived, if only barely. His breath was a bubbling wheeze in his lungs. The mage had not spoken since he'd asked for Kelida's help, but only lay still and silent.

He was not dead, but it would not be long before he was. Both of his hands and several ribs were broken, too much blood stood in his lungs.

Tyorl, who had left to quickly scout the glade for signs of the young man's attackers, returned now. He carried his longbow, an arrow still at nock, in his left hand; in his right, he held an old cherry wood flute. This he silently offered to Stanach.

Stanach took the instrument, running his thumbs down the smooth length of polished wood. After a moment's hesitation, he laid the flute beside Piper's broken right hand. "Where did you find it?"

"A little way off. Stanach, I have to talk with you."

Stanach nodded and climbed wearily to his feet.

The elf, his long blue eyes unreadable, glanced at Piper, then looked around for Kelida. He saw her standing with Lavim at the edge of the glade and motioned for her to join them.

"Stay with him, Kelida."

Kelida said nothing. Green eyes wide with pity, face paled by fear, she settled beside the mage. Lavim, silent for once, crouched down opposite her. Stanach sighed heavily and followed Tyorl into the deepening shadows of the forest until they were well out of the others' hearing.

Tyorl returned the arrow to his quiver, but did not unstring his bow. "He looks like he was set on by a mob."

Stanach nodded.

"I found no sign at all that anyone else has been here. I found no track or mark that even he had come into the glade. How do you suppose he got here?"

"I don't know. He's magi and—" Stanach swallowed against the tightening of his throat. "—and known in Thorbardin for his transport spells." Memory caught him and he smiled. "He gets you where you want to go, but the magic always feels like its going to pull the day's dinner out of your belly. He's—known for that, too.

"I don't think it happened very far from here, though. He wouldn't have had the strength to transport any great distance. Is the road into Long Ridge near?"

"Five miles, maybe a little more," Tyorl said.

"Then, that's where it happened. Or near there. It's where he was waiting for me."

"I'm sorry."

"Aye," Stanach muttered roughly, "so am I." He turned and started back to Piper. He didn't get two steps before Tyorl caught his arm.

"What about the sword?"

"What about it?" Stanach tangled the fingers of his right hand in his beard and closed his eyes. "I don't know," he said bitterly. "I didn't get to Piper in time, did I? He can't help me and I—I can't help him. Let me at least sit with him while he dies."

So saying, the dwarf turned and left the shadows for the sun-dappled sward. Tyorl followed silently.

Kelida moved aside when Stanach came to sit beside her. "He's still breathing, Stanach. He's still alive."

Stanach said nothing, only drew the back of his hand across his mouth and nodded, his eyes on Piper's broken hands.

Kelida, following his gaze, whispered, "Why?"

"So he couldn't defend himself with magic." He touched a finger to the flute. "They didn't know about the pipe. It got him away, but not in time to save his life."

Ah, Jordy, Stanach thought. I'm sorry, Piper!

"We might as well camp here." Tyorl said, "It's a muddy hole to pass the night in, but I've a feeling we'll want the lee of the hill to shelter our fire tonight. We'd better set our night watch fireless on the hilltop." Tyorl motioned to the kender who looked like he wanted to ask questions. "Fuel and kindling, aye?"

Lavim rose stiffly and, with one look at Stanach, slipped into the woods. The elf climbed the hill to walk the watch. Alone, Kelida sat beside Stanach. She, who had watched her family and friends fall before a dragon's rage, saw the deep and desolate sorrow in the dwarf's eyes and knew that he mustn't sit alone.

Solinari, as it always did, rose first above the horizon. Lunitari did not lag far behind. Night, deep blue and cold, flowed into the glade. Shadows and firelight turned the naked brush to glowing black webbing.

When the red moon's light crested the hill and ran down

into the woods, Stanach realized that he hadn't heard the thick, rasping sound of Piper's labored breathing for many moments. He leaned forward, gently placed his hand on the mage's chest. There was no movement. The lifebeat in his neck was stilled. Stanach sat listening to the thunder of his own heart.

"I'm sorry," Kelida whispered.

Stanach nodded. He looked at her for a long moment, then at the Kingsword she still wore at her hip. Gold caught the fire's light, and shadows glided over the silver. The five sapphires winked coldly. Stanach thought he could see the crimson heart of the steel glowing through the shabby leather scabbard.

Kelida covered his right hand with her own.

Stanach still said nothing.

The music that had enchanted the dwarven children of Thorbardin was flown. The magic was gone. Jordy was dead and Kyan was dead.

In that moment, Stanach didn't let himself feel a thing for fear that his grief would overwhelm him and he would weep.

CHAPTER 13

Where is the sword?

The voice, as hard and cold as black obsidian, became the darkness. The darkness became the voice. Hauk did not know whether he saw the dwarf with his eyes or felt him, like a shape-shifting nightmare, in his mind.

Where is the sword?

Hauk answered carefully. The dwarf could see into his mind. Or he stood inside his mind. "I don't—I don't know."

The questioning had become like a defensive sword fight. Parry and deflect, retreat, then parry again. Like a fighter whose back is to a cliff's drop, Hauk knew that he could not retreat much longer. His answer was true. He didn't know where the sword was now.

Who has the sword?

"I don't know." I don't, he told himself. I don't know her name. He cached the picture of the red-haired barmaid behind the wall of his will.

It's mine, he told himself over and over again. I own this memory. I own it! He buried it deep and far, as a miser does who hides a treasure of immeasurable worth.

Realgar's laughter washed sickeningly up against the edges of Hauk's soul. Like a miner with a sharp pick, the mage dug and scraped at Hauk's mind and held each memory up to cold, white light.

Hauk smelled smoke in the air of a tavern's common room.

Realgar laughed again. The white light vanished, it's afterglare throbbing and pulsing. Between one heartbeat and the next, it leaped high, a column of flame. Stormwinds howled.

Hauk tasted ale in his mouth, the rise of bile in his throat. A silver flash cut the smoke. He saw Tyorl's blue eyes, amused and tolerant of his young friend's follies.

His dagger's steel blade quivered in the exact center of a wooden serving tray. The sound of the blade's vibration rose, high and humming, and Hauk felt it. The floor of the cell trembled as though an earthquake shook the stone.

Darkness fell hard, and Hauk, his heart trembling, let it settle over him and told himself that the darkness was good. It hid treasures.

Realgar's laughter became the raucous noise in the tavern's common room. Hauk had found Tyorl in his mind, and he clung to the image of his friend. He filled his mind with all the memories of the years, boy and man, that he had known the elf.

Blood tapped on stone. It slid across a shadow-pocked, rock floor. Tyorl lay dead at Hauk's feet. The elf's fingers stiffened in death, still clutching the mortal wound in his belly.

Stormblade, sapphires breathing like soft twilight, hung from Hauk's hand, blood hissing down the blade.

Where is the sword?

Hauk threw back his head and howled in grief and rage and denial.

He never, not even for a moment, allowed himself to remember the girl with the copper braids and eyes like emeralds. She was no real girl to him now. She was only a light, bright memory in the darkness. That memory was his and he clung to it the way a drowning man clutches the last splintered board from a storm-whelmed ship. He had nothing else.

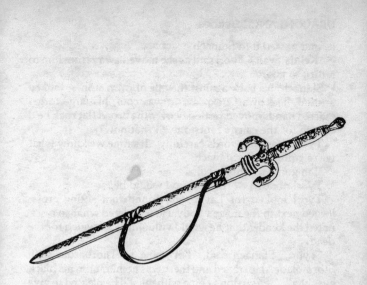

CHAPTER 14

Before the moons had set, Stanach began to build Piper's cairn. Tyorl, walking watch on the hill, thought the dwarf worked with all the dispassion of a mason constructing a wall. Stones littered the hill's crest, and Stanach used these to lay the base for the mage's tomb.

The dwarf asked for no help, but he offered no protest when Tyorl asked Kelida to relieve him at watch and, instead of seeking his own rest, bent his back to dragging stones for the cairn. Neither said a word to the other, each was tired and wrapped in his own thoughts. By the time dawnlight turned the dark sky a soft, cool blue, the tomb was laid and ready to accept Piper's body.

By that time, too, Tyorl had made some decisions. He gratefully accepted Kelida's water flask, took a hard pull on it, and passed it to Stanach.

"Kelida, wait," Tyorl said as she moved away from him to return to guard.

Stanach, his back against the pile of cairn stones, looked around. The dwarf's expression was cool, his large forge-scarred hands moved restlessly over the broad flat rock he'd chosen for the cairn's footstone. "What now?"

Tyorl chose his words carefully. "It's time we know what we're going to do, Stanach."

"I'm going to Thorbardin."

Tyorl nodded. "I thought you would be."

Tyorl looked for Lavim and found him sitting cross-legged next to the mage's body. He wondered what so fascinated the kender that he would voluntarily sit watch for the dead.

"Tyorl," Stanach said, "I'm going to Thorbardin with Stormblade." He smiled and there was no humor in his black eyes at all. "If you don't come with me, I'll be pleased to give your greetings to Hauk. If he lives."

"You've played that tune one time too many, dwarf," Tyorl snapped.

"He could be alive. Care to risk it?" The dwarf jerked his head at the empty cairn waiting in the morning shadows for Piper. "You build these things awkwardly still. You'll get better with practice."

"You're skilled enough at it," Tyorl said coldly. "Your friends don't seem to live very long, Stanach. How many cairns have you built since you left Thorbardin?"

Kelida, standing in silence between them, clutched Tyorl's shoulder. "No, Tyorl, no."

Stanach held up his hand. "People are dying for this sword. More will die because of it if I don't fetch it back to where it belongs. True, Tyorl?"

Tyorl said nothing for a long moment. Stanach spoke truly and the elf would not deny it. He looked up at Kelida, still standing between them. The day's new light ran like gold through her thick red braids, sent her shadow leaping out before her. In that moment, dressed in the gray hunting leathers he'd found for her in Qualinost, Stormblade at her hip, the frightened girl he'd known seemed to vanish. Mud-stained leathers, hand resting on Stormblade's hilt, she looked like she would be at home in Finn's company of rangers.

Aye, but she wouldn't be! The girl could barely use a dagger and had only yesterday learned how to walk with Stormblade on her hip without tripping over it. She was no ranger, no warrior woman. She was a farmer's girl turned barmaid.

Tyorl shook his head and got quickly to his feet. "I'll tell you this, Stanach: I don't know if Hauk is living or dead, but I believe your tale about the sword. Stormblade is no longer his. The sword should go to Thorbardin." He heard Kelida's sigh of relief and saw it mirrored deep in Stanach's dark eyes.

"However, it goes someplace else first." He cut off the dwarf's protest with with an angry gesture. "My ranger company is nearby. You weren't the only one hoping to meet friends on the road, Stanach. Finn will want to know what's happened to Hauk, and he'll need to know something I was sent to Long Ridge to learn."

Quickly, with spare detail, Tyorl told Stanach what he and Hauk had discovered in Long Ridge of Verminaard's plan to move supply bases into the mountains.

Understanding moved like pain across Stanach's face. "Verminaard plans to attack Thorbardin?"

"Oh, yes," Tyorl said dryly. "Did you think your precious mountains would be safe forever? Did you think the war would part around them like water around an island? The first supply trains are likely moving around Qualinesti's borders now. The season advances and Verminaard will want to have his bases in place for a strike before winter. It will be a good idea, don't you think, if we get to those hills before a horde of draconians arrive? And before whoever killed the mage finds us?"

The sun, now above the tree line in the east, poured its light over the hill and gilded the stones of Piper's cairn. The dwarf rose slowly and started down the hill with no word to either Tyorl or Kelida.

Kelida watched as Lavim scrambled to his feet and went to meet Stanach. Her eyes were sorrowful and her expression softened by pity. When she looked at Tyorl, the sorrow was gone. The pity remained and Tyorl had the uncomfortable feeling that it was for him.

"That was cruel, Tyorl."

"What was?"

"What you said about his friends dying." She left him abruptly and jogged down the hill.

Standing alone, Tyorl shivered in the sunlight.

The high, tuneless squeal of a flute, soared up from the foot of the hill. Down in the hollow, Lavim yelped as Stanach snatched Piper's flute from his hands.

Tyorl bounded down the slope, his doubts and misgivings forgotten. Draconians and murderous seekers after god-touched swords paled when compared with the nightmare of a kender with an enchanted flute.

The dwarf Brek ran thick fingers along the side of his face. The tic near his right eye jumped again. "Where's Mica?"

"I saw his tracks this side of the road. He'll be back." Chert shifted uneasily from foot to foot and offered the only piece of information he'd discovered. "The mage is dead."

The noon sun, thick and as sickening as the stench of something lately dead and rotting, rebounded in golden darts of light from Chert's blood-hued helm and mail, and stained the rocky hills with light. The southern road to Long Ridge was only a thin, brown ribbon seen from these low fells; the dark forest a smoky border, its shadows reaching out to pool around the high fall of rock and debris that looked like a giant's cairn. The smaller one, the real cairn, could not be seen from this distance. Behind them to the east, the broad blue heights of the Kharolis Mountains reached for the sky. Beneath those mountains lay the Deep Warrens and home.

Brek spat and wondered if he would be dead of the light or the Herald's dagger before he ever saw the warrens again. He looked sidelong at Agus the clan-reft. He'd been reading his death warrant, glittering in the deeps of the Gray Herald's one eye, since Hornfel's pet mage had vanished yesterday.

"How do you know the mage is dead?"

"There's a newly built cairn in the woods," Chert offered.

There won't even be that for me, Brek thought. My bones will rot and crumble in the sun if I don't recover that sword!

He glanced at the Herald again. Realgar did not tolerate incompetence and it would not matter at all to him that Brek had given good and faithful service for the twenty years past.

"I don't care about cairns," he snapped.

"Aye, but someone must have built it. Who would take the time but a friend? I saw the signs of three, maybe four people." Chert grinned and scratched his tangled beard with a battle scarred hand. 'Warrior's silver,' the Theiwar named the scars earned in battle. Chert was wealthy in it. "One was clearly a dwarf."

Wulfen, standing apart from his companions, laughed low in his throat. The sound reminded Brek of vulpine snarling.

"Aye, who but a friend? Hammerfell's apprentice. Could you tell where they were heading?"

"East into the foothills."

East into the foothills . . . Hammerfell's apprentice, tracking home to Thorbardin, was afoot and without the mage's spells to protect him. Brek relaxed and smiled.

Chert's hand slipped to the crossbow slung across his shoulder. "Do we follow?"

"No," Brek said. "We cut him off. Wulfen! Let's go."

Not right in his head, Brek thought again as the slim dwarf loped up the hill. Eyes like iced-over mud, Wulfen raised his head and laughed, an eerie howling. He scented prey.

As though Wulfen's howl were a signal, Mica crested the hill. Brek hailed him and motioned for him to fall in with his fellows.

The Herald, one-eyed Agus, said nothing as he followed the three north across the hills.

Tyorl welcomed their return to the forest. Out on the hill, even in its lee, he'd felt exposed and vulnerable. He breathed easier in the shade and shelter of the woods. The berms they had seen the day before, softened by a thin covering of earth and fallen leaves, were now naked gray stone outcroppings, thrusting up from the ground and often half the height of the tall pines. The trail was only an uneven winding path through stone and thick, gnarled tree roots.

The forest, though it looked like part of Qualinesti's border, was in fact the beginning of what Finn termed his 'run.' The rangerlord, and his company of thirty elves and humans, hunted the narrow strip of land between Qualinesti and the Kharolis Mountains. Their best prey were draconian patrols.

Finn's Nightmare Company had been restless, deadly predators since the first draconians had fouled the forests with their presence. 'Border-keepers' some in the remote villages and towns called them. The people gave the rangers aid when they could. Sometimes it was only a loaf of bread and a drink at the well. Sometimes aid came in the form of information or, more precious, silence when a squad of draconians passed through in search of those that had savaged a hapless patrol of Verminaard's soldiers.

Much as he did in Elvenwood, Tyorl felt at home in these stony woods. In a day or two, if not before, he would find Finn.

Or, he thought, Finn will find me.

Tyorl walked ahead, an arrow nocked and ready on his bowstring. He looked over his shoulder, caught the wink of sunlight on the dwarf's silver earring, and saw that Stanach had dropped back to last position. Though Stanach's old sword still rested in his back scabbard, Tyorl knew that it was within easy reach. He'd made no comment at all about Tyorl's plans to seek the rangers, but Tyorl supposed the fact that Stanach was still with them was acceptance enough. Stanach would go where Stormblade went, and, though she had castigated him for what she called a cruel remark, Kelida had to agree that Tyorl's idea was a good one.

Tyorl scowled. Piper's flute hung by a thong from Stanach's belt. Though Tyorl had tried to convince him to entomb the instrument with the mage, Stanach would have none of it.

"I've buried him," Stanach had said stubbornly, "I'll not

bury his music. Piper was Hornfel's man. The flute I'll give to him."

As far as any of them knew, Lavim's piping had done no mischief. But the potential for mischief, for danger, was real. According to Stanach, the mage had not only invested the flute with several spells, the instrument possessed a magic of its own.

"Piper used to say that it has its own mind," Stanach had said. "Sometimes, it chose its own song, and then it wouldn't matter at all what Piper wanted to play. Or so he liked to say."

The dwarf had said nothing more, only slipped the thong through his belt and run the palm of his hand along the polished wood.

Tyorl looked at the kender, jogging along beside Kelida, spinning some disconnected tale of improbabilities. As often as Lavim looked up at Kelida, that often did his attention wander back to Stanach and the cherry wood flute. Tyorl would have been as happy to lose the kender as the flute. He knew, watching Kelida's smile, that she would have none of that.

He did not stop then to wonder why it mattered to him what Kelida wanted.

Shadows lengthened and the sun's light was losing its warmth when Tyorl waved Stanach forward. Kelida, her expression telling clearly of aching muscles, sank to a seat on a lichen-painted boulder and only offered a thin smile when Stanach, passing her, dropped a hand onto her shoulder in a gesture of encouragement.

Lavim, uninvited and not caring in the least that he was, followed Stanach. "Why're we stopping, Tyorl?"

Tyorl ran his thumb along his bowstring. "We're stopping to hunt, Lavim. You're stopping to make camp."

"But I don't—"

"No arguments, Lavim. There's a hollow beyond those rocks." Tyorl gestured with his bow toward a cobble of trees and stone rising to their left. "You'll find a beck for water and likely the wood you'll need to make a fire." He tossed his water flask to the kender and motioned for Stanach to do the same. "Fill the flasks, then get kindling and fuel."

Lavim scowled, his face a mass of wrinkles and puzzlement. "You know, all I've been doing lately is making camp! How come Stanach gets to go hunting and I have to skin catches and drag around wood and kindling?" He slipped his hoopak from his back and looked from one to the other. Kender-quick, his expression changed to a guileful smile of assurance. "I'm an awfully good hunter."

"No one's doubting that, kenderkin." Tyorl drawled. "What I'm doubting is whether we can trust you to come back with dinner when some bird or bush or cloud catches your eyes."

Lavim bristled, about to argue, when Stanach held up a hand.

"He didn't mean that the way it sounded, Lavim. He meant—" Stanach faltered. Tyorl had said exactly what he'd meant. He tried another approach. "Well, someone has to stay here with Kelida."

"Yes, but—"

"That someone is you. You wouldn't want to hurt her feelings, would you?"

"No, but I don't see how me not staying would—"

Tyorl moved restlessly, impatiently, but Stanach waved him to silence. "If Tyorl or I stayed, she'd be sure that she was being, well, looked after. She'd think maybe we don't trust her to take care of herself."

"You don't?"

"If she could, I would. She can't. But you can manage the thing better than we could. You're good at that, Lavim."

The kender dug in stubbornly. "Kelida knows how to use her dagger. I taught her and—"

"Ah, she's that quick a study, is she? We'll all be taking lessons from her soon, I guess."

Lavim drew in a chestful of air and let it out in a gusty sigh. "No, of course not. I haven't taught her my over-the-shoulder double-trouble trick yet—among other things. But Stanach, I—"

"Well, then? Are you going to leave her by herself to make camp and maybe just hope she's there when we get back?" He sighed deliberately. "I guess I was wrong about one thing."

Lavim wore the look of one who suspects he is being led, but he couldn't resist the question. "About what?"

"I got the idea that you'd taken Kelida under your wing. You know, teaching her to use the dagger, telling her stories to keep her mind off being tired and frightened." Stanach, his dark eyes as wide and innocent as any kender's, shrugged. "I guess I was wrong."

Tyorl swallowed a smile as Lavim, dragging his heels and kicking at small stones, returned to Kelida. "I never heard of anyone trying to actually reason with a kender before; I certainly never heard of it working," said Tyorl.

Stanach shrugged. "He really is fond of Kelida. I figured I could take a chance on that. I don't expect that ploy will work every time." He jerked a thumb at Tyorl's longbow. "I suppose I get to flush the grouse?"

"Not unless you'd like to chase a squirrel or two with your sword."

Stanach said nothing, but followed the elf into the woods.

The stars promised a clear day. The moons, both red and silver, rode high in the midnight sky, spilling light through the forest. Shadows wavered like ghosts across the ground.

Someday, Lavim told himself, I'd like to be able to move around as quietly as a ghost. He crouched down by the stream's edge and scooped up a handful of icy water. Without, of course, actually being one. Still, there would be advantages.

Moonlight sparkled on something just beneath the water's surface.

Lavim slipped his finger back into the water and pried a gleaming stone about the size of his fist from the stream bed. Brownish red and shot through with green striations, the rock seemed to shimmer in the faint moonlight. Flecks of yellow and and white danced on the stone's surface.

Like gold and diamonds! Well, they're probably not bits of gold and diamonds. They're probably something with some name that only gnomes or dwarves would know.

Lavim tucked the stone into one of his pouches. He sat back on his heels and watched the moonlight rippling through the water. A gray fox barked in the thickets behind

him. A nighthawk screamed high in the sky beyond the roof
of the forest and a rabbit dove for its burrow in skittering
panic. All around the kender, leaves rustled with the com-
ings and goings of night creatures, stalked and stalking.

Why do you suppose, he asked himself, that people
always say silent as a forest at night? This place is noisier
than a market fair!

The kender laughed silently. He'd lately fallen into the
habit of talking to himself. Probably because I'm getting
old, he thought. People always said that the old talk to
themselves because they know they're the only ones who'll
give themselves a good answer.

Lavim found a more comfortable position and settled
back to watch the forest and think in the moonlight.

That's what I'm really doing: I'm thinking, he thought.
I'm not talking to myself because I'm not all that old. Sixty
isn't really that old. Maybe my eyes aren't what they used to
be, but I still managed to save young Stanach from all those
draconians!

He smiled. Right. And as long as we're talking about
Stanach . . .

Lavim knew—and recognized the matter with only a
careless shrug—that what he'd really been doing all along
(as well as talking to himself) was trying to find a good
answer to the puzzle of how to get his hands on Piper's flute.
Stanach had kept it close and never once let it out of his sight
all day.

All I want to do, Lavim assured himself, is just borrow it
for a minute or two. I could see, he went on, why the flute is
really important to him, seeing as it was Piper's and they
were such good friends. Poor Stanach. He must be lonely
without Piper. He was really looking forward to seeing Piper again. He's a long way from home and probably would
have appreciated seeing a friendly face. Though you'd think
he'd be happy he's getting the sword back. Now what was I
saying? Oh, right. The flute. He'd be really happy to find
out afterward—if I managed to get my hands on it in the
first place—that he didn't lose it but that I only borrowed it.

Lavim grinned up at the moons. He hadn't the least doubt
that he'd be able to get his hands on the flute. It only

required the right time and place.

Red and brown cherry wood, long and light, the flute had haunted the kender ever since he'd first seen it. He'd managed to squeek just a note or two out of it before Stanach had grabbed it away. He wondered now what kind of spell must live in a mage's flute. The kind that teaches you songs, maybe?

Lavim wrapped his arms around his drawn up knees. Aye, the kind that teaches you songs. He understood nothing about playing songs and music, but he just knew that if he ever got his hands on Piper's flute again that would change.

The kender climbed stiffly to his feet. The ground was cold and he hadn't caught anything for breakfast yet. It was about the only thing anyone let him do besides make camp, find wood, fill flasks, and break camp.

He slipped into the shadows, thinking about enchanted flutes, rabbits, and hot broth made from what was left of the grouse.

The smoke drifting up to the top of the cobble still smelled sweetly of roasted grouse. Stanach looked down at the camp and wondered when kenders slept. Lavim was nowhere to be seen. Kelida slept close to the fire. Tyorl, his back against a hawthorn, slept with his head resting on drawn up knees.

Not for long, Stanach thought as he started down the rocks. Tyorl should have taken the watch before now, and the dwarf wasn't going to wait any longer for him to wake. All Stanach wanted was the fire's warmth for a few moments and then a place to sleep that wasn't too stony.

The fire threw black shadows against the trees and made them seem to sway in a silent wind. Stanach caught a glint of fire on steel and saw Stormblade under Kelida's outflung hand. The peace strings on the scabbard were loose and the blade lay half outside its sheath. He knelt to slide the sword back into the scabbard.

His palm touched the rough place on the chasing. He'd been smoothing that silver when the Kingsword was stolen, when the walls of the forge had shattered before his eyes.

Fire had exploded in his head and he'd felt blood running down his neck, before darkness swallowed the world and he'd fallen, senseless, to the floor.

A crimson light pulsed in the steel that was not the reflection of the fire. Stanach slid Stormblade from the scabbard so quietly that Kelida's breathing never hitched. He stood slowly and stepped away. He held Stormblade across both palms.

Kyan Red-axe had died for this sword. Piper had died for it, too.

Realgar's men would have searched for the mage. They would have seen the cairn. I shouldn't have built it, he thought. He shook his head. No, the Theiwar would have found Piper's body sooner or later. By the carrion crows. Stanach shuddered.

Do what you have to do. It was the last thing Piper had said to him.

I'm doing it, Stanach thought.

It was what he'd planned all along. Find Piper, take the sword, and get back to Hornfel. Now, by taking the sword, he would be leaving his companions to their deaths if the Theiwar caught up with them.

Stanach looked down at Kelida. Her heart was so simple to read! He wondered when she would realize that she had fallen in love with the half-drunk ranger who had given her his sword.

When she knows that he's dead, his mind's voice whispered. She'll know it when she finally knows that he's dead.

Stanach looked at the Kingsword in his hands. He would happily have taken the sword that first night in Qualinesti. He would gladly have left her, Tyorl, and Lavim behind in the forest and made his own way to Thorbardin. Because he couldn't do that, he did the next best thing: he'd given Kelida a reason to carry Stormblade to Thorbardin. He'd given her a dead man to love.

I'm sorry, she'd said as he sat mourning for Piper. She'd stayed with him for a long time, her hand on his, warm and silently telling him that, for this moment at least, he was not alone. The comfort she offered had been as simple as a kinswoman's, a sister's silent understanding.

Knowing that he ought to leave now, make off into the forest with the Kingsword and hope that he could buy time by leaving these three to the Theiwar, Stanach knelt and slipped Stormblade into the scabbard again.

Aye, Stanach thought, you understand, don't you? You've lost kin and friends. You understand, *lyt chwaer*, little sister.

He tied the peace strings, two leather thongs on each side of the sheath, and silently rose to wake Tyorl.

CHAPTER 15

Finn watched dawnlight glint on his dagger as he cut the draconian's throat. He jerked his hand back quickly, pulling the blade free of the creature's scaly flesh before the steel could be caught in the corpse's transformation from flesh to stone. His stomach pulled tight with disgust, as it always did. He hated these misbegotten beasts living; he loathed them dead. Their kind killed his wife and murdered his son. He couldn't kill enough of them.

The stenches of battle, blood, and fire filled the small clearing. Rising high on the cold morning breeze, the smoke from burned supply wagons swirled around the tops of the tall pines and slid down toward the nearby river. It caught the currents of air over the water and drifted back to the glade where the draconian patrol and the supply train of three wagons had been caught just before dawn by Finn and his rangers.

Before dawn, Finn thought, and just in time to fill their sleep with the last nightmares they would have.

Thirty strong, the ranger company had not lost a man, though a few were injured. Finn smiled cold satisfaction and looked around for Lehr. Dark shaggy hair lifting lazily in the small breeze, Lehr sighted the rangerlord and trotted across the clearing, jogging around the charred wagons bristling with arrows, and leaping nimbly over bodies turning to stone and dust.

"Any sign of more?"

Lehr shook his head. "Only these, Lord. I've been up on the ridge. You can see for miles up there. Nothing moving but the crows, and they're only wondering when we'll be gone so they can have breakfast." Lehr's eyes lighted with dark humor. "Poor birds. Nothing to pick here but what's left of the draconians' dinner last night. Unless they want stone and dust."

Finn grunted. "Make camp by the river, Lehr. When your brother is finished with his work, both of you join me here."

"Aye, Lord?" It was an invitation to explain further. When Finn did not accept it, Lehr shrugged and went to find his brother. Finn did not often explain his motives. Lehr didn't often expect that he would, though he didn't mind trying for an explanation now and then.

He found Kembal already tending the worst of the wounded and gave him Finn's word. "Something's up, Kem. What do you think?"

Kembal, healer and ranger both, looked up at his brother mildly. "Don't know, but I'll bet it has something to do with the signs you picked up yesterday." Kembal eased the arrow from a man's leg with gentle hands. The man flinched. His face paled, then settled into grim lines of resignation as the blood began to pour from his wound. He knew, as well as Kembal did, that draconian arrows were often poisoned. The blood flow now would be a cleansing, and, though he didn't like to see it, he accepted it. Kem worked swiftly to clean the wound and didn't watch as his brother left.

Both knew that Finn had not appreciated the surprise of

stumbling upon a draconian patrol and supply train. He knew, too, that though the rangerlord had sent Tyorl and Hauk to Long Ridge to discover just such news of Verminaard's movements in the foothills, the two had not returned from the town.

It was Lehr's thinking that the signs he'd seen earlier were Tyorl's. Kembal expected that Finn agreed. He wrapped the wound and rose to move on to the next man awaiting his attention. He supposed that Finn was going to take this time to let his men breathe; and to track back along the trail and satisfy himself that the tracks Lehr had seen were or were not Tyorl's.

But what would the elf be doing with such an oddly assorted party as the signs had indicated? A dwarf, a kender, and a light-stepping human or elf?

And where, Kem wondered, was Hauk?

The late afternoon sun, freakishly hot as it sometimes was in autumn, appeared as white splashes on rocky outcroppings. Old brown leaves rattled across the rocks in the light, cool breeze. Stanach wiped sweat from his face with the heel of his hand and dropped to one knee in the shadow-crossed path. Someone had passed along the trail not long ago. The dwarf glanced up at Tyorl standing at his shoulder.

"Your rangers?"

Tyorl shook his head. He pointed to a white-scarred rock in the path. The stone had been scraped by steel. "No ranger in Finn's company wears steel-capped boots. Look at that foot mark over there."

Off to the side of the path, the moss, still cool and moist in the shade of a tall larch, held one well-formed impression. No woodsman, Stanach shook his head, frowning.

"A dwarf," Tyorl said patiently. "Look, the size almost matches your own."

Stanach closed his eyes thinking of Piper's cairn crowning the hilltop a day and a half's journey back through the forest. The Theiwar must have seen it and picked up their trail. It wouldn't be hard to guess where the four companions were heading now. "Realgar's men."

"It's likely." Tyorl passed silently up the path, eyes to the ground, and returned after only a moment. "They're headed for the river. It looks like they passed here at dawn."

The path, such as it was, led to the only fording place within a day's walk. The next closest ford lay ten miles south. Stanach rose and tugged absently at his beard. "Damn!" he muttered. "They mean to cut us off!"

"Where's the kender?"

"Back with Kelida. Why?"

"I want to get across the river today. More than that, I want to know these mage-killers aren't waiting at the ford. You've a steady hand with your sword, Stanach." The elf slipped his longbow from his shoulder. He strung it quickly and drew an arrow from his quiver. "At best, we'll be three against four, with Kelida to protect. That won't be easy. The sword marks her as their target. Can you convince Lavim to stay with her again while we scout?"

"I wouldn't even try. Don't worry about it. He's talking to Kelida, he'll be occupied for a few minutes. Let's check the ford while we can."

Hesitating, Tyorl glanced back down the trail. The bend in the path hid the place where Kelida and Lavim had stopped. The girl, unused to walking and climbing all day, spoke no word of complaint, but wisely took each chance she could to rest. Lavim, never one to lose an audience, kept pace with her.

Sunlight glinted like gold in Tyorl's hair as he ploughed his fingers through it. Stanach watched as the elf considered.

Kelida's soft laughter drifted to them on the cool breeze. Lavim's deep tones ran as counterpoint to her light voice.

Tyorl and Stanach moved down the path, their footfalls on the rising path sounding loud in the still forest. Ten yards beyond the place where they'd found the tracks, the path angled east, narrowing so they could no longer walk abreast.

The path climbed steeply now. Dark, damp earth clung to overturned stones in the path. Moss showed on the tops of some, the sides of others, and in many places the thick, green cover was scraped and scored. "They were hurrying," Tyorl said, "and not bothering to cover their trail. They cut onto the path just where we first saw their sign." He looked back over his shoulder. "We shouldn't have left her alone."

The breeze quickened, and the shadows sprawled across the path swayed and danced. Stanach tried to catch the sound of Kelida's voice and heard nothing but the scratching of old leaves against stone. "I'm thinking you're right. Go back. If Lavim's still there, send him ahead and tell him to catch up with me."

Tyorl frowned and Stanach, seeing his doubt, snorted. "I'm no ranger, Tyorl, but I'm not blind either." He nodded to the signs on the path. "I can follow this, and I can keep quiet enough when I have to."

He didn't have to say it: the elf's longbow could defend Kelida better than a lone sword. Tyorl nodded. "Leave the track here, Stanach. Keep it in sight and follow it from the woods. If they're waiting up ahead, they'll have a guard posted along here soon. If you sight him, get back here quietly and quickly. If we can take them, we will."

"And if we can't?"

Tyorl shrugged. "We try to cross the river someplace else. However, I don't want to worry about these mage-killers cropping up in front of us again."

"Go on then. I'll be back."

Stanach watched him go. The dwarf picked his way as quietly as he could through rustling underbrush whose slim branches clawed at his beard and scratched at his face and hands. He paralleled the path for a dozen yards, then was stopped by the broad, high face of an outcropping of stone. Around or over? he wondered, eyeing the obstacle. The stone was hard and old, rough with good grips. Stanach, who had seen nothing but forest for too long, grinned. Over, he decided.

He ran a careful hand over the stone, testing hand- and footholds. The holds were good, and he climbed swiftly, gaining the crest of the outcropping in a few moments. A foolhardy young pine clung to the the top of the rocks, with a few scrawny bushes for company. Except for these, the stone was gray and naked. Crouching low, Stanach kept to the north side of the pine's trunk. From this cover, he saw the empty trail below. No guard.

Several yards beyond the outcropping, the trail turned again to the right, ran just below the rock where Stanach crouched, and dropped off suddenly. Stanach shifted position a little to gain a clearer view.

The trees ended abruptly here, and the path snaked down into a stony river valley. The river itself was a narrow silver ribbon, the ford a shallow place at the path's end, fringed with browning reeds. There was no sign that whoever had come up the trail before them lingered now in the stony vale.

A hawk wheeled high over the valley and slid down the wind on long, lazy spirals, searching for prey. The water's wind-ruffled surface split as a small bass leaped high, a silver flash in the sun. Before the fish reached the height of its arc, the hawk dove hard and caught it with a triumphant cry.

Aye, dinner for you, Stanach thought, and likely you've left some for us.

The vale was empty, the river full of fish, and the fording would be easy. Smiling, he rose and turned.

He stood face to face with the one-eyed Theiwar known in Thorbardin as the Gray Herald.

Cold fear filled his belly. Trapped! Even as he understood that, Stanach instinctively ducked his right shoulder and pulled his sword free of the scabbard across his back. The high, singing whine of steel coming free was overwhelmed by the Gray Herald's hard, brittle laughter. Stanach, fearing that he had already lost, knew it was so when his mighty double-handed blow rebounded inches from Agus's neck. The air around the mageling flared scarlet, spat hot, fat sparks, and Stanach's arms ached to the shoulders as though he'd struck mountain stone.

Agus, laughing still, lifted his right hand, caressing the air. He whispered a word, then another, and the sun-filled air around Stanach became cold as a winter night. The sky, blue a moment ago, became heavy, smelled of fear and despair. As though a huge hand had struck him from behind, Stanach crashed to his knees. Dimly, he heard the clatter of his sword on stone and saw Agus reach for the blade and snatch it up from the boulder.

Stanach tried to find air to breathe. There was none. It was as though the Gray Herald's spell had sucked all the air out of Stanach's lungs.

This, Stanach thought, is how Piper was taken. Ambushed by a Theiwar mageling.

Thinking of Piper, he remembered his friend's flute hanging from his belt. Though Piper had invested it with several spells, though the flute possessed an inherent magic of its own, it was useless to Stanach, who was not versed in magic. He knew instantly that it would be a powerful tool in the hands of the Gray Herald. The Theiwar would surely fathom its use if he had the time to study it. Under the guise of struggling to move, Stanach freed the flute from his belt and shoved it fast and hard into a crack in the boulder.

Agus lifted his hands again, and Stanach knew the gestures he made now. The words he spoke, only three, were oddly gentle ones which gave Stanach no comfort at all. They were the words of a transport spell.

Agus reached down, touched Stanach's head, and smiled into his eyes. Caught in the familiar wrench and grab of a transport spell, Stanach doubled over as all feeling drained from his arms and legs, all sense of being fled his heart and mind.

Lavim perched on a boulder just off the trail where he could see up the path and down. His hoopak balanced across his knees and a large leather pouch containing stones ranging from smooth pebbles to rough-sided, fist-sized rocks lay between his feet. He examined the stones one by one, the way an archer will check his arrows. He held up a reddish brown and green stone mottled with shining bits of yellow pyrite and white calcite for Kelida's inspection.

"This rock," he said, watching the sun catch the pyrite and calcite, "killed a goblin at a hundred paces."

Kelida eyed him doubtfully. "A hundred, Lavim?"

The old kender nodded casually as though his veracity had not been questioned. "Maybe a hundred and ten. I didn't have time to count, you understand."

"But you fetched back the rock after it killed this goblin?"

"Oh, yes. It's a good rock, a lucky rock. I've had it for a

long time. It was my father's, and he had it from his father."

Kelida swallowed a smile. "Sort of a family heirloom, is it?"

Lavim tucked the stone back into his pouch. "Well, I never thought of it like that, but yes, I suppose it is."

The picture of two generations of kenders dutifully retrieving this rock each time it flew from a hoopak's sling was too absurd to consider. Though she hid her smile behind her hand, Lavim saw it in her green eyes.

"What's so funny about that, Kelida?"

"Oh, I'm not laughing, not really. I'm—I'm smiling because it's nice that you have something to remember your father and grandfather by."

Kelida drew her legs up tight to her chest and rested her chin on her knees. She watched the kender continue his inspection of his weapons. Thin sunlight ran like silver down his long, white braid. In his weather-browned and wrinkled face, his green eyes shone like spring leaves in sunlight.

"I was just thinking I don't have anything to remember my family by—no lucky rock, at least."

Lavim looked up. "Oh, there are plenty of them in Khur. Have you ever been there? That's where I was born. It's a nice country, all hills and mountains. Some pretty valleys, too. You should see it sometime, Kelida. I'd like to go back there myself. I always mean to but—I dunno, something always tugs me in the opposite direction. Like this Stormblade, although I'll be darned if I can figure out what it is, exactly.

"You didn't always used to be a barmaid, did you? You used to live on a farm with your family, right? Before the dragon—uh, well, before you were a barmaid. Well, if you like farming, you'd love the valleys in Khur. I'd be happy to take you there. That way I'd get back, too. For a while, anyway. After we take care of Stormblade." He paused. "Say, you don't suppose this Hauk fellow is going to want to come to Khur, too, do you?"

Kelida watched sun dazzle on stone. "Why would he want to?"

"Well, if you were there he might. He probably knows

you're coming to Thorbardin to rescue him, and he'll probably be grateful. I wonder if they've got him in a gaol or a dungeon? Gaols are all right, I guess, for limited duration. The food's usually really nasty, but it's pretty regular.

"Dungeons? I don't like them so much. The food's not much worse, but you don't see it as often. The people who put you there tend to forget about you after a while.

"You know, Thorbardin's a really big place. Not one city—six of 'em. They're all sort of connected somehow. Maybe with bridges. And it's built right *inside* the mountain. Can you imagine that?

"There's gardens, too. Did you know that? But, if they're inside the mountain, how do they get sunlight? How do they get rain? Well, I suppose they could save up the rain and water their gardens, but that would be a big job, don't you think? Even if they did—water the gardens, I mean— that still doesn't solve the problem of sunlight. You can't carry that in a bucket."

Lavim rambled on. Kelida only half heard him. She was thinking of dungeons and gaols and wondering if Hauk did, indeed, know that someone was coming to help him.

He must know, she thought. He must know that Tyorl is searching for him. She ran her hand along the sheathed flat of the Kingsword. He has to know his imprisonment is because of this sword.

"Of course, if you were going to carry sunlight in buckets, the buckets would have to have a tight lid, wouldn't they?"

If he's alive, she thought, Hauk knows. Can he still be alive? It had been six days since the night he'd walked out of Tenny's. She thought of Piper, the mage, and the cairn on the hill in the forest, and of Stanach's eyes when he spoke of his kinsman's death. She closed her eyes and rested her forehead on her drawn up knees.

She tried to hear Hauk's voice, find the little break in it that told of a gentleness hiding behind the bear's rumble. She imagined that if she could always hear his voice in her memory, he would still be alive. If she could always see his eyes as he laid the sword at her feet, he would not be dead.

She had built, of the few moments she'd spoken with him, an image of gallantry and kindness, and she no longer remembered that, in those real moments in Tenny's, she had feared him.

". . . And they'd have to be dark buckets—maybe lined with lead or something like that—so the sunlight wouldn't always be leaking out. Hmmm. I wonder if they've thought of that."

Kelida closed her fingers around the scabbarded sword. Kingsword, Stanach called it. Stormblade. For Kelida it would always be the sword of the man who risked her life for a gamble and then gambled with his own to keep her safe.

Bushes rustled, a stone skittered on the path, and Lavim scrambled from his rocky perch, scooping rocks back into his pouch. Kelida looked around and saw Tyorl standing beside her. She moved to get to her feet, but the elf waved her back.

"Not yet. Lavim. Get up the trail and catch up with Stanach, will you?"

The kender slung his hoopak across his back. "Sure, Tyorl. What's going on?"

"Nothing. Go find Stanach. And don't wander."

Grinning happily, the kender loped away up the trail, pack and pouches jogging.

"I heard him halfway up the trail." Tyorl said. He settled on the boulder that the kender had abandoned. "What was he on about?"

Kelida smiled. "Thorbardin and sunlight in lead-lined buckets."

"Sunlight in—?" Tyorl scratched his jaw. "Why?"

"Oh, for the gardens. He says there are a lot of gardens in Thorbardin. Are there?"

The elf shrugged. "I don't know. The city's inside the mountain so I don't see how there could be. Kender-talk is half dreams and half imagination."

Kelida watched in silence for a long moment as Tyorl ran his thumb along the longbow's string. "Where is Stanach?"

"Up the trail." Tyorl shrugged again. "Running scout."

"Shouldn't we catch up with him?"

Tyorl looked into the shadows. Though he heard nothing but wind in the trees, he shook his head. "In a minute. It's a long climb up the trail. We can wait here still."

Kelida nodded and fell silent, watching the shadows weaving on the trail. Tyorl watched the sunlight running like gold thread through her hair.

You see, the thing about the buckets, Lavim told himself, is that they might work and they might not. But you never know until you try, right?

The wind sighed in the treetops, and Lavim trotted up the trail.

Right, he thought. Of course, if they do have gardens in Thorbardin, then they must've figured something out about the light.

Lavim had decided that he wasn't going to worry about this new habit of talking to himself. Besides, he enjoyed it almost as much as talking to someone else. For one thing, he never interrupted himself. Besides, it seemed as though Stanach and Tyorl just couldn't be happy unless they were cutting him off in mid-sentence. Kelida listened, sometimes. But, all in all, he was beginning to enjoy his conversations with himself. He gave and got good answers.

He left the path where broken bushes and trampled underbrush showed him Stanach's trail.

Just like a dwarf! He cuts a path a mile wide so everyone can see where he's been. They're not real good in the woods, dwarves, are they?

A stone outcropping rose tall and gray before him. Lavim grinned. I'll bet he went this way. Why didn't he stick to the path? Oh, well. I'll ask him when I find him.

He grabbed for hand- and footholds and scrambled up the stone. Oh, yes, Stanach had been here. The lichen clinging to the rock was scuffed and torn. Lavim shook his head. Might as well paint a sign in red that says, I WENT THIS WAY.

Sunlight winked on something smooth and red-brown where it lay in a narrow crevice in the stone. Lavim reached for the gleam and frowned when he picked up Piper's flute.

Lavim drew a long breath and let it out in a low whistle. Piper's flute! What a find!

He raised the flute to his lips, ready at once to make good

his resolve to see if the flute would teach him songs. He tried a note and then another. Before he could draw another breath, he was stopped by a sudden thought.

Now why, he thought, would Stanach leave this up here? He's always real careful not to leave things lying around—annoyingly careful—and here is Piper's flute, just tossed aside.

The kender rubbed his thumbs along the smooth cherry wood, then held the flute up to the sunlight, watching the red and brown glints deep inside the wood. Had the dwarf dropped it?

Lavim snorted. Not likely! It was Piper's flute and, so Stanach said, magic. You don't just drop a magic flute that's been hanging from your belt for two days and that you check every six minutes to make sure is still there.

Lavim peered closely at the stone beneath his feet. Someone else had been here, too. The dirt around the small pine at the crest of the stone showed two sets of footprints.

Not Tyorl's footprints, the kender thought. He dropped to his haunches and laid his hand along the prints. One set was narrower than the other, but both were of a length. Another dwarf.

Now why do you suppose there'd be another dwarf way out here in the middle of the woods? Oh, he thought, right, the whadyacallems.

Theiwar.

"Right," he said, "Theiwar. That means—" Lavim snapped his mouth shut and looked around. Wind sighed in the underbrush. The river in the valley below whispered and laughed. A jay scolded from the top of an oak and took noisy wing. There was no one around, but he'd heard a voice, hollow as the wind or a distant flute song. "Uh, hello?"

Lavim, Stanach is in trouble.

Lavim turned this way and that, frowning into the valley, scowling at the thickets back down the trail. "Where are you?" he said aloud. "For that matter, who are you? How do you know Stanach's in trouble?"

You have to help him, Lavim.

"Yes, but—Now wait a minute! How do I know you're

167

not one of those, uh . . ."

Theiwar.

"Right! How do I know—"

Why would I tell you he's in trouble?

"Why don't you show yourself? How about that? Where are you?"

Right behind you.

Lavim spun around. No one stood behind him. He turned back. No one stood there. He couldn't be hearing a voice if no one was there to speak. Was he talking to himself again?

This didn't sound like his voice. He squeezed his eyes shut, trying to remember what his voice sounded like when he was talking to himself. (*Thinking*, he reminded himself.) But he couldn't recall, and on the chance that he wasn't having some strange conversation with his own mind, the kender opened his eyes again and peered around.

"Now listen—"

The voice, behind and on all sides of him now, had changed from wind-hollow to steel.

Lavim, you called me. Now listen to me! Go get Tyorl!

Lavim sighed. If he was still talking to himself, he'd picked up Tyorl's and Stanach's annoying habit of interrupting himself.

"I called you? I didn't call anyone. I didn't —"

We'll talk about it later! Go!

Lavim scrambled down the outcropping and headed for the trail. Fear didn't send him running. Neither did obedience.

What caused him to run, as noisy as a dwarf through the underbrush, was the sudden and complete realization that, this time, it was not his voice and he had not been talking to himself.

Well, he amended, I might've been talking to myself, but someone else was answering!

Lavim laughed and brandished the old wooden flute high as he ran. He guessed who had been answering him.

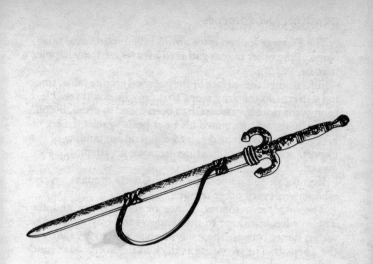

CHAPTER 16

Gneiss heard the newly lighted braziers in the council chamber hiss, then sigh and settle to slow, steady burning. He massaged his temples, realizing as he did that the
gesture had become as much a habit as his headache seemed
to be. The cause of that headache, the eight hundred refugees who had been the subject of council meetings for too
many days now, waited in the valley outside Southgate.
Their representatives, glimpsed only briefly as he had
entered the council chamber, were a half-elf and a tall,
lovely Plainswoman. Gneiss rubbed his temples more gently. The two waited now in an antechamber for the decision
of the council. On the council's word, they would either
take their eight hundred elsewhere or—Gneiss sighed
wearily—settle them into Thorbardin.

The Daewar looked once around the broad, oval table. None of the other thanes gathered here seemed any happier than he.

Tufa studied the surface of the polished granite table, tracing patterns in the gray stone that only he could see. He'd been silent since the council had been called to order. Bluph, the gully dwarf, drummed his boot heels against the leg of his chair. As though he'd gained a dim understanding of the importance of today's meeting, he made an attempt to stay awake.

If you can call someone awake, Gneiss thought sourly, who yawns every other minute!

The two *derro* thanes, Rance of the Daergar and the Theiwar Realgar, kept to the shadows the way a fish likes water, Rance because these days he was never very far from the Theiwar. The two were as thick as fleas on a dog's hind end.

Hornfel, his eyes speaking of sleepless nights, rose from his place at the head of the table.

"We have agreed that there will be no further debate on the issue of admitting the refugees to Thorbardin." Rance drew a breath to interrupt. Hornfel, as though he hadn't seen, continued smoothly. "The refugees' representatives await our word. I will keep them waiting no longer. This council has other matters to attend to."

A silence, pensive and waiting, settled over the chamber. Bluph settled for swinging his legs in the air and not permitting his heels to thud against the chair.

"We will vote." Hornfel turned to the Klar. "Tufa, give us your word."

The thane of the Klar declined with a slow shake of his head. "My thinking hasn't changed. I will abide by the council's decision." He shot a quick, and for him defiant, look at Realgar. "Whatever that decision is."

Gneiss sighed. Unless any of the others now voted differently than he'd previously indicated, his would indeed be the word that would determine the council's decision. As he'd told Hornfel on the Southgate battlements, he'd come to a decision. Though he'd spoken to no one about it, his solution was the best he could devise.

Hornfel closed his eyes, drew a breath, and then nodded to the gully dwarf. "Bluph, turn them away or admit them?"

Bluph straightened in mid-yawn and stopped scratching. He blinked, then grinned widely. "Admit them." He narrowed his eyes and looked as though he might reconsider.

Hornfel spoke quickly. "Rance."

"No! No! And no!"

"I thought not," Hornfel said wryly. "Realgar?"

The Theiwar shrugged. In that moment his eyes reminded Gneiss of a cat's, narrow and hungry. "I'll save you the trouble of reading my mind, Hornfel. Turn them away. We've no place for them, no liking for them, and no need of them."

Gneiss looked up, met Realgar's eyes steadily. The same, he thought, might be said of you, Theiwar. Aloud he only said, "We can put them in the east farming warrens. These have gone unused for three years. We don't know these people to like or dislike them, so that hardly matters. Need them?" He swept the table with a swift glance. "We can always use farmers. That's what these people are. I say admit them, and they'll work for their keep. As halfcroppers, they'll pay for it, too."

Again Gneiss looked to Hornfel. "Your vote?"

Hornfel's voice held quiet triumph. "Admit them."

On his words, Realgar rose with silent grace and stalked from the council chamber. Rance, snarling dark curses, followed on the Theiwar's heels. There was nothing the two *derro* thanes could do now to prevent the admittance of the eight hundred humans.

The council had voted, and the vote was something to hold even Realgar. For now.

Gneiss watched the two leave and Tufa and Bluph after them. He sighed, half-listening to Bluph wondering how the vote had turned out, then turned to Hornfel.

"You've got your vote, my friend."

Hornfel nodded, but did not look like one who has just secured a victory.

"What now? Did you perhaps think that your ragged eight hundred should spend the winter sleeping and lounging?"

Hornfel ignored the sarcasm. "Tell me, Gneiss, how are

we going to make allies and friends out of the sick and hungry people we've just put to work half-cropping in our fields?"

Gneiss sighed tiredly. "They don't have to start today, Hornfel. Take what you've won and tell your refugees they winter here. If it comes to fighting a war from the Outlands, they'll be well by then and likely happy to defend the place they're living in. If it comes to . . . revolution in Thornbardin, you've my Daewar and the Klar. We'll need none else."

Yet even as he said it, Gneiss remembered the cat's look in Realgar's eyes. He didn't like the chill skittering up his spine. "Will you tell them now?"

Hornfel drummed his fingers on the table. "I want a minute to breathe."

"Breathe? Aye, go right ahead. But have a care where you do it. I don't like the look of the Theiwar these days."

"Neither do I." Hornfel said. Gneiss understood then that his friend had not been losing sleep only to the matter of the refugees.

Hornfel was careful where he did his breathing. He went to the garden outside the Court of Thanes. He paced the fine gravel paths, a measured march.

He was happy for the victory he'd won. And no, he'd had no plan to let "his ragged eight hundred" lounge and sleep the winter away. Nor had he wished to offer what looked, even to him, like indentured servitude. It was no way to win allies, and he knew he would need allies soon. He'd seen the confirmation of that in Realgar's eyes today.

He paused in his measured pacing. His circuit of the garden brought him to the largest areas of planting. Here, the wildly colored mountain flowers of summer bloomed, as they did all year round, in the carefully controlled climate of the underground gardens.

Slim-leafed bell heather and the gray-green mountain everlasting blossomed side by side. Royal fern spread wide fronds, more gold than green. Hearty yellow-flowered gorse poked through those sweeping fans as though caring little for the prerogatives of royalty, and rosebay crept up the border of the planting in low growing mats.

Hornfel touched a finger to one of the rosebay's delicate flowers. The soft pink petals were wide in the light shining down from the many shafts of crystal leading to the surface. The rosebay's tender flower shivered a little.

Hornfel drew back his hand and looked up at the light shaft positioned almost directly above him. The lavender glow of approaching twilight drifted down to the garden, but during the day, a diffused golden light nourished the plantings.

The same system of crystal shafts illuminated the six cities as though they lay in sunlight and provided the light needed to grow the crops that fed hungry Thorbardin.

We may love the mountains and all their deep secrets, thought Hornfel, but we love the light, too. At least, some of us do.

A soft footfall and a roughly cleared throat startled Hornfel. He turned slowly, not showing his surprise. As he met the black eyes of the Theiwar's thane, Hornfel had the clear impression that Realgar, squinting in what to him must seem the bright glare of the garden, had been watching him for some moments. He saw the shadow of dark thoughts in Realgar's eyes. The back of his neck went cold as though the breath of winter mourned through the garden.

"Your . . . guests await you," the *derro* mage said. He spoke the word as though naming a plague. With a scornful smile, the Theiwar left as silently as he'd arrived.

Dark thoughts and red fury, Hornfel thought. Realgar had fought to the last moment of a long and exhausting council session, insisting that no good would come of admitting humans into the mountain kingdom.

He used to think that he would be the first Realgar would murder if he could. Hornfel thought now that if the chance presented itself, Realgar would certainly murder him. But not before he killed Gneiss, whose temporizing had opened the doors to the refugees just as effectively as a firm commitment.

He supposed that the only reason they weren't dead yet was Realgar hadn't found the Kingsword. How long before he did? Or how long before he tired of waiting for the symbol and mounted his revolution without it?

Hornfel was no longer certain that the sword would be found. It had been too many days since word first came that Stormblade had been seen. Last night, in the dark of midnight, Hornfel began to consider what must be done if Kyan, Piper, and Stanach were dead; if Stormblade were lost again. All his plans were for defense.

Gneiss, he realized, must be considering the same plans. Three of Gneiss's Daewar warriors seemed always to be nearby. Yet, how would they defend him against magic should Realgar swerve from his usual path of assassins and daggers in the dark?

Not at all, Hornfel thought bitterly, as he left the garden and prepared to dole out his ragged hospitality.

Gneiss's guards did not enter the Court of Thanes with Hornfel, but stayed behind at the door within sound of his call. Three others, their weapons close to hand, waited in the council chamber. They made no pretense to politeness, but stood within an easy hand's reach of the refugees' representatives.

Hornfel, studied the two messengers carefully as he walked the length of the great hall. One, a red-bearded half-elf turned at the sound of the dwarf's footfalls. He wore a sword at his hip and a longbow over his shoulder. His green eyes were hard and sharp.

His companion, a tall woman dressed in the buckskins of the Plains, laid a slim hand on the hunter's arm as she heard Hornfel's approach. Hair that was both moon-silver and sun-gold glistened in the glow of newly lighted torches when she moved. She murmured a word, no more, and the half-elf relaxed.

At least, he seemed to. Those green eyes never softened. Here's one, Hornfel mused, who doesn't like playing the supplicant! Aye, well, I can't blame you, hunter. I wouldn't care for the role myself.

At Hornfel's open-handed gesture of welcome, the guards moved back a pace or two.

"I thank you for waiting," the dwarf said.

The half-elf drew a breath to speak, but the light hand on his arm moved in a way meant both to be gentle and, unconsciously, to command. The woman spoke and her voice was low and soft. The soothing whisper of a dove's wings lay behind that voice, the whisper of a heart at peace. "We have been enjoying the beauty of your hall."

I doubt it, Hornfel thought, or at least your friend hasn't been. He motioned toward an alcove off the main hall, large enough to hold a map table made from a single cut of rose-streaked marble.

"Lady," he said as he lifted a torch from a nearby cresset, "be comfortable."

She nodded graciously, and when she stepped into the shadowed alcove and took a seat, Hornfel thought he couldn't be convinced to lay wager which dispelled the shadows, the lady's own beauty or the light of the torch. The hunter followed her closely, as though he were her bodyguard, with the three Daewar on his heels. Hornfel drew an impatient breath as he observed their maneuvering. He spoke as he positioned the torch on the wall.

"You," he said to the half-elf, "go hover behind your lady if that makes you comfortable." He jerked a thumb at the guards. "You can all crowd in here behind me or go ward the door, whichever makes you happiest."

The Daewar looked confused, but they knew a command when they heard one. They left the alcove. Though the half-elf finally grinned sheepishly, he went to stand behind the lady.

"Do they guard you against us?"

Hornfel shook his head and dropped into the chair opposite the woman. "They guard me, but it hasn't to do with you or your lady. We don't guard ourselves against friends."

The Plainswoman considered this, then nodded. "We are happy to be named friends." She gestured gracefully to her guardian. "This is Tanis Half-Elven." She smiled. "Though I am not his lady, I could be no safer with him if I were. I am Goldmoon, Chieftain's Daughter of the Que-Shu." Her eyes lighted with dawn's own softness.

"The goddess I serve is Mishakal," she said, "and I am her cleric. In her name we have come to learn if you will help the homeless refugees from Verminaard's slavery."

Hornfel shook his head. "Lady, there hasn't been a true

cleric in Krynn for these three hundred years past."

"I know it, thane. Not since the Cataclysm. There is now."

The dwarf closed his eyes. Mishakal! Mesalax, the dwarves called the goddess, and they loved her no less than they loved Reorx, whom they named Father. For, if he was the maker of the world, Mesalax was the fountain from which its beauty sprang.

Hornfel looked from Goldmoon to the one called Tanis. Was it true? He thought it might be. Gods moved in Krynn now, lending their fire to Kingswords and their dragons to Highlords. Why wouldn't Mesalax grant her blessing to a woman out of the barbarian Plains?

Goldmoon smiled, and it might well have been Mesalax's own light the dwarf saw in her eyes.

Hornfel glanced at Tanis. The half-elf's determined jaw relaxed a little beneath his red beard when he looked at the Plainswoman as he did now.

"My lady Goldmoon," Hornfel said at last, "be welcome in Thorbardin."

He would figure out what to do about the farming warrens later. He didn't know if Goldmoon were, indeed, what she claimed to be. He did know that he wouldn't permit her to languish in a cobbled-together fieldkeeper's hut any more than he would allow her to languish in a dungeon's cell. And she, he knew, would go where her people went.

Darknight spread its wings to half extension, admiring the play of its shadow stetching up the black, gleaming walls of its lair and nearly spanning the width of the rough, high ceiling. It snaked its neck to its full length and stretched its jaws wide. Though it could not see the effect, it imagined that the light of the small brazier near the far wall made its fangs appear to be gleaming daggers of flame.

It turned its head and spoke to a shadow on the wall.

"My Lord, all in all, I prefer the sunny lairs in the cliffs of Pax Tharkas to these wet, cold warrens beneath this wretched Thorbardin."

That doesn't surprise me, the shadow whispered. Verminaard threw back his head and laughed in his chamber in Pax Tharkas. His shadow-image on the cave wall did the same.

Darknight lashed its tail impatiently and rumbled deep in its massive chest. It preferred the iron-fisted martial order of Pax Tharkas under Verminaard's rule to the tempestuous storms of dwarven politics in a kingdom under no one's rule. "Highlord, I heartily wish that Realgar would mount his wretched revolution and be done with it, so that I can be done with him."

The shadow sharpened to knife-edged clarity. Darknight could almost see Verminaard's eyes as red lights on the stone.

He's still wasting his time on the ranger?

The ranger had given Realgar no good answer to the question of the Kingsword's whereabouts in all the days he'd been the Theiwar's captive.

"Aye, Lord. It's the difference between you," the dragon snarled as it listened to its belly rumble. "Were the ranger your prisoner, I would have been sucking the marrow out of his bones days ago." As it was, Darknight had to forage at night for mountain sheep while Realgar marched bloody-footed through the ranger's soul for nothing but enjoyment.

Darknight snorted and closed its eyes. "Simple enjoyment is all he's getting from it now. He admits that if there is an answer to be had, the ranger isn't going to provide it. Enjoyment, and a soothing revenge for time wasted."

Shadow eyes flared red and it scraped its claws on the stone floor of its lair. It doubted that the ranger had ever known where the sword was, and if he had, there could be nothing left of his mind now in which to sift for an answer.

"Lord, how go your own plans?"

Well enough. The troops move into the mountains and the bases will be in place. Ember will fly tonight as cover for the last of them.

Ember! Flying with fire and fear as its weapons, and it was lodged here in this dank, foul hole! Darknight gnashed its teeth.

"Cover, Lord? Does Ember—" Darknight caught itself. Haughty Ember would never admit to needing assistance. "—want company?" By the Dark Queen! Its legs were cramped, its wings aching for a night flight!

The shadow seemed no shadow at all, but an image reflected on polished ebony. The dragon saw Verminaard's face now—coldly handsome that face was, ice-eyed and hard as stone.

Ember needs nothing more of company than it'll have, good Sevristh, and that is me. It's a small matter of rangers.

He might have said a small matter of gnats. Darknight sighed.

Verminaard laughed, ice booming in a frozen river.

Patience, Darknight. Stay with your new lord for a time yet.

And the shadow was gone. The red lights faded as though they'd never been.

The black dragon growled. In Darknight's estimation, its new lord was an ass. Realgar commanded an army of anarchists and commanded them well. It was not any easy task to control a race of murderous *derro* whose most pleasant dreams were of torment, revolution, and death. Still, Realgar was an ass.

Sevristh was not a political creature and had little understanding of—or patience for—Realgar's need to acquire this Stormblade, this Kingsword. It sighed and the air shivered. These dwarves, and the Theiwar most especially, were mad for talismans and symbols. Realgar would not light revolution's fire in Thorbardin until he held Stormblade in his greedy, white-knuckled grip. And Verminaard seemed content to wait.

What matter, it thought scornfully, whether Realgar wields the Kingsword or some humble, nameless blade? Hornfel must be killed and it could hardly matter whether he died by a Kingsword's stroke or a dagger's blade. The one who kills him owns history. He can write the tale to his own preference later and name himself king regent or high king of the dwarves, if he wishes.

Aye, as long as he can manage to stay alive. Darknight smiled and felt a little better. That wouldn't be long, no matter how Realgar styled himself.

The dragon felt the feathery vibrations of footsteps in the stone of the cavern's floor and heard the distant whisper of breathing. It closed its eyes. That breathing was Realgar's, and the dragon picked up the high, bright excitement in his scent.

Please the Dark Queen, he'd found the miserable sword!

Sevristh opened its eyes and sighed. He hadn't. Or had he?

Darknight looked a little closer. Aye? Maybe.

Realgar came close and smiled, a cold pulling of his lips across his teeth. "I greet you, Darknight."

"And I you, Highlord."

The title did nothing to warm the new Highlord's smile. It never did. High king was what he wanted to be called, and anything else would not do.

"The Kingsword has been found."

Verminaard's gift ran a forked tongue over sharp teeth. No it hasn't, Darknight thought scornfully. It knew the look in his eyes by now. He only *hoped* it had been found. The dragon rustled its wings. "Aye? Shall I fly, my Lord?"

And then, the Theiwar surprised the dragon. "Yes, fly. The Herald is expecting you."

Sevristh stretched its lipless mouth in a wide grin. Fly it would and, in flight, apprise the only Highlord it truly acknowledged that his plans might well be moving forward with more speed than even he thought.

CHAPTER 17

"Where are you?" the kender had asked.

Piper didn't know where he was. He'd told the kender he was right behind him. It was a good enough answer. He might have been, since he seemed to be both nowhere and everywhere at once. There were no landmarks in this fog-bound drifting plane, it all seemed to run on forever. The things he "saw" he didn't see with his eyes, but rather with his mind. It was not magic that showed him these things. There was no magic left to him but the spell he was caught in now.

Piper was a ghost, made so by his flute's magic. He was dead. He stopped thinking for a moment. It was rather like holding his breath. But, like breathing when he was alive, thinking was not something he could go long without doing.

Tentatively, like a man running gentle fingers over a healing wound, he reached for the memory of his last living moments.

There had been all the pain and all the bone-deep exhaustion. He'd heard the young woman call for help, heard her cry Stanach's name. He hadn't heard anything else after that for a long, long time until Stanach's thoughts, grieving and heavy, brushed up against the edges of his mind.

Ah, Jordy! I'm sorry, Piper!

He'd wanted to speak then, to find some way to warn Stanach about Realgar's men. He hadn't the strength. He had only the need.

When Stanach laid his flute beside him, he saw the instrument, though he could see nothing else at all. The flute held his music and his magic. It sang his own songs to him with a friend's voice and gave voice to songs he'd never imagined. He found the small strength to work one last spell. The magic was the flute's.

Was this ghostly state more or less than being dead? He reached around him with his mind. He couldn't "see" everything the way he'd imagined a ghost would be able to. He saw—or knew—only a little more than he would be able to see were he alive. However, that was changing even as he tried to extend this new sense. Like the potential he'd once sensed in his strong body, he knew that the ability to "see" farther would increase with using it. He would have to explore this netherworld the way he would have done the physical world, a little at a time. He was not alone here.

The souls he sensed behind the fog were few and showed no interest in him at all. They were, like he, beings moving to their own purposes and only brushed past him like sighs.

Piper laughed ruefully and the fog shivered. How many of the spirits here were bound to a kender for the rest of his natural life?

That's what the flute's spell had done: tied him to Lavim, the person who had triggered it, for as long as the kender lived. The spell not only gave Lavim a ghostly companion, but because of the connection to Piper, access to the flute's magic.

Of course, he hadn't imagined that the kender would be

the first to play the flute. He'd thought Stanach would. The dwarf hadn't and Lavim had. The summoning spell had called Piper back, all right, but it had called him to a kender's attention. It had taken Piper all night and half the day to make his way through the labyrinths of Lavim's confusing mental chatter and get to a place in the kender's mind where Lavim could hear him.

Stanach, when he was taken by the Theiwar, had dropped the flute for fear that it would end up in a Theiwar's hand. He couldn't have known that the flute's magic would work for no one but Lavim now.

Piper hoped he wasn't in for more trouble than he could handle. He'd have to convince Lavim to give Tyorl the flute.

The fog seemed to thicken and grow dark and heavy with Piper's fear. Soon it would be too late to help Stanach.

Lavim danced impatiently from one foot to the other. As delighted and surprised to find himself in conversation with Piper, he'd come to his senses before he'd come to the place where Kelida and Tyorl waited near the path. He had tucked the cherry wood flute into the deepest pocket of his old black coat, certain that Tyorl was going to want to snatch it right out of his hand.

Now, he had Tyorl plaguing him with questions in one ear and Piper whispering directions in the other. He didn't know who to answer first.

Tell him about Stanach and give him the flute.

Tyorl clamped both his hands on the kender's shoulders and held him still. "Lavim, tell me about Stanach!"

"I will. In a minute." Lavim blinked, not exactly sure who he was answering.

Tyorl's blue eyes flared with sudden anger. "Tell me now!"

Tell him now! Give him the flute!

Lavim squirmed away and put Kelida between himself and Tyorl. Though he was a lean, slim fellow, the elf had a bear's grip and looked as though he'd like to shake all the information out of him.

"All right, all right, I am! There's some rocks up ahead and I found, uh, footprints and some of them were Stanach's and some of them weren't. Stanach isn't there now, and I don't know where he is, but I came back here because—"

Because you're going to give him the flute. Tell him about the flute!

"Because I figured you should know."

Lavim! Give him the—

Lavim steadfastly ignored the voice in his mind. "Tyorl, what do you suppose happened to him? The other footprints were a dwarf's and he was probably one of those, um,—"

Theiwar, Piper muttered.

"Theiwar," Tyorl said.

Lavim blinked. He was getting a headache. "Right. Those are the fellows who're looking for Kelida's sword, aren't they?"

Tyorl reached for his bow. His mouth a grim, hard line, he drew an arrow from the quiver on his back. Kelida looked from one to the other of them.

"Tyorl, they'll kill him," she whispered.

The sunlight on the path had deepened to gold. Shadows gathered in the thickets and under the trees, soon to spread through the forest and become night. The breeze sighed colder now.

Aye, Tyorl thought, they will. Sooner or later.

"They couldn't have taken him far," the ranger said.

He's in the river caves.

Lavim nodded. "He's in the river caves, Tyorl."

"How do you know that? Damn, Lavim! What else do you know?"

Lavim didn't know what else he knew. He hadn't even known that till just now. "Tyorl, I—" He started to try to explain, then he snapped his mouth shut as Piper bellowed *No!* right inside his head.

But, he demanded silently, how am I going to tell him if I don't tell him about you? Stop yelling, would you? I've got a headache already and—

You can tell him later. There's no time to go into the part about me now, Lavim. The way you tell it, you'd be explaining all day. Stanach doesn't have all day.

But what am I going to say?

Piper sighed heavily. *Tell him you saw the caves.*

But I didn't see any—

Don't get virtuous on me now, Lavim.

"I saw the caves. Where else could he be?" With Piper's prompting, he told the rest of the tale. "There's five of 'em. Not caves, dwarves. There's only three caves. They're this side of the river and—"

Tyorl knows where. He's been here before. Finn caches weapons in a cave in the forest, but he doesn't know that this one connects with the river caves.

Lavim nodded. "Oh, Finn caches—"

No! Don't tell him that! And give him my flute!

Lavim shoved his hands into his pockets and grasped the flute. He wasn't going to give that up yet. "—Uh, stuff in the forest, doesn't he? Like weapons and things?"

Has he ever . . . ?

"Has he ever used those ca—I mean, any caves around here?"

The elf shook his head, impatient again. "Aye, Lavim, he has. But those are woodland caves, and they're too far south of here to connect to caves in the riverbank."

"Yes, they—I—well, I mean, maybe they do." Lavim curled his fingers around the flute. He was beginning to get the knack of talking to two people at once. He hoped.

You heard something about caves . . .

"I heard something about the caves in these woods. I don't know where I heard it, but I did. Something about, um, right, caves that start out at the river and end up back here in the woods.

"They were saying back in Long Ridge that bandits used to hide out in 'em and sometimes they'd go to ground here in the woods because they wanted to lose whoever was chasing 'em. You pick up all kinds of stuff like that if you just listen and—"

"Tyorl," Kelida's hand trembled as she laid it on the elf's arm. "We've got to help Stanach."

Tyorl let his breath out in a frustrated sigh. He was caught between having to believe something a kender had 'heard'—which meant he could have heard it, or thought he'd heard it, or imagined the whole idea right now—and the realization that if Stanach was made to tell his captors where the sword was, Kelida's life now stood in danger.

The proverbial bear and the cliff's edge, he thought bitterly.

We've got to help Stanach, Kelida had said. That was another matter. He couldn't leave her behind, alone and with the sword to mark her as the dwarves' target, but he didn't want to take her into danger with him either.

Hands tied by circumstance, Tyorl cursed. Where was Finn? Thirty rangers in these woods and he should have run across their trail by now. He damned the sword, damned the dwarves, and made the only decision he could make.

Cautioning the girl and the kender to follow him as silently as they could, he slipped off the path and headed south.

Piper's gusty sigh of relief made Lavim's ears pop.

Horror crawled all over Stanach with clammy, plucking fingers. Trapped in the one-eyed *derro's* magic, he wasn't breathing well, nor was he thinking well. Like the echoes of dreams, he heard voices, thin and distorted.

No clear blue sky stretched above him now, only a rough, low ceiling of stone, smelling like mud and the river. Stones dug into his shoulders and back as he lay on a rocky floor. Though his hands were not bound, he could not move.

No, he thought, it wasn't that he couldn't move. He hadn't the strength to move, or he didn't want to move. Like thick, wet fog, lassitude seemed to have seeped into his muscles, his very bones.

Light, soft and fading toward gloaming, shimmered around the edges of the cave's mouth. Stanach didn't remember coming here. He had no memory of anything beyond the cold glitter in the Herald's one black eye, the sudden, wrenching sickness that accompanied a transport spell, and a long, sickening slide into sleep.

And the distant voices.

They wanted Stormblade.

A dwarf, thin and holding an arm stiffly at his side, moved into Stanach's field of vision, cutting the soft light with shadow. Wulfen they were calling him. Stanach knew him as one of the Theiwar whose blood he'd wiped from his sword in the grass on the side of the road to Long Ridge.

A cold lump of fear lay heavily in Stanach's belly. He saw hunger for revenge in Wulfen's eyes and heard it in his low, vulpine laughter.

Stanach was no mage, as Piper had been. He had nothing arcane with which to defend himself. He had only his ragged strength and the hope that his companions would not try to rescue him.

Tyorl, he thought, get the Kingsword out of here! Find your rangers and get it to Thorbardin!

But would he? Or had he finally counted his friend Hauk as dead?

Aye, maybe. But Kelida hadn't. Stanach had made sure of that. He'd given her a brave ranger to love, and she didn't know that the ranger was dead. Stormblade would come to Thorbardin and Kelida would carry it there. The elf would go where she went.

Stanach stared hard at the roof of the river cave. He would not lose Hornfel's Kingsword again. He'd do what he had to do, as Kyan Red-axe had, as Piper had.

Wulfen rumbled low in his throat. Stanach told himself that he was no longer a swordcrafter. He was a merchant, one who was in the business of buying time.

The cache was empty. Tyorl and Hauk had helped store the quivers of arrows, the swords, and daggers the night before they'd set out for Long Ridge. By the signs, Finn had been here only recently to gather supplies.

Tyorl wished again that he knew where the rangers were. An empty cache place meant they'd had a need for the weapons. They were fighting somewhere and he'd seen no sign that any battle had taken place nearby.

Damn! he thought. I need them and they'd likely appreciate my bow. Where in the name of the gods are they?

Tyorl smiled wryly. Likely Finn knew about the dragonarmy supply bases by now anyway; likely the dragonarmy knew about Finn and his Nightmare Company by now, too.

The cave wasn't high enough for Tyorl to stand comfortably and only deep enough for him and Lavim to enter. Kelida stood watch. Tyorl listened for her footstep scuffing on stone, caught a glimpse of gold-shot red braids, and turned to Lavim.

"There's no way back to the river from here," he said irritably.

The kender nodded vigorously, his long white braid bobbing on his neck. "There is, Tyorl. It's, um, just behind the back wall."

"Lavim, there's nothing behind that wall but dirt and stone."

Tyorl ran a hand over the rock, his thumb over the cracks forced there by the thick roots of the pines that lived on the cobble above. The place smelled of rich, dark earth and stone. Tyorl missed the warm fall of the setting sun's light. Caves were fine for secreting stores of weapons, but they were too dark and heavy with the weight of the earth for the elf's taste.

Lavim squeezed past Tyorl and dropped to his heels before the widest of the fissures. He shoved his right hand into the crack and curled his fingers around the stone as one would around the edge of a door. He smiled up at the elf, green eyes gleaming.

"There's air moving back there, Tyorl."

Lavim ran his left hand along the wall at arm's length and shoulder height and followed the thin crack he saw there down to the floor. He peered up at the ceiling, squinting mightily, and saw a narrow fissure there as well. His smile became a grin as he eyed the distance between his outstretched arms. "We could fit through here easily."

"Aye," Tyorl drawled, "if we could walk through stone."

"No, we don't have to do that. There's . . ." Lavim cocked his head as though listening for something, then nodded. "I think I hear echoes. Kind of like water—the river—and if we can get this stone to move, we can get right to the water. The cave back there runs . . . uh, the river smell means it heads straight and straight is east and . . . uh, that's probably where Stanach is."

"Guesses, kenderkin."

"Oh, no, they're not guesses I—" Lavim cleared his throat and nodded. "You're right. They're guesses. I hear the river, Tyorl, and I can feel the edge of this stone." He withdrew his right hand and held it up for Tyorl's inspection. "This wall's no thicker than my palm, and the edge of the crack is smooth. I'll bet if we can just get this stone to move . . ."

Lavim pressed his shoulder to the wall and shoved.

"Lavim," Tyorl sighed heavily.

The kender braced his feet against the stone floor and squeezed his eyes tightly shut, all his weight behind his efforts.

"Lavim, I don't think—"

The kender grunted. "Could you stop thinking for a minute, Tyorl, and give me a hand here? Or a shoulder? Put your weight against the right of the stone."

If only to disabuse the kender of his foolish notions, Tyorl lent the weight Lavim asked for. Amost immediately, the stone began to move. Air, dank and heavy with earth smells, moved lazily through the opening. Beneath the scent of dirt and stone drifted the odor of the river: fish, silt, and decaying vegetation.

"Bandits' caves!" Lavim cried. "See! We—I was right!"

He dove for the opening, and Tyorl quickly caught him by the collar of his shapeless black coat. "Wait, Lavim!"

But the kender was waiting for no one. He squirmed away from the elf's hold and darted into the newly opened cave.

Tyorl called quickly for Kelida. She slipped into the cave, eyed the dark, narrow doorway into the earth and then the light over her shoulder. She looked as doubtful as Tyorl felt.

"Where's Lavim?"

Tyorl jerked a thumb at the fissure. "Where you'd expect. Ready?"

Kelida nodded.

"Stay close then, and let's see if we can catch up with the kender."

He hadn't meant it as a jest, but when Kelida's emerald eyes lighted with a sudden spark of laughter, Tyorl smiled and stepped aside as though ushering her into a safe and comfortable chamber. Unthinking, she laid her hand on his shoulder as she passed. He felt the light touch of her fingers long after he'd left the opening and the faint light behind.

Three!

Stanach clung to the idea of the cipher through another red-hazed spin into darkness. They'd snapped three of his fingers. Seven, he thought, seven to go. Or two if they only want to leave me one-handed. Seven or two . . .

The lethargy of the sleep spell had worn away, but he still couldn't move. It was as though invisible bonds held him to the stone floor. More of the Herald's work, he thought.

The red star, the ember from Reorx's forge, hung low in the purpling sky. The only thing Stanach could move were his eyes. These he kept fixed on the star.

Seven or two. It doesn't matter . . . it doesn't matter . . . soon I'm not going to be able to feel this at all.

Wulfen, his black Theiwar eyes like bottomless pits in the shadows of night, leaned forward. "Where is the sword?"

Stanach did not have the heart or the strength to wonder why Wulfen's tone was so coolly reasonable. The midnight wings of pain rustled around him. He swallowed back bile and vomit.

"I told you," he whispered, his voice hoarse and thin, "I don't know. I didn't . . . find it."

The Herald nodded, smiling.

Stanach screamed and the sound almost drowned out the searing pain and another dry snap.

Four! Six, his mind panted, six or one . . . six or—

Five!

When his thumb was finally broken, Stanach's scream almost sounded like triumphant laughter in his own ears. His right hand was a swollen, blue mass of flesh on the stony floor.

Those don't look like fingers, his mind's voice observed thinly, not at all. Now there's a hand that won't be lifting a hammer again.

Behind him, the Herald made a sound like rumbling laughter. Another of the Theiwar drifted past the cave's mouth as he walked his patrol, paced back again, and turned. Faint as old memories, Stanach smelled the smoke of the guards' watch fire.

The red star winked and vanished and appeared again. Icy sweat trickled into Stanach's eyes, slid down his cheeks and into his beard like cold tears. He closed his eyes, then opened them, only to find the cave faded a little around the edges.

Wulfen took a dagger from his belt. The only light in the cave was fading twilight reflected in the mirror of the blade's steel. Creeping and tentative, smoke wafted into the cave, stinging Stanach's eyes as it passed him, clutching at his throat.

Stanach looked to the side, saw the fingers of his left hand, whole and straight, and closed his eyes. In the darkness he saw the Kingsword, red-streaked steel, four sapphires the color of twilight, a fifth like a midnight star. He'd seen the steel born in fire, and he'd seen Isarn's wonder, his dawning understanding when the reflection of the forge fire hadn't faded. He'd watched in grief and pity as the old master became slowly mad when Stormblade had been stolen. Kingsword!

Kingsword, he thought. Kingsword, Realgar! By the god's forge, you won't have it!

Steel, like winter's ice, touched the thumb of his left hand at the first joint in cold caress. Stanach drew a long breath and let it out in a tattered sigh.

He'll crack that knuckle like a tightly closed nut, Stanach my lad, with a thrust and a snap . . .

Stanach opened his eyes and saw only his own fear reflected in the dagger's blade.

"Where is the sword?"

Stanach thought he might be a little mad. He laughed, and the laughter kept perfect time to the beat and thunder of the fire consuming his right hand. "I—told you. I don't have it."

No! That was the wrong answer! Stanach saw it in the flicker of interest in Wulfen's eyes.

The Theiwar's voice was soft as the smoke now. "Who does?"

Stanach couldn't see the star anymore. The guard stood between him and the sky. He closed his eyes again.

If Realgar's men found Kelida with the sword they'd kill her before she'd have a chance to scream.

Lyt chwaer, he'd named her, little sister. She'd tried to

ease his grief for Piper's death with understanding and a kinswoman's gentle silence. *Lyt chwaer*, who has a dead ranger to love.

I do what I have to do. I lie to friendless barmaids, and I watch my own friends die. How does it balance, how does it balance?

Wulfen's breath was hot against Stanach's face. His strange *derro* soul shone in the madness reflected in his eyes. He was close now, and his dagger's steel lay at the base of Stanach's jaw. "Who has the Kingsword?"

The Herald moved forward. Stanach heard his breathing, soft as a snake hissing.

Stanach looked at his right hand, twisted and swollen out of recognition. He'd never lift a hammer again. He'd never again know the magic of crafting. His own masterblade lay lifeless, stillborn amid the wreckage of his broken fingers. Wulfen had stolen that. In that way, he and his mad *derro* kin would rob all of Thorbardin, twisting and breaking everything beautiful under their trampling reign.

The dagger's tip traced a thin, bleeding line up to just below Stanach's right eye. The muscles tightened across the back of Wulfen's hand.

"I'll ask again, but this will be the last time. Who has Stormblade?"

Stanach spat, and prepared to lose his eye.

CHAPTER 18

THE LOW CEILINGS OF THE CAVES GREW HIGH BEFORE Lavim had gone several yards past the entrance. The river's moisture glistened on the rock walls and plastered the dust to the smooth stony floor. Dim light filtering in from the rangers' cache place did little to illuminate these interior caves and only served to cast confusing shadows. Behind him, Lavim heard Tyorl and Kelida stepping carefully in the darkness.

"Piper," he whispered, as something that looked like a spider with too many legs scuttled across his boot. "I don't suppose you can do a little magic from where you are and give me some light? That looked like a spider, but I'm not real sure and—"

No, I can't. Don't waste time stumbling around in the

dark and getting lost. Go catch up with Tyorl.

"Oh, don't worry. I never get lost. I just find new places to be. I—hmmm, I wonder what's over here?"

Dirt. Lavim, Tyorl and Kelida are getting ahead of you now.

"Uh-huh. Thanks for telling me. I'll catch up."

The kender intended to—in a minute. Though he couldn't see very well, Lavim still had his hands and his curiosity. He'd told Tyorl that these were bandit's caves and, in the course of convincing the elf that this was so, he'd convinced himself as well.

He made his way around a pile of heaped rubble, felt around a small chamber, backed out of it when he found nothing of interest, and edged into another. With a sound like restless wind in the tree tops, the far wall began to rustle.

"Piper! Look! I think that wall way back there is moving!"

Bats, Piper warned, *get out, Lavim!*

"Bats? So? I'm not afraid of—"

They're afraid of you and when they fly they'll warn everyone in sight that you're in here. Get out!

Lavim sighed. He supposed Piper was right. He backed out of the cave, moving as silently as only a kender can.

Tracking east, following the scent of the river, Lavim veered aside—only a little—to squeeze himself into a spider-webbed corner.

Piper, who in life had thought himself the most patient of men, lost his patience for the fourth time in a quarter hour. *Lavim! Get moving!*

"But these are bandit caves, Piper, and I—"

They're not bandit caves. Go catch up with Tyorl. And give him my flute!

Lavim poked at the rubble and dust in a natural alcove. Tyorl and Kelida had passed him by a few moments ago, but he was sure that he could catch up with them again. All he had to do was follow the scent of the river and the sound of their breathing.

"You said they were bandit caves." Though he did think, even as he said it, that Piper might have been mistaken. The alcove held nothing but scatterings of rock. Not even a tumble of old bones.

*What were you hoping for, a skeleton? And you said
these were bandit caves, I didn't.*

Lavim sighed heavily. He wasn't at all certain that he liked
having someone right inside his head and reading his every
thought. "No, Piper, I really do think it was you who said
these were—"

Damn it, Lavim!

Not only a ghost, Lavim thought sourly, but a testy ghost
who's as bad as Stanach and Tyorl ever were about letting
him finish a sentence.

*Aye, testy! When you start a sentence that makes sense,
then maybe you'll get to—*

The scream shivered through the darkness, a hollow, for-
lorn echo of pain. Like what a ghost *should* sound like,
Lavim thought. All hope of finding bandit treasure fled as
the kender suddenly remembered why he was here.

"Stanach?" he whispered. Up ahead he heard Kelida's
gasp and a low, murmured word from Tyorl.

Aye, Stanach. Lavim, stay back a minute.

"But you just said to catch up with them. Piper, how am I
supposed to figure out what you want me to do if you don't
even know?"

Stay! Wait here.

"Yes, but—"

Take out my flute.

Lavim grinned. Aye, that he'd be happy to do! Though he
thought it a little odd to be playing music now when
Stanach needed his help, he dug into his pocket, pulled out
the flute, and raised it to his lips.

No! Piper bellowed. *Not yet! Put it down and listen to me
very carefully.*

Reluctantly, Lavim lowered the flute.

*Aye, now do exactly as I say, Lavim. The gods know I
must be half-mad, but if you listen—very carefully!—and
do just what I say, exactly the way I tell you—*

A second scream, like horrible laughter, tore through the
cave.

*Listen, now. The flute knows I'm near—no, don't start
asking questions! It senses my mind—my spirit, I guess is a*

*good word, eh? It will lend its magic to my needs. Take a
deep breath—no, deeper than that. Aye, that's it. The flute
will play the tune, and the tune is the magic, but you have to
supply the air and the intent.*

Aye, Lavim thought (because he couldn't very well speak
while holding his breath), and what do I intend? Can I sum-
mon monsters? Am I going to be invisible? Can I turn all
Tyorl's arrows into fire?

None of that, now, Lavim. Piper said sternly. *This is what
you intend—and only this.*

Lavim felt Piper smile and, because the mage seemed to be
in such a good humor, he quickly decided to try a little idea
of his own.

The low-roofed, narrow-walled tunnel connecting the
woodland cave to the one opening onto the river held the
echo of the scream for many moments. Tyorl shuddered
and glanced over his shoulder at Kelida. She stood where
he'd told her to, in the webbing of shadows and darkness
where the tunnel bent left and back in the direction they had
come. Her eyes bright in the darkness, her mouth a hard,
determined line, Kelida grasped her dagger in a firm and
steady hand the way Lavim had taught her.

The tunnel stank of musty earth, and rank, stagnant
water pooled in the center of the floor. The litter of rubble
and mud lay mostly undisturbed but for a footprint or two.
If the Theiwar had explored this corridor at all, or the cave
beyond, they'd likely been turned back by the seemingly
impassable wall at the back of the woods cave. Tyorl wondered fleetingly how Lavim had found an entrance.

Aye, but a kender will find his way into a miser's purse if
he wants to. No reason why solid rock should stop him.

The half-rotted carcasses of beached fish, washed into the
tunnel from a high tide swollen by storm rains, shimmered
with the strange, evil light of putrification. His back to the
wall, Tyorl edged around the water careful not to cause
even the faintest whisper of a splash.

A second scream, a deep-throated and terrible roar, made
the muscles in Tyorl's belly wrench sickeningly. Under cover of the echo, the elf inched forward until he reached the

entrance to the river cave. Narrow, barely wide enough for Tyorl to get through sideways, the entrance was blocked by a cloaked and hooded dwarf who stood with his back to the ranger.

The dwarf shifted his stance, moved aside and forward, and Tyorl closed his eyes. He hadn't seen much, just an arm and a hand.

Tyorl trembled with a cold rage. Each finger of the hand had been twisted and broken. His own fingers tightened around the hilt of his dagger. The hooded dwarf stood within striking distance, and Tyorl knew he'd smile to feel his dagger's blade slide between this one's ribs. Before he could move, the sound of a flute's voice, hollow and chased by its own echoes, floated through the tunnel. From behind.

No! Gods, no! The kender has the mage's flute!

The Theiwar turned sharply. One eye, he had, filled with hatred and the love of death. He snarled a curse when he saw Tyorl. His hands groped at the cold, damp air of the river cave, and took sudden flight in magic's winged dance. Tyorl barely had time to see the Theiwar's hands falter, like arrow-shot birds, before his own knees went weak and watery.

Back in the tunnel, Kelida cried out, her cry torn by gagging and choking.

The music, a perversely light and merry air, drifted toward the elf on currents of the vilest odor he'd ever smelled. The stench of middens years uncleaned, eggs rotting, dead rats under a tavern's floor, and vegetation moldering and turning to thick, greasy slime, filled the tunnel. Tyorl dropped to his knees, helpless to do anything but wrap his arms tightly around his belly, and clamp his back teeth against the overwhelming urge to vomit.

From within the river cave, and more distantly from without, came gagging and the sounds of wrenching pain. A voice, one that could only have been Lavim's, echoed from behind the elf in deep, booming laughter. Small hands pounded at the elf's back and pulled at his arms.

"Tyorl! Doesn't this smell *awful*? Everyone's just about throwing up everything they've eaten in the last week! Isn't it great? Hey, Tyorl! Get up, would you? Tyorl! You ought to run in there and rescue Stanach and get rid of those wad-dayacall'ems while they're all—uh, Tyorl?"

"Kender," Tyorl gasped weakly, "I swear by every god there is I'm going to—" Caught by a stabbing belly cramp, he doubled over and knew very suddenly that trying to speak had been the wrong thing to do. He finished his threat in groans and gagging. When he was able to look up again, Tyorl was alone.

I am going to kill him, he thought as he wiped the back of his hand across his mouth. He staggered to his feet, braced his back against the wall, and tried not to breathe. I am going to lay that damned kender open from neck to gut and kill him!

A hand, shaking from the sudden and violent attack of nausea, gripped Tyorl's arm. Kelida, dazed and weak-kneed, leaned against the elf. Shuddering, she whispered, "Are you all right?"

"Aye." Tyorl lifted her chin. Then, surprised by his own gesture, he dropped his hand and held her gently away. "You?"

She shrugged and managed a wan smile. The noxious odors were beginning to drift in the direction of the river, dragged reluctantly away by damp, cold breezes. "Tyorl, what happened? What is this horrible smell?"

"The damned kender has the mage's flute! Did you see where he went?"

Kelida looked quickly around then shook her head. "Those screams—" Her face was white. "Stanach."

Within the river cave, the hard, bitter noises of retching and choking had fallen still. Lavim's laughter rose and then stopped with ominous suddenness. Tyorl stepped into the cave, Kelida right behind him.

The freshening night wind cleared away the last of Lavim's malodorous spell. Tyorl took a tentative breath and then another. The aching nausea left him. He looked around the cave and saw Stanach lying in the shadows against the wall. Kelida slipped past him and ran to the dwarf.

Realgar's assassins lay on the stony floor and did not rise again. The skulls of two were crushed and the rock that killed them lay near Tyorl's foot, smeared with blood and brains. The third was dead of a dagger in the ribs. Tyorl quickly checked outside and saw a dwarf lying far down the river, sprawled half in the water, half out.

"Lavim," Tyorl said, his voice low with astonishment, "you killed all of them?"

Lavim, crouched in the darkest shadows of the night-filled cave, looked around. "I wish! One of 'em got away, Tyorl, and he was my favorite, or, he was the one I wanted to kill the most. I should have waited for you, I suppose, but you seemed to be having some temporary difficulty and—"

"Stanach!"

A small and pitying sigh on her lips, Kelida dropped to her knees and laid light, hesitant fingers on Stanach's throat. She nodded to Tyorl; she'd found a faint lifebeat.

Tyorl's belly went tight with what the dim starlight showed him. Blood and dirt matted the dwarf's black beard. A dagger's trail scored his face between eye and chin. It was the wreckage of Stanach's right hand that sickened him.

If he had been schooled in the craft of war, Tyorl had also been schooled in other things. An artisan's hand, someone once told him, is sacred. Without it, there is no bridge between what he envisions and what he can ultimately create. Stanach's bridge lay in twisted ruin.

A low, bubbling moan, thick with pain, startled Tyorl. Stanach, his blue-flecked black eyes flat and dull, looked at Kelida. When Stanach spoke, his voice was only a thin whisper.

"I don't—I don't feel my hand."

A glimmer of panic broke the dullness of his eyes. He shifted a little on the ground and tried to move his fingers. When not even his smallest finger responded, Stanach closed his eyes again.

"Is it there? I feel my arm—but not my hand."

Kelida tried to speak but found no words. She stroked his head gently, brushed his blood-matted hair away from his forehead. Tyorl, his heart aching, caught the glimmer of tears on her cheeks.

In a voice strangely thick, Lavim said, "Aye, young Stanach, your hand is there."

"I don't—feel it."

For Stanach's sake, Tyorl mustered a crooked smile and dropped to one knee beside him. "You may thank some god that you can't just now, but your hand is there, Stanach." Tyorl's heart went cold and aching. All the better for you that you don't feel it, he thought. Aloud he only said, "Rest easy now."

Stanach's breath shuddered in his chest. "Piper. They killed Piper. They want—Stormblade."

Tyorl saw understanding darken Kelida's eyes. Aye, Hauk, she hopes you're alive. Lad, I hope you're dead. They had a few hours at the dwarf. They'll have been a week or more at you. Gods, I hope you're dead!

Kelida's hand dropped to Stormblade at her hip and then jerked away as though her fingers had been seared. She knew she would be dead now if Stanach had not somehow managed to keep silent through the agonizing ruining of his hand.

"No," she murmured. "Oh, Stanach, no!"

How do you bear the weight of knowing that you live because others are suffering and dying? Tyorl shook his head. You tear your cloak for bandages, you cool the unbearable fire with the water from your flask. Watching Kelida's gentle hands, listening to her soft words of comfort as she cleaned Stanach's face and soaked the strips of green cloth for bandaging, Tyorl understood that he had fallen in love with Kelida just as surely as she had fallen in love with Hauk.

No, he thought, no. I'm tired, half sick still, and I don't know where we're running to next. I'm a lot of things, but I'm not in love with a barmaid, and a human one at that. No, and not with the woman who loves Hauk.

Tyorl nudged Lavim and walked slowly to the cave's mouth. He needed air to clear his lungs and his head. The kender rose slowly and followed.

"Lavim, you said one got away?"

Lavim nodded. "He was fast, that one-eyed piece of gully dwarf—" He glanced over his shoulder, saw Kelida, and shrugged. "Lucky for him. Besides, I had my hands full with the others."

"Aye, you must have." Tyorl looked downriver. "And

that one?"

"Uh, he's dead, too. Pretty near, at least."

"So I see. You were a busy fellow for a minute or two."

"Oh, yes, really busy, Tyorl. There wasn't a whole lot of time, but did I ever tell you what a good cave-fighter I am, unless I'm outnumbered too badly, and my hands are tied, and I've lost my knife, and—"

"Where's the flute?"

Lavim studied the night sky. "Um, the flute?"

"The mage's flute." The elf held out his hand. "Give. And don't waste any breath telling me that you don't have it."

"But, Tyorl, I don't—uh, I think I lost it back there in the cave." Lavim dug into the deep pockets of his old black coat, searched a couple of pouches, and even patted himself down, eyes puzzled and innocent all the while. "I, um, I must've lost it back there somewhere. That smell-spell was awfuller than I thought it would be, and, well, to tell you the truth, it kind of startled me. Didn't it startle you? You looked pretty startled when I caught up with you. You were kind of green, Tyorl. Not a lot green, you understand, but sort of. Around the edges, so to speak."

Around the edges! Tyorl had no doubt that he'd been as green as moldy bread. He didn't want to argue the matter or even think about it now. He knew he should go look for the flute himself, but there was something about the dwarf by the river that piqued his curiosity.

"Go find it, Lavim, and bring it right to me."

"Well, sure, but I don't really know where I'd look."

"Look in the cave!"

"Oh. Right, in the cave. Which—?"

Tyorl didn't hear the rest of the question as he stalked away from the river cave. There was something about the way the dwarf lay sprawled on the bank, arms wide and hands frozen in a grasp at the air that made Tyorl think he hadn't died of a broken skull or a dagger in the ribs, and that he hadn't been killed by the kender at all.

Stanach wanted the windswept ledges above Thorbardin. He wanted the peace. His dreams were filled with endless searching for the feel of ancient stone against his back, the

frosty scent of gold autumn. He longed for the heatless wash
of starlight, the silver spray of Solinari's light on the early
snow, and Lunitari's glow, edging the crags and peaks of the
mountains with crimson.

He found none of these in his fevered dreams, and none in
his few moments of waking. All he had was pain.

Pain was what he was made of. Not bone and flesh, nor
blood and breath. Each time he tried to climb to the sky,
pain stood, a grinning demon with Wulfen's mad eyes, to
block his way. He could not reach the golden sunlight, the
diamond night, the sapphire twilight. He was lost in darkness, listening to the weeping of moisture down a black
stone wall. When he cried out none heard and no light was
brought. He was alone with no way back, no path to Thorbardin under the mountain.

Lavim returned to the river cave. As he did, he dipped his
hand into his pocket and touched the smooth cherry wood
flute. He was almost surprised to find it. Lavim did not consider himself a liar, or even a temporizer. What he said, he
believed wholly. At the moment he said it.

He cocked his head, listening for Piper's comment. The
mage, it seemed, always had something to say about what
Lavim was thinking.

Piper had nothing to say now.

Piper, he thought. Piper?

Nothing.

Lavim dropped to his knees beside Kelida. He supposed
Piper might be just the least bit annoyed about his improvi-
sation.

Well, he told himself, the flute hadn't seemed to mind.

Apparently it had played exactly the melody needed to
produce what Lavim had come to consider the smell-spell.

A nice little spell it was, too, he thought for the benefit of
the silent mage.

Kelida had wiped the blood and dirt from Stanach's face,
cleaned the dagger cut, and covered him with her cloak.
With one hand she was carefully lifting his head, with the
other holding her water flask to his lips. When he didn't
swallow, Lavim leaned forward and stroked the sides of his

throat with his gnarled old hands. The dwarf swallowed once, and then again, though he never opened his eyes.

"Sometimes that helps," Lavim said. He looked at Kelida and shook his head. "Poor Stanach."

The girl looked ragged and tired. She brushed straggling wisps of red hair away from her face with an absent gesture. "We—we should do something about his fingers, Lavim, but I don't—I don't—" She stopped, unable to find words to express her reluctance to tamper with that swollen ruin of a hand.

As though he sensed her feeling, Lavim drew in a long breath and let it out in a sigh. "You're afraid you'll do something to make it worse?"

"That," she whispered, "and—oh, Lavim, whatever I do is going to hurt him so much!"

"It's a shame we don't have any dwarf spirits. I've heard that if you have enough of that stuff in you, you probably couldn't feel a tree if it fell on you. We don't, so you'd better do what you have to do before he wakes up. I don't think he's going to want to watch you straighten and bind those fingers." Lavim shook his head. "As a matter of fact, I don't think I want to watch you, either."

"Lavim, will you help me?"

Lavim certainly didn't want to do that. His stomach went all squishy when he thought about it. "Kelida, I don't think—well, that is, I'm not really very good at this sort of thing and—"

Help her, Lavim.

Oh, but I don't think—

Hold his hand at the wrist and straighten the fingers as she binds them.

Lavim's stomach was really acting up now. Leftover smell-spell, he told himself and didn't choose to remember that he, as the spell caster, hadn't been affected by the odor at all.

No, Piper, he said silently, I don't think I want to do that.

Piper's voice was very gentle inside his head.

Lavim, he's never going to have the use of that hand again. But you can help Kelida ease the pain.

"All right," Lavim whispered.

Something was eating Stanach's hand. It gnawed one finger, chewed flesh, spat out bone, and moved on to the next. Voiceless and surrounded by hollow voices that should have been familiar, but were not, he tried to scream and failed.

Three!

(Two or seven . . .)

Four!

(One or six . . .)

Reorx! I beg you! Grant me grace or strike me dumb!

Fire ran along the edges of Wulfen's dagger; the steel of its blade sent fear rebounding around the cold, wet walls of the cave the way the echoes of pain and old, spent thoughts echoed around Stanach's mind.

"Where is Stormblade?"

Pieces of twilight and a midnight star.

"*Lyt chwaer.*"

"Now, one more, Stanach."

Stanach heard a distant scream. Faint and very thin, it shivered the darkness surrounding him.

Five!

"Rest easy, young Stanach," the god said with the voice of an old kender. "Rest easy."

Stanach sighed as the clean, cold wind of the mountains dried his sweat and tore through the echoing voices, shredding them the way it would smoke.

CHAPTER 19

Tyorl walked along the frozen mud by the river's edge. The wind off the water blew cold out of the mountains from the east. The elf thought it smelled of snow. Instinct told him that though many hours remained to the night and they should put some distance between themselves and this wretched place, what was needed was a fire, some food, and a chance for Stanach to gain whatever strength he could before dawn.

Inclination told him to get Stanach on his feet somehow. The one-eyed Theiwar might still be about somewhere. Though he was alone, he was what the dwarves called *derro*. Tyorl had spent enough time on Thorbardin's border to pick up a good store of dwarven words. He knew what *derro* meant: half-mad and seemingly able to thrive on nothing but hate. He was magi and dangerous as well.

Tyorl kicked a small stone into the water and regretted it the moment he heard it splash. Childish behavior like that will get us all killed before dawn, he thought. Childish behavior like that, and the unlooked for change in his feelings toward Kelida. He'd held himself back in the tunnel because of her, because he was concerned for her. Lavim could have used his help, and, if he'd been there to give it, the Theiwar would be no problem now; he'd be dead.

Damn! The woman isn't tracking through the forest, putting her life at risk, because Hauk is important to you! She does it because he's important to her. Hauk left Tenny's without his sword and with the barmaid's heart. Did he know that?

Tyorl shook his head. He didn't think Hauk was alive at this moment to know. For his friend's sake, he hoped that he wasn't.

The elf ground a curse between clenched teeth and broke into a run. The dead Theiwar lay just before the river's bend.

An arrow protruded from the dwarf's chest. Four thin blue bands marked the shaft a thumb's length above the fletching notch. He knew the mark well and the gray fletching and black cock feather even better. Finn!

He looked around quickly. The river, never silent, ran whispering on his left. Black shadows and blacker trees, the forest crowned the rise on his right. Tyorl drew the arrow from the dwarf's chest and rose, sending the red-shouldered hawk's shrill *keee-yeeer!* echoing against the forest's wall of trees. There was only one answer to that cry, a thrush's reedy, upward spiraling song. Tyorl heard it almost at once and laughed aloud for sheer relief.

Finn, tall and thin as fence rails, stood on the rise between two trees. Tyorl didn't see his smile, but he heard it in his question.

"Where've you been, elf?"

"Looking for you, Lord, and hoping you'd find me." He kicked at the body lying near his feet. "Have you seen another one of these around?"

"Only this one. He raised that crossbow too fast when he

saw me. Gave me no time to ask after others."

Finn left the rise, jogging down the slope. Two shadows, dark as night, left the forest and followed. Lehr cut ahead of the rangerlord and Kembal, his brother, drifted behind.

Lehr, dark eyes shining with the light of his grin, shaggy black hair ruffling in the cold wind, slapped Tyorl's shoulder in greeting. "Where's Hauk? That one's owed me three gold or twelve steel for a week and more. I figured you two've been dragging your heels getting back because he didn't come by it in town."

Tyorl shook his head, the brightness flown from the reunion. "He's not here, Lehr. "He gestured toward the river cave. "Kem, you're needed back there. Go with your hands on your pack. There's a kender in there who claims to have killed four dwarves."

Tyorl glanced at the arrow still in his hand. "I know he killed three of them. Three or four. He's likely grown bored of being proud of himself and will be looking around for trouble to get into."

Lehr laughed, but his brother only nodded and loped toward the cave.

"Go with him, Lehr," Finn said quietly. When they were alone, the rangerlord accepted his arrow from Tyorl and checked the fletching. He found it still good and returned it to his quiver. "Good to see you, Tyorl."

The elf looked back to the forest. "And you, Lord. Are the others with you?"

"No. I left them six miles north of here. Lehr crossed your trail yesterday. We'd have come looking sooner, but it seems that Verminaard is quick-pacing his war on the borders. We've been busy these three days." Finn smiled coldly. "Raiding supply trains."

"Have we lost anyone?"

"No, though Kem almost heaved himself inside out from the stink of this place a few minutes ago. Where did that come from? If you tell me the Abyss, I'll likely believe you."

Tyorl sighed, suddenly realizing how tired he was and how strange a tale he had to tell. "It's a very long story."

"No doubt." Finn looked at him sharply. His eyes softened a little. "Tyorl, we saw no sign that Hauk's with you. Is he dead?"

"I don't know. I think he's in Thorbardin."

Finn said nothing for a moment, only looked across the river and to the foothills rising in the east. Thorbardin was nearly a hundred miles away. "Odd place for him to be, dead or alive, isn't it?"

Odd? Oh, yes, Tyorl thought, damned odd.

"I'll have your report now."

"Aye, Lord, but you may not believe it."

Finn stepped a pace away from the dead Theiwar and dropped to his heels. "Tell me."

Tyorl sat down beside him. He watched the wind slide across the water's black surface, shivering through the dwarf's brown hair and beard, and thought, as he had not since the first night in Qualinesti, that Takhisis the Dark Queen was moving in Krynn.

Dragonqueen, they called her in Istar and Ergoth. She was that. The folk of Icewall knew her as Corruptor. She was that, too. In Thorbardin, the dwarves named her Tamex, the False Metal.

She's proved false enough to you, he told the Theiwar silently. May she prove as false to your master!

Quietly, Tyorl told his tale of Kingsword and revolution, rangers and barmaids, pursuit and escape.

In the high, star-frosted sky, the two newly risen moons, the red and the white, combined their light into a garish purple spill. Darknight was a black lance against the red moon. Ember, Verminaard riding high on the dragon's long, powerfully muscled shoulders, cut like a huge distorted shadow across Solinari.

Its eyes hooded as much against the bitter cold of the heights as against the moons' glare, Darknight laid its broad wings against its back, darting down and under the red. Swooping high again, the black dragon rolled and returned to Ember's side, roaring loud laughter at the red's disdain for its antics.

Darknight cared not at all. The dank walls of the Deep Warrens no longer confined it and it was incapable of anything but high, fierce joy.

Ten miles clear of Thorbardin, at the southwestern edge of the Plains of Death, Darknight had sensed Ember gliding over the eastern forests. It'd gained speed with powerful thrusts of its wings and caught up with the Highlord and his mount over the Hills of Blood. Darknight had flipped its wings in casual salute to Ember and given the Highlord a swift mental picture of the situation at Thorbardin.

Such was the connection between Verminaard and Takhisis' dragons, both empathic and telepathic, that the Highlord had not only the sense of Realgar's plans, but a clear sense, too, of Darknight's estimations for their success.

Aye, bring him his Kingsword, Darknight. Help him cut the first stroke of revolution. Verminaard's satisfaction rippled through Darknight's mind like shadows on black ice. *Then, give me his Stormblade when you give me his head. They'll both be fine ornaments.*

Ember craned its long neck around, and, by the brilliant light of a gout of flame shot from its narrow-jawed maw, Darknight saw their shadows, small and sharp, sliding over the foothills of the Kharolis Mountains. The black cut its wings back again and dove low over the rolling dun-colored hills. A long-sighted creature of the night, it saw what Ember was looking for before the red did and sent the image of a clutch of rangers directly to the Highlord.

Several miles south of the rangers, it picked up the dark cloud that was the Gray Herald's mind. Darknight loosed a thundering roar, wheeled, and then dove.

Down the dragon arrowed toward the thin silver line of a river west of the hills. Several hours remained before dawn and Darknight expected to be back in ancient Thorbardin before sunrise. Before the sun set again, Realgar's shout of triumph would ring through the dwarf-realms.

The moons rode low in the sky, dipping toward the forest and the western horizon. Tyorl, watching their strange purple light touch the tops of the trees, thought about Finn's reaction to his story. Tyorl knew that the rangerlord did not think Hauk was alive. The elf had not been able to convince Finn of that.

"If the girl's hope can keep someone alive, aye, he's alive."

Finn's eyes told Tyorl that he already mourned Hauk as dead. "You want to go to Thorbardin."

"Aye, Lord, I do."

Finn had said nothing for a long moment, only looked from Stormblade, still scabbarded at Kelida's hip, to the ruin of Stanach's hand as Kem unwound the makeshift bandaging and gravely complimented the girl on her work.

Tyorl poked at the small fire. Lavim, without having to be asked, had found kindling and fuel and set the fire outside the cave and away from the entrance. The kender still hadn't found Piper's flute.

Lost, aye, Tyorl thought. It's lost in your pockets, imp! Enjoy your night ranging, Lavim. By all the gods, I'll tie you down and search every pouch and deep pocket you have when you get back.

Tyorl turned suddenly at the soft scuff of a boot on stone, the whisper of a cloak against hunting leathers. Kelida, her eyes darkly shadowed with exhaustion, stood hesitantly behind him.

"Am I disturbing you?"

Tyorl shook his head. "No. Lehr caught some fish for dinner. Are you hungry?"

"No. Just tired." She sat beside him, her back against the cave's outer wall.

"How is Stanach?"

"Sleeping. Really sleeping. Kem got him to drink some mixture of herbs and powders. He says it will help him find his strength again."

"It will. Kem's a fine warrior and a better healer. Is he sitting with him now?"

Kelida nodded. She stared out across the river, listening to its ancient travelsong. "You've spent a lot of time on these borders, haven't you?"

"A few years."

"When I was cleaning Stanach's hand, binding it, he said something. It was in a language I didn't understand."

"Dwarven, likely."

"Maybe. 'Leet Kware,' he said."

"*Lyt chwaer*, eh? Little sister. Well, he was hurting and maybe a little out of his head. It isn't strange that he'd call out for kin." Tyorl shook his head. "So, Stanach has himself a younger sister, does he? He did say that Kyan Red-axe was his cousin, but, somehow, I never thought of him having kin, or being connected to anything other than his wretched Kingsword."

The river lapped and sighed at its banks. Tyorl tossed a branch into the small fire. He smiled at Kelida and gestured to the stocky youngster pacing the watch at the riverside with long, restless strides. "That one sometimes reminds me of Hauk. Finn calls us his Nightmare Company. We call Lehr, Finn's Nightmare."

"Why?"

"Because he's impulsive, restless, and too well loves a good fight."

The wind was growing steadily colder and swept across the water with a mourner's voice. Kelida huddled into her green cloak. "Aren't those good traits for a ranger to have?"

Tyorl answered her question with another. "You see no difference between him and Hauk?"

"I don't know Hauk but from that one night in Tenny's. But then, I . . . "

Tyorl stared at the fire. "What?"

"I don't know, Tyorl. I thought that he might be something—someone—I could like."

Like, he wondered, or love?

The wind shifted, blowing from the northeast now, straight down the river's path. Lehr stopped his restive pacing and stood still at the waterside.

"He's a likable fellow, our Hauk."

"But, he too well loves a fight?"

Tyorl shook his head. "No, not at all. He has a cool enough head most times. He's a good man to have at your back, but, like Finn's Nightmare over there, he's young. I suppose that's really why Lehr reminds me of him."

Kelida remembered what seemed now a long ago night in Long Ridge, the night Hauk had given her Stormblade. She remembered Tyorl as he'd been that night, tolerantly amused by his friend's extravagant apology. He'd watched her scrubbing at ale and wine stains on the bar, and she, as she worked, had compared the two rangers: Hauk thick and stocky as a bear, Tyorl like a silent-stepping stag. She'd thought, then, that it was difficult, if not impossible, to determine an elf's age from the look of him.

She looked at him now, sun-colored hair stirred by the cold wind, blue eyes soft with his thoughts, long legs crossed tailor-fashion as he leaned toward the fire. Lean and fit, a border ranger's air of danger and, aye, romance hung about him. It was impossible to think that he was anything but a few years older than Hauk.

"I think," she said hesitantly, "that we all seem young to you."

"Well, sometimes you do. I've seen one hundred summers, Kelida. That makes you and Hauk seem young to me. I'm a young man by the standards of my own kin." He smiled and shrugged. "It only gets confusing when I'm not with elves. There's all the years lived." He tapped his chest, suddenly tight and aching. "Then there's this, this heart, which reminds me how young I truly am."

Lehr abandoned his watch path and trotted north upriver, head low like a hound scenting trouble. Tyorl, who knew the look, got to his feet. "Kelida, go get Finn."

She felt the sudden tension in his voice and scrambled to her feet. Before she could ask a question, he was gone, running down to the water.

Lavim smelled the smoke just as the wind shifted. Stretched at full length on his stomach by the riverside, he thought of campfires and warmth. He'd certainly appreciate some warmth now. His old black coat lay nearby on the bank and he was wet to the shoulders from trying to catch fish with his hands as he'd seen Lehr doing earlier.

You'd think, he told himself, that it would be as easy as it looks!

Nothing is as easy as it looks, Lavim.

Lavim said nothing, only plunged his hands into the icy water again. Too late! The bass flew through his fingers, tickling his palm as it darted out of the shallows under the bank and into the center of the river. Lavim jerked his hands out of the water and, shaking off the icy water, tucked them under his arms.

It's all a matter of perspective, Lavim. When you look into the water you don't see what you think you see. Neither does the fish, for that matter, when he looks up.

"Uh-huh," Lavim muttered. "You'd know that, having been a fish most of your life, eh?"

All in all, Piper growled, *I think the wrong one of us is being testy. After all, I'm the one who's dead. If anyone has a right to be testy, it's me.*

"I'm not being testy. I'm trying to catch breakfast. Piper," he said suddenly, "I'm sorry that you're dead. I didn't know you when you were alive, but—I'm sorry. What does it feel like, being dead?"

Piper was silent for a moment. *It doesn't really feel like anything.*

"Where are you?"

I'm inside your head, and in the netherworld.

"What does it look like?"

Piper laughed. *It's foggy—in both places. Lavim, you've got another chance at a fish.*

A brown trout, nearly as long and plump as the bass, glided into the still water of the shallows. A lazy shrug of its tail put the fish into the thick grasses waving just below the water's surface. Lavim grinned and raised his hands to strike again.

Aim a little ahead and to the side.

"Why?"

Because you want a trout for breakfast.

Judging this to be a good enough reason, Lavim did as Piper suggested.

"Hah!" he crowed as his fingers curled around the trout. He yanked the fish from the water, dripping and glistening in the moonlight. "Gotcha!" But the trout wriggled, squirming against his palms, and Lavim, fascinated by the feel of scales against his skin, loosened his grip slightly. As though winged, the fish leaped from his hands and flopped back into the water.

"Damn!" Lavim flipped over onto his back, disgusted and too cold to plunge his blue-knuckled hands into the water again. The smell of wood smoke thickened on the wind. "What are they doing with that fire, anyway? They're going to—"

Lavim!

"Gods, Piper, don't bellow like that! It makes my ears pop! What?"

Dragons!

"Where?" Lavim snatched up his coat and hoopak and scrambled to his feet, his eyes on the sky. "Where?"

North! Get back to the camp, Lavim! There's one over the forest and heading for the river!

Grinning, Lavim ran for the river camp. Everyone was always talking about dragons: red ones, black ones, blue, and green, a whole rainbow of them. Lavim had only ever seen one—the one red that'd flown high, daily passes over Long Ridge.

The kender laughed aloud as he dashed toward the cave, trying to watch the sky and the ground at the same time. His luck was about to change!

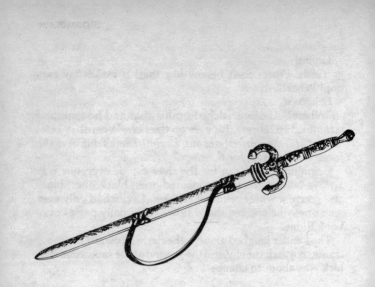

CHAPTER 20

HAUK'S DREAMS WERE MADE OF STONE AND MOVED LIKE ghosts, silently on the near wall of his prison. When they'd first come, he'd thought them a sign of approaching madness.

He didn't care anymore. He was waiting to die, and to truly die this time. Though Realgar asked no more questions, showed him no more twisted visions, he still amused himself with his game of death. Sudden as a hawk dropping for prey or lazy as a vulture wheeling and waiting, death lived in this dank tomb, whispering his name and sometimes clawing him with cold, cold hands, dragging him through black gates to a realm where the air gnawed at his lungs with teeth of ice.

Hauk had long ago lost count of his deaths and only lay in

darkness watching dreams on 'the wall as they slid across rough stone.

He saw the forest. Qualinesti, the green and shadowed homeland of the elves, was lit by thick, honey gold columns of sunlight. Like a dream within a dream, Tyorl drifted through glades and thick stands of pine and aspen. A strange look haunted his eyes, long blue eyes that Hauk knew well: a friend's eyes. Pain lived there, and grief and—almost—resignation. He followed paths known only to the elves and he was always searching.

Like smoke drifting on the wind, the dream shifted and he was once again in the tavern in Long Ridge. A girl with copper braids and leaf-green eyes smiled at him.

Aye, he thought, but she never did, did she? She'd only shrunk from him in fear and then, suddenly angry, spat in his eye. When the anger had fled, wariness crept into her eyes. Never a smile.

What was her name? He'd never known.

He looked closer at the wall, trying to see the dream and see her face more clearly. Tall, she was, or tall for a girl. She'd stood only a hand shorter than he. The girl. The barmaid. What was her name?

The scene on the wall shimmered, wavered, and afraid that he would lose sight of this girl who made up the only memory Realgar had never pried from him, Hauk reached out, his hand crabbing toward the wall.

Aye, tall, he thought as the dream became suddenly sharper. She appeared as a hunter or even a ranger, carrying a sword and wearing a cloak the color of her eyes, with hunting leathers the color of a storm sky.

Hunter-girl, ranger-girl, what is your name?

As he asked the silent question, she turned, her face white, her emerald eyes dark. She held out her hand, a graceful gesture of welcome. A cold spill of light winked on sapphires and gold.

She wore his sword, the one Realgar called Stormblade, at her hip.

The dream shattered, splintered by a bolt of white hot pain striking hard at his eyes, running in jagged edges down the length of his spine. Hauk cried out in grief for the dream killed and the cry echoed around the prison.

Someone held a lantern high, spilling light like fire all over the floor. Old and dry, choking with its own kind of mourning, a voice haunted the shadows behind the light.

"He won't have it. He won't."

Hauk knew the voice. Mad and old, held together with whispers like spider webs, he'd often heard it rustling around the edges of his nightmares, laughing or sobbing as he died.

Groaning, Hauk asked the question that had never yet received an answer. "Who are you?"

Before, the voice had always vanished with the question, carried away on the shuffling and scraping sounds of retreat. This time it didn't.

"He won't have it. Up, boy, up!"

Hauk couldn't rise. Gnarled hands, shaking and rough with scars, touched his face ancient frames for his pain.

"My Stormblade, he wants my Stormblade. He thinks he's found it, boy. He thinks he's found it!"

Fear lanced through Hauk. Smoke from the oily lantern streamed like the banners of the dead. Orange light splashed across the darkness. Hauk rolled onto his back and looked into the face of a dwarf. White hair hung, long and unkempt, to his shoulders. A beard, thickly tangled, spilled almost to his waist. Tears lay on his face, terror in his brown eyes.

Though it took every shred of strength that he had, Hauk lifted his hand, frightened by the sound and the creaking of his muscles. He grabbed the dwarf's wrist. Horror twisted the old, bearded face as it gazed into the eyes of the one it had seen killed by Realgar many, many times.

Cavern followed cavern: rock walls soaring up to shadow-draped ceilings; the cold, heavy scent of water; the smell of stone in an endless chain of caves.

He was strong, the dwarf, for all that he seemed as ancient as the mountains themselves. The dwarf flinched every time he had to bear Hauk's weight or the grip of his hands on his arms. He didn't take Hauk's weight easily, but he did take it. He badly wanted the ranger out of that prison cave and to a place that he imagined would provide a safe haven from Realgar.

In that way, they came at last to the final cavern. The dwarf led Hauk to a rough pallet on the floor against the far wall. Four blankets thick, it was warm and, despite the cold stone beneath, felt as fine and welcoming as a lord's bed. Torches lined the walls of the cave, their intricately worked iron brackets evenly spaced. The ventilation in the place left hardly a trace of their smoke.

The dwarf, quietly muttering to himself as though he would not, for any price, disturb Hauk's rest, went about the place checking small piles of food supplies and water flasks. A low brazier stood in the center of the stony chamber, and, from time to time, the dwarf stopped to tend it. Each time he did, he looked over at the ranger and his muttering stilled.

Hauk studied him carefully. The brown old eyes were surely mad, but something new flickered in them now, seen for the space of a heartbeat and then gone, chased away by pain, longing, and fear. The new thing was recognition. Hauk didn't know why it was there, he couldn't begin to guess what it was that the dwarf recognized.

He didn't care. He gave him nothing back, not even blinking to break the cold steady stare he knew terrified the ancient dwarf.

Little by little, like the tide creeping back at dawn to a barren shore, Hauk's strength returned. As his strength grew, so did his rage and hatred. He would wait patiently for revenge, for as long as he had to wait.

Then, he would rise up and drag the heart out of the old bastard with his bare hands and grind it into the stone.

CHAPTER 21

Stanach lifted his right hand with his left. Beneath its bandaging, the broken fingers lay as heavy and senseless as steel bars in his palm. His knees watery and weak, still he waved off the support Kem offered and took one, then two faltering steps. Drawing a deep breath, he walked to the cave's mouth. The ranger had assured him that he'd find his strength soon enough.

Stanach leaned against the cave's stone wall and looked out to the water. He hoped Kem was right. Smoke, like dark fog, drifted upriver, shepherded by the cold, heavy wind. The sky throbbed red, high above the top of the forest. Kelida, Stormblade still at her hip, ran a short distance along the bank to meet Lavim. The kender fairly danced with excitement. Kelida snatched his arms, holding him still enough to hear what she had to tell him. Then, pouches jouncing, Lavim scrambled downriver to where Tyorl ranged the water's edge.

As Stanach watched, two other rangers broke from the forest's cover and joined the elf at the water. One, Finn, pointed north.

Stanach turned back to the cave. "What is it?"

Kem, his face sculpted of shadows and finely drawn with worry, looked up from packing his healer's kit. "Forest fire, they say. We're getting out of here, Stanach. Are you all right to walk? Finn wants to ford the river here and put it between us and the fire as soon as we can."

"Aye, does he? Then I'd better be all right to walk." Stanach softened his growl with a shrug.

Lehr, shaggy hair tumbling in the wind, stepped into the cave. He and his lord had been well into the forest, and Lehr smelled of smoke and burning. He eyed Stanach sharply, then slapped his shoulder hard enough to make the dwarf grateful for the wall behind him. "Aye, you'll do it on your own legs, eh? Good. Kem, let's get moving."

Kembal threw his healer's pack over his shoulder. "How far north is the fire? Damn, Lehr! What started it?"

"Not very far, and it's moving fast." The ranger checked the cave, saw that nothing had been left behind, and cast a quick look back to the river. "We figure the leading edge is between us and the rest of the company, but we don't know where the flanks are and we didn't have time to look. Finn says the only place we'll find the company—or them us—is on the eastern bank."

The ranger was gone before either Stanach or Kembal realized that he hadn't answered the question of what started the fire. Kem grimaced impatiently.

Stanach left the cave carrying his sword on his back and a hard lump of dread in his belly.

"It's not much of a river here," Tyorl said, "and maybe only waist high. Can you do it, Stanach?"

Whether his returning strength was a result of the healer's draught or the impetus of the distant, whispering growl of advancing fire, Stanach knew that he would be able to keep

up with his companions in the river. He cast an eye sky-
ward. The moons had set. The crimson glow over the forest
looked like vengeful dawn.

"Aye, I'll do it."

Though the elf nodded, Stanach saw doubt like shadows
in his eyes. "I'll be right behind you. Kem says you'd better
keep your hand dry if you can."

Finn entered the water first, longbow high over his head.
The smoke channeling upriver hid him from sight before
he'd waded very far.

Bandaged hand well out of the water, trusting to his well-
oiled leather scabbard to protect the sword slung across his
back, Stanach followed Finn into the river.

He gasped as the icy water caught him, tugging with insis-
tent strength at his knees, then swirling high and clawing at
his chest. The cold ached in his bones and muscles and
quickly numbed his feet as though they were not stoutly
booted.

Tyorl and Kelida waded in next. Taking her cue from
Finn, the girl brandished Stormblade, wrapped in her cloak,
high over her head both for balance and to keep the sword
dry. Kem cut out to the side, flanking the crossing and ready
to assist any who needed help negotiating the quickening
current. Lehr kept close to Kelida, offering a hand to steady
her when she needed it. Once, he wrapped an arm around
her waist and pulled her close when the current tangled her
feet.

Lehr laughed aloud as he set Kelida on her feet again. The
ranger clearly did not mind a pretty girl in soaked hunting
leathers clinging to his neck. Tyorl looked as though he
minded greatly. Surprised to hear himself wondering if the
flat of his sword would teach the impudent young ranger
some manners, Tyorl passed Stanach, who readily dropped
back to let him by.

Lavim held no place in the line. Giving himself up to the
inevitable, he plunged into the icy river, cutting through the
black water with all the enthusiasm of a fish and none of
that creature's grace.

When Stanach finally stumbled onto the rocky eastern
shore, clumsy with cold, heavily awkward and bound to the

ground again, he turned to look back the way he'd come. Like the breath of ghosts, wavering and dark, the smoke veiled the far bank. Kelida dropped light hands onto his shoulders.

"Are you all right?"

"Aye," Stanach said, though he wasn't sure. The river crossing had sucked the warmth out of him.

Finn jerked a thumb toward the low, stony hills. Kem took the right point, and Tyorl insisted that Lehr accompany him on the left. Lavim, shaking himself like a soaked hound, scurried on ahead and quickly left the rangers behind.

The thick odor of burning forest followed them into the foothills. The ground on the eastern side of the river was rocky and rising. Low scrub growth huddled in widely spaced thickets. Hills and then tall fells marched eastward. Kelida, quiet with her own thoughts, matched her pace to Stanach's. Each time they looked back over their shoulders they saw the crimson stain of fire in the sky.

"*Guyll fyr*," Stanach whispered, stopping to watch the fire ignite the brush only a mile from the river cave. Despite the biting wind and the cold pre-dawn air, sweat trickled down the sides of his pale face, glittering along the edges of his moustache and clinging to his thick black beard. Kelida, seeing his need to rest and restore his failing strength, stopped with him.

She silently tried the words he'd used, then looked up and tried it aloud. "Gueel fire?"

Stanach smiled crookedly. "Close enough. Wildfire." The dwarf pointed southward along the line of the forest. "The brush is up, but most of the fire is in the treetops. If the wind changes, it will cross the river."

"That's wildfire?"

Stanach searched the dark ahead of them. Kembal waited at the foot of the first of a series of fells. "No," he said, starting out again. "It will be *guyll fyr* when it hits the Plains of Death about thirty miles from here."

If the wind's right, he thought grimly, it will do that tomorrow.

He said nothing further, about the fire or anything else.

The task of walking needed all his attention now. Kelida went a little ahead of him, her eyes on the dark ground, always finding the rubble in the path, the dips and holes in the stony ground, in time to catch his arm before he stumbled.

His right hand hung at his side like iron stock, feelingless and heavy. Stanach remembered the fire that had burned remorselessly in that hand only hours ago. He didn't remember it in his hand, he didn't feel the echoes of recent pain there. He felt it cold in his chest, tightening in his stomach.

When, he wondered, would Kembal's salves wear off?

Tyorl, on his heels at the top of the fell, searched the sky for signs of the dawn. He found none. The fading stars told him that the horizon should be graying, but the light of the fire had spread across the sky as the forest caught the flames and sent them speeding south and east, overwhelming the whisper of faint dawn.

Had the fire crossed the river yet? Tyorl didn't think so. He got to his feet and stretched aching muscles. He couldn't remember when he'd last slept. He didn't know when he would sleep next.

Finn, his sharp eyes on the ground at the foot of the hill, nudged Tyorl. Kem jogged back down the slope to help Stanach and Kelida. "The dwarf is going to have to rest soon. Aye, and from the look of him, it'll be at the foot of the hill, too."

"We can't stop here. The fire could jump the river."

Finn snorted. "It will jump the river."

They stood silently for a long moment. Tyorl searched west, wondering if the thirty rangers of their company had escaped the flames. He glanced at Finn and saw the same question in the rangerlord's weathered face. And he saw the answer in his eyes.

They couldn't have escaped. The river ran foaming in wild, treacherous white water six miles north and could not be forded. The fire looked to have started where Finn said the company had been camped. What had happened?

Gods, Tyorl, who did not do so often, prayed, *grant*

some of them life if you can't let them all live!

Kerrith. Bartt. Old G'Art. The names and faces of the thirty men and elves who had been his friends for so many years seemed to be written on the smoke. Tyorl shivered. That fast would they die, those friends, and as easily as wind scatters smoke.

Finn paced the top of the fell then returned. "I wonder where the kender's got to?"

"Keeping out of my way, no doubt," Tyorl said.

Finn grunted. "Will he return?"

"He's a night rider, but he always comes back. Worse luck for me."

"Aye?" Finn eyed the elf shrewdly. "I thought he was a friend of yours. Trouble between you two?"

"One doesn't cancel out the other," Tyorl said wearily.

The moons were long set. No starlight remained to cast a shadow. Still, Tyorl suddenly saw the shade of dread and danger in his heart as though he had seen it cutting along the ground.

Finn bellowed a curse. As an echo, Lehr's cry of shock and alarm sounded from the foot of the hill as he roared a warning to his brother.

A piece of midnight, shrieking like a banshee's war cry, a black dragon arrowed from the sky.

The moment the dragon's cry sounded was like a fragment separated from the line of time itself. Kelida's heart crashed against her ribs, sickening her with the force of her fear. Cold to her bones, her muscles frozen, she watched, helpless to move, as the creature's wings cut back along its glittering ebony sides, watched in horror as it touched the ground, its massive head reared high. With terrifying speed, the dragon's forelegs shot out as though reaching for something.

Reaching for her!

Stanach's howl of horror slashed the bonds of Kelida's terror as though it were a hard-edged sword. She flung herself to the side.

Stormblade!

She didn't stop to think that she, untrained and without

skill, would likely injure herself with the sword before she could ever wound the dragon. Dagger-sharp claws, black and curved, hung over her like a cage waiting to close. Kelida fumbled with the peace strings, trying to haul the sword from its scabbard. Red-hearted steel and ice blue sapphires, Stormblade's weight would drag at her wrist muscles as she tried to raise it aloft. It didn't matter. She had to try.

A hideous cry of triumph shivered the night before she could pull the sword free. The dragon bore a rider! Dark cloaked and hooded, a dwarf sat astride the beast.

Stanach roared, a sound like a wordless curse, and dove between Kelida and the beast. The dragon's huge wing caught him hard and swept him to the ground. He rolled instinctively, came up staggering, and fell to one knee. Fast as lightning's strike, the dragon's long neck whipped to the side, its teeth bared and dripping, eyes murderously bright.

"No!" Kelida screamed. "No! Stanach!"

Heavy as a falling tree, a flying weight caught Kelida from behind. She hit the ground hard, all the breath flown from her, and tried to scream again. There was nothing in her with which to scream, no air, no voice. A hand clamped roughly on her arm, dragging, dragging, and Kelida came to her knees, sobbing and gasping. Lehr, unruly dark hair tangling in the wind from the dragon's wings, stood between the beast and Kelida. Sword high, the ranger lunged, though he must have known that his blade would never pierce the dragon's scaly armor.

Lehr's steel struck and turned on ebony hide. The dragon rumbled deep in its great chest. The low thundering sounded horribly like amused laughter.

With a careless stroke of dagger claws, it's eyes already on Kelida, the black tore heart and life from the ranger. Lehr's blood, like hot rain, spattered Kelida's face and hands. She screamed and heard only a moan. She tried to run and only fell.

Like a cage, she'd thought when she first saw the dragon's claws. Like a cage they closed around her now, and then drew tight, scraping against each other as they captured her and dragged, then lifted her high.

No! her mind screamed. No!

The dragonrider reached for her arm, yanked hard, and dragged her over the beast's neck. Her head snapped back and her stomach lurched with sickening force.

Kelida had nothing of sense left, only the need to free herself. She kicked back hard, heaved herself to sitting, and clawed at the dwarf's face. Her fingers dragged the hood away and she saw that he had only one eye.

As the dragon thrust hard against the ground and leaped for the sky, wings wide to catch the wind, Kelida struck at that eye with a mountain cat's instinct. Dimly, she felt a hand close quickly, with desperate strength, on her ankle, then just as quickly loose her. Thick and strong, two arms wrapped around her waist. The right hand, wrapped in bandaging torn from her green cloak, slipped and then pressed hard against her ribs. Stanach!

Blood streamed down the dragonrider's face, caught in his grizzled beard. He flung himself away from her hands. Kelida hardly recognized the high triumphant cry ringing in her ears as her own. The sky dove for her, then turned sickeningly at the wild thunder of wind under the dragon's black wings.

Slim and light, still she was a farmer's girl and stronger than she looked. Kelida balanced across the dragon's slick, scaly neck the way she would on a horse. Again she lunged at the dragonrider and didn't see his dagger until a forge-scarred hand clamped on the dwarf's wrist.

Stanach!

Kelida looked around wildly and found him clinging to the dragon's ridged back behind the dark-cloaked dwarf.

Bones snapped, the dragonrider screamed. The dragon's powerful muscles rippled under Kelida's knees as it leaped high and wheeled again. As in a dream where there is no sound and everything moves slowly, Kelida felt her balance slip, saw the dragonrider slide down the long black slope of the beast's shoulder, and saw his mouth stretch wide in a futile scream as he found no grip. Clawing at nothing but air, he fell away in a sprawl of rigid arms and legs to the ground far below.

Her hands were nerveless with reaction to the horror, her legs too weak now to keep their grip. Kelida doubled over the dragon's neck and waited, helpless to move against the force of the rushing air. The dun-colored sweep of hills and stone would rush up at her, snatch her the way it had snatched the one-eyed dwarf.

It never did.

Stanach caught Kelida quickly around the waist, his arms shaking, his breath thin clouds in the icy air of the heights. He dragged her back and held her tightly against him. She felt his beard against her back, thick and warm. She watched, as from a distance, as he reached around her with his left hand and grasped the dragon's spiny crest.

The beast thundered and soared high, cutting through the wispy, gray clouds of dawn. Kelida felt Stanach's sigh ragged in his chest, heard him whisper something in a choked voice.

Lyt chwaer, it sounded like. Little sister.

She sagged a little, closed her eyes against the sickening pressure of the dragon's speed, and marshaled all her strength to hold on until they reached whatever destination the dragon chose.

Lehr's blood still stained Kelida's gray hunting leathers, still speckled her hands and arms. She shuddered deeply. The shudder became a wrenching sob and she wept, her tears freezing to ice on her cheeks.

Darknight roared, stretching for the sky. Far below it, Realgar's mageling, called the Gray Herald, dropped like a stone from the cold blue height.

A flight of a different kind! The black dragon howled its laughter. It'd hated the mageling's imperious commands, hated the sound of his thoughts, the smell of him. It craned its neck back to see the two who rode now where the Gray Herald had. Another dwarf, light as Agus had been, and a human girl. *Sevristh* narrowed its eyes against the wind. The dragon's tongue, long and forked, flickered around dagger fangs. It scented their fear and it smelled sweet indeed.

Nothing was tougher to chew than a muscular, sinewy dwarf. Nothing was more tender than young human flesh. The girl carried the Kingsword, and Darknight looked forward to Realgar's pleasure, if only for the chance to claim these two as a reward. As, it thought, dinner.

The black dragon made every effort to keep its riders on its back. Its flight was smooth, and it avoided the rougher wind pockets the way a ship's captain would run his craft through the trough of the sea to keep the waves from broadsiding his hull.

Stanach felt nothing, not the exhaustion, not the terror, not Kelida's violent sobs, until the dragon swept out across the Plains of Dergoth, the Plains of Death. Then, as the black climbed high to catch a favorable wind current, canted its flight to put the wind at its back and under its broad wings, he saw the carpet of flame advancing east.

Kelida shook against him, an aspen in a windstorm, and he had no words to soothe her.

High in the southeastern sky, the new sun glinted on what seemed a long crimson arrow. A second dragon, a fire-breathing red, shot through the rolling black smoke above the forest and, wings folded, dove for the high, dark spine of the southern mountains and Pax Tharkas.

Stanach knew then what had set the forest aflame. He didn't know why. If Verminaard's troops and supplies were moving into the mountains, why would he risk firing the forest and destroying the lines of attack he had only recently set in place?

The dragon caught a lower current, dropping with stomach-wrenching speed, and Stanach pulled Kelida hard against him. Off to the side, Stanach saw the answer to his question. Broad, deep fire breaks, looking like plough scars from this height, scored the foothills in a straight, narrow channel right to the plains themselves.

Channels, he thought bitterly, protecting the forests to the north and south and leading the flames right out onto the Plains of Death.

From there the fire—*guyll fire!*—would march on Thorbardin like the savage advance raiders of a raging army.

Stanach groaned aloud. No army's hungry raiders could do more damage.

A hundred years ago, wildfire had swept across the boggy

marshes of the Plains of Death. Then the dwarves had tried to stop it, tried to save the marshlands. Stark and ugly those marshes were, but they were part of the wilds of dwarven lands, the places where birds nested, beasts watered, and fishes dwelt. The marshes formed a large link in Thorbardin's food chain.

A century ago, the marshlands had not been saved. It was true that the farming warrens deep below the mountains were able to feed Thorbardin. True, too, was the real danger that should blight threaten the crops and disease take the stock, famine would result.

We are under siege!

Kelida, limp with exhaustion, half-turned and buried her face in Stanach's shoulder. He shifted his grip on the dragon's crest, hitched his bandaged and still nerveless right hand higher to assure his grip on the girl. She said nothing, but her weeping had stilled a few moments ago. Stanach tried to see her face, but could not.

The dragon dropped lower, slowing its speed. Thorbardin was below and to the southeast. The city lay within the high peaks of the mountain just now taking the sun's gilding. Snow blushed rose on the highest peaks, where it was already winter. As the dragon slid along the currents, Stanach was able to make out the still shadowed defile that led to Northgate, shattered and ruined three hundred years before in the Dwarfgate Wars. Gaping wide, stones silently screaming of pain, the mouth of the gate itself opened onto a thin and treacherous ledge. In three hundred years, that gate had never been closed, its mechanism destroyed in the war. Northgate was guarded more heavily than the still operable Southgate.

Wind thundered around them as the dragon glided still lower, dropping below the defile, below the ledge, and finally descending into the last shadows of night at the mountain's foot.

Cold fear crept through Stanach. Northgate was guarded, warded by strong and fierce Daewar warriors. However, the caverns below, secret holds the Theiwar called the Deep Warrens, lay far beneath the gate.

Realgar had a dragon to do his bidding, likely to call him

Highlord. Now, he waited in the Deep Warrens for Stormblade. The Kingsword would make him more than a Highlord; it would make him king regent of the dwarves and ruler of Thorbardin.

Stanach closed his eyes.

He felt the jolt of the dragon's landing in his bones and heard the scrape of claws on stone. Kelida stirred, then sat away from him.

"Where are we? Do you know?"

Stanach knew. His eyes on the glittering sword at her side, he wanted to say that they had come to the place where they would soon die. He didn't say that, but only shook his head.

"Home." The word passed his lips hoarsely, as though it were a lie. "We are in Thorbardin."

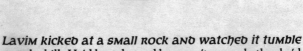

CHAPTER 22

Lavim kicked at a small rock and watched it tumble down the hill. He'd heard—and he wasn't sure whether he'd heard this from Piper or someone else—that all this desert, all this rolling, dry, dusty, empty, shadowless, and boring place they called the Hills of Blood, had once been a grassy plain.

You forgot 'dull.'

"What?"

You forgot to mention that the hills are dull.

Lavim sighed. "I didn't think I'd have to. Kind of speaks for itself, doesn't it?"

Piper smiled.

Lavim kicked at the dirt, watching the puffs of dust being carried away by the knife-sharp wind. He thought it was curious that he could tell when Piper was smiling.

He dove into his pocket and pulled out a map made of carefully folded, cracked parchment. "I used to have a map case for these, but I don't know what happened to it. I had it not so long ago, about a month or so before I went to Long Ridge. It's gone now. Lots of things tend to disappear just after I'm running to or from some place."

He dropped to a crouch and laid the map out on the ground, smoothing the creases carefully. "Look at this place, Piper. It's even ugly on a map." He traced the map for the benefit of a ghost who could now see well behind them and well before them.

Piper said nothing and let him go on.

"See? Back here to the east is Qualinesti." Lavim looked up, squinting at the sky. "Kind of odd, isn't it, that I spent most of my time there looking for ghosts and didn't find one until I was out of the place. Well, there it is, Elvenwood, all green and pretty. Here's the river we crossed, that blue squiggly line." He snorted in disgust. "And here's where the map gets ugly and the land gets even uglier. Just little hills, the map says. Huh! These aren't hills, they're little mountains."

No, they're hills.

"Easy enough for you to say; you're not walking them." Lavim folded his map and tucked it back into his pocket. "It would be a whole lot easier to get to Thordardin if we could cut across the Plains of Dergoth—or the Plains of Death as the dwarves call 'em. Why do they call 'em that, Piper?"

Because thousands of dwarves, hill dwarves and mountain dwarves, died there during the Dwarfgate Wars.

Lavim rose and stretched. The wind cut sharply from the east now, pushing the wildfire ahead of it. Though the sky was clear of the *guyll fyr's* smoke, the currents over the plains for the most part sucked the roiling smoke along the channel of the marshland. Still, he could scent it.

With no further word, he jogged off to the south, climbed the highest hill he could find, then dropped again to his heels.

The fire was miles distant and looked from his hilltop like a broad red snake slithering toward the mountains in the east. The smoke overhung the marshes, a thick black pall. When he tried very hard, eyes squeezed shut and shoulders hunched, Lavim imagined he could hear the roar of that fire like distant thunder.

Piper, silent for all this time, spoke suddenly and Lavim jumped. *Why don't you go talk to Tyorl?*

"No, I don't think so." Lavim glanced over his shoulder and down the hill. "He's still real upset about Kelida and Stanach being snatched up by the dragon. I could see why he would be. I don't—I don't like to think about it much myself."

I've noticed. Maybe Tyorl needs to talk about it.

Lavim shook his head darkly. "Not to me, he doesn't. Look at him."

Tyorl was sitting on his heels, watching the sky. He'd had his eye on the hard blue heights since the dragon had snatched Kelida and carried her and Stanach into the dawn. Lavim sighed. He'd missed nearly the whole wonderful thing and only come back to the others in time to see the dragon, looking like nothing as much as a sharp black tear in the sky, winging eastward toward Thorbardin with Kelida and Stanach and without its rider.

They'd found the one-eyed dwarf in a gully between two fells. Bone-smashed and bleeding, he was not dead. Lavim supposed that Finn had been moved by revenge for Lehr's terrible death when he cut the dwarf's throat. Piper had said such a killing was a mercy.

Lavim glanced at Finn now. Forehead on drawn up knees, the rangerlord sat unmoving in the shelter of the hill, seemingly unaware of Kem's restless pacing. Kembal, always quiet, hadn't said a word since his brother had been killed by the dragon. He prowled the base of the hill, head up and ready, like a hunter waiting to resume his prey's trail. He was sharpening his arrows on the stone of revenge, Piper said.

With the change in the wind's direction just after dawn, the fire had spread fast through the hills and, racing south and north as well as east, threw up a wall of flame behind them. They'd headed for the desert hills on Finn's advice. There wasn't much to burn here and the rangerlord figured they'd be safe. It had been a hard run and now, as the shadows grew longer and darker with imminent sunset, the four had stopped to rest before pushing east again.

Go on, Lavim. Talk to Tyorl.

"And?"

And what?

"And give him the flute, right? It's what you've been nagging me about all along. Give him the flute, give him the flute."

I'd be happier if you did.

"But he can't use it and I can!"

Piper sighed. *As long as I tell you what to do, yes.*

"Then where's the sense in giving it to him?"

Lavim! Go!

Lavim squeezed his eyes closed and clapped his hands over his ears. Wishing that Piper had never developed this nasty habit of yelling right inside his head, he went to join Tyorl.

The elf never looked around, even when Lavim's small shadow cut across his. Lavim cleared his throat loudly.

Tyorl got to his feet and scanned the eastern quarter of the sky. "We've an hour or so before dark, Lavim. Let's not waste it talking." He nodded to Finn who rose and signaled Kem that they were ready to move again.

Kem, as was his custom, took the northern point, covering ground with his long-legged lope. Finn jogged a little ahead to the south and east, setting their course. Soon, the smoky pall from the Plains of Death ran high over their heads. Lavim trotted beside Tyorl, stepping quickly to keep up.

"Uh, Tyorl, I want to tell you something."

Tyorl made no response.

"I want to tell you about Piper."

"He's dead," Tyorl grunted. "What more do I need to know about Piper?"

Lavim sighed patiently. "I know he's dead. But I think you think that if you had his flute when the dragon grabbed Stanach and Kelida, you'd've been able to do something about it."

Tyorl said nothing.

233

"You wouldn't have. You couldn't have."

"Aye? And why not?"

"Because the flute only works for me, Tyorl. Piper says that it won't—"

"Piper says?"

Lavim nodded. "You see, he's a ghost, Tyorl. He talks to me in my head and he tells me things—"

"Lavim—"

"Please, Tyorl, let me finish. He really is a ghost. He told me when the red dragon flew over the forest and set the woods on fire. Well, not that he—the dragon, I mean—was going to do that, but that he was flying. And—and he told me about the black dragon, too." The kender sighed and picked up his pace. The sand and red dust seemed to drag at his feet. "But—but I was too far away to do anything about it. I tried! I really did, but Piper says that spells have ranges and—I'm sorry. I'm really sorry. I wish I'd been closer. I wish I hadn't been out in the hills. But I was. And—and I know you think that you would have been able to help Lehr and Kelida and Stanach when the dragon came if only you had the flute, but you couldn't have. You don't have Piper in your head."

"And neither do you. Kenderkin, sometimes I think you're half mad and—"

Tell him you are not mostly senile.

Indignantly Lavim snapped, "I am not mostly senile! Not even partly!"

Tyorl stopped. It was the phrase he'd been about to use "What?"

"I—Piper said—I mean I said—I am not mostly senile." Lavim drew a shuddering breath and stopped. Hands on his knees, head low and panting, he closed his eyes and tried to catch his breath, still talking. "And Piper says, too, that right now you're thinking that you'd better find a way to keep me quiet before Finn hears."

Tyorl blinked. "Aye? Does he?"

"Yes, and he says that now you're thinking that the last thing you need is a crazy kender on your hands. I'm not crazy, Tyorl! Do you understand? I'm not making this up. It's true. It's real. Here." He groped through his pockets and dragged out the flute. He pressed it into Tyorl's hand before he could decide not to. "Try it. Play something."

"What will it prove? I can play the instrument, but I don't know the notes for any spell."

Lavim whistled the quick, light notes he had played to trigger his smell spell. "Try those." He whistled the tune again. "Got, 'em?"

Tyorl held the flute gingerly. "Lavim."

"Try it! Go ahead. Piper says it's all right."

The elf looked at the flute, glanced sharply at Lavim, and drew a quick breath.

"Go on."

Tyorl tried the tune, braced for disaster at worst, for the unimaginably foul odor that had sickened him in the river cave at best.

Nothing happened but that the breeze quickened a little.

"Piper says that the wind has nothing to do with the flute. Something about the air currents over the fire or something. See? Try it again."

Tyorl did. The breeze blew at the same strength and the air still smelled of the wildfire's smoke, but nothing else. He stared at the flute in his hand and saw, just a moment too late, the kender's own hand dart out and snatch the instrument back. It was secreted in deep pockets before Tyorl could protest.

"Lavim! Wait! Give—"

But Lavim was gone, trotting ahead to catch up with Finn, the flute once again in his possession.

Tyorl started after him. If Lavim had been on the fell when the black dragon had struck, he might have been able to help. But, he was night ranging and hadn't been there. Blaming him for that now was as fruitless as blaming himself for missing his shot at the dragon when he did.

Tyorl ran faster. He was not thinking about ghosts or chances missed. He suddenly realized that Lavim had proved that the flute's magic worked for Lavim alone. The implications were frightening.

From the hill where he walked the dark watch in the hours after midnight, Tyorl saw the fire rampaging in the marshes and bogs on the Plains of Death. The wind from the west had calmed after sunset, but the wildfire no longer needed the wind's push to speed it on its way to the mountains. The marsh grass might as well have been lamp oil; nothing would stop the fire now.

Tyorl cursed bitterly and looked up at the stars, tiny chips of glittering ice scattered across the black sky. Solinari, high and bright, was girded by a hazy silver ring. Lunitari's light crimsoned the dark hills to the east and sent indigo shadows running down to the lowlands. The red moon's ring was pink as water-washed blood. Tyorl smelled snow in the air.

We'll not be making the mountains before the fire does, the elf thought, and that means we won't be making Thorbardin at all.

He ran his thumb along the polished wood of his longbow. Smooth as silk the yew felt under his thumb, and familiar. And useless, useless to defend Kelida against the dragon.

Tyorl winced as pain and regret clawed at his heart. That, too, was familiar. His straight, true arrows had bounded off the ebony dragon's scaled hide as though they'd been repelled by steel. A bolt through the creature's eye would have slowed it, might have killed it, but the dragon moved too fast and had flown well out of Tyorl's range before he could sight and aim. For a moment, as the dragon leaped for the sky, he'd thought that Stanach had pulled Kelida free. He watched the struggle on the giant beast's back, praying, then cursing as the beast took to the sky.

Stanach, the elf thought bitterly, Stormblade has cost you kin, friend, and hand. You say Reorx blessed the blade; I say he cursed it. But you tried. You fought like a wolf for it.

He turned his back on the lurid glare of the *guyll fyr* and, his eye caught by the small, tame glow of the campfire in the hollow, watched the shadows of its smoke playing across the ground below. Red beneath the sun, the rocks and thick dust of the desert floor gleamed strangely purple under the eerie glow of the moons. Lavim, as ever, was nowhere to be seen. Tyorl hadn't caught up with him before the camp was made and hadn't been able to find him since.

Night riding, he thought, or communing with his ghostly

mage.

He veered wide of that thought. He was certain that Lavim believed that dead Piper spoke with him. Tyorl didn't know what he himself thought. Yet, it was true that Lavim had known his words before he'd half-thought them himself. When he'd tried to discuss the matter with Finn, the rangerlord had shrugged and expressed nothing but the most caustic disbelief.

Tyorl glanced over the camp again. Finn lay wrapped in his cloak and slept near the fire. Kem, whom Tyorl had relieved from the watch an hour ago, sat staring into the shadows. Tyorl wondered when he would sleep.

Kem's silence had always been a thing of good-natured, amused observation. Quiet by nature, the healer had left most of the talking to his voluble younger brother. Now it seemed that Lehr's death had stolen away the gentle, humorous light in Kem's eyes. Kem wanted revenge and so, too, did Tyorl.

Tyorl was suddenly cold to his bones. It was the first time he'd admitted, even to himself, that he believed Kelida dead.

The black dragon had flown out of the east. Out of Thorbardin. It could only mean that the revolution Stanach had feared was a thing accomplished. Realgar reigned in the dwarven kingdom and had dragons at his command. Aye, and Verminaard as his ally.

Again he whispered a curse, this time against the sudden tightening of his throat. Last night he'd been wondering whether he was in love with Kelida, hiding from the idea and yet waiting to catch the soft sound of her voice, hoping to feel the warmth of her casual touch.

Tonight, and too late, he knew that he loved her. Now he could only look to memory to hear her voice, to feel her hand light on his arm, or catch the sun glinting in her hair.

Would he have told her? Aye, in a minute!

And what of Hauk?

The elf smiled bitterly. It hardly mattered now. They were both dead, and he had only a handful of moments, now memories of a farmer's girl turned barmaid. It was too late to worry about what might have grown from those moments. They were gone.

Tyorl resumed his watch walk, the wildfire on his left and shadows before and behind him. Too late for anything, he thought coldly, but vengeance. No matter at all who ruled in Thorbardin now. He'd find a way to the mountain cities, and he'd find his vengeance for Kelida, and for Hauk whom they'd both loved.

From a night-filled ravine west of the campsite, Lavim watched Tyorl pacing on the hilltop. He'd recovered kender-quick from his desert run and, knowing that Tyorl would be after the flute now, had slipped into the shadows of the twilight and avoided all three rangers. He wanted to talk to Piper without being bothered with Tyorl's demands for the flute. Lavim had some questions that needed answering.

He wriggled to a more comfortable seat on the rocks and scowled into the night. The problem was that Piper hadn't been giving him many answers at all. He'd stopped giving answers right about the time the kender took out the flute. Lavim ran his fingers along the smooth red cherry wood and smiled slyly. He suspected that Piper's lack of response to his last question was an answer in itself.

"I think," he said, pointing the flute to where he imagined Piper would be standing if he were anywhere but inside his own head. "I think that I can use this flute any time I want to."

Piper said nothing.

"I think it doesn't matter whether or not you tell the flute what magic tune to play."

Piper still said nothing.

Lavim grinned. "That's what I think. You know why? Well, I'll tell you: because that smell-spell was my idea, and the flute played the song I needed when I needed it. That's why you want me to give the flute to Tyorl, isn't it? I can use the magic and I don't need you to tell me how to. I just need you to be inside my head so the flute will work. What do you say to that?"

I say that you're an ass, Lavim.

Lavim refused to be insulted. "Might be, might be. But

I'm an ass with a magic flute."

Piper's voice was cold inside Lavim's head. *Aye, and I couldn't think of anything more foolish or dangerous.*

Lavim watched the moons' light run along the satin-smooth wood. "You're mad, aren't you? Strange, since it's me who should be mad at you for telling me that I needed to have you tell me how to work the magic." He nodded solemnly. "Friends don't lie to friends."

Friends don't steal from friends either, Lavim.

Stung, the kender slid off the rock. "I didn't steal the flute! You gave it to me!"

I asked you to give it to Tyorl.

"And I said I would. Pretty soon, too!"

Lavim, I don't know what you have planned, but it had better not involve the flute. There are only a handful of spells you can work with the flute's magic, and you don't know what they are.

Lavim chuckled. "I know what two of them are. A smell-spell and a transport spell. And I don't need a smell-spell now!"

He left the ravine, scrambling up the steep sides, and dashed toward the campsite.

"It'll be easy!" he crowed. "We'll just transport to Thorbardin and save Kelida and Stanach and maybe this Hauk fellow, too!"

No! Lavim, no! That spell takes words, too. You have to know them as you play the notes. If you try that spell without the right words, you'll be standing in the middle of nowhere with three piles of dust who used to be your friends!

Lavim stopped, head cocked and frowning. Then a smile smoothed the wrinkles on his weather-browned face. He had the solution to that problem, too. "That's all right, Piper. Just tell 'em to me when I have to know 'em."

Piper, who might as well have been riding a runaway horse down a mountain, wished desperately that he had something to hold on to. He'd need it. There was no way to stop Lavim now.

Tyorl knew he believed in Lavim's haunting the instant he

saw the kender pull out the mage's flute. Puffing like an old bellows from his run up the side of the ravine, Lavim waved the elf down from the hilltop.

"Tyorl! C'mere! I've figured it all out! I can get us to Thorbardin before you know it!"

At once he heard a voice from memory. Stanach's, low and rough with grief, whispering, "Piper's known in Thorbardin for his transport spells."

Piper! Tyorl begged silently, Piper, don't let him do it!

Tyorl scrambled, tripping over a jutting stone and sliding most of the way down the hill on his heels. The gods only knew what would happen if Lavim misinterpreted the instructions for a transport spell. The words and gestures of a spell were delicate things. How much more precise must the notes be when a spell is enacted with a mage's flute! What manner of spell could be mistakenly loosed?

Tyorl dove for Lavim.

So did Finn.

And so did Kem.

The kender went down in a welter of arms and legs, kicking and squirming, but held the flute with a sure grip.

"Hey! Wait! What's the matter? Let me up! You don't understand I—"

Tyorl pulled himself out from under Finn's knee, keeping his grip on Lavim's ankle. Finn twisted away from Kem's elbow and never relinquished his hold around the kender's middle. Kem tried to haul Lavim to his feet. No one held his hands and no one thought to clamp a hand over his mouth.

Lavim, certain that his companions had somehow misunderstood what he'd said—clearly if they'd understood him they'd all be much happier than they were now—dragged air into his lungs and raised the flute to his lips.

He'd thought, somehow, that the tune for a transport spell would be just a little more exciting than three little notes. As he heard the first of them, Piper bellowed in his head. Lavim thought probably the spell should have sounded more delicate, somehow just a little more gentle, than curses.

He seemed to fade, to stretch, and suddenly his stomach twisted around inside him and tied itself in knots.

Very strange, he thought, as all sense of feeling drained out of him. (Through his fingers and toes, it seemed.) I think when I come out of this spell, I'm going to need to find a place to get sick for a minute or two. I suppose I'd better send us outside the city. It would be a little embarrassing to lose your dinner in front of a whole lot of—

Suddenly Lavim felt nothing at all.

Tyorl hit the ground with a teeth-jarring thud. When he tried to catch his breath, smoke filled his lungs. Fire licked across his fingers, and he would have cried out had he the breath to make any sound at all.

Damned kender's set us on fire!

"Get up! Tyorl! Get up!"

That was Finn. Tyorl tried, from long habit, to obey. He dragged a knee under himself and slipped, splashing into cold water.

Damned kender's put us in the middle of the ocean!

"Tyorl, please get up!" That was Lavim, and though Tyorl was not prepared to swear that he heard fear in the kender's voice, what he did hear there made him flounder and splash and finally push himself to his feet. He dragged a hand across his face, wiping away thick mud and slimy, clinging grasses. Staggering, he rounded on the kender. Lavim was only a small indistinct form in the smoky night.

"Name of the gods," he snarled, "where are we?"

"I—I'm sorry, Tyorl. I didn't mean for us to end up here, really I didn't. I just wanted to end up outside the city because I was feeling a little, uh, queasy, and I thought it wouldn't really be polite to turn up in somebody's house without a specific invitation. And then I kind of didn't know what to do and there was no one to ask and the whole spell just sort of fell apart about—" He scratched his head and looked around at the flames marching ever closer. "—uh, here. Are you all right?"

"Where's the flute?"

Lavim shrugged. "I don't know, I—"

"Where is the flute?"

Lavim drew a deep breath then smiled sheepishly "I have it."

"Give it to me."

"But Tyorl, I—"

"*Now!*" Tyorl roared.

Lavim meekly handed over the flute. "All right. But Piper says—"

Tyorl's voice was low, dangerous, and challenging. "Piper says what?"

"Not to throw it away. He says we might need it."

The smoke was thicker now, and, when he looked around him, Tyorl saw Finn helping Kembal to his feet. The four stood in water up to their knees, surrounded by tall marsh weeds. Only a quarter mile away, flocks of cattails, like tiny torches, were ablaze as far west as Tyorl could see. Embers from the fire and clumps of burning grass flew, wind-blown, through the thick black air. He grabbed Lavim roughly by the shoulder and jerked him around hard.

"Look."

Lavim squirmed. "I see."

"We're in the bogs, Lavim, and we're surrounded by wild-fire. Is this your idea of a little way outside the city?"

"No, but—"

Finn slogged through the mud and foul standing water. He grabbed Tyorl's arm and pointed east. "This way. I don't know a thing about these swamps, but heading for the clear is about all we can do." His blue eyes hard, he flicked a glance at Lavim, then back to the elf. "I think we should kill the little bastard and then get out of here."

Lavim, about to apologize, snapped his mouth shut. He watched as Finn vanished into the smoke and waited until Kem sloshed past before he looked up at Tyorl. "You don't think he really meant that do you?"

Tyorl didn't answer but herded Lavim ahead of him.

Piper, Lavim asked silently, you don't think Finn meant that, do you?

If he doesn't, Piper said, his mental voice sounding decidedly weak and hoarse, *I do!*

But—but, Piper, he thought, I was only trying to help. I was only trying to get—Piper?

The mage did not respond.

Aw, c'mon, Piper. Really, I only wanted to help!

Look around you, Lavim. Piper snarled. *You haven't done anything but make sure that you and your friends are going to be roasted before you get anywhere near Thorbardin.*

Lavim glanced over his shoulder and stumbled a little trying to see behind and walk ahead. The sheets of fire raging behind them were closer now, leaping and snapping and sending wild sprays of embers into the black night sky.

Lavim wisely decided to wait until they got out of the fire and the bogs before he reminded Tyorl and Piper that, while they might not actually be in Thorbardin, they were probably whole days closer.

CHAPTER 23

GNEISS OF THE DAEWAR MADE his way through the crooked alleys and paths created by the hastily built field-keeper's huts that lined the walls of the East Farming Warrens. There will not be air enough for a dwarf to breathe, he had said. Even he admitted that the complaint was hyperbole, but each time he came into the farming warrens the thought growled in his mind.

The eight hundred human refugees had managed to settle quickly. The youngest children, those who were not out in the fields with the men, scampered through the tangle of huts, their cries high and loud, echoing around the cavern walls and flying up to the roof many hundreds of feet above. Women tended the stock, the few dozen horses needed for ploughing, a rowdy herd of goats, and far, far too many chickens and ducks.

Damn place looks and smells like a ragged border town on the edge of nowhere! A note of reluctant admiration crept into the Daewar's thoughts. Reorx knew, it didn't take them long to recover from their trek across the Outlands.

Though the fields were not at all what these human farmers were used to, they'd adapted quickly to the level acres of deep black soil transported into the warrens many years ago and replenished and refreshed seasonally from the valley outside Southgate. No stone fouled the plough blades, not even the smallest grade challenged the horses or their ploughmen.

Gneiss stopped at the edge of a newly furrowed field. The dark soil glistened under the light from the many crystal shafts high above. Boys with large, heavy canvas seed pouches slung over their shoulders followed the carefully laid lines of the furrows, sowing to the left and right as they walked. Soon the wealthy black soil would be covered with a tender green carpet of new-growing wheat. Beyond this field they planted corn, and in the cavern into which this one led, millet, hay and pasturage for the stock would soon thrive.

Yes, they were doing well, Goldmoon's people. One could almost believe that Mesalax had blessed their efforts. One could almost believe that the Plainswoman did, indeed, have the goddess's favor.

Almost. Gneiss snorted. He hadn't heard that one of the gifts Mesalax granted her clerics was the ability to enchant thanes. And Hornfel was enchanted. These days it seemed that he spent more time here among the refugee farmers than in the upper cities.

And me, the Daewar thought, I have to drag down here after him like some errand lad each time I want to speak a word to him! Courting allies, he says. The best way to gain an ally is to know him, he says. Hah! What kind of allies will these ragtag refugees make? Damn poor ones, I'll wager.

Raucous and high, a child's shriek of laughter preceeded her as she pelted out from behind a hut, head down and arms flailing. She bowled into Gneiss before the Daewar could turn, staggering him, and she tumbled to the ground.

He snatched up the child by her elbows and dumped her unceremoniously on her feet again. "Easy with your wild running, lass! You've two eyes—use them!"

The two eyes so noted, wide and blue as the sea, stared at Gneiss as the girl edged cautiously toward the field.

All skinny legs and skinnier arms, Gneiss thought. Someone ought to think about feeding the thing. And what have they cut the creature's hair with? A saw's blade by the look of it.

"Hold still a moment, will you?"

The girl stopped where she stood and pushed ragged black hair back from her face.

"I'm looking for Goldmoon and—" He smiled sourly "—her prisoner Hornfel. Where are they?"

"Prisoner?" The girl's eyes grew, if possible, wider with sudden laughter. "Oh, yer jokin', Grandfather."

"Grandfather!"

She pointed with a grubby finger to his long, graying beard.

Gneiss's eyes narrowed against an unbidden smile. Impudent little scamps shouldn't be encouraged, aye, by no means.

The impudent scamp's face split in a grin. "I know where they are. I'll take you."

"Aye," the dwarf growled, "and then you'd better be taking yourself off to your mother for a wash and a combing, eh?"

She shook her head and shrugged in the most matter-of-fact manner. "Can't do it, grandfather."

"Can't you? Why not?"

"The lady Goldmoon says m' mother an' m' father have gone to be with Mishakal." The child's expression clouded. "I think they're dead."

So saying, the girl scampered away, and Gneiss had to step quickly to catch up. The children of war are fatalists, he reminded himself. He'd seen it often enough and had never become used to it, warrior though he was.

Gneiss followed the child through the winding, newly made streets to a field-keeper's hut, low-roofed and featureless, no different than all the others. Inside the tiny hut, he found Hornfel seated with the Plainswoman at a table. The half-elf was on his heels by the door, there being no place else to sit, fletching arrows with the absent skill of one who performs the chore as much to pass the time as to keep his weapons in good order. Though fox-haired Tanis and Gold-moon were often seen together as the leaders of these refugees, rumor had it that there was a great and brooding Plainsman about somewhere who might well have the right to call Goldmoon his lady. In fact, there were nine people in this motley band who had rescued the slaves from Verminaard's mine. Gneiss had only met and spoken with the half-elf and Goldmoon. The other seven either had business of their own or were happy enough to leave the matter of negotiations to these two.

It's just as well they did, Gneiss thought. He'd heard that one among the party was a hill dwarf of the ill-famed Fireforge clan. He'd no interest at all in speaking with a hill dwarf, let alone in being in the same room with one whose grandfather had fought against the mountain dwarves in the Dwarfgate Wars.

Yes, and here sits Hornfel, the Daewar thought, taking a cup of spirits with Outlanders! As though there were nothing else to concern him or the council but finding a pleasant way to pass the afternoon!

Gneiss regretted his assessment when he saw his friend's eyes. The dark shadows in the Hylar's eyes told of heavy matters discussed.

Goldmoon smiled and gestured Gneiss into the hut as though the tiny place were hers and she were proud to welcome a guest.

"You are looking for your friend? You may accurately accuse me of selfishness, Thane Gneiss. I have kept him here too long."

Chieftan's daughter was her proper title. Gneiss thought that he would like to have known her father, if only to meet the man who so well trained Goldmoon to this regality.

"Aye, lady. We've had a need of him. Hornfel," he said, "word has come from the border. *Guyll fyr*." He'd spoken the words in Dwarven and was surprised when the half-elf reacted.

"Wildfire?" Tanis, his green eyes sharp, addressed Gneiss. "Where?"

"Running down the hills west of the Plains of Death. Two border patrols reported seeing it last night. It has the wind behind it now and is moving fast."

Faster than the wind before which it ran, Gneiss thought. He'd seen the fire at dawn from the Northgate walls. Garish light leaping for the soft opal sky, the *guyll fyr* had looked like a sea of flame, its waves lapping at the forest shore of the mountains' feet. Smoke, thick and black, rose in columns to the sky or streamed out ahead of the rampaging flame as it danced with the cold winds whirling above the Plains of Death. It's lurid glare and deadly smoke had made the dawn's light seem a pale and sickly thing.

Gneiss turned to Hornfel. "You're needed in the council chambers, my friend. That and other matters want your attention."

Goldmoon, she of the silver-gilt hair and wide blue eyes, rose from the shaky-legged table where she sat. "The fire."

Gneiss nodded gruffly. "Aye, lady?"

"How did it start? Do you know?"

"No, lady, but you and yours are safe enough here." He saw Hornfel grimace and shrugged. "That was your concern?"

"No," she said softly. "I know we are safe here. I know, too, what happens when wildfire hits the plains. I've seen it, but never this late in the season."

"You're thinking of Verminaard's dragons, are you?"

"I am."

"Aye, well, I've had the same thought, lady." For Hornfel's sake, for his friend seemed to value this Plainswoman, this so-called cleric of Mesalax, Gneiss tried for a more formal tone. "Lady Goldmoon, this is a council matter. I hope you will grant us your leave."

Goldmoon said nothing, but when Hornfel and Gneiss left the cramped little hut, Tanis went with them. Hornfel seemed to have no objection and Gneiss did not protest, but only kept a little ahead, preoccupied with wondering why his words had sounded so churlish in his own ears.

Thorbardin was made up of six small cities deep inside the mountain. These cities connected to each other and the several auxiliary halls and two great gates by a series of roads and transport shafts, which the two dwarves knew well. They took their roads seemingly without thinking, as those do who are born and have lived all their lives in such a place. The noise of the merchants square and the quiet of the gardens moved around them like sunlight and shadows.

Tanis walked quietly behind the two thanes, well content with his observations and his own thoughts. As the three stepped onto a short, narrow bridge spanning the fathoms-deep main cavern in which the cities were built, Gneiss, hearing the half-elf's softly drawn breath, looked up and then around.

The bridge, its arching roof and broad floor constructed of perfectly square cuts of dark and light granite, was empty of anything but shadows and the sound of their own breathing. From the esplanade ahead came the shouts and laughter of dwarven children at play. The gardens behind were silent as shadows.

"What is it?" Gneiss whispered.

Tanis held up a hand, head cocked to listen. Leather on stone, they heard the scuff of a footstep. The half-elf reached for his short sword; Hornfel's fingers closed around the grip of the small dagger at his hip.

"In the shadows," the Hylar said.

Even as he spoke, the shadows, which seemed to perch on the edge of the bridge, flowing up from the cavern yawning below, took on substance and form. A superstitious chill skittered along Gneiss's neck. He recognized the dwarf who stepped away from the darkness and, seeming not to have seen the three, turned and entered the esplanade.

A Theiwar, one of Realgar's *derro* magelings.

Tanis, his thumb absently stroking the hilt of his short sword looked from Hornfel to Gneiss. "Who is it?"

"Don't know his name," Gniess grunted.

"Dhegan," Hornfel said. "Aye, Dhegan. One of Realgar's—underlings."

He might well have said "assassins," Gneiss thought. He shook his head and headed toward the esplanade and light.

As he walked, the Daewar noted that Hornfel gave Tanis no word of explanation. Adept at understanding what his old friend did not say, as well as what he did, Gneiss realized that the half-elf did not accompany them for the opportunity to see the city. At some time in the past day or night, Hornfel must have discussed the political climate of the dwarven kingdom with the two leaders of the refugees. Tanis Half-Elven, Outlander and stranger, walked with them not only as a companion but as a bodyguard as well.

Aye, well, they're protecting their interests. The first thing the damned Theiwar will do after he begins his revolution is get rid of these refugees.

Suddenly, the Daewar wanted to see the light, to feel it. Soon he would have to fight. He did not want to fight in the shadows.

Darknight had no love for the fire's light. Realgar ignored its impatient snarl and turned his back to the torch in the wall cresset. His shadow, black and ragged, leaped out before him, crawling across the rough stone floor of the dragon's lair. A thread of fury raced through the Theiwar like a line of flame. His right hand moved to the scabbarded sword at his hip, fingers tracing the silver chasing and the pattern of the inlaid sapphires on the hilt. As though he touched some calm-giving talisman, his anger cooled. He signaled to the two guards waiting behind him in the shadows. Between them, the guards dragged a heavy, unyielding burden into the light.

Dead meat! Darknight growled, a jagged sound of protest and anger. Beyond its reach, in the smaller cavern outside its lair lay better food: the one-handed dwarf and the human girl Realgar had taken prisoner at dawn. The dragon thought of the live meat and then eyed the corpse of a dead dwarven guard.

"Is this what you are feeding me?"

Realgar laughed, a sound like breathing ice. "Are you still hungry, then? A goat and calf were not enough? Aye, dragon, you've an endless appetite." He rounded on Darknight, his eyes flaring anger. "The ranger is gone! I found this one in the prison cave where he should have been! You're hungry? Well and good. Blunt the edge of it on this carcass and find the ranger for me. Then you'll have better meat. Not before."

Darknight snaked its neck forward, its great nostrils distending. Carrion was an insult, but its belly rumbled with hunger. It sank dagger fangs into the shoulder of the dead guard, bit down hard and snapped bones.

Realgar took no notice, but jerked his thumb at the two guards and spoke a word of curt dismissal. He turned his back on the dragon and the corpse at its feet. He drew the Kingsword from the scabbard.

Oily torch smoke streamed across the jeweled hilt.

The god-touched heart of the blade quickened beneath the sliding light of the flame. Realgar lifted the sword high in both hands, brought it slowly down to eye level. His breath, short and quick, clouded the steel. Through the veil, the crimson heart glowed, undiminished.

A Kingsword, Stormblade was innocent of any rune or marking.

"Those," he whispered to the sword, "those will come later to mark the deeds of my reign. King regent?" His eyes narrowed. "No. High king."

No regent, he thought now as he lowered the blade; no caretaker for the throne of high king, waiting to the last days of my life for a mythical Hammer to be found. I will be high king!

Darknight stretched its neck again and brought its head, low and almost touching the damp stone, to within reach of the dwarf. The great beast's eye was almost at a level with Realgar's. "What do I guard them for, Lord, if not my own dinner?"

Realgar smiled coldly, his eyes strayed from the Kingsword to his prisoners still lying in the darkness where his guards had thrown them. His sleep spell would wear off soon enough. He smiled again to think of them waking to find the dragon brooding hungrily over them. The swordcrafter's apprentice, Stanach, and the human girl would be saved for better things than Darknight's belly.

Saved for my crowning ceremonies, he thought, where I will thank them for bringing me the Kingsword, then cut their hearts out for seeking to keep it from me. To the dragon he said nothing, only shrugged.

Darknight raised its head, its great fangs dripping, its breath stinking of its recent kills. "Lord?"

Realgar held himself perfectly still, though his skin crawled to have the dragon's fangs so near his neck. "You guard them at my command. It should be reason enough."

The dragon contented itself with imagining how pleased Verminaard would be to hang the sword on the wall of Pax Tharkas's throne room above the skull of this arrogant lordling.

Realgar smelled victory the way a wolf smells prey. It was near and he only had to leap to catch it. His assassins stalked the other thanes, lesser wolves but as hungry. Darknight curled its tail tightly around its flanks and stretched its lipless mouth in silent laughter.

These stalkers, too, would be denied their prey until Realgar gave the word to feast. That word would not be given until Hornfel was dead.

The dragon watched as Realgar, his captives forgotten, held the sword up to the flame again, watched his eyes track the light down the edges of the blade. Crimson light and glittering, it splashed like the shadows of blood across the dwarf's hands.

The Hylar would die soon, fallen to Realgar's dark schemes. Aye, coward, the dragon sneered, you kill your great enemy in the dark and the shadows, secretly with a sword's blade through the back. Do you really think that the deaths of lesser folk, achieved in the light and before the eyes of whoever remains in this wretched kingdom, will prove your courage?

Realgar sheathed the sword with slow, almost ceremonial motions. He turned back to the dragon, a strange, knowing smile on his lips. "You hear my thoughts, do you, Sevristh?"

Darknight stretched its wings with preening grace.

"Aye, you hear them and that's good. Keep listening. I'll need you to fly once more before this is done, and it will likely be that I can't call you any other way."

Wings settling tightly over its sleek ebony flanks, the dragon snaked its tongue, flickering, around the edges of its fangs. "Oh, aye, Lord. I am, as always, yours to command."

Darknight watched him leave, listened to the confident voice of his thoughts, and found not even the smallest trace of doubt in his plans or in the dragon's intentions. He was thinking about a high kingship and the dark road leading to his goal.

Well and good, Darknight thought, using his own phrase. It ran the edges of its claws scraping along the stone floor and nuzzled the half-eaten carcass of the dwarven guard and imagined that the bones it snapped between its powerful jaws were Realgar's.

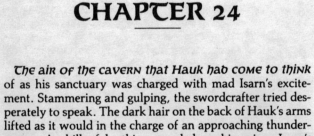

CHAPTER 24

The air of the cavern that Hauk had come to think of as his sanctuary was charged with mad Isarn's excitement. Stammering and gulping, the swordcrafter tried desperately to speak. The dark hair on the back of Hauk's arms lifted as it would in the charge of an approaching thunderstorm. A chill of loathing crawled up his spine. Isarn's efforts to control his excitement made his face writhe and contort so that he could barely force an intelligible word past his lips.

Hauk got his legs under him and sat, putting his back against the stone wall of the cave that was their sanctuary. "Easy and slow," he whispered. "Tell me again."

"The lad. The elfmaid. The lad."

Hauk didn't know how to answer. He didn't know what

Isarn was trying to tell him. Yet, for all the panic he saw in the dwarf's eyes, he thought the swordcrafter was more clear-minded than he'd been in days.

"Tell me," he said again. For the sake of uncovering Isarn's information, Hauk made his own voice as gentle as he could, trying not to communicate his own urgency. He didn't know how long it would be—a matter of moments or an hour—that Isarn would remain sane enough to talk.

The pattern of the dwarf's lucid moments had gradually changed over the time they'd been in hiding. The light in his eyes was sometimes sharp and focused for greater lengths of time, but at less frequent intervals. When he was mad, he trod a frantic, pacing path around the cavern. Then he reminded Hauk of a sparrow caught in a closed barn, fluttering to find escape, battering himself against the walls. Nothing could calm him but some inner word from himself.

When he was sane, as he seemed to be now, his eyes were as quiet as shady pools under a stream's banks. His hands were at rest, his pacing not even a thing he remembered. Then, he would sit beside Hauk, speaking in low tones as one would to a friend who had been long ill but looks now to recovery.

His solicitous care did not make Hauk want any less to kill him. The ranger was not thinking of killing now, though he could and did, still long for it.

Isarn drew a long, steady breath. He leaned forward, his eyes eager, and Hauk feared that the eagerness would precipitate another one of the dwarf's frantic pacing fits of insanity. "Stormblade has come home!"

Hauk sat perfectly still and almost didn't breathe.

"Listen," Isarn whispered, "listen to me. The masterblade is here. The Kingsword is back in the heart of the world where it was born!"

Hauk still didn't move.

"Do you hear me?" Isarn's hands worked in quick, jerky motions, scrubbing and scrubbing. The stillness of the pool was about to be shattered.

"I hear you," the ranger whispered.

Ranger-girl, he thought, little barmaid! He's found you! Ah, gods, no! He's found you!

"Aye, back where it belongs, back with me, who gave it heart and life. Back with me for the thane. Aye, the thane, the king who will be. Returned with the lad."

His heart filled with fear, Hauk asked a quick question. "What lad?"

"The boy, the boy I trained. The boy. Young Stanach."

"An apprentice?"

"Aye, aye, the lad. And a girl, dressed as an elf and tall as one. But no elf she! No. A fire-haired girl with jade eyes."

Isarn screamed as Hauk grabbed his wrist. A fire-haired girl with jade eyes had carried Stormblade to Thorbardin! His ranger-girl, his barmaid!

"Tell me about the girl! Tell me!"

The dwarf pulled back, but a rabbit might as well have tried to pull back from a wolf's jaws. Squirming, he gasped something, a panting that Hauk didn't understand.

"Tell me!"

"Realgar," he cried. Fear shot through Hauk like the lightning's strike. He ground the bones of the dwarf's thin wrist in his grasp. "Realgar has them! Realgar—has my sword and the lad and the elfmaid who is no elfmaid!"

"Where?"

"In *derro* tunnels. In hiding."

"Why?" Hauk snapped. "Tell my why!"

"I don't—I don't know."

"Take me to them, old one, or I'll snap your wrist like a twig."

It was never much of a battle. There was that in his eyes which lead Hauk to think that Isarn's surrender was planned. He understood suddenly that the old dwarf wanted him to retrieve his precious Stormblade.

Anger, like fire, seared through Hauk. His ranger-girl, his barmaid had been taken. He didn't stop to think why he thought of her as his now. Perhaps because she had, for such a long time, represented the only thing Realgar had not taken from him. It didn't matter. He'd find Isarn's Stormblade for the girl's sake.

CHAPTER 25

Stanach stared into empty darkness, listening to the rumble and gusting of the dragon's breath. Like a small echo of the dragon's breathing, he heard Kelida's shuddering sigh. Unmoving, as she had been since they'd been brought to this place, the girl lay huddled beside him. His eyes on the dragon, Stanach moved his hand slowly to the side. He slipped his fingers around her wrist and tried to feel her lifebeat. Slow and steady as it was, it did not ease Stanach's fear. Realgar's sleep spell was taking far too long to wear off.

He put his back to cold stone again, his heart lurching each time the dragon yawned or stretched, each time Kelida stirred and the huge beast looked their way.

Dual chambered, the cavern held the small cave where Stanach sat now and the broad, high-ceilinged lair of the dragon. The separation of the chambers was marked only by a broadening of the stony floor and a sudden high leaping of the walls. The walls, he realized, did not soar to a ceiling but to what surely must be the sky. From the high entrance to the dragon's lair, echoes of the wind sweeping the mountainside moaned in the caves.

His own natural dark-sight showed Stanach the dim red outline of the dragon where it lay in its lair. He tried to estimate the distance and thought that nearly fifty yards of rough stone floor lay between them and the beast.

Aye, he thought, and it can cross that in an instant!

A smoldering fire burned from his right wrist to his shoulder. Realgar's guards had not been gentle. Yet, for all the awakened fire in his arm and shoulder, Stanach's hand, still bandaged, had no feeling at all. He now knew that he had not Kem's salves to thank for the absence of pain. He would never again feel anything in that hand. No, not even pain. Broken bones, aye, even twisted bones, could be mended. Shredded muscle could never be healed.

Stanach saw the yellow, malevolent gleam of the dragon's eyes.

Its breathing quickened, like the pumping of a bellows. He felt its hunger as a dread deep within his bones, and he felt it waiting. It had been commanded not to dispatch Realgar's prisoners yet, only to guard them. And so it waited.

Darknight, Realgar called it. Some time ago it had been brought two goats and a screaming calf to sate its appetite. Stanach still smelled the blood, a thick, coppery reek on its breath. Among the animal's bones lay the shreds of the black and silver uniform of a Theiwar guard.

Kelida stirred, a small moving of her hand, and fell still again.

Too long, Stanach thought. She's been unconscious too long.

How much time had passed? He had only scattered memories of waking in this place deep below the cities. For a time his mind had been thick with confusion and the aftereffects of Realgar's sleep spell. Then, as in dreams, time had little meaning. Even now, listening to the dragon breathing,

Stanach only remembered the few moments after Darknight set down in a deep ravine below the Northgate ledge.

A squad of six Theiwar, Realgar at its head, had poured from the mouth of a cave like bats seeking the night. Each of the six had crossbows trained on Stanach and Kelida, bolts anchored and ready to be loosed at their thane's command. Realgar had issued no such order. He bade the two dismount and they did, both expecting every minute to feel the shock of a bolt flying home.

Three of the guards had surrounded Stanach the moment his feet touched stone. They disarmed him neatly and in seconds. While one guard kept Stanach well in his bow's range, two others grabbed his arms and hustled him toward the gaping hole of darkness that was the cave's mouth. At the entrance, despite his captors' holds, Stanach dug in his heels and wrestled himself around to see Kelida similarly surrounded.

Realgar approached her, strange dark eyes alight, hands twitching restlessly as though anticipating the feel of Stormblade's cool, golden hilt.

His guards' hands tightened on Stanach's arms. They yanked his arms tightly behind him, sending white-hot bolts of pain shooting from his elbows to his shoulders. Stunned by the pain, Stanach watched Kelida's disarming through a dizzying, red-shot haze.

Stanach's stomach turned over as he remembered Realgar's slow reach for the Kingsword, saw again how he almost touched the sapphired hilt, then drew back. He had motioned the guards away. Very gently, Realgar unbuckled the sword belt from Kelida's waist.

Stanach closed his eyes now, trying not to hear again Kelida's soft moan, trying not to hear his own cry of outrage and horror as Realgar buckled on the swordbelt and smiled.

Now, in an echo of that thin despairing moan, Kelida's breath caught once in her throat. Stanach reached for her hand again, covered it, and leaned close to her.

"*Lyt chwaer*," he whispered, so low that he barely heard the words himself, "easy, now. I'm here."

The cave was blacker than a moonless midnight and she, a human, had no dark-sight. Stanach felt her hand quivering in his.

Darknight rumbled deep in its chest and snaked its neck around, a baleful yellow light in its eyes as it observed the prisoners. Then, as though disinterested, the huge black dragon backed away. Kelida's hand went cold and limp in Stanach's as the rough sound of scales dragging on stone, dagger claws scraping, echoed in the cave.

Stanach closed his fingers around Kelida's hand again, holding her still and silent until Darknight withdrew completely. How long would Realgar's command hold the dragon?

Slowly, as silently as he could, Stanach shifted his position and released Kelida's hand. She caught her breath and grabbed his arm, a drowning woman clinging to her only hold in a black, cold sea. Her voice was low and thin, tight with panic. "I can't—I can't see."

"Oh, aye, you can, Kelida. You just can't see here. Quietly, now, hold on to me and sit up."

She moved slowly. She got the stone wall against her back and pushed herself straight.

"Better? How is your head? Hurts, I'll wager." He tried for as careless a tone as he could, hearing it ring false in his own ears. "Aye, it's the sleep spell. All the headache of a good flask of dwarf spirits and none of the fun."

In its lair, Darknight moaned low and deep, scales whispered again on stone. Kelida gasped, then held perfectly still.

"Just the dragon." Stanach said as he might have said just the rabbit. "We're safe enough for the moment."

"Where—where is it?"

Stanach shrugged. "In its lair, playing watchdog." He lied smoothly. "It's not interested in us."

Did she believe it? Stanach didn't think so.

"Why can't I see?"

Stanach snorted. "Because there's no light. In the Outlands there's always light. Even on the cloudiest night, it gets caught between the ground and the sky. Here, in the heart of the world, there's no light unless we make it."

"But—you can see me."

Darknight sighed a gust of breath reeking with blood.

Stanach spoke quickly to still the panic he sensed rising in Kelida.

"All living things give off warmth. Things not having life, stone and mountain, those hold the day's light. That's what I see, the outline of that warmth. You're a dimensionless form, but I see that very well. If you could see my eyes right now, I don't think you'd like them. The pupils are so wide, expanding to get the little bit of light, that they look like bottomless pits."

Kelida drew in a long breath and let it out in a slow, almost silent sigh. "What's going to happen to us?"

Stanach didn't know how to answer. He shook his head, then remembered that she couldn't see the gesture. "*Lyt chwaer*, I don't know. Realgar has Stormblade now. I don't know why he hasn't killed us already."

Kelida was silent for a long moment. Stanach felt her fingers tighten again around his hand. He knew what she'd say next.

"Then—then Hauk is dead."

Stanach swallowed hard and said nothing.

"Stanach?"

"Aye," he whispered. "Hauk's dead."

How could he read such grief, such pain, in a depthless outline of red light?

"*Lyt chwaer*," he whispered.

She buried her face in his shoulder. Stanach felt her tears warm on his neck as she silently wept. *Lyt chwaer*, he named her, little sister. She'd comforted him in his grief, cared for him after his maiming, her hands gentle, her ministrations tender as a sister's.

Stanach held her tightly as she wept. Over her shoulder, he saw his right arm, outlined in the red glow of his body's warmth. His hand, bandaged in the torn strips of her cloak, lay heavy and nerveless against her back. Lifeless as it was, no light edged the place where his hand should have been.

"I'm sorry," he whispered. "Kelida, I'm sorry."

Kelida suddenly went stiff in his arms, then limp as though unable to bear the burden of some new grief. Her voice thick and ragged with silent weeping, she said, "I—I killed him."

261

Stanach caught his breath, not certain he'd heard her correctly. He held her away, trying to see her face, her eyes, and saw nothing but a trembling red outline.

"Kelida, what are you saying?"

"I should have—I should have guarded the sword better." Her hands, like the ghosts of red birds, covered her face. "No. I should have given it to you or Tyorl. If I'd kept it safe—if you could have brought it to your thane—" She drew a rough breath. "Oh, Stanach! If I hadn't been such a fool about carrying it, about—about holding on to it, he'd still be alive!"

"No," Stanach whispered. "No, Kelida, that's not true. There's nothing you could have done."

"If I'd let you have the sword instead of pretending that—that because I had it, I had something of him. Oh, instead of pretending that he gave it to me because—because he cared. That he would remember me and maybe he would—"

"No!" he cried harshly.

The echo of that cry rebounded from the walls of the small cavern, thin protests. Claws scraped again on stone. Darknight rumbled deep in its chest. Yellow eyes gleamed from across the cavern. The beast didn't move, yet Stanach was sure it was laughing.

He held Kelida's arm with his left hand and let his feelingless right hand fall.

"Kelida, I'm sorry. Oh, gods, I am sorry! Hauk's death—it was never a thing you could prevent."

She swallowed hard and shook her head. "Yes, if I—"

"No," he whispered, "no. Hauk is dead, aye, but you had nothing to do with it. Kelida, he was likely dead before we left Long Ridge."

She drew away from him, slowly as though edging away from a suddenly drawn dagger. "But, you said . . ." Her voice dropped to a shuddering sigh as she groped for understanding. "No, Stanach. You said . . ."

"I lied. I needed the sword. I lied to you."

She moaned softly.

Stanach leaned his head against the stone wall and closed his eyes. He didn't say that he was sorry, though only Reorx knew that he had never in his life been sorrier for anything.

Aye, not even for the loss of the Kingsword. He couldn't find the words for how he felt; he didn't think they existed in any language.

After a long time spent listening to the growling breath of the dragon and the stilling of Kelida's sobs, Stanach felt her hand light on his right arm. She lifted his hand, wrapped in the rags of her cloak. Because he heard the faint whisper of her fingers passing over the bandage, he knew that she held his ruined hand.

Guyll fyr raced madly across the windswept Plains of Death. Long narrow fingers of flame charged ahead of the main body of the fire, blazing outriders bearing pennons brighter than the sun. Greedy for pillage, the fire raged through swamp and marsh, feeding on thin grasses and brittle, dry bracken.

Standing before the worktable in the Chamber of the Black Moon, Realgar watched the fire in the smooth, clear surface of the glass. A simple spell of seeing had called the vision to the glass, and like a man on a mountaintop, he watched the fire's advance.

Well satisfied, he whispered a word as he passed his hand over the table. The scene shifted, becoming more focused and sharper.

A marsh rat scuttled to ground beneath a shallow, reedy pool and died a length from its nest, its blood boiled in water suddenly heated.

An emerald-headed duck caught in an airless pocket burst its lungs with a last effort to rise to flight and escape the flames.

A long-legged crane and a prowling silver fox fled the advance of a common enemy. Pitiless, the *guyll fyr* caught and killed them as it did every creature in its path. The once cold air above the Plains writhed under the heat of the fire's passing. The wind, ever a lost and mad traveler across the Plains of Death, twisted the path of the flames.

To the mage, the fire appeared as a furious and deranged beast, rearing and bucking in explosive sheets of flame. The *guyll fyr* charged toward the foothills of the mountains, hissing over the marshes and roaring toward the fuller feast of a forest thick with sap-rich pines and panicked, fleeing wildlife.

Realgar turned away from the scenes of destruction. They wove a tapestry of lurid and violent death, but there was one thread more to be woven in order to make the picture complete. Realgar had that thread in his hands now.

Though no regular Guard of Watch had been set in ruined Northgate in many years, one had been now. The crumbled gate, useless since the ruinous battles of the Dwarfgate Wars, was unofficially sanctioned as a Theiwar holding. Realgar dropped to a seat behind the glass table and laughed. The watch was composed of Gneiss's faithful Daewar.

Faithful all, he thought. Or almost all. Anyone can be corrupted, even a Daewar guard.

One such was even now looking for Hornfel with the word that Gneiss wished to meet him on the Northgate wall. The treacherous guard would bring the message that the Daewar thane had seen the *guyll fyr* sweep down to set the Plains of Death ablaze. The message would rise in urgency as the false guard relayed Gneiss's supposed anxiety about the danger to Thorbardin's food supply.

Reluctant as Hornfel might be to enter even unsanctioned Theiwar territory, the Hylar knew that Northgate was the only place to track the fire's progress. He'd be comfortable enough in the belief that he was going to meet Gneiss.

Only it was not Gneiss who would be waiting for Hornfel in Northgate. It would be Realgar. And Stormblade.

Realgar ran his palm along the scabbarded sword at his side.

"Aye," he whispered, "you've searched long for the Kingsword, Hornfel, and you'll find it in Northgate. You'll see it at last and you will die on it!"

The hand of the goddess Takhisis, the Dark Queen, was extended to him. He need only reach to take it. The spark of revolution that would ignite tinder-dry Thorbardin would give life to the start of a *derro* reign.

Realgar closed his eyes, slipped easily into the language of the mind, and called the black dragon.

Have you found the ranger?

Darknight had not. A thread of impatience drifted through the Theiwar's mental speech. *It doesn't matter now. This will be over soon. We'll find him then.*

A thought, a command, and Realgar sent the black dragon flying for the mountaintops. Darknight would stand ready to back up his attack on Hornfel and then on Gneiss's guards at both Northgate and Southgate.

Gneiss paused in the center of the garden outside Court of Thanes. The air was thick with the scent of white dog rose and scarlet queen's plume. He had no inclination to admire either and was uncomfortable with the gentle serenity suggested by the garden. Beyond the green boxwood borders, Thorbardin had a strange and brooding air. In that way that a city's people have, the populace scented trouble. Though few could identify it, all seemed to be reacting to it with shortened tempers and anxious looks.

Gneiss turned to leave, taking the shortest path back to the street. When he walked past the small pond at the garden's east border, he realized that the garden was not as empty as he'd thought it. The Outlander Tanis Half-Elven crouched at the water's edge, idly pitching pebbles into the water.

Tanis turned sharply at the sound of the dwarf's approach and visibly relaxed as he recognized the Daewar.

"If you're looking for Hornfel," Tanis said mildly, "he's not here."

"I can see that." Gneiss eyed him carefully. "Something you need here?"

The half-elf shook his head. "Just enjoying the garden." When Gneiss's careful look became one of slight suspicion, Tanis smiled. "Easy, Gneiss. Hornfel was here a moment ago. We were talking and a guard—one of your own by the livery—called him away."

"Say where he was going?"

"Not to me."

An awkward moment of silence fell between the two. Tanis, his long green eyes hooded, scratched his beard. "Gneiss, you don't like me, do you?"

Caught off guard, Gneiss stammered, "I haven't an opinon one way or the other."

"Oh yes, you do." Tanis settled back on his heels and pitched another pebble into the pond. "You don't like Outlanders, and you especially don't want them in Thorbardin. Tell me, why did you finally vote to shelter those refugees?"

"Because all of Hornfel's arguments made sense." Gneiss said curtly. He narrowed his eyes. "What do you want, Half-Elven?"

"Safety for the refugees." Tanis got to his feet with easy grace and let the pebbles fall from his hand.

"You've got it."

"Aye? Not as long as they're in danger of being caught between the anvil and the hammer. Or both sides of a revolution." Tanis looked out beyond the fragrant boxwood hedges to the street outside. "They're nervous out there, Gneiss. Tell me you can't taste it in the air."

Gneiss said nothing. He did not consider Thorbardin's politics and problems fit matter for discussion with an Outlander.

"It's very uncomfortable in the middle, Gneiss. Before you came, Hornfel and I were talking about that. The refugees will fight if they have to. It would be better if they were fighting with you, and not in spite of you. If a revolution does break out here, you are going to need our help."

Gneiss shook his head. "Not the help of untrained farmers, I don't."

The half-elf ran a gentle finger along the edge of a half-blown spray of queen's plume. The featherlike blossom left a faint dusting of golden pollen on his knuckle. "What about the help of the people who freed those refugees from slavery—snatched them from under Verminaard's nose, Gneiss!—and brought them here all the way from Pax Tharkas?"

Eight hundred, Gneiss thought. Maybe half of them would be able to fight, or at least defend the East Warrens if it came to that.

But he didn't think it would come to that. Realgar would not mount his revolution if he were not certain that he would win. Yet, if Realgar did strike, it would be because Rance had thrown in his lot with the Theiwar. The first strike would have to be hard and disabling. The two *derro* thanes would not waste time trying a first strike on the remote farming warrens in the east of Thorbardin. There was no need to involve the half-elf or his refugees.

Or was there?

Gneiss eyed Tanis again. This time there was no suspicion or mistrust in his gauging. He smiled slowly. There was not any certain way to know when, or even if, the *derro* would strike. But there was a way to assure that their blow, if struck, would be weakened.

The East Warrens opened into Rance's Daergar city from the north and the south. Pinned in their city like rats in holes, the Daergar would find it difficult to support Realgar's attempt at revolution.

He looked at Tanis and raised an eyebrow. "I don't know much about farmers, Half-Elven. I'd imagine that they have to be good at trapping vermin to protect their crops."

Tanis shrugged. "I would imagine."

Gneiss stroked his silvered beard. "Then I might have a job for your farmers after all." He bent to retrieve one of Tanis's pebbles and pitched it into the pond. Like echoes, the ripples of the stone's strike sighed out to the edges of the water.

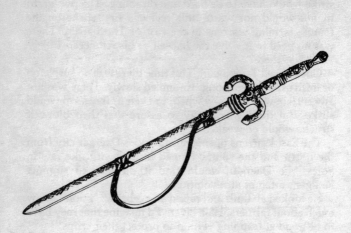

CHAPTER 26

Tyorl sagged against the rough barked trunk of a tall pine. His hunting leathers hung wet and heavy on him, covered with mud from the bogs, smeared with black ash and mud. His legs strengthless, his arms and back a mass of aching muscle and bone, he knew that if it were not for the tree's support he would fall.

Smoke and ash sent hot tears running down his face. Shivering with cold, Tyorl wiped his eyes with the heels of his hands, smearing soot and mud across pale cheeks in the horrible semblance of a mourner's ashes.

Behind him raged a swiftly advancing wall of flame. *Guy-ll fyr* rioted in the bog, flames shooting high into the sky. Pillars of fire pierced the thick roil of smoke billowing toward the foothills. There would not be more than a few moments for him and his friends to rest.

"Finn," he rasped. The word caught in Tyorl's hot, dry throat. "Finn, what do you know of these mountains?"

Finn shook his head, his lips twitching in a bitter, cynical smile. "I'm no dwarf. I know as much as anyone does of this arm of the mountains—which is about nothing. I hear the dwarves call these foothills and mountains the Outlands. But then, they have never been ones to encourage visitors. Pity you don't have your broken-handed friend with you now."

A pity, indeed, Tyorl thought. While the young dwarf had never been a favorite companion, he would be useful now. But Stanach, ever cold and silently brooding, was likely dead.

Tyorl winced at the callousness of the thought. Cold Stanach had always been, and distant, but Tyorl knew that Stanach had leaped for the dragon and hauled himself, one-handed and exhausted, onto the beast's back more for Kelida's sake than for that damned Stormblade.

Tyorl shook his head, tired with running and tired with thinking. His companions were both dead now. They were part of Stormblade's bloody toll.

Finn coughed in the thickening air and Tyorl looked up. "We are guideless, Finn. We'll have to do the best we can and make outrunning the *guyll fyr* our goal."

"Not all of us will see the goal." Finn gestured toward Lavim.

The kender, too, braced against a pine's supporting trunk. His head low, Lavim's heaving gasps for breath shuddered through his small body, rattling in his chest like wind in the reeds. He'd been limping the last mile, muttering about stones in his boot.

There was a big enough hole in one of the kender's old boots to support the excuse. Still, it was an excuse Tyorl did not believe. Even now, thinking himself unobserved, Lavim bent over his right knee, rubbing it with slow, careful strokes. He'd wrenched it hard coming out of the bog.

Tyorl glanced at Finn. The rangerlord shook his head again, a light of pity in his smoke blue eyes. Though Finn had argued for cutting the kender's throat and leaving him in the swamp, his anger, as always, had been short-lived. It was he who hauled Lavim, cursing and sputtering, out of the last and deepest waters.

We are the last of four who set out, Lavim and I, the elf thought. And none of us really knew a thing about the others but their names. He suddenly realized that, in a handful of days, these people had become important to him. The deaths of two of them—aye, even grim Stanach!—would echo darkly in his heart for long years.

Tyorl pushed away from the tree.

"We're wasting time. Stanach isn't with us. I know the direction he intended to take. South of the bog and east. I know little about Thorbardin, but I do know that we must be yet north of the place. The winds are pushing the fire north and east. It will be a hard road up and south to Thorbardin. We'd best get moving now while we still can.

"As for Lavim, he'll get as far as I do, Finn, because when he can't go any farther I will carry him."

Without a backward look, Tyorl left the rangerlord and went to join Lavim. Dropping to one knee, he laid a hand on the old kender's shoulder. Lavim looked around and flashed his ever-present grin. It took him a moment, though, to get that grin rightly in place.

"How are you, kenderkin? Are you ready for another run?"

"I'm ready, Tyorl, whenever you are. And I think—well, that is Piper thinks—"

"Piper thinks what?" Tyorl said warily.

"He thinks that he can guide us to Thorbardin from here. He sort of recognizes some of the landmarks, and he says you're right about heading south and east. He wants to know if you'll let him be the guide for a while."

A ghost as a guide? Tyorl sighed tiredly. Why not? When fleeing a house afire one abandons everything in an effort to get out alive. He turned to look at the western sky, crimson and roiling with thick black smoke.

"Well, we've no guide at all now. Tell Piper I'd be grateful for his help." Tyorl smiled. "But let me tell Finn about it, aye?"

Lavim nodded, grinning. "He's not real fond of Piper, is

he?"

"Let's say he's not fond of the idea of Piper."

Tyorl ran the flat of his hand absently along the smooth cherry wood flute at his belt. He'd snatched it from Lavim in the bog and fastened it to his belt by its leather thong. He hadn't let it out of his sight since.

Tyorl smiled.

He'd make Finn understand somehow. It was time to abandon everything, including all the good sense he once credited himself with having.

Hauk had no idea where he was, and he was quickly growing tired of the feeling. There was no way of determining direction under the mountain, with no landmarks to follow and no light but that spilling from Isarn's leaping torch. He followed that torch through dark and deep corridors the way he would follow the pole star in strange lands.

Isarn had drawn, from among the supplies he had in the sanctuary cave, a dagger and a sword. These he'd given to Hauk with a proud light in his mad old eyes.

"I made them," he said simply, watching Hauk test the balance of the finely crafted weapons. "Carry them. I will carry the torch."

The dagger in his belt, the sword in his hand, Hauk felt better than he had in many long days. Weaponed, he felt almost whole again, almost strong. He'd accepted the steel with a curt nod of thanks.

The tunnels through which Isarn led him seemed labyrinthine, winding and turning with no pattern or reason. Some were wide, with cressets for torches on smooth, high-reaching walls. Others were narrow and cramped and so low that Hauk had to stoop to get through. The smoke of Isarn's torch coiled back and caught in Hauk's lungs, choking him. At the end of one of these, shoulders aching and back stiff, he caught Isarn by the arm and halted him.

"How much farther? And where are we?"

The old swordcrafter slipped away from Hauk's hand. "Deep Warrens. Not much farther. Only a few tunnels."

"Aye? If they're no higher than the last, I'll be no good to anyone."

Isarn said nothing, only shrugged as though to suggest that the tunnels hadn't been delved for tall Outlanders in the first place. They hadn't been delved for the common traffic of Thorbardin either. In many places, Isarn found them a tight passing as well. When, at the end of another corridor, Hauk saw the dwarf bend low, he groaned inwardly and dropped to his hands and knees.

I'm going to be on my belly, he thought, before I ever come to where this crazy old bastard is taking me!

So low was the ceiling in this tunnel that Hauk imagined he could feel the whole weight of the mountain pressing down on him. So narrow were the walls that rough stone scraped against his shoulders and arms. The smoke of Isarn's torch poured back over his shoulder and then suddenly eddied ahead, caught by a cold crosscurrent of air.

Hauk realized then that this was no corridor at all but a kind of passage between corridors. He dragged himself out of the tunnel on his elbows and cautiously climbed to his feet.

Isarn, calm and almost steady till now, shuffled from foot to foot. His breathing quickened, his hands trembled so that the torchlight was useless for anything but making the walls of the corridor seem to dance and sway.

"What is it?" Hauk whispered.

"Here. They're here. The lad and the girl."

Hauk's heart lurched suddenly, leaping hard against the cage of his ribs. "Where?"

Isarn didn't answer but to press the torch into Hauk's hand and slip into the weaving shadows and darkness ahead. Hauk followed, his mouth dry, his blood singing high in his ears.

She was here! The fire-haired girl whose name he'd never known. The memory of her, straight and slim, green eyes shining, had kept him whole and sane through all the torments that Realgar had inflicted upon him. When he couldn't tell whether he was dead or alive, when he'd seen and felt Tyorl's death, known that he'd killed him and known that he hadn't, the girl's eyes had shown like emeralds in his heart.

She was here.

Slowly, following the sound of Isarn's agitated breathing, Hauk edged around a corner. Orange light from the torch spilled across the far wall, revealing the dwarf where he knelt before a jagged crack in the stone. Just barely wide enough for Hauk to fit through, the gap reached from the floor to well out of the ranger's sight.

"In there?"

Isarn nodded. "Aye. The lad and—"

Low and ominous, a rumbling filled the corridor, rising to a high scream in which Hauk somehow recognized dark, fierce joy. The stone itself seemed to vibrate with that cry, to sing echoes back to whatever voiced the soul-chilling scream.

Isarn wailed, a thin, high shriek of terror. The terrible bellowing struck Hauk like a blow and dropped him to his knees, He hung on to the torch with both hands while the sword fell to the floor. He didn't hear the ring and clatter of steel on stone. As though the thing that made the cry were rising, the roar grew. Shadows from the torchlight spun madly across the walls and floor. Light, thin and orange, flickered around the corridor, alternately showing him the rough walls and the niches where darkness pooled.

There was no sign of Isarn.

Hauk shifted the torch to his left hand, grabbed up the fallen sword with his right. "Isarn!" he called softly. "Isarn!"

Nothing moved in the stony corridor but the trembling light and madly dancing shadows thrown by the torch. Urgent fear crowded into Hauk's mind and raced through his heart. Isarn was nowhere to be found. Hauk caught his breath, listening. He heard nothing but the hiss and sputter of the torch. Where was the dwarf?

Then, he had no thought for Isarn at all. Soft, like wind sobbing, a low, moaning sound came from beyond the crack in the wall. Even as he recognized it for a woman's voice, the moaning faded and died.

Heart racing, not stopping to think, Hauk bolted through the crack in the wall. Isarn lay, huddled and small, to the left of the entrance. Hauk noted only peripherally that the old dwarf didn't move. The cave was cold and filled with the dry, musty stink of reptile. In the far corner, memory made real, crouched a girl with hair like thick copper.

She was huddled over her knees, her hands high and fisted, green eyes wide in a white face splashed with shadows. A dwarf, black-bearded and thick-armed, stood over her. He reached for her with a bandaged hand.

Hauk roared, a bear's battle cry, and charged across the cave. As he ran, he realized that the dwarf was too close to the girl for a sword thrust. He reversed his grip on his weapon and raised the pommel high.

She saw him and recognized him in the instant he brought the sword's grip thundering down between the dwarf's shoulders.

"Hauk!" she cried. "No!"

Her cry echoed in the vibrations of the blow, echoed in the dwarf's gasping, and the sound of his body hitting the rocky floor. And it echoed in the horror and anger in her green eyes as she flung herself across the dwarf as though to protect him from the glittering steel of the sword.

His hand trembling, his heart hammering painfully in his chest, Hauk lowered the sword. The torch guttered and died. Darkness leaped to fill the cave. The only sounds Hauk heard were the murmur of wind from some far, high place and the girl's raggedly drawn breath.

He reached for her shoulder, touched her gently. When she pulled away, her cry of fear cut right to his heart.

After a long time of sickening darkness, a hand, fingers trembling, stroked the side of Stanach's head.

"Oh, please," a familiar voice whispered. "Oh, please, Stanach. Please, my friend, be alive."

It was a child's plea, made without any concession to logic and from the heart. The plea was typically Kelida's.

The cold air gasped as fire sprang to life.

There was light in the darkness behind Stanach's eyes and it confused him. He remembered very little beyond the sudden roar of the dragon. Kelida had cried out in terror. His own heart had stopped beating. He hadn't expected to feel anything but the rip and tear of Darknight's fangs. He certainly hadn't expected to feel a sword's grip crash down between his shoulders.

"*Lyt chwaer,*" he sighed, unable yet to open his eyes, "there is no sense in pleading with the dead to live."

She caught her breath in a sharp, startled gasp and took his left hand firmly in her own.

Stanach opened his eyes then, his head aching from the sharp invasion of light. Wavering light from the reanimated torch cast black shadows across Kelida's face. Her green eyes seemed to flicker to the flame's cadence.

"Stanach?"

"Aye," he sighed, gratefully. "What hit me, Kelida?"

Shadows separated from shadows behind Kelida, and a young man, black haired and black-bearded, stepped into the light. His brown hunting leathers hung awkwardly from a frame that should have been thickly muscled and stocky.

Stocky, Stanach thought, when he is eating regularly. This one has not been eating regularly or often.

"I hit you, dwarf."

There was nothing of regret in that cold voice. A feral light gleamed in the young man's blue eyes; the eyes of a wolf held too long captive, the eyes of a wolf cut off from the pack and afraid.

Stanach pushed himself up to sit. The young man watched his every move. Stanach shivered and thought for one long moment that he was looking at a ghost. Ranger's garb and the look of a hungry predator. He knew, suddenly, who this young man was. And yet, how could he still be alive? How could he have survived the torments Realgar must have inflicted upon him?

Those had to have been horrible torments, indeed. The heart Stanach saw reflected in Hauk's dark eyes was gaunt and needy.

The dwarf looked quickly to Kelida. She wore the wary and confused look of one who has found what she's lost and now, for some reason she cannot determine, hears instinct clamoring that she must fear it.

Stanach got to his feet, aching in every muscle. Hauk, head up and tense, watched him, tracking his every move with cold, deadly eyes. The dwarf forced what he hoped was a wry and appreciative smile.

"You are Kelida's Hauk. You struck a good blow."

The hard set of Hauk's jaw softened and Stanach realized that the ranger hadn't even known her name.

"Aye," he said, rubbing the back of his neck with a careful hand. "Kelida."

Kelida swallowed dryly and got to her feet. Her gestures quick and nervous, she brushed her straggling hair from her face, smoothed her wrinkled and stained cloak. "Do you— do you remember me?"

His lips moved, though he made no sound. He nodded.

"Will you—will you put up your sword, please?"

He stiffened and tightened his grip on the weapon.

"Please." She took a small step toward him, her hand out. "We've been looking for you."

Hauk shot a sharp, suspicious look at Stanach. He lowered the sword. "Tyorl?"

Kelida laid her hand on his wrist and lowered the sword. "All right, I think." She looked at Stanach.

"I'm fine." He smiled, an ironic twist of his mouth. "You'd better tell him about his sword, Kelida. And if he found us, maybe he knows a way out of here. That dragon leaving so suddenly certainly means trouble."

Stanach looked around the cavern. A figure lay hunched in the black shadows near the cavern's entrance. He drew a sharp breath.

"Isarn," Hauk said evenly. "I don't think he's dead. I—he led me here, and we heard that screaming, that roaring. He went in before me and must have caught a glimpse of the dragon leaving."

As Hauk had guessed, the old master was not dead. Not yet. He lay in the shadows, drawing thin, rasping breaths. Stanach hardly recognized him. The madness that had for so long ravaged his mind, the grief that had for as long ravaged his soul, left their external marks. The old dwarf was thin, his once strong wrists and arms nothing but bones for weakened muscle and scanty flesh to cling to. His beard, once full, clean, and white as snow, was ragged, tangled, and filthy.

His eyes, gently staring, did not blink or track when Stanach approached.

Stanach dropped to his knees beside him. Once those dull

brown eyes had seen the vision of a masterblade. Once they had watched the first light shine from the blade of the Kingsword. Stanach's heart tightened. He felt the shadow of impending grief.

"Master," he whispered. The old title came easily to his lips. "Master Isarn."

His was a voice the old one knew well, and one not heard for a long time. Isarn ran a dry tongue over cracked lips. "Lad," he said distantly.

"Aye, Master, it's me. I've come back."

He saw the dirty green bandaging binding Stanach's right hand. Grief filled his eyes like tears. "What have they done to your hand, boy?"

Stanach winced but did not know how to answer.

He didn't have to; the question faded from Isarn's mind. When he spoke again, his voice rang out strong with conviction. "Stormblade will kill the high king!"

Stanach caught his breath and held it. The words sounded like prophecy! They rang with foretelling, and Stanach felt the foretelling as cold fear along the skin of his arms.

It will kill the high king.

But there was no high king in Thorbardin. None had sat upon that throne for three hundred years. Aye, and no Kingsword had been forged in Thorbardin in three hundred years.

"Master," he whispered, "I don't understand."

The vacant, staring light in Isarn's eyes changed, glimmered faintly with sanity. He looked directly at Stanach, his lips moving in what could have been a smile.

"Always, lad, you tell me you don't understand. And always, you do."

Like ghosts, Stanach heard well remembered words from the long past of his life, from a time when his hands were filled with discovery, his head with learning.

Your hands have the knowledge, Stanach my lad, and your heart has the desire. It remains for your head— sometimes harder than the stone for which you are named!—to understand.

So saying, Isarn would impart another bit of knowledge to guide Stanach's hand at the forge.

Stanach leaned closer. "Master, there is no high king now. I don't understand what you—"

Isarn's brows contracted in an expression Stanach well knew. It was the fearsome scowl he turned upon an assistant or apprentice who has failed to listen to instruction.

"There is a king, boy," he whispered hoarsely, impatiently. "There is a king. I made the sword for him. Stormblade, I called it—there is a king."

Hornfel! Stanach trembled with exhaustion and sudden understanding of what Isarn was saying. Hornfel would be high king.

Stanach closed his eyes, trying to think. Isarn was inarguably mad. Was this more rambling? Some said Isarn's descent into madness began when Stormblade was stolen. Stanach knew his master had begun that long descent when he saw the unquenchable heart of fire in Stormblade's steel and knew that he'd created a Kingsword.

Aye, but not for a high king. For a king regent. Even Hornfel himself did not look to claim more than a regency. The old swordcrafter was confused and wandering in the murky hazes of madness and death. He could not know what he was saying.

"Master Isarn," Stanach said, very gently.

Isarn made no response. Stanach looked at him closely, his heart racing. The old swordcrafter's eyes were no longer wide and staring, but hooded and still. "Master?"

"I made the sword," Isarn whispered, "for a thane. Realgar will use it to kill a high king." His hand, gnarled with age, pitted with forge scars, crabbed across his chest. When his fingers touched Stanach's they were dry as ancient parchment. "You brought the sword home. Find it again. Find it."

A knot of pain, like tears, choked any reply Stanach would have made.

He closed his fingers around the old dwarf's hand. "Please, Isarn, no. Don't charge me with . . ." His words died in a whisper and a sigh.

Isarn Hammerfell was dead.

Slim, shaking fingers touched his shoulder. Stunned by the death of his kinsman and friend, Stanach turned blindly.

Kelida dropped to her knees beside him.

Wavering in the torchlight, a black shadow cut across the girl and the corpse. Stanach looked up to see Hauk standing behind Kelida. His eyes, feral once, were tamer. But they were still haunted. Images of torment lived in them.

The dwarf made to rise, then dropped back to his knees. He was too tired, it seemed, for even this. How was he going to bear the terrible weight of Stormblade?

Kelida reached to take his hand. "Let me help you."

Stanach moved to accept her help. Before she could take his hand, Hauk's came between them.

His was a large hand, fingers hard and scarred with the marks of sword and dagger. When he pulled Stanach to his feet, he did not, as the dwarf expected, immediately free his hand. Instead he closed his fingers around it in a warrior's long clasp of companionship.

Stanach said nothing. There was nothing to say.

"I heard what the old dwarf told you," Hauk said. "I don't know anymore whether this sword, this Stormblade, is mine. I think it's not.

"But I've been a part of this. Realgar—" Hauk's voice dropped low. "Realgar has done things to me—he showed me Tyorl's death, and he made me believe that I had killed him. I know—I know you say he's alive, but the memory of—murder is still in me. He has made me die, and he has brought me back." He kept his eyes on Stanach's now because he didn't want Kelida to see the naked emptiness in them. "And he made me die again. Stanach, Realgar owes me something."

Stanach looked down at his broken-fingered hand. He closed his eyes and saw crows in a hard blue sky, heard wind mourning around a cairn in the cold hills. Isarn's last words had been madness, ghost-dreams of myth and legend. The reality was that friends and kin had died for Realgar's poisonous longing for power. More would die, still.

Stanach watched with a chill of fear as Hauk handed his dagger to Kelida. "You, too? No, Kelida."

"Yes." She shivered, looking around the cold cavern. "I won't stay here. I go where Hauk goes. Where you go." She stroked the hilt of the dagger with her thumb. "You were the one who insisted that I learn how to use this. I think our friend Lavim was a good teacher. I still don't know if I can kill with it, Stanach. I do think I can defend myself. I'm going with you."

She touched his bandaged hand gently. "People have allowed themselves to be harmed for my sake. I have to go with you."

The dwarf looked at Hauk and saw some of the emptiness vanish from his eyes. He saw fear for her there, too. In that moment, a silent understanding passed between the ranger and the dwarf. Come with them she would, but both agreed that she would not come to harm.

CHAPTER 27

Bitter wind cut across the narrow, crumbling ledge. Screaming like the abandoned souls of the damned, the wind dragged behind it the black smoke of the burning Plains of Death.

Like funeral shrouds.

From this ledge, one thousand feet above the pine forested valley, Hornfel saw the fire as a bolt of golden silk unfolding like a banner, rippling and shifting to the vagaries of a capricious breeze.

As Hornfel watched, the fire left the Plains. Leaping with uncanny speed, it gained the thickly forested slopes of the mountain. Like a rampaging army of conquerors, it made waste of everything in its way.

The wind shifted suddenly, as it will in the steep corridors of the mountain peaks, howling now from the northwest. The wall of flames followed the wind's trail, galloping madly through the valley below Thorbardin.

Gneiss's message had been to meet at the gatehouse. Hornfel had waited, speaking with the captain of the guard for a moment or two before the scent and sound of fire rampaging in the valley drew him out onto the ledge.

Now, Hornfel stood alone on the ledge, or as alone as his guard would permit. Behind him, in the wide empty place where once the Northgate had warded this entrance to Thorbardin, four strong dwarf warriors stood, two facing the Hylar thane, two watching several yards farther into the gatehouse. The eyes of those two were not on Hornfel, but on the inner courtyard and the shadows of the rubble-strewn, ruined gatehouse itself. Their hands hovered near the hilts of their swords. None of them forgot for an instant that Gneiss had given them charge of Hornfel's safety.

Northgate was, after all, an enemy holding. Though some of the gate was occupied now by Theiwar, most of the great hall leading from the gatehouse to the North Hall of Justice was thick with the dust of centuries. The hall itself, a sometimes active guard station, was clean and repaired to the point of easy use. But the structures of the temple and residences beyond seemed unchanged from the time of the Dwarfgate Wars. The marks of ancient battle scarred the stone walls and floors. In some places, huge black stains, the shadows of old blood, fouled the cracked, shattered tiles of the floor.

Until the Theiwar had laid claim to the area, none but the skeletons of the dead, dwarf and human, occupied Northgate. Some still did as falls and scatters of bones and ancient armor in black, lightless corners. The Theiwar, that strange *derro* race of dwarves, took perverse pleasure in sharing quarters with the dead.

A song of steel ringing on mail, booted feet on stone, sounded in the corridor between the gatehouse and the North Hall of Justice. The Guard of Watch was changing.

Deep voices murmured questions. Hornfel imagined that the new watch was inquiring as to the state of the *guyll fyr*. Hornfel sensed a palpable unease in the voices of the retiring guards.

Hornfel stepped back from the ledge. Impregnable Thorbardin was not at immediate risk from this fire, but the destruction of the marshes and woodlands would exact a toll on the mountain kingdom's food supply in the spring.

We won't be hungry, he thought bitterly, but we will be lean. What will convince the Council of Thanes that we should not only continue to aid the refugees sheltering here now, but open our doors to others?

Hornfel sighed.

Like ghosts, thoughts of the anguished days of the Dwarfgate Wars haunted Hornfel. Then, the Cataclysm had driven the dwarves into the mountain kingdom. The devastation of that time had reshaped the face of all Krynn.

The years after the Cataclysm were plague years, and the Neidar, the hill dwarves who before the Cataclysm had left Thorbardin for the Outlands, for what they called the freedom of the hills, wanted to come back to the mountain kingdom. They were hungry and they could raise no crop, hunt no game, in lands burned sere by endless drought and fouled by plague.

They needed allies, the Neidar, and they found an ally in the great mage Fistandantilus who, at the head of an army of ragged humans, laid seige first to Pax Tharkas, and then to Thorbardin. The humans believed there was treasure stored in the mountains.

Duncan knew, and so did the hill dwarves, that there was indeed treasure: there was food. But not enough to feed even those who lived in Thorbardin.

High King Duncan knew that his duty lay with his people. He and Kharas, his friend and champion, laid plans for what history would come to call the Dwarfgate Wars.

Kin made war against kin as Duncan, the last king of the dwarves made his choice to feed and shelter what relatively few people he was able to within ancient Thorbardin.

War again raged in Krynn. Hornfel knew, however, that, though war's brutalities were the same from century to century, this war was not the same as the one Duncan had fought.

For one thing, he thought, staring out into the fire-

___

283

threatened valley, we are not fighting this one. My people have chosen to hold themselves comfortably apart from this war. For another, the refugees we shelter here are not of the dwarven race.

No, they are humans. Is that really a difference? One could not, in any seriousness, call those over-tall and truculent, short-lived creatures kin. Yet, in the warlands, humans and elves had allied, if uneasily, against the dragonarmies. An old proverb had it that the wolf at the door will make brothers of strangers.

"And so is another old saying still good, King Duncan," he whispered to a dwarf three hundred years dead. *"Who does not learn from his fathers will learn from no one.*

The wolf is howling for your children's blood, Duncan. I can smell his breath in the *guyll fyr's* smoke. We have to turn these strangers into brothers now.

So thinking, he turned away from the ledge, from the fire, and passed between his two guards and into the gatehouse. He didn't know where Gneiss was, and he couldn't wait for him any longer. He would leave word with the captain of the guard that he been here and—

An indrawn breath whispered, and Hornfel looked around. Realgar leaned against the shaft of the gate mechanism, arms folded and at ease. He wore a dark, heavy cloak against the biting wind. The cloak did not hide the shape of a sword worn, as always, at his hip. His narrow-pupiled, black eyes glittered.

"It's like an army," Realgar said, "and it comes closer."

Fire without and fire within! Hornfel remembered Dhegan shadowing him and Gneiss on the dark bridge, and he looked to his guards. Their eyes cold, Gneiss's Daewar closed ranks.

"Like an army, aye," Hornfel said. He resisted the urge to drop his hand to the dagger at his hip. "I'm going to call a council. Plans will have to be made; it'll be a lean winter."

Realgar shrugged. "As you say." He stepped aside to let Hornfel pass and waited, too, until the four guards fell in behind their charge.

As he made his way through the muttering guards, Realgar amused himself with thinking about his plans for

murder and revolution. His army of bloody-handed
Theiwar were ready to begin the fight for the cities, and
Stormblade was heavy in the scabbard beneath his cloak.
The Kingsword seemed to breathe with restless, hungry
power.

He closed the distance between himself and Hornfel's
guards.

The chill, damp corridor opening on the bridge across
Anvil's Echo was not absolutely lightless, though to Kelida
it seemed so after the warm, comfortably lighted streets of
Thorbardin. It took long moments for her eyes to adjust to
the faint gray light leaking into the stone hallway. This was
not light from outside the mountain, but a whisper of the
stronger illumination from the glittering shafts of crystal
that guided and enhanced the sun's light in the city proper.

When her eyes adjusted, she shrank back against Hauk,
who stood close behind her. The bridge spanned a cavern so
high and so deep that Kelida, who could see neither roof nor
floor, could not imagine boundaries. Low stone rails lined
each side of the wide bridge. As though they stood sentinel,
small carvings of dwarves held up the rail with strong, stone
arms.

"Stanach," she whispered. The whisper echoed endlessly
around the cavern. Kelida swallowed hard and touched
Stanach's shoulder to get his attention.

His hand on the sword he'd picked up in the city, Stanach
turned and Kelida gasped. As he had said in the caverns far
below the cities, his eyes were only wide, black pupils now,
empty and ghostlike. A chill swept down her back.

The dwarf grinned, a comical mock leer. "Aye, didn't I tell
you? Frightening to see if you're not accustomed to the look
of them, eh?" With his bandaged right hand, he patted her
arm. "It's me, little sister, only me."

. . . me, only me . . . me . . . me . . .

Kelida shuddered, then felt Hauk's hand tentative but
warm on her shoulder. His words chased themselves around
the cavern, too, when he spoke.

"I don't like this hole, Stanach. What's Hornfel doing
here? We should have gone to your Council of Thanes for

aid."

It would have been Stanach's first choice, but the Theiwar guard they'd overpowered in a cold dark corridor near the dragon's lair had responded to their questions about Realgar and his plans with only a hard laugh and a boast he seemed happy to make: "Hornfel's dead on Northgate now!"

By grim, silent agreement, Stanach drew Kelida on ahead with him as Hauk lingered with the Theiwar guard just another moment before catching up to them. He'd left the Theiwar dead in the shadows of the corridor.

The dead guard's gleeful boast had filled Stanach with anger and despair that hadn't abated until the three reached the upper levels of the city. It was Hauk who pointed out that what the guard had said could not be true. Or not yet.

"Look," he'd said, gesturing toward a merchants' square, a tavern, a park. "These people are nervous, Stanach, but they aren't behaving like people who have heard that one of their leaders is dead."

Stanach agreed and felt the easing that hope brings. They might not be too late to help Hornfel. The mood of Thorbardin was one of waiting and simmering fear.

Thorbardin scented a storm and knew the lightning would strike very soon, though it didn't know which quarter of the sky would bring it.

Stanach, roused from his thoughts, gestured to the darkness around them. "This is a Theiwar holding and even the adventurous don't come here. The bridge should be safe enough."

Followed by the echoes of their footsteps, echoes like stealthy ghosts, the three set out across the bridge.

Kelida started out counting steps as a way to keep her mind off the seemingly endless drop below. Though the bridge was wide enough for them to walk abreast, it seemed all too narrow for Kelida's comfort.

The whispers of their footsteps grew thicker, as though they were rebounding from closer walls. Kelida sighed, the sound like the wind wandering through canyons. The bridge over Anvil's Echo was behind them. Stanach glanced over his shoulder and then wordlessly waved them forward.

His sense of direction below ground, as keen as an elf's in

a forest, kept them heading unfailingly north. They passed walls black with the marks of fire and white with the scars of battle. In dark corners lay the skeletal remains of warriors three hundred years dead. The leather and fabric of their clothing had long since rotted, but the brittle bones of hands still clutched shattered swords. Rusted mail and pierced armor still hung about what had once been bodies.

Kelida kept close behind Stanach and took a little comfort from the sound of Hauk's even breathing behind her.

After a time whose passage seemed slow in the unmarked blackness, light, like gray fog, eased the dark around them.

Kelida made out the tall broad shape of a dome-capped building to which wide stone steps led. They were no longer in the stone walled corridors, but a kind of plaza or square.

"The temple," Stanach breathed. "We are close to the gate-house. Listen!"

Echoing flatly, like whispers from the long past, came the sound of mail jingling and metal-shod boots scraping on stone. Fear spidered along Kelida's skin. Hauk's hand, warm on her shoulder, made her gasp and start.

"Easy," Stanach hissed. "It's only the Guard of Watch changing. And likely a good thing. Whatever Realgar plans, he can't possibly carry out Hornfel's murder in front of two full watches."

At one time the temple must have been as beautiful as any within the precincts of the cities. Though the domed ceiling was gapped and shattered now, it had once soared across the temple. Some of its pieces lay on the dusty black marble floor and stars, carved deep into the stone and blacker than the marble, showed from beneath shrouds of dust.

At first Kelida wondered why the artisan who'd made this dome would show the stars as blacker than the sky. Then she realized that these stars had originally been deep etchings filled with gleaming silver. That silver, tarnished now with age, must once have reflected the lights of torches and braziers in such a way as to mimic the dance and play of true stars.

Columns of rose-colored marble, some split and fallen, some still whole, lined the wide, crimson tiled walk leading to the central altar. There an anvil stood, seven feet high, its face five feet across. The whole altar had been carved from a single block of obsidian. At the anvil's foot lay what seemed to be the helve of a giant's hammer.

A temple to Reorx, Kelida thought, how beautiful it must have been! She shuddered to think that murder was being planned so close to what had been a place of worship.

Stanach slipped behind the altar and found a cleric's door.

"This should lead us out into the great hall itself. This whole place is part of the North Hall of Justice. At one time, the temple was for the convenience of visitors to the kingdom. Now, it's only a ruin. From here on, the going should be easier. Theiwar may like the rubble and filth, but the gatehouse is kept clear in case a watch is mounted."

Hauk moved close beside him. When he spoke, his voice was a barely heard whisper. "What lies beyond?"

Before Stanach could reply, a scream, high and filled with a terrible agony, rang from without. The echoes of that horrible cry had not fully settled when a shout of alarm and then another followed.

Like a bolt from a tightly strung crossbow, Stanach was through the cleric's door.

Hauk grabbed Kelida's wrist. His eyes mirrored both fear for her and a strange, fierce longing that had nothing to do with her at all. Kelida fell back a step, recognizing the lust for battle.

Stay," he snarled. Then, perhaps hearing the harshness of his command, or recognizing that no order of his could hold her if she took it into her head to follow, Hauk said, "Defend the door. If we can still help Hornfel, likely this will be our only way out."

He did not stay to see that she obeyed.

Alone, the sound of battle rising and swelling close now, Kelida swallowed back an urge to call after him, forced herself to stay where she was and not run to follow. He had looked like some strange, heartless warrior whose purposes all had to do with killing.

Kelida's fingers were cold and dry around the grip of her dagger. The little weapon felt both heavy and absurdly light in her hand.

Faint memory ghosts from what seemed a long, long time

ago, Lavim's incongruously cheerful instruction in the art of
the dagger, whispered to her.

Another thing a dagger is for is stabbing.

Kelida tried hard to ignore the roiling sickness in her
stomach, the weakness of her knees, and crept closer to the
doorway. Stabbing . . .

The great hall beyond the temple was only a little less
dark than the disused sections of Northgate, but the illumination there was more diffuse and even. There was enough
light for Kelida to see that Realgar had indeed attempted
Hornfel's assassination during the change of the Guard of
Watch, and that for a very good reason. Dwarven warriors
wearing the black and silver of Realgar's service filled the
place, falling upon the Guard of Watch and outnumbering
them almost two to one.

The battle thundered through the hall. Steel clashed
against steel, voices soared high in almost indistinguishable
cries heralding death or triumph. The stench of blood and
fear hung over the place as though it were the clouds from
which the storm fell.

In the center of that storm, its eye and its focus both, a
badly outnumbered, embattled dwarf fought for his life.
Nothing marked him as the Hylar's thane unless it was the
storm raging around him, and perhaps the innate nobility of
one who knows himself beaten but fights on.

Hornfel had long been a warrior before he was thane.

There was one guardsman left to him, a young dwarf
wearing the scarlet and silver of what Kelida imagined must
be the Guard of Watch. His back to Hornfel's he kept off all
comers with a wolfhound's valiant ferocity. It was for this
eye, this focus, that Stanach ran. Behind him, Hauk defended Stanach's back.

Kelida moved without thinking. She was not a half dozen
yards into the hall before the tide of battle swept between
her and her friends.

Something hit her hard in the back, an arm caught her
around the knees and, too breathless to scream, she fell. Terror tightened her hand on the dagger's hilt or it would have
flown from her grip. Twisting hard, kicking out with her
right foot while she got her free hand and left foot under her,

Kelida lurched to her knees.

She screamed then, but not from terror. She screamed with the rage of one who sees her own death in the eyes of an opponent.

Stabbing is funny stuff . . . Don't stab down if you're in close. All you'll do is hit bone and make someone mad. Stab up from below. That way, you stand a really good chance of hitting something important, like a liver or kidney . . .

Two handed, Kelida drove her dagger's blade hard and up. Steel rasped on mail and the blade turned. Panting desperately, Kelida adjusted her aim without thinking and plunged the dagger with all her strength up and into the dwarf's throat.

Blood, like an ugly crimson fountain, spurted high and the Theiwar guard fell away.

Retching from the coppery reek of hot blood, Kelida scrambled to her feet. Again something hit her from behind. Blindly she spun and struck, missed her mark, and simply kicked low and dirty. Her attacker fell, gagging. Instinctively, Kelida brought her knee up hard. She heard and felt the dwarf's jaw shatter.

Heart thundering now, Kelida spun and found herself, for a moment, in the clear.

Quelling urges to vomit, scream, or run, Kelida searched the bloody hall for her companions. The guards of the black and silver, though not as many as before, still outnumbered Hornfel's defenders. Tall among them all, like an enraged bear among the battling dwarves, Hauk still fought to keep any enemy away from Stanach's back.

Stanach, now an arm's length from his thane, swept the head from the shoulders of a Theiwar guard with his sword. He kicked the corpse away and reached with his right hand, the bandage stained with blood and dirt, for Hornfel.

As he did, the valiant guardsman, Hornfel's only defender, died with a Theiwar dagger sunk to the hilt between his ribs. When Stanach touched him the thane spun.

Splattered with the blood of the dead guardsman, his eyes wide and blazing with maddened fury, Hornfel swung his sword high for a double-handed blow.

Kelida screamed.

CHAPTER 28

"Friend!" Stanach roared, "Hornfel! Friend!"

It was not Stanach's bellowed assurance that convinced Hornfel that he was not an enemy. It was the mere fact that while roaring "friend" Stanach proved his claim by slicing the arm from a Theiwar lunging for the thane's back with a deadly shortsword and, on the back swing, opening the belly of another of Realgar's warriors.

Hornfel bared his teeth in a warrior's welcoming grin. Aye, this was a friend. So was the broad-chested human protecting Stanach's back. The blade of his sword was crimsoned with blood. The light in his eyes shone like *guyll fyr*.

Stanach looked wildly around the great hall. He searched the place like a wolf caught in a canyon by hunters. Like the wolf, he wanted a way out of the trap, and that want made every muscle quiver. When he found the way, the bolt hole, his eyes lit.

The Guard of Watch had driven Realgar's Theiwar, for a moment, away from Hornfel. In doing so, they had left him unguarded by none but these two.

"Who holds the gatehouse?" Hauk yelled.

"No one." Hornfel drew a long breath and looked down at the Daewar guard who had died defending his life. "It's where we were trying to make for when Realgar attacked."

The young man shrugged and grinned, the grin oddly out of place and chilling. "Let's go, then. Stanach?"

Stanach nodded, still checking the great hall as though searching for someone. Hornfel heard him curse low under his breath. Stanach elbowed his companion in the back and pointed with his blood-stained, bandaged right hand.

A human girl, with blood smeared on her hands and a face as pale as Solinari, stood with her back to one of the tall support columns. She fought off three black and silver liveried dwarves with a dagger and, when the dagger missed its mark as it often seemed to do, with vicious kicks. The girl was outnumbered and could not hold out much longer against her attackers.

"Hauk! There's Kelida! Get her and make for the gatehouse!"

Stanach hefted his sword in his left hand for a better grip and nodded once to his thane. "I've got your back, Hornfel."

Stanach was the only defense he would have, but Hornfel thought it would be enough. He ran for the gatehouse.

Piper explored the boundaries of his netherworld as often as he could and found, each time, that he was able to extend himself a little farther than the time before. It was not so much a matter of being able to go farther as it was a matter of being able to know farther.

He was bounded by no sense of dimension now, no forward or back, no up or down. He could hear what his companions could hear and more; he could hear the thoughts of those around him.

It was how he became aware that, though they thought they were, Lavim, Tyorl, and the rangers were not alone in the defile.

The soaring rock walls of the narrow defile formed a perfect channel for the smoke, a chamber to carry and magnify the roar and snap of the fire raging along the sides of the mountain below and above them. Tyorl cursed bitterly.

The air was already thick with smoke, heavy and black, reeking of burning, clogging his lungs. Tears streamed down his face as the smoke burned his eyes raw.

Tyorl wondered if Piper were still reading his mind, then laughed mirthlessly. Finn would say it was better to wonder if he were out of his mind for depending upon the guide work of a ghost.

Somewhere ahead, unseen but known by their deep, wracking coughs, Kembal and Finn ran scout. Lavim, following behind, made no sound but for a light wheezing.

Tyorl did not like the sound of that reedy wheezing. When he turned to check on the kender's progress, he knew at once that Lavim was not going to make it to the end of this defile without help.

Tyorl caught his arm to stop and steady him. He went down on his heels beside Lavim. "We've no time to rest, Lavim. Let me help you."

Lavim shook his head. "No," he gasped, "I'm fine, Tyorl, really, I am."

He was nothing like "fine." The soot blackening his face did not hide its grayish pallor, nor did the smoke-stung tears disguise the dullness of his eyes. The dirty, weighted air seemed to get only so far into his lungs before he coughed it out again.

"Lavim, please." He took the old kender's shoulders in a gentle but firm grip. "Please. I don't have time to argue. Now, climb up. Piggyback it will have to be until we can find our way to better air."

Lavim shook his head, his cracked, dry lips thinned to a tight line of both stubbornness and wounded pride. "I can make it, Tyorl. I—"

Something cut loose inside Tyorl and it snapped painfully hard, like a whip lashing.

"Don't argue!"

In that moment, he did not see Lavim, stunned to silence and staring at him with wide green eyes. He saw the faces of all the people who had become lost to him, snatched away by the cold hands of death and war.

Hauk and Kelida.

The companions he'd fought beside in the spring, dead now and only raw, naked bones fleshed by nothing but his memories.

Young Lehr who had challenged the black dragon and died for it. Mule-stubborn Stanach!

Aye, and the mage Piper.

I walk with ghosts!

"No more!" he shouted, his voice cracking hard in his dry throat. He saw Lavim flinch and hardly understood why, so caught was he in the tide of fear and grief washing through him. "Listen to me, Lavim! No more!"

Tyorl saw his white-knuckled grip on the kender's shoulders and realized dimly that it must surely hurt. Though he tried to relax his grasp, he could not. He did not know how to do anything but what he was doing: hold the kender in such a grip that not even death could snatch him away.

Lavim squirmed, and then, with a sure and fine instinct, held still. He reached up and covered the elf's hands with his own. Nodding slowly, as though suddenly he understood something, Lavim found a smile.

"All right, Tyorl. All right. I guess I could use a rest. Piggyback it is. But we'd better hurry or we'll lose Finn."

His arms around Tyorl's neck, his legs around his waist, Lavim tried to settle his weight as evenly as he could. Probably, he thought, I'm not really very heavy.

He's thinking you weigh about as much as a half-starved child, Lavim.

"Aye, well, the part about being half-starved is right."

Tyorl looked around. "What?"

"Piper says we're almost there."

I did not. But you're right, we are. You can tell him for me that I haven't lost my mind, or my way. Just another mile down the defile and we'll be at Northgate.

"Just another mile, Tyorl. I can—"

And don't offer to walk. Helping you is about the only

thing he can do now to make any difference. So he thinks. Let him help.

"I can really use the rest, thanks." Lavim sighed. "Piper says to tell you that he hasn't lost his mind, or his way."

He felt the elf's surprise in an involuntary hitching of his breath. When he spoke, Tyorl's voice was heavy with sarcasm.

"I wouldn't mind if he wanted to stop reading my thoughts."

"Sometimes," Lavim said, "I know what you mean."

Piper wasn't quiet long. Lavim had no more than settled into the uncomfortable rhythm of Tyorl's gait—like a three-legged mountain pony who limps on one of 'em, he thought—when Piper interrupted his thoughts.

Dragon!

"Dragon!" Lavim yelped.

"Dragon," Tyorl demanded, "where?"

On the mountain!

"On the mountain!" The old kender scrambled down from Tyorl's back, fumbling for his dagger and calling for the rangers. "Finn! Kem! Dragon on the mountain!"

Tyorl snatched Lavim's arm and his attention. "Where on the mountain? Where, Lavim?"

Lavim shuddered and squeezed his eyes tightly shut, caught between Tyorl's questions and Piper's answers. He did his best to sort them out, but his head seemed to be filled with the confusing echoes of Piper's voice, his own thoughts, and the demands of Tyorl and the rangers.

Talking to everyone at once and feeling like he was talking to himself, Lavim tried to answer. "Where? Tyorl, on the peaks . . . high . . . behind the crest of the mountain . . . What? What are you saying? All right! All right!"

As from a great distance, the kender heard Finn mutter something and Tyorl answer. Lavim clutched the elf's arm, his heart pounding hard now, his breath coming in ragged gasps. "He's going to kill the Hylar's thane! That fellow that Stanach was always talking about!"

"Who, Lavim? What are you talking about, and where is the dragon?"

Lavim shook his head hard to clear it. "The dragon is on

the mountain, behind the peaks over Thorbardin. There's a mage, a dwarf, and he's going to kill Stanach's thane. He's thinking about it now, Tyorl. He's going to do it soon—and—and there's going to be a battle or something.

"Stanach's there! And Kelida!"

Stunned, Tyorl could do nothing but stare. It was Finn who spoke.

"Kender, what are you talking about? Stanach and the girl are dead."

Lavim turned to Tyorl, tugging hard on the elf's arm.

"Tyorl, Piper knows what he's talking about. It's happening now—what Stanach's been afraid about all along!"

Tyorl did not doubt the veracity of Piper's report. He looked around them, along the smoky channel of the defile and at the shadows gathering high on the mountainside. The shadows of a dragon and war. He sensed Finn's disbelief and confusion.

"Lavim," he said, slowly, carefully, "calm down now. Ask Piper if it is really happening now."

No, but soon.

Lavim shook his head. "Not now—but soon. Tyorl, we have to get—"

"Where are Stanach and Kelida?"

"In Thorbardin. They're there, Tyorl, with—" Lavim cocked his head, listening to Piper's soundless words. His eyes went wide with amazement. "They're with Hauk. He's all right! Piper says we're real close to Northgate now. Just another quarter mile down the defile. We could get there in time, Tyorl, maybe."

Finn snorted. "Aye, maybe. Maybe we'll miss our way. Tyorl, the smoke is so thick now we can't see a yard ahead. Chances are very good that we'll miss the gate completely."

Lavim answered quickly. "Oh, no, we won't miss it. The defile becomes a ledge right in front of the gate, and it's real narrow. Five feet wide, maybe. We couldn't miss that."

Finn stared at the kender as though not certain if he was joking. "We'd better not, eh? It's a thousand feet to the valley below. What does your ghost say about that?"

Nothing could have been more innocent than Lavim's expression then. "He says you'd better not miss your footing. He says you probably won't want to be caught outside the gate in case the dragon notices us, so we'd better get going."

Rage coursed through Realgar the way the *guyll fyr* tore through the valley below Northgate. His attack on Hornfel had failed! Like a bloody haze across his vision, fury clouded everything. He heard nothing but his own raving thoughts and was only dimly aware of the groans of the dying, his own guard and the Daewar who had defended Hornfel, as distant whispers. Then, cold and black, Darknight's mental voice growled from the heights above Thorbardin. Realgar heard that bad-tempered growling as a deep rumbling in his mind and grabbed it. The Theiwar slipped, staggering, into the language of the mind.

Are you ready?

Aye, ready. I am hungry and I smell blood.

Realgar smiled then. *Patience, my friend. There will be food enough for you soon. You'll have your pick of the Hylar's kin.*

Darknight subsided. Thin wisps of its longing drifted through Realgar's soul and twined with his own.

Realgar ran his thumb along Stormblade's guards, feeling the blade's red heart of fire as a wild song in his own heart. The great hall was still now and, but for the groans of the dying and wounded, quiet. New blood stained the cracked and shattered paving stones of the court, spattered the walls and broken columns. He counted twenty dead from among his own guard, thirty from Hornfel's defenders.

He had not killed all of them. Realgar cursed bitterly. He should have killed the two humans, should have made certain that Hammerfell's apprentice was well and truly dead!

Aye, Hammerfell's apprentice, he was the one who had fouled the coup. Without his aid, the two humans would still be in the Deep Warrens, dark-blind and secure until Realgar could finish his business with them.

Without that damned stripling of an apprentice to interfere, Hornfel would not now be holed up in the gatehouse.

Realgar closed his eyes and breathed deeply, seeking a calm place within where he might think. Slowly it came, and with it came an ordering of his thoughts. With order came a solution.

Though twenty of his own men were dead, there still remained six, uninjured and, by the look of them, eager to avenge the deaths of their comrades. Though they were not enough to rush and take the gatehouse, there was an easy way to increase their ranks. It would take time, but not so much that Hornfel and his three defenders would become so emboldened as to try for a renewed engagement in the hall.

Soon, he thought, soon he'll tire of his bolt hole. There is no way out of it. The whole of the two Guards of Watch are dead, his own guards are dead. Now, there is no way for him to send for aid. Realgar laughed aloud. In short order, anyone who might think to aid Hornfel would be busy fleeing the fire of revolution.

Secure in the knowledge that the thousand-foot drop to the valley below the Northgate wall would keep Hornfel tightly trapped—and if it did not, Darknight would!—Realgar called a guard to him.

"Five squads, I think, to the Northgate. Move them fast."

The guard ran, ducking back into the North Hall of Justice and into secret passages beneath the ruined temple. There were Theiwar ready to attack the Klar city. Among them he would find the *derro* to fill his thane's need.

Realgar stroked the flat of Stormblade's bloody blade.

Hornfel listened to the final cries of the dying. Here in the gatehouse, he could not tell whether those cries were made by friends or enemies. Muscles quivering with the exhaustion of a battle's aftermath, his lungs thick with the encroaching smoke of the *guyll fyr*, Hornfel leaned against the wide shaft of the huge, ancient gate mechanism. It hardly mattered whose cries they were. They were the cries of the dying. Treacherous Theiwar or Gneiss' faithful warriors, they were dwarves.

He shuddered. Whether or not they chose to acknowledge the fact, they were kin. And kin had raised steel against kin, as they had in the Dwarfgate Wars.

Then, he thought bitterly, they were fighting for the right to eat. Today, we fight for the right to rule.

The sword Realgar wielded was the Kingsword. Hornfel had never seen Stormblade before today. Fire-hearted steel and blazing sapphires, Stormblade had cut through Gneiss's warriors like a scythe through wheat. The Kingsword had come back to Thorbardin.

Behind him he heard the restless pacing of the hungry-eyed human warrior they called Hauk. He was well named. In battle he struck with a raptor's instinct to kill and kill fast, a hawk's wildfire in his eyes.

The girl, possessed of a starveling's thin, pale face, they called Kelida. Hornfel wondered who had named her and if they had known that if they softened the *d* in her name she would be known as Wanderer in dwarven speech. *Kelye dtha*: the one who wanders.

A hand, thick with bloody bandaging, touched Hornfel's shoulder lightly. He looked up and met the eyes of a son of Clarm Hammerfell, black, and flecked with blue lights.

Hornfel sighed. "I owe you my life."

"You'd best not take an accounting, Hornfel Thane, until we find a way out of here."

"Sound enough advice, young Stanach."

Stanach crooked a smile. Bitter though it was, it softened the harsh, red line of a knife's trail.

"Aye. According to our restless Hauk, we're neatly trapped and only have to wait for the hunters to finish us," Stanach said. "And according to you, Thane?"

"Me, I think he's right. The only way out of here is into the great hall or out the gate. We can't fly and we're only four. You know that Realgar is calling up more warriors even now. I say if the hunters want us they'll have to come in and get us. If they do, let them make their peace with Reorx.

"They'll have to earn their prey, those hunters. If we suffer a lack of numbers, we have all the weapons we want; this is a guard hall as well as a gatehouse."

Stanach nodded solemnly.

"Wait." Hornfel drew a short breath as though reluctant to ask the question. "Kyan Red-axe and Piper?"

"Their cairns are in the Outlands, Thane," Stanach said simply. He needed to say no more. Mountain dwarves know that there is no bleaker way to describe a death.

"Go arm that girl with something more suitable than a dagger," Hornfel said softly. Then his voice hardened. "No mail or helm of ours will fit Hauk, but there may be some to fit her. See if you can find something for us as well. Realgar may find us few, but he'll find us ready."

Kelye dtha. One who wanders. Dressed in a cast off elven hunting costume and a borrowed dwarven mail shirt too big in the shoulders and too short at the waist, Kelida shifted from one foot to the other seeking a balance for the new weight of the mail.

The west corridor of the gatehouse was apportioned into guards' quarters. Spare, comfortless bunks were built into the back walls, racks of spears, crossbows, and swords lined the side walls. On either side of the door were coffers filled with quarrels for the bows.

Little sunlight leaked into the stone-walled room from the gate, though the air was thick with ashy scent of smoke.

Guyll fyr, Stanach thought. He'd seen the blaze from the gate, a great sea of fire. With only the thin ledge of the wall between himself and the thousand-foot drop into the burning valley, Stanach had felt that he was standing at the edge of the world.

Stanach shook his head as Hauk fitted a glittering steel helm on Kelida's head. The nose guard gave her trouble, crossing down into her line of vision. She made a face something like a grimace, almost like a sheepish smile.

"*Lyt chwaer*, look beyond the nose guard, the way you'd look beyond your hand when you shade your eyes from the sun. Try not to see the guard."

She nodded, the gesture awkward with the helm's unaccustomed weight. "I feel foolish, Stanach. Like a child playing at dress-up."

With a gentleness Stanach had not seen in him before, Hauk adjusted the helm and stroked Kelida's face, lifting her chin to kiss her lightly.

Stanach saw her shoulders tremble, looked away, and said, "Foolish or not, Kelida, this is one of those times when the costume is dictated by the event. I would be happier if you would take a sword."

Kelida, eyes bright, thumbed the hilt of her dagger. "No. I can't use a sword, Stanach. I can use the dagger. Sort of."

The phrase held an echo of Lavim's equivocating. Stanach smiled in spite of himself.

"Aye," Hauk said, "and failing that, there are those who have cause to regret getting in the way of her kick." He pushed her gently toward the door. "Kelida, take some swords from the rack and bring them to Hornfel. Choose the best, for he is thane of the Hylar. Stanach and I will make do with what remains."

When she was gone, Hauk dropped to a seat on one of the hard bunks. Whatever tenderness had been in his expression when he spoke to Kelida had vanished as though it had never been.

"Stanach, we're going to die here."

"I wouldn't put odds on anything else."

Hauk smiled grimly. "Neither would I. I hear you call her *lyt chwaer*. What does it mean?"

"It's dwarven for 'little sister.' "

"Good, if you mean it."

Stanach looked around then. Aye, he thought, she taught me how to mean it. "A dwarf does not claim kin lightly."

A ghost of a smile lighted Hauk's face. "I'm glad. This is a dirty game we're engaged in, friend Stanach. She goes out there to your thane with a warrior's intent, but not with a warrior's skill. It won't matter to those she fights against. She's going to be one of the first to fall, and you know it. Is there a way out of here for her? A place to run to, to hide?"

Stanach shook his head. "The only thing she could do is bolt herself in here."

When Hauk's expression told him that he thought this a good idea, the dwarf added, "You'd never get her to agree to do it. I'll tell you this about her, Hauk: she survived a dragon raid on her home, the occupation of Long Ridge, and a dragon flight across the Plains of Death. She is not going to be easily convinced that she must hide in here now. And I don't think you should try. She deserves that respect."

Out in the corridor Hornfel called softly. "It's time, Stanach. They're here, and they are many."

CHAPTER 29

SMOKE, DRAGGED UP BY THE WIND FROM THE GREAT burning in the valley, channeled through the defile and filled Tyorl's lungs. Black, hopeless dread fill his heart. Though it was only the wail of the bitter wind on the heights, he imagined that the shrieking he heard was a dragon's battle cry.

I don't smell dragon-stink, he told himself firmly, I couldn't possibly smell anything in this smoky reek but ash and burning!

Still, he could not banish the dread, the sense that something huge and deadly, taloned and fanged, watched him and patiently waited for him to come within reach.

Fear of the dragon, however, seemed like a child's warrantless night fears compared with the ranger's terror of the heights upon which he now walked.

Tyorl cast a quick look over his shoulder. He and Lavim were running scout. Lavim's strength had increased with the degree of his fascination. Like all kender, his fascination grew in direct proportion to the degree of danger. Tyorl was the only one who could curb Lavim's inclination to scramble too far ahead of his companions, peer out over the ledge, or climb just a little higher up the sheer face of the wall to see down into the burning valley.

His legs weak and trembling with both fear and exhaustion, the elf pressed his back against the ice-sheathed stone of what must once have been the wall of Thorbardin's Northgate, waiting for Finn and Kem to climb with painfully slow care over a tumble of rocks and gravel. The slither and clatter of falling stone found echoes in the thumping of Tyorl's heart.

Ahead, Lavim amused himself kicking stones into the wind-torn depths from a ledge no wider than his foot was long.

Tyorl closed his eyes against a sudden wave of vertigo, found that darkness was worse than sight, and swallowed. He forced himself to open his eyes again.

Though the might of the gods, unleashed during the Cataclysm, had sheared away huge portions of the Northgate wall, the destruction had been capricious. In some places, like the place where Tyorl now wedged himself for balance, the raw stone of the mountain gaped like open wounds. In others, the smooth curved masonry of the wall could still be seen. The ledge was most treacherous in the niches and the gaps, strewn with the rubble of centuries.

At times, the ledge narrowed to barely three feet across. No perch for the rubble to collect, Tyorl thought, and barely a perch for an eagle to land!

Lavim sidled up beside him, his green eyes wide, his sooty face alight with a grin of complete delight.

"Tyorl, isn't it wonderful? You can see the whole world from here! You can see everything! I saw the bog, and I think I saw Skullcap, too. It's not burning anymore—the bog, I mean. Skullcap couldn't burn, anyway, it being stone.

"I'll bet a person could see straight to Long Ridge if there weren't all those mountains in the way. I'll bet he could see all the way to the sea and to Enstar and to whatever is beyond that. If there's anything beyond there, that is. I don't know if there is.

"My father, he once said that there are other places beyond the sea, but he never knew anyone who'd actually been there. Me, I figure there probably are other places. Maybe people have gone there, and they liked it so much they just didn't bother to come back."

The wind screamed across the ledge. Lavim cheerfully raised his voice to be heard.

"Back in the hills, when we came off the Plains, I thought I was going to give up this business of going places. I don't think so anymore, Tyorl. I think—once we save this Hornfel and find your friend Hauk and Stanach and Kelida again—I think I'm going to look for the places beyond Enstar."

There was more, a happy kender's speculations about what these imagined places beyond Enstar must look like, what the people who lived there must be like, how long it would take to get there, whether there were other kender there . . .

Tyorl sighed and let Lavim ramble, only half listening to him play with his dreams and spin his plans. There was no sense trying to silence him. If there were a dragon perched on the heights, as Piper had warned, it knew perfectly well that they were approaching the gate.

Anyway, it would be easier to quiet an avalanche. The kender hadn't been so voluble since they'd left the bog. Tyorl was surprised now to discover that he had missed the sound of Lavim's chatter.

Sweat freezing on his face, wind-stung eyes streaming with tears, Finn edged up beside Tyorl. Behind the rangerlord, Kembal picked his way carefully around the last of the rubble blocking the ledge. Tyorl waited until the two were steady and balanced again before he spoke.

"Lavim, how much farther to the gate?"

The kender shrugged. "Just around the next bend. I'd just caught a glimpse of it when you called me back that last time. We're really almost there, now, Tyorl."

"And where is this supposed dragon?"

Lavim's eyes went vague and unfocused. Then he grinned again, nodding as though in response to Piper's information. He pointed straight up the cliff's face.

"Right up there. It's in a big cave in the mountain and Piper says it's not very happy. It's a black, and they don't like light, he says. There's too much light coming into the cave now."

"A black. Is there a chance that it won't fly because of the sunlight?"

"Oh, no," Lavim said with the infuriating cheerfulness of a kender hedged upon all sides by approaching disaster. "Piper says that it hates the light, but it'll still fly. Probably the light's just making it more annoyed. He says that's why you feel the dragonfear; it's really unhappy now and just throwing around little fear spells out of sheer bad temper. If it were really mad and doing those fear spells for real, you wouldn't be able to move." He cocked his head again, then nodded. "And Piper says that it knows very well that we're here, too."

Finn looked like he could happily murder the kender for his light-hearted delivery of such information. Kembal slid his sword from the scabbard as silently as he could and flattened against the cliff.

Tyorl only sighed. "All right, Lavim, give the rest of it."

"The rest of what?"

"Why hasn't the dragon attacked? Does Piper know that?"

"Uh, I didn't ask—"

"Ask!"

"Right. I—oh, I see. Piper says its because the dragon's waiting. It knows we're here, and it knows it can pick us off any time it wants to—" Finn snarled something and Lavim shrugged, managing to look both innocent and offended. "Well, I'm sorry, but that's what he says the dragon thinks. It's waiting." The kender glared at Finn. "And don't ask me why, because I don't know because Piper doesn't know. All he knows is that it's waiting. I dunno, maybe it's waiting for something to happen or—"

Lavim swallowed whatever it was he meant to say. His voice only a shaking whisper, he said, "I think we're too late."

So pale was the kender that Tyorl, afraid that Lavim's legs would buckle under him, grabbed the kender's arm. "Lavim, what? What is it?"

"We're going to be too late—oh, Tyorl, we're going to be too late!"

"Lavim, what are you talking about?"

Lavim twisted out of Tyorl's grip and bolted, scrambling and limping along the rubble-clogged ledge.

"Lavim! No! Wait!"

Instinctively, Tyorl lunged for him.

And missed.

Caught off balance, Tyorl's ankle twisted and he fell hard to one knee. He only dimly felt the pain as distant fire shooting through his knee and leg.

He was aware of nothing but the long, terrible drop into the fiery valley a thousand feet below, felt nothing but the cold, empty certainty of his death. Though he wanted to, there was not enough air in his lungs to scream.

With a hoarse cry, Kembal grabbed his arm. Hauling with all his strength, the ranger had Tyorl's back against the cold rock of the cliff face before Finn could move.

"Damn the kender!" Finn snarled. "Damn him!"

Stone and bits of the crumbling ledge slid over the edge of the cliff, rattling down to the valley below. A cold wind clawed at Tyorl's face and hair. He hardly felt it for the roaring of his blood, the thundering of his heart. Nausea roiled in his belly, hot, acid bile stung his throat. He wanted to vomit but hadn't the strength for it.

His hand trembled so badly that he needed two attempts before he could clutch Kembal's arm. Tyorl gasped for what breath he needed to speak.

"Forget about the kender," he whispered, wanting for some reason to laugh when he heard the thin croak that used to be his voice. "The gate is around this bend. Give me a hand up if you can."

Finn shook his head. "No, sit here a moment, catch your breath. Your legs won't hold you if you try to stand now."

His back pressed hard against the cliff face, Tyorl pushed himself up, sliding along the rock as though he would never allow as much as an inch of air between his back and the stone again. "We haven't any time now, Finn. Something's happening in the mountain."

"According to that damn kender's dead mage?"

"Yes," Tyorl panted, "according to Piper. Believe it or don't, Finn. You cannot deny that Piper—or Lavim, if you choose—has been right about everything so far."

Finn didn't deny it. Nor did he openly accept it. He only sighed with exaggerated patience. Finn found it easier to look down into the burning valley than at the heart-shattering terror in the elf's eyes. He gestured to Kembal. "Take the lead."

Kembal edged carefully past them. When he was safely past, Tyorl, his face white as death, followed. Behind him came Finn, and Tyorl felt the rangerlord's eyes on his back.

Watching, the elf thought, to see that I don't slip, but I swear, I can hardly bear the weight of his look!

The sun was failing, its light gray through the filter of smoke rising from the distant valley. Lavim, his back to the stone and his dagger in hand, kept himself in the shadow of the mountain as he approached Northgate's opening. When he spoke to Piper he did so silently.

It must have been a very big door!

Piper said nothing.

"I said," he whispered aloud, "it must have been a—"

I heard you, Lavim. Hush! There's no time for chatter now. They've got a few minutes—you'd better get in there while you can.

"Who's got—"

Will you hush!

Who's got a few minutes?

Hornfel and Stanach and Kelida and—

Stanach! And Kelida? What about Hauk? Is he there, too? I've heard so much about him, and it would be nice to finally meet him. Piper—

Footsteps, slow and heavy, sounded from within. Lavim peered very carefully around the edge of the doorway. He squinted into the darkness and held his breath.

A dwarf, his shoulders broad, his chestnut beard thick

and long and shot through with silver, walked slowly down the narrow corridor. In his right hand he carried a sword, in his left a dagger. The clothes he wore were blood stained and torn.

That's Hornfel, the Hylar thane.

Is it? Really? That's what a thane looks like? He needs a good night's sleep and—

The dwarf paused by a half-opened door and leaned against the stone wall. Then, as though chiding himself for resting, he quickly straightened. He looked at his sword and went back down the corridor the way he had come. After a moment, he toed open the door.

"It's time, Stanach. They're here, and they are many."

"Stanach," Lavim whispered.

It was Stanach who entered the corridor, followed by a thick-chested, stocky young man who looked like he needed not only a good night's sleep, but several very good meals.

Abandoning caution like unnecessary baggage, Lavim whooped joyfully and scampered into the gatehouse.

"Hey! Stanach!"

The young man turned, sword in hand, and lunged for the kender.

"No!" Stanach shouted, "Hauk, no!"

Yelping in shocked protest, Lavim ducked, barely in time to miss being spitted by Hauk's sword. His eyes on the glittering blade, Lavim picked himself up very slowly and put his back to the wall.

"Hey, Stanach," he whispered, "do you think you could tell him I'm a friend of yours?" He glanced at Hauk and nodded with what he hoped was reassurance. "I really am, you know. Once, in Long Ridge, there were twenty-five draconians chasing him, and they would have caught him, too, but I saved his life. Then, when the—the waddayacall'ems caught him in the river caves, me and Tyorl and Kelida rescued him.

"And, well, Stanach probably doesn't know about this—but it's true, you just ask Tyorl when he gets here!—I used Piper's magic flute, and we wouldn't be here now at all if I hadn't transported us right to the mountains. Or—well, maybe not right to the mountains. You see, the spell makes you a little sick in your stomach, and I didn't want to turn up in somebody's house or right in the middle of the city and, ah, make a mess. So, we kind of ended up in the bog and—gods!—that place is really burning!"

Squeezed nearly breathless in Stanach's embrace, Lavim had no further chance to list the rest of his credentials.

CHAPTER 30

The broad bay of windows in the west wall of Gneiss's study looked out onto gardens simply designed and laid out in the forms of interlocking rectangles. The study within had been decorated in sparse, military fashion. What few wall hangings there were depicted legendary battles and campaigns in careful detail. Weapons, both ancient and contemporary, bristled in cabinets and showcases. The furniture of stark wood and stone would be inviting to few but old campaigners accustomed to the hard fields of war.

Yet, the gardens, deep and no wider than the length of the study itself, formed a maze of flowers, herbs, and shrubbery that was one of the Daewar's secret delights. However, lush and beautiful as the carefully planned landscaping was, this was not the lure that brought Gneiss, as it always did, to the window.

From where he stood, he could hear the cries of dwarven children at play, among them his own grandsons. These sounds, and the sight of the youngsters' rowdy and raucous games, drew a sigh and a contented smile from the old warrior that might have surprised even his friend, Hornfel.

Aye, Hornfel! Where have you been these hours past? You should have been long back, my friend. Does your silence, he wondered, herald the revolution we've been braced for?

None had seen Realgar for about the same amount of time.

Armor chimed against stone, and Gneiss turned from the garden to answer the peal of battle. Two humans and the half-elf Tanis waited with discernible impatience at the map table. Tanis and the knight, Sturm, stood studying the map of Thorbardin. Dark-eyed and intense, the knight traced the streets he knew and carefully connected them to access ways and transport shafts, familiarizing himself with the infrastructure of the city.

One a planner, Gneiss thought, and the other a careful hunter.

Their companion, the helmed and armored warrior Tanis had introduced as Caramon, lounged in a seat nearby. All long legs and brawny arms, he was the biggest human Gneiss had ever seen.

The three seemed odd and out of place here.

Too big! Gneiss thought. All of 'em are just too damn big!

The dwarf cleared his throat roughly. Gneiss was, above all things, a war chieftain. He was never an orator. He cut right to the heart of the matter at hand.

"Hornfel is too long gone in the Northgate." He nodded to Tanis. "Three hours now since he's left. I don't like it. My runners and scouts report that the cities are too quiet. All but one. They are buzzing in the Theiwar holding like hornets about to tear out of the nest." He held out a hand to the map table. "To work."

He briefly made the three familiar with the six small cities of the kingdom known collectively as Thorbardin and then outlined the plan of defense he and Tanis had hammered out earlier.

"I still don't know whether Rance will rise to fight with Realgar's Theiwar," Gneiss said. "Troops of my own Daewar and the Hylar will keep the northern roads out of their city blocked." He jerked a thumb at the southeast quarter of the map and nodded to Caramon. "With this giant and half the refugees defending the access between the Daergar city and the East Warrens, and Sturm holding the southern route with the other half, I think Rance's warriors are going to be spending most of the revolution caged, eh?"

Caramon chuckled low in his throat. "Depend on it."

"I am depending on it, lad," the thane said quietly.

Gneiss then turned to Tanis. "You will do me a kindness," he said with awkward courtesy, "if you would command your folk and the refugees. Any questions so far?"

Tanis nodded, his own smile wryly appreciative. "Just one. That takes care of the possibilities." He ran a finger over the northwestern part of the map, tracing the areas marked as Klar and Theiwar cities, running up to the ruins of Northgate. "What about the probabilities?"

"Call 'em certainties. That's what they are." Gneiss stabbed a finger at the Theiwar cities. Its shadow cut like a dagger across the finely detailed map. "Here and here is where the trouble will start. Tufa has already got his Klar between the Theiwar and Urkhan Sea. They won't be enough to hold the sneaking bastards, but I'll reinforce them with my warriors." He looked up then, his eyes hard with warning. "Two fields of battle, and between them is the remainder of the refugees.

"You know those people best," Gneiss added. "Assign them to whichever of your two captains here you think appropriate, but keep them as much out of the cities as possible."

"A little hard on your allies, aren't you?" Caramon drawled.

Gneiss said nothing for a long moment, straining for the patience he would not otherwise have wasted on a human. By the Forge! He wished he had the manpower to do this by himself!

"You are allies," he said, slowly, distinctly. "But, my people are edgy and likely won't work with strangers until it's too late. Do you understand?"

Caramon's eyes flashed with sudden anger. Tanis dropped a hand onto the big warrior's shoulder. The gesture itself warned Caramon to silence.

Gneiss had wondered why the half-elf, likely unwelcomed by either humans or elves by the fact of his mixed blood, was the one to lead not only these two humans, but all nine companions who had single-handedly freed eight hundred slaves from Verminaard's mines. There was, after all, this fine, young knight among them. He glanced at Sturm. At best, one would characterize the look in his eyes as one of impatience.

The dwarf snorted as Caramon settled back, hard-jawed but silent. The hasty giant had at least half a brain.

"Are there any more questions?"

There were none. After another few minutes at the map, the three left and Gneiss was alone. He crossed to the windows again and realized that the shouts and laughter of the children had fallen silent. The gardens were empty. He listened carefully for the sounds of the streets beyond the garden wall. He found nothing but an eerie silence.

The captain of Gniess's own guard found him a moment later with word that an attempt had been made on the life of the Klar's thane. Tufa, only slightly wounded, had gone to join the fighting that had broken out at the southern end of the Theiwar holdings between the Urkhan Sea and the Klar city.

"Thane," the captain said, his eyes grim, his fist closing on the grip of his war axe, "the Klar says that the Theiwar have split their forces and nearly fifty of them have fallen back toward Northgate. He and his warband can hold those who remain, but he fears that the squads making for Northgate are acting on some order."

Gneiss buckled on his sword belt and assured himself of the deadly sharpness of the blade. He knew now where Hornfel was, and he knew why Realgar hadn't been seen in hours. A trap had been sprung in Northgate.

"Ten squads to me," he snapped. "Four of archers, the rest swordsmen. You are under Tufa's command now. Take the rest of our warriors and support the Klar where he thinks best."

Gneiss held no hope that he could get to the ruined gate in time to prevent Hornfel's death. However, one hundred strong Daewar, forty archers and sixty swordsmen, would cut through the Theiwar like sun through fog. He would at least avenge his friend's murder.

A bone-snapping hug from Stanach, a hearty kiss from Kelida, and the reunion was over. Lavim tugged his old black coat into order as Stanach fixed him with a look.

"You say Tyorl is here?"

"Oh, yes." Lavim nodded vigorously. "He's on his way and should be here soon." He looked around as Hauk ran toward the gate opening. "Do you think you could be just a little more careful greeting him? There's two rangers with him, and Tyorl might not be the first one you see. Do you remember that ranger Finn that Tyorl was always talking about, Stanach? He's here, too, and Kem.

"It's all right," the kender assured Hauk, much the way he would assure a hasty watchdog that the visitors approaching the door were not to be torn limb from limb. "They're friends."

Hauk grinned. "Aye, old one, I know they are."

"He's mighty quick with that sword," Lavim muttered when Hauk had left. "I thought for a minute there that it was going to get a bit drafty around my middle.

"Sir," he said, addressing Hornfel, "did you know that there are people trying to kill you?"

Hornfel, quiet during the reunion of friends, now fixed the kender with a hard look. "I know it, Lavim. Tell me, how do you?"

Lavim had the feeling that the dwarf's look was not meant as grimly as one might think. Still, he thought it a good idea to answer as best he could. "Well, Stanach told me some of it. All the part about Stormblade and how it was made for you, but this other thane wants it, too, and that you're all fighting about who is going to be the king something-or-other—"

"Regent."

"Yes, that's it. Sort of like a king and sort of like the fellow who watches the store while the shopkeeper has his dinner, right?"

Bemused, Hornfel nodded.

"That's what I thought. Piper told me the part about how this other thane is trying to kill you now. He—"

"Piper?" Kelida shook her head. "Piper, Lavim? He's—"

"Well, yes, he is. He's dead. But he told me. You just ask Tyorl. He knows. It's kind of a strange story, Kelida. You see, it all started back in Qualinesti when Stanach was building the cairn for Piper and—"

A confusion of cries, some from Hauk and Tyorl at the gate and some from the south end of the gatehouse, brought Stanach to his feet.

"What is it, Stanach?"

"They're coming to kill the thane, Lavim. How are you weaponed?"

"My dagger. I lost my hoopak in the bog, but—"

"You'll find plenty of weapons in the guards' quarters over there. Arm yourself well and come back here to me."

As Lavim scurried toward the guards' quarters, Stanach caught him back by the collar. "Wait. What do Tyorl and these rangers have?"

"The rangers have bows and swords. Tyorl lost his bow in the marshes."

"Show them the weapons lockers and get them armed fast."

Stanach was thinking quickly now. An increase of four in the ranks of Hornfel's defenders would make little difference at all if Realgar stood ready to bring several squads of warriors against them. Stanach smiled coldly. But we have archers now. That should count for something.

He touched Kelida's arm with his broken-fingered right hand.

"*Lyt chwaer*, send Tyorl up here and—" Stanach stopped, suddenly aware that he was speaking without authority.

Hornfel nodded to Kelida. "*Kelye dtha*, when you've done as Stanach asks, give Finn my welcome to Thorbardin. Tell him that I'm in need of good archers, and I'd be grateful if he would put his men at the command of my young captain here."

Stanach watched her sprint down the corridor with Hornfel's message.

"Stanach," said Hornfel, breaking the momentary silence, "If I'm to die, it will not be like a rat in a hole."

"Every sword is welcome here, Hornfel Thane, and yours not the least."

Stanach turned and, with a whispered word, gave his plan of defense to the six waiting in the gatehouse.

Outside in the great hall, the murmuring of the Theiwar fell silent, the rattling of their swords against mail and breast plate was stilled.

Like the voice of winter, Realgar's order to attack rang cold and high.

There was only room in Stanach for a last prayer, and he made that as he lifted his sword and instinctively found its balance.

Please, Reorx, please defend us now . . .

The two archers, placed out of sword's reach on the ancient gate mechanism's shaft, kept the air thick with arrows. Kelida knew no difference between her terror of being impaled on an opponent's sword and her terror of catching a friend's arrow in the back.

More frightening than the rangers' arrows were the bolts from Tyorl's crossbow. Those split the air with a wailing shriek that was always echoed by an enemy's high, dying scream.

"Leave the aim up to the archers," Hauk had said. "That's their business, Kelida. Yours is staying alive." He'd started to say something more, but there had been no time. The battle dragged them apart.

Kelida fought with no more skill than she'd had in the great hall, but with as much, if not more, ferocity. It did not take a tactician's skill to know that their backs were to the last wall now. There was nothing behind them but the burning valley a thousand feet below the city.

A black and silver liveried guard lunged from her right, a second from her left. Kelida drove her dagger into the throat of one and kicked out, breaking the knee of the second. Blood was everywhere, steaming from her dagger's steel and running between her fingers.

Someone, she thought it was Lavim, bellowed a warning to duck and she did, only realizing as she dropped to the blood-slick floor that the warning had not been meant for her. A length from her and to her left, a Theiwar, bolt cocked and ready in his crossbow, dropped to one knee and took aim. His target was Hornfel.

"No!" she cried as she launched herself at the dwarf's back, dagger high. She plunged the blade between the bowman's shoulders, and she knew she'd killed him when his scream vibrated in the dagger's steel.

Before Kelida had time to react, Lavim roared warning again. A dagger flew over her head, missing by scant inches. Kelida heard a horrible, bubbling moan and turned.

She knew at once that turning had been a mistake. A heavy weight toppled her from behind. Hands pinned her arms to her side, a knee driven hard into the small of her back sent a sharp pain lancing through her. Nausea churned in her stomach, her vision grayed.

Panicked and weak, Kelida heard someone scream her name.

There was nothing she could do to free herself, no breath to take to even answer. She heard the rough grating of a steel blade scraping on bone.

Had she been struck?

She didn't know. There was no pain . . . until the blade was withdrawn. She knew then that she had been stabbed, and knew it only a moment before she knew nothing at all.

The screams filling the gatehouse echoed the screams tearing through Hauk's soul. Like a starving raptor, he fell upon the Theiwar as though they were nothing more than prey. He killed silently, a voiceless creature seeking death and hoping those deaths would amount to vengeance and that vengeance could amount to cleansing. Those who died on his sword and were luckless enough to look into his eyes as they did, carried an image of fire and ice with them through eternity.

317

"Kelida!" someone screamed.

Hauk yanked his sword from the belly of a Theiwar.

Kelida!

She was down, lying in a spreading pool of blood, her left arm outflung, her hand reaching wide as though for help or pity. She didn't move. A Theiwar lay half across her back, staring up at the dark vault of the ceiling with sightless eyes. His body bristled with arrows, and protruding from his neck was a crossbow bolt.

But there was no getting to her. Realgar's guards swarmed through the gatehouse, and the waves of battle carried Hauk far from the blood-stained floor where Kelida lay, still and silent as the dead.

"Kelida!" Tyorl howled warning, but too late. Too late!

The bolt he loosed flew true, taking the Theiwar guard in the throat. But too late! He looked wildly about the gatehouse, searching for someone who was in the clear and close to her. Lavim was, but only for the second it took Tyorl to draw a breath to call to him. One of Realgar's dwarves jumped him from behind, dragging the old kender down in a tangle of arms and legs.

His mind worked on two levels now: the level of searching for someone to help Kelida, and the level of attack and defense. Tyorl sent a steel-tipped bolt through the heart of the dwarf who rose up to plunge a dagger into Lavim's back and shouted for Stanach, who was just dragging his sword from the gut of another.

The wailing of the dying, the screams of the attackers and defenders both dinned in his ears. Tyorl couldn't be sure that Stanach had heard him, but he no longer had the attention to spare. Four Theiwar, their cold black eyes gleaming with a wild blood lust, rushed him.

Too close to his attackers now to make any use of the crossbow, Tyorl abandoned the weapon for his dagger and sword. Steel in each hand, roaring Kelida's name as though it were a war cry and a talisman both, he leaped among the dwarves.

Stanach kept his back so close to Hornfel's that a sword's

blade could not have passed between them. The thane fought with deadly skill and a cold fury, and no Theiwar would take him from behind while Stanach still lived.

As short as that span may be, Stanach thought grimly.

Realgar had called up fifty warriors. The enemy outnumbered them by odds Stanach didn't care to reckon. Still, the entrance to the gatehouse was narrow, and the three archers within exacted a deadly toll. Stanach thought they could hold the gatehouse for a time, if all of his seven could fight with any skill. But one was an untutored girl, one an old kender, and the three rangers were exhausted before they'd ever picked up their weapons.

And I am one-handed and failing fast . . .

Stanach staggered as Hornfel, hard pressed by two opponents, fell back against him.

"Break," Hornfel panted, "break the form, Stanach! I can watch my back. You're needed in the gatehouse!"

"I'm needed here," Stanach growled.

He sliced the arm from his opponent. Bone glared white and obscenely naked. No sound came from the Theiwar but a thin, gasping with no voice behind it.

Stanach read the scream in his eyes.

Blood sprayed high, steaming in the cold air. Stanach ducked to avoid the blood and kept a firm control over a rising urge to vomit. When Stanach recovered his stance it was to face yet another opponent.

Realgar!

Sapphired Stormblade raised for a killing blow, Realgar's eyes shone with a hatred like the heart of a raging fire. Stanach saw his death in those eyes and in the red-shot gleaming silver of Stormblade's steel.

He swung his own sword up to counter and didn't know the defense had gone well until he heard the ring of steel on steel and felt the numbing vibration of Stormblade's strike against his sword. Stanach threw his whole weight behind his blade, pushing with all the strength he had left.

His strength was not sufficient. As inevitably as the moons rode the sky eastward, so did Stormblade push closer and closer.

Stanach smelled the rusty stench of blood and saw that

319

blood, thick gouts of someone else's life moving in slow sliding trails down Stormblade's smooth steel.

In some far place in his mind, Stanach thought that a pattern was coming right, a circle closing. He would die on the blade of the sword for which he had risked his life and the lives of those who had become his friends.

Realgar hissed, and Stanach, feeling the first tremors in the muscles of his sword arm, knew the hiss for laughter.

Someone bellowed wildly and tackled him low around the knees. Stormblade's steel cut the air where Stanach's neck had been.

He crashed to the broken tiles and slid with the force of the tackle on the blood-slicked floor. Gasping for breath that would not come, Stanach groped blindly for his sword.

"Up!" Lavim yelled, "Up, young Stanach! C'mon! Get up! There's more of 'em! Look!"

Stanach lurched to his feet, still gasping. He looked wildly around. More, aye! He laughed aloud. The most of the dwarves he saw wore Daewar scarlet and silver!

"Friends, Lavim! Those are Gneiss's warriors!"

Stanach sucked in a long breath and realized then that the deep song of bow strings and flown arrows was stilled. The clash of steel on steel rang now only in the great hall. The gatehouse behind him was silent. He stared numbly at the old kender who had once again saved his life. "Where's—where's the thane?"

Blood crimsoned the kender's hands nearly to the elbows and his old black coat was slashed. A bruise purpled his wrinkled cheek and the mark of a dagger scored his forehead. But he was still on his legs, his green eyes gleaming.

"I'm not sure," Lavim said. "He might be in the gatehouse. He ran back toward Tyorl. Stanach, that crazy-eyed dwarf who was going to slice off your head followed him! Piper says he's the one who wants to kill Hornfel."

"Piper says—" Stanach shook his head. Piper says . . . But there was no time to think about dead mages. He had to find Hornfel.

"Who's still standing?" Stanach asked.

"Finn has a sword cut in the leg. Hauk is all right. Kelida's hurt but I saw Kem a minute ago and he says she'll be all right." Lavim fell silent, tugging at his long white braid.

"Lavim," he said, strangely calm, "who else is hurt?"

"I—I don't know if Tyorl will be all right—"

"What happened to him?" Stanach snapped.

"That dwarf with the crazy eyes—he was chasing Hornfel and Tyorl got between 'em and—Stormblade—"

As though he hadn't heard the old kender's words, Stanach looked slowly around the hall. Twenty-nine Theiwar lay dead or dying. Realgar was not one of them, and Stanach didn't know where Hornfel was.

Lavim didn't know if Tyorl would be all right.

Stanach spoke harshly, his throat thick with fear and impending grief. "I have to find the thane. I—I have to, Lavim. Is Hauk with Kelida?"

"Yes."

"Get him. We owe him a debt of vengeance. Tell him I know where he can collect it."

Lavim watched him go and only too late realized that in the excitement of finding his friends again, of the battle, he'd forgotten to tell Stanach about the dragon.

CHAPTER 31

HORNFEL HAD NO SWORD. HE HAD NO DAGGER. HE HAD only his life, and that he would not have for long. Hornfel lifted his head and spoke with a simple dignity.

"Murder me now, Theiwar, and be known as the Cursed King." His brown eyes glittered. "And no curse carries more weight than that of a murdered man. Meet my challenge. Here above the kingdom you want to rule is where we'll decide the matter. Have you the courage to face me without your warriors?"

They faced each other on the ledge like statues carved from the living rock of the mountain, Hylar thane and Theiwar. Though bitter wind tore at them, whipping their hair and clothes wildly around them, Stanach had no sense that they were anything but some stone cutter's monument to strife.

Grounded on the stone of the narrow ledge, the blood-darkened swords Realgar held reflected the eerie twilight only thinly. Though they must have heard Stanach's approach, and Hauk's a moment later, neither Realgar nor Hornfel looked around.

Stanach heard his own voice, his words, before he was aware of speaking. "We can take him, Hornfel Thane."

Hornfel did not take his eyes from Realgar's as he accepted the weapon the Theiwar passed to him. When he spoke, he spoke to Stanach.

"So you can. But, I've made a challenge, and he's accepted it."

Yes, Stanach thought, but will you be the one to survive this? We need a king regent, and not the mad rule of a *derro* mage. Hornfel Thane! Don't do this!

Like a ghost's whisper, Isarn's strange words echoed in Stanach's heart: *I made the sword for a thane. Realgar will use it to kill a high king.*

In the Deep Warrens, Stanach had been reluctant to believe the old master's words, had refused to hear the prophecy ringing behind them. Now, standing on the ledge a thousand feet above the fiery valley, the Kingsword's crimson steel heart shining with the reflected light of Reorx's forge, Stanach wondered if Isarn had spoken truly.

Reason tried to dissuade him. Where was the Hammer of Kharas? Where was the legend that would consecrate a high king? No one knew. No one even looked for the mythical hammer anymore. Yet Isarn Hammerfell, who had crafted a god-touched Kingsword, spoke of Hornfel and called him high king, as though, in the last moments of his life, the old master had seen legends become real.

Behind him, Hauk moved restlessly. Stanach stilled the ranger with a gesture.

"We can take him," Hauk whispered. "Stanach, we can end this."

Stanach shook his head. "This is the thane's business. We'll wait, Hauk."

Hauk heard nothing in Stanach's words but a brave warrior's death sentence. His hands tightened on the grip of his sword. "We'll wait for what?" he said harshly. "For Hornfel to die?"

"He's a good fighter. He won't die."

Realgar's smile was cold as ice. He lifted his head a little, as though scenting victory. In the gray twilight, the Theiwar's eyes were like a snake's, the pupils narrowed to slits to protect his retinas from what to him must seem a blazing glare.

Stanach shivered with sudden fear in the wind.

His eyes! No light-hating Theiwar would choose to fight even in the dim twilight if he could avoid it. Why was Realgar here? Why hadn't he maneuvered Hornfel back into the darkness of the gatehouse?

Realgar lifted a hand and moved his lips in a soundless word of magic.

Fear, like sudden sickness, shot through Stanach and filled him with dread.

"Hornfel—!"

His cry of warning came too late.

Twilight became midnight, starless, moonless, and as complete as the darkness of the tomb. A dragon's battle cry thundered against the cold sky. All heart and strength sucked out of him, Stanach fell to his knees. Stunned with dragonfear, blinded by the dragon's spell of darkness, he only dimly heard Hauk's cry and Hornfel's shout of anger.

Realgar's triumphant laughter soared through the darkness as though on the wings of the dragon.

"Bastard!" Stanach snarled. "Treacherous bastard!"

The wind of the dragon's passing flung him back against the face of the cliff and sucked the breath from his lungs. Suddenly dizzy, disoriented, and numb with fear, Stanach was reft of his will and helpless. Caught in a web of darkness, in a swamp of horror, he was incapable of moving. A thousand feet below the valley still burned. The flames, leaping high, seemed to reach for him with certain confidence that they would have him. The wind of the heights, the blast of the dragon's renewed passing dragged him so close to the cliff's edge that Stanach knew he must fall.

Hauk screamed his name. With the unbreakable strength of panic, a hand clamped on his right wrist. Though

Stanach couldn't feel the grip, he felt the pull in his shoulder. Hauk had him and dragged hard, hauling him back from the drop and into the gatehouse.

Echoes from a nightmare, the belling of steel clashing against steel rang in the darkness.

The thane! Oh, Reorx, the thane!

"He's fighting blind!" Hauk cried. The young man's horror ran like lightning through his hands and set Stanach's bones vibrating.

Tyorl pulled himself up, leaning heavily all the while on Lavim's shoulder. He'd seen men do it, stand when they should have been incapable of even breathing. Once he'd wondered what that must feel like, and now he knew. A slow draining of life, his blood seeped from the jagged sword wound in his belly.

It had happened fast, all in a moment. The rage and fury of the battle had risen to a mad pitch as red and silver uniformed Daewar poured into the great hall and the gatehouse. Tyorl, back on his vantage point on the gate mechanism, had seen Realgar, Stormblade leveled to plunge into the Hylar's unprotected back. There was no time to load a bolt into the crossbow. The elf had moved without thinking.

Tyorl had put himself between Realgar and Hornfel. Stormblade had been like ice tearing through him, like fire when Realgar ripped the steel free. Now, he felt no pain. By that, more than even the lifeless cold, he knew he was dying.

And what was dragonfear to one who was dying?

"The—the crossbow," he whispered.

Lavim swallowed hard. "Tyorl, I don't think you—"

"Please. Help me now, Lavim."

"No, Tyorl! You have to wait here for Kem." Desperate hope made the kender's voice ragged. "He'll make you better. You'll see. You'll see, Tyorl."

Tyorl leaned his face against the stone wall and braced his legs. These small movements, this trying to talk, only left him colder. He slid the flat of his hand along Piper's flute, still on his belt.

Lavim had once claimed that Piper could read his thoughts. Tyorl clutched the flute.

Piper, he thought, tell him to help me. I can kill that dragon if he'll only help, Piper . . .

Do as he asks, Lavim. Do as he asks.

As he heard Lavim's frantic objections, Tyorl's fingers tightened, white-knuckled, on the kender's shoulder. "Please."

Even as he pressed the crossbow into Tyorl's hand, Lavim protested again. "Tyorl, you have to stay here. You have to wait for Kem. He's with Kelida now—"

"Kelida!" Tyorl whispered. "Lavim, she's all right?"

Lavim nodded vigorously. "She'll be fine. Kem says so. Please, Tyorl, please let me help you sit until he can get here."

Tyorl shifted his grip on Lavim's shoulder.

"Help me onto the ledge."

"No, Tyorl!"

The pain he should have been feeling snarled within him, not felt yet, but stalking him like a relentless wolf.

Piper, tell him.

Tyorl watched the kender, head cocked and listening while Piper spoke soundless words.

Lavim. It's like when you had to help Kelida set Stanach's fingers. I know you don't want to, but you have to. There's no time to argue. Do as he asks.

"But what are we going to do? He has to stay here! He has to wait for Kem! Piper—!"

The kender's voice faded and became the howling of the wind. The stone Tyorl now braced his back against was the mountain wall, and he didn't know how he'd come to be outside the gate. Gnarled hands gentle and trembling, Lavim still held him up. The cold on the ledge seemed almost warm when compared with the emptiness filling him.

Close, and yet seeming so far away, steel whined on steel. Blackness shrouded the ledge. Distantly, like an old, old memory, fear of heights whispered in Tyorl's heart. But it only whispered. As he did not feel the dragonfear, he did not feel the clutch and drag of the fear of heights.

"Lavim, nock the quarrel."

He heard Lavim ground the crossbow and grunt with the effort of drawing back the string. Shrieking higher than the wind, the black dragon flew high and wheeled for another pass at the ledge.

Hauk's voice, harsh and thick with fear, cried: "Stanach! He's fighting blind!"

Steel sang, boots scraped on stone.

Tyorl opened his eyes when he felt the bow pressed into his hand again.

I can't see in this darkness!

"Piper can." Lavim whispered. "It's all right."

Guide me!

"He will—"

"Have you loaded the bow right?"

"Of course I have, Tyorl!"

Tyorl drew a thin breath and stiffened as pain finally found him. A blast of wind, like thunder, filled the darkness. The dragon dove, screaming with savage and terrible joy. The ranger's arms had been so heavy before. They were light now. Hardly knowing that he'd lifted the crossbow, Tyorl gave himself over to Piper's direction, ready to shoot at a dragon he could not see.

Darknight's fear spell lay like a deadly weight on Stanach's heart. Hornfel was blind in magic's darkness and somehow finding the courage to battle both the dragonfear and a relentless enemy. Blind against Stormblade and the murderer who wielded it. Blind at the edge of a thousand-foot cliff!

Before he could think, before he could remember that he was not supposed to be able to move under the paralyzing constraints of dragonfear, Stanach broke Hauk's grip.

Dizzy and disoriented, his head aching with his eyes' efforts to see where no sight could function, Stanach forced himself to stop. He, who could see in places where no light ever came, was blind.

Dragging bitterly cold air into his lungs, Stanach managed to ease the reeling dizziness. He strained to hear and found at once that he could place the fighters by their hoarse breathing, the clash of steel on steel.

Somewhere in the icy sky, the dragon still flew. Waves of dread, like the restless motion of a horrible sea, churned the air around the ledge. Concentrating only on the sounds of the fight, Stanach inched forward, praying for some clue to tell him which of the combatants was Hornfel, which was Realgar.

The high whine of one blade sliding along another sounded in the darkness. Loose stone slithered, and Stanach heard a boot scrape on stone, a tightly drawn breath.

Then, Stanach heard the deep, vibrating hum of a crossbow bolt in flight.

They were nothing, the elf and the kender on the ledge. Hardly anything to whet an appetite. Certainly they wouldn't satisfy Darknight's hunger for anything but cruelty. That cruelty became simple rage when the dragon saw the crossbow in the elf's hands.

Did the puny creature really think to do it harm with that toy?

Darknight cut its wings back and reared high, forelegs reaching for the elf on the ledge, screaming laughter as it dove.

It heard the hum of the crossbow's string as nothing more than a stirring of the air. The steel-tipped bolt tore like silver lightning through its left eye, and the black dragon's scream of joy became agonized shrieking. There was room for nothing in its mind but surprise, and then panic, as its wings fouled in an updraft and fire ran along its spine. No sooner had the dragon recognized the pain, when all sense and feeling vanished from its huge body.

There was nothing left to it but one small part of its mind, and that part was filled, for the moment it had left of life, with astonishment.

Darknight dropped with the echoes of its death scream into the burning valley.

Like fire in the darkness, the dragon's scream tore through Stanach's blindness, reverberating in endlessly wailing echoes from the mountainside.

Slowly, like ice melting under the sun, the terror of dragonfear fell away, and the darkness of the dragon's spell dissolved like smoke before the wind. Darknight was dead!

Gasping for breath, Stanach looked wildly about him for Hornfel.

Hauk bellowed warning. Steel clattered on stone, and Stanach spun to see Hornfel, unweaponed and his back to the burning valley. Dark cloak whipping behind him, mad *derro* eyes aflame, Realgar held Stormblade in an easy grip.

"The fire," he whispered, "or the sword? The fall or the steel?"

Hornfel's expression, deadly cool and steady, warned Stanach off. "Give me the steel," he said to Realgar and crooked a finger in a mocking "come ahead" gesture. "Let me see if you can."

Realgar firmed his grip on the red-hearted Kingsword and leveled Stormblade. Under the guise of shifting his stance, he lunged for Hornfel's throat.

Stanach dove for Realgar the moment Hornfel dropped low and shouldered in under his guard. The two hit the Theiwar at the same time, Stanach high and grabbing for his wrist with his left hand; Hornfel low and toppling him hard to the ledge.

Stanach caught an elbow hard under the jaw and fell away. He tried to scramble to his feet, but didn't make it. The Theiwar, Stormblade still in his fist, struggled to free himself from Hornfel's hold and kicked back hard. Stanach felt the boot heel like lightning on the side of his head and heard the blow as resounding thunder. Almost at once, two hands, large and strong, hauled Stanach to his feet. Knees weak as water, Stanach still tried to break Hauk's hold.

"No room," Hauk said, pinning Stanach's arms behind him. "No time."

Realgar had broken free of Hornfel. Stormblade high, he launched himself at the Hylar thane, swinging the Kingsword as though it were an axe. Hornfel rolled back against the mountain and threw himself to the left. Steel screamed on rock, a high, chilling shriek. Realgar, staggered by the blow, struck and missed, reeling toward the edge of the cliff. Hornfel growled low in his throat and then roared a furious curse. He was on his feet before the curse had begun to echo.

Realgar staggered on the brink of the ledge, Stormblade clenched in his right fist. Stanach saw panicked astonishment screaming in the *derro* mage's eyes the instant his foot missed the crumbling stone.

Panting raggedly, Hornfel dove for Realgar's arm and caught it in both hands. He fell to his knees, dragged to the stone by the weight of the struggling mage.

"Let him go!" Hauk cried.

With all Realgar's weight pulling on him, Hornfel gritted his teeth and pulled back.

"Let him go!" Stanach whispered.

Hornfel's grip slipped, his hands slid up Realgar's arm to his wrist, his fingers touching the hilt of the Kingsword just as Realgar threw back his head and screamed. The mage fell and Hornfel lunged for Stormblade.

Steel flashed, fiery heart catching the last gray light, as Hornfel snatched it back from the void.

Stanach closed his eyes, sharp tears clawing at his throat. For a long, dizzying moment, he didn't know if his heart tightened for regret or for rejoicing.

They weren't Hauk's hands on Stanach's arms now, but Lavim's. Hauk had rushed to Hornfel. Still staggered by the Theiwar's kick, Stanach looked around at the kender in confusion. Lavim was saying something but Stanach couldn't make it out.

"Slow," the dwarf whispered hoarsely. "Lavim, go slow."

Lavim tugged at Stanach's left hand. "Come with me now, Stanach," he urged. "You have to come with me now."

The dwarf said nothing. He wasn't up to arguing with Lavim and simply went where he was pulled. He heard Kelida's voice, low and weary. He looked around for her, his vision skewing a little.

The dwarf found her on her knees at the gaping door to Northgate, supporting Tyorl. Her hunting shirt was torn where she'd been struck, the gray leather slit neatly where Kembal had cut it away to clean and bandage her wound. She spoke a word to Lavim, and the kender, his wrinkled face white, bolted for the gate, shouting for Kem.

From where he stood, Stanach could see Kelida's grief-stricken expression, the shaking of her hand as she rested her fingers on Tyorl's throat to feel for a lifebeat that, if it still existed, could not be strong. Too much blood stained the elf's hunting leathers.

He heard Hauk's voice behind him. Stanach turned. Hauk looked down at Stormblade in Hornfel's hand.

Slowly, Hornfel laid the sword down beside Tyorl. The flash of loathing in Hornfel's eyes toward the Kingsword, momentarily seen and instantly hidden, chilled Stanach's heart. Stormblade's sapphired hilt caught the fading light. The fire of Reorx's forge pulsed in the flat of the blade.

Wordlessly, Hauk took Lavim's place. He placed shaking fingers on Tyorl's arm. His lips moved soundlessly, repeating the name of the friend who had traveled so far to rescue him from Realgar's torments. Hauk's were the bleakest eyes Stanach had ever seen.

Stanach touched Kelida's shoulder gently. "*Lyt chwaer.*" He went to his heels beside her.

"I sent Lavim for Kembal." Grief made a tattered thing of her low voice. "It won't matter. Tyorl is dying, Stanach."

He wrapped his arms around her, supporting her while she held Tyorl. "I'm sorry," he whispered.

Kelida leaned against Stanach's shoulder and buried her face in his thick, black beard.

Stanach stroked her shoulder gently and looked up to meet Hauk's eyes. The ranger's disbelief, and his struggle to understand that his friend was dying, made him seem suddenly very young.

Tyorl stirred. His lips moved as though he tried to speak. When his hand moved in Kelida's she turned, green eyes shimmering with her tears. Gently, so that she didn't jar him, Kelida bent and lightly kissed him.

"Ah," Tyorl whispered, "you kissed me for luck and farewell once before—in Long Ridge." He lifted his hand, touched her face, her hair. "Kelida."

Stanach felt her move as she caught Tyorl's falling hand. Kelida sobbed, and Stanach's heart ached with stunned grief.

Tyorl was dead of Stormblade's steel.

CHAPTER 32

Stormblade.

Kingsword made from pieces of twilight and a midnight star.

Though it was his, Hornfel had not buckled on the sword, not felt its weight on his hip, in all the three days since the battle in Northgate. Though the dwarves of Thorbardin acknowledged him, cheerfully some and sullenly others, as king regent, his investiture would not take place for seven nights. It would not be appropriate for him to wear the Kingsword before then.

Hornfel lifted the lid of the coffer that held Stormblade. Lined with velvet the color of smoke, satin the color of the steel's red heart, this coffer had held the Kingswords of generations of high kings.

Now it holds that of a king regent, he thought, and holds it here in the Court of Thanes, well under guard, but here for all to see, wonder at, exclaim over.

They had come like people seeking the blessings of a relic. The Court of Thanes had never been so well guarded as it had these two days past. The house guards of each of the six thanedoms stood shared watches for all the hours of the day and night.

Hornfel stepped back from the coffer, away from the long display case, which looked more and more like a bier each time he saw it. He wondered if any Kingsword had ever cost so dearly as Stormblade had cost.

When word returned to the Theiwar fighting at the Klar city that their thane was dead, they had fallen into confused disarray and fled back their dark cities.

It was a confusion, Hornfel thought now, that would not find resolution until the Theiwar found time to stand back from the bloody waters of their own internal politics and choose a leader from among those still living.

Though Rance would not admit to a death count, in the farming warrens Rance's Daergar had moved swiftly and savagely against the refugees. Sturm had pinned them neatly in the south entrance to the farming warrens and Caramon had closed them in from the north. Tanis and his captains had stood true.

It was the end of the revolution. Rance stood by his claim of defending his holding when he'd thought it surrounded by Outlanders taking advantage of the Theiwar uprising to loot and pillage. None could prove he was allied with Realgar.

Hornfel shuddered and found his eyes drawn to the sword. Silver chased gold hilt, perfect sapphires, and a flame-hearted blade of finest steel: it was the price of so many lives!

His weariness was soul-deep and he didn't know how he was going to make his regency worth the lives of the kin, friends, and strangers who had died for it.

He heard a footstep behind him. Hornfel turned, thinking suddenly of Piper. He almost called the mage's name aloud, but stopped himself when the kender, Lavim, rounded a broad, high column.

Hornfel stared at the kender. He had gotten past twenty-four armed warriors and none of them could have so much as thought a shadow was passing!

The kender, cheerfully unconcerned, greeted Hornfel with casual goodwill. "You know, sir, they've been looking for you all over the place. It's almost sunset now. They'll be waiting for you in the Valley of the Thanes. Me, I figured this was where you'd be, so I came to get you. Besides, I kind of wanted to get another look at Stormblade." He cocked a thumb at the Kingsword. "I've been looking at that thing for a couple of weeks now. I have to tell you, it doesn't look like itself in there."

Hornfel smiled. "What does it look like?"

"Well, bigger, I guess."

Lavim stepped closer to the coffer for a better look. Hornfel kept close beside him. Amusing and ingenuous as he was, Lavim was still, after all, a kender.

"No," Lavim said, revising his opinion. "Not bigger. Just— I dunno, not like Kelida's sword. Or Hauk's. Or whoever's it is." Lavim shrugged and then looked up at a deeply shadowed corner of the far ceiling, his eyes narrowed. "Right. His."

A shiver of something partly fear and partly anticipation slid along Hornfel's arms. "Lavim," he said slowly, carefully, "who are you talking to?"

Lavim's face, a weathered mass of deep wrinkles, brightened. "Piper, of course."

Piper. Hornfel had heard the story in the gatehouse, Lavim's fast-talking explanation as to how he came to be entering Northgate by a five-foot ledge a thousand feet above a burning valley. The kender claimed that he spoke with Piper's ghost. To his credit, Finn grudgingly backed Lavim up. Hornfel did not know what to believe.

Lavim, his eyes full of mischief, cocked his head again, listening to some voice Hornfel could not hear. "Oh," he said as though reminded of something, "right. I forgot." Hands kender-quick, he reached into a deep pocket of his old black coat and rummaged only a little. What he produced from that pocket made Hornfel smile. Cherry wood, polished smooth as satin, and so very familiar, the kender held up Jordy's pipe.

"You know this, don't you? Piper's flute. It's magic. I know because I used it twice. Once to save young Stanach from the—the waddayacall'ems—"

"Theiwar."

"Right. And once to transport me and Finn and Kem and—" Lavim hesitated only a little, his eyes darkening. "— and Tyorl out of the Hills of Blood. Stanach was going to bring it back to you because he said that you and Piper were particular friends."

"Particular friends, eh? Stanach said that?"

"Well, no. I just did. But Stanach would have said it if he'd thought of it."

Hornfel reached out and ran a finger down the flute's length. "Does he really talk to you, Lavim?"

Lavim nodded vigorously, white braid bobbing. "Oh, sure he does. He told me all about how you kept him out of the dungeons and how light gets into the city from outside and about the gardens and farms." Lavim's eyes twinkled. "And he told me something else, too. He told me—oh. Well, I can't tell you that." He shrugged. "But never mind, you'll know all about it soon anyway. There's one thing I can tell you."

Amused, Hornfel smiled indulgently. "What is that?"

Suddenly solemn, Lavim tucked the flute back into his pocket. "He said you should bring Stormblade to the Valley of the Thanes when you come for—when you come."

For Tyorl's funeral. There had been funerals enough in the last few days. Hornfel had attended those he could. This one, small and private, would be different. Tyorl's funeral would serve, at least for Hornfel, as Piper's, too. And Kyan's. Elf, dwarf, and human mage, they had died for Stormblade. And for him.

Though it would be fitting for the Kingsword to be present, Hornfel would not be able to wear it until his investiture. Not even for this.

The dwarf shook his head. "I can't do that, Lavim. I can't wear it yet."

"Mmmm. You really can't? Would it just be impolite, or is

it some kind of law or something?"

"Both."

Lavim thought, or listened, for a moment. "So, then don't wear it. Just bring it."

"Lavim, I don't think—"

"Now you see," Lavim said earnestly, stepping closer to the coffer as he spoke. "That's just the problem everyone seems to have. They say 'I don't think,' and they really mean they're thinking. It's no good, thinking. Just gets you into trouble."

Quick as a trout darting, Lavim took up the Kingsword and tossed it to Hornfel, who caught it. "There! Now you've got it. If you've broken some law or been impolite—though I think you've certainly been polite enough all along—you might as well do it for an hour or so as do it for ten seconds, right?"

Stormblade balanced perfectly in Hornfel's grip. It had been made for his hand and fit well there.

"Piper says to bring it?" Hornfel asked.

Lavim nodded solemnly.

"All right then, I'll bring it. What about the flute?"

"Oh, that." Lavim patted his pocket. "You've got that heavy sword to carry. Don't worry about the flute. I'll keep it for you temporarily, right here in my pocket."

CHAPTER 33

Home, Stanach thought. I'm home!

Using his left hand and his shoulder, he rolled another cairn stone to the growing pile. He'd been reminding himself since dawn that he was, indeed, home. Now, with the sunset light red on the walls of the Valley of the Thanes, he still needed reminding. It wasn't that Thorbardin had changed. Stone and steel, the place was still the same. He had changed.

Stanach shied from the memory of his reunion with his parents, with his friends. He didn't like to recall their shock when they'd seen his ruined hand, or the way they'd looked at him when they realized he was not the quiet, peaceable forgeman they'd known only a few short weeks ago.

He'd been in the Outlands, and he'd come home changed.

The difference had not to do with his injury. It had more to do with the stranger they saw in his eyes. Dark-eyed, he was, and knife-scarred, changed somehow by looking at horizons more distant than those many dwarves had seen.

The wind cut, sharp and cold, through the Valley of the Thanes. The valley was the only part of Thorbardin open to the sky. In ancient times, it had been a cavern. Now, the cavern long since collapsed, the sinkhole had become a valley, holding a small lake and carefully tended gardens on the water's edge. The barrows of lesser folk lined the edges of the valley. The cairns of thanes and high kings stood in the gardens.

If the Valley of the Thanes was where the dwarves buried their dead, it was also where they, normally great mistrusters of magic, rejoiced in the working of enchantment. High above the lake, its shadow cutting always across the water and the valley, hung Duncan's Tomb. Nothing supported the tomb but the spell of some long-dead mage.

Here Duncan was entombed, the last High King of the Dwarves. None had reigned in Thorbardin for all the three hundred years since his death. Despite the lives lost to regain the Kingsword Stormblade, none would reign in Thorbardin again. Kharas, Duncan's friend and champion, had hidden his war hammer with the aid of magic and the god who had made it. None had found it since.

Hornfel would be high king, Isarn had said.

Stanach shook his head. No, Hornfel would not sit on the high king's throne. He was king regent, though Reorx knew he'd guard the kingdom as though he were high king. That would have to be enough.

Stanach leaned against the pile of stone and dragged an arm across his face. Sweat and dirt grimed the loose, white forgeman's shirt he wore. He'd not stand before a forge again, but he knew no more comfortable clothes than this old shirt and the brown leather breeches he'd once worn for forge work. There were people who would have done this cairn building for him, stonemasons and diggers whose job it was to do it. Stanach would have none build Tyorl's cairn but himself.

Of Piper's cairn, built on the lonely edge of Qualinesti,

Tyorl had said: *You're skilled enough at it. Your friends don't live very long, Stanach. How many cairns have you built since you left Thorbardin?*

Then, Kelida, standing watch on the hilltop, had murmured protest at what she perceived as the elf's cruelty. Stanach had not thought the words cruel then, he didn't think them cruel now. Only true.

The dwarf's lips twitched in a crooked, humorless smile. Piper's had been the first cairn he'd ever built. Tyorl's would be the second.

"And the last," he whispered. "Aye, the last, Tyorl. Though I'd never thought to be building yours and never here in the Valley of the Thanes, in the shadow of a high king's tomb."

The wind whistled high and then dropped low around the walls of the valley, a slow, sad dirge. Stanach thought of Piper's flute. They were mourning in Thorbardin and not the least for the mage Jordy, whom the children had named Piper.

Lavim, perverse and adamant, still insisted that though Piper was dead, the mage spoke to him, whispering inside his head. Mostly lecturing and scolding, according to the kender.

Stanach bent to his work again. He hadn't the heart for believing in ghosts. Piper was dead. He'd buried him just as he was preparing to bury Tyorl now.

They were seven who gathered in the Valley of the Thanes, under the shadow of Duncan's Tomb and in twilight's fragile glow, to honor Tyorl.

It was a measure of Hornfel's gratitude toward the elf who had died in saving his life that he had commanded that Tyorl's cairn be erected in the gardens that had been, until now, the inviolable precincts of thanes and kings. It was a measure of his respect that he would speak Tyorl's eulogy.

Why, Stanach wondered, did Hornfel carry Stormblade with him into the Valley of the Thanes?

Grimy and sweating still, Stanach watched as Kelida, with Hauk beside her, took her place beside the grave. The dwarf smiled, for the first time genuinely. The two had been together only a few days. They moved in concert now as though they'd known the way of each other for years.

Kembal and Finn carried Tyorl's body into the valley and laid it within the grave that Stanach had made. The piles of stones seemed like heaped darkness beside the frame of Tyorl's cairn. The rangers went to stand beside Hauk. They were the last of the Nightmare Company, come to bid a brother farewell.

With a quiet deference to the friends gathered here, Hornfel grounded Stormblade's point as though in salute and leaned the Kingsword against the piled stones before he took his place at the foot of the cairn. Lavim, green eyes quiet and solemn, came to stand beside Stanach. The dwarf hoped he wasn't going to start talking about ghosts now.

Lavim reached up to gently pat Stanach's shoulder. "You did all this?"

Stanach nodded grimly.

"It's very nice," he whispered. He cocked a thumb at Duncan's Tomb. "But the shadow of that big floating thing kind of gets in the way, don't you think? Piper says it's Duncan's Tomb and—"

Stanach closed his eyes. "Hush, Lavim. Not now."

The wind, cold and thin, fluted through the Valley of the Thanes. Its song did not disturb the silence of those gathered by the cairn but framed it.

When he spoke, Hornfel quoted the wisdom of the proverb he'd remembered on the Northgate wall with revolution boiling at his back and *guyll fyr* raging at his feet.

"The wolf at the door," he said softly, "will make brothers of strangers. The wolf's been snapping and howling outside Thorbardin, and for too long we've bolted our doors against him, believing that there is no wolf if we don't hear him.

"We hear the howling now, who have too long ignored it. We hear it in the mourning of the kin-reft, in the cries of those who die under the claws and fangs of war.

"We hear the wolf's howl in the wind of the dragons' wings. Tyorl silenced it for a moment, but we will hear it again."

Hornfel lifted his eyes then and looked at each person

gathered at the cairn.

"But we see, too. We see brothers where we once thought strangers stood. We see kin, if not kind. And kin we've too long turned away from, kin who have tried to silence the wolf's bloody howl while we waited for it to leave, to hunt some other ground.

"The wolf won't leave; Verminaard still ranges our lands, and the war will not go away until it has stolen everything and everyone. As it has stolen Tyorl.

"I mourn with you for the death of a friend."

Lost in his sorrow for Tyorl's death and the echoes of past mourning; Stanach didn't realize that Hornfel had finished until he felt, and then heard, a change in the wind's tenor. He looked up at Kelida, directly across the cairn. Head cocked, the last light catching in her red hair, she seemed to have noticed the change, too.

Hauk glanced at Kembal. Finn tilted his head back to look up at the dark rim of the valley.

Lavim drew a short breath and let it out in a soft, wondering sigh. Stanach turned in time to see the kender take an old flute from his pocket. Piper's flute.

Listening for only a moment, as though to assure himself of the melody and his proper place to join it, the kender raised the flute to his lips and began to play. The hard walls of the Valley of the Thanes became faint and gray as ancient memories.

Sunlight danced down a silver river, and Stanach not only saw the jeweled play of light, he smelled the rich, dark mud on the water's banks, tasted the sweet river itself.

Diamond ice sheathed winter trees, melting at the touch of a hand and sliding away to make new jewels. Kelida lifted her hand, touched a finger to her lips, and Stanach felt the cold on his own lips.

Dew drifting back to the sky on the summer sun glistened on Hauk's face; like tears it crept into his dark beard. Like a wraith, or only the dew that it was, it vanished under the sunlight. It took a moment longer for the tears to dry on Stanach's face.

In days after, he would try to capture the melody of that song. Always, though he would remember and see again the images of the forest he saw in the shadowless light of gloaming, the song would elude him except as the half-remembered laughter of wind in the trees.

Lavim dropped to his heels, and watched as Hauk, Kembal, and Finn arranged the last of the cairn stones over Tyorl. The sound of that sad building echoed hollowly throughout the valley.

"I didn't mean to make them cry," the kender whispered.

Aye, spellcaster? Piper's voice was very gentle. *What did you mean to do then?*

"I wanted to make a song for them to remember Tyorl by, that's all." He sighed and shook his head, listening to the wind that was only wind now. "And—and I know that Stanach built this cairn here all by himself, and that Hornfel said he could be buried with kings and thanes. But it seemed kind of sad that Tyorl wouldn't be in his woods anymore. I wanted them to remember Qualinesti for him."

And they will. You crafted a fine song, Lavim.

Lavim frowned then. "I did? All by myself? It wasn't you or the flute?"

Who's was the intent?

"Mine."

Then it was your song, aye?

He'd done magic all by himself! Lavim scrambled to his feet, eyes wide. "Piper! Did I—"

Hush, now, Lavim! It's not over yet. Watch—quietly! — for a moment more. And then, just do as I tell you.

Stormblade sang the high song of steel as Hornfel withdrew the Kingsword from its scabbard. Though the last light had fled from the Valley of the Thanes, the blade's red steel heart shone. The light of Reorx's forge pulsed gently, spilling it's crimson glow across the faces of those gathered by the completed cairn.

Like bloody shadows, Stanach thought.

Then, caught by the glow, caught by the light of the Kingsword he had helped to forge and remembering suddenly the joy of Stormblade's making, the promise of its steel heart and the hope it represented, Stanach thought again.

Not like bloody shadows at all, though Reorx knew enough blood had been shed for Stormblade. Bloody shadows would be cold as death. The light of the Kingsword shone bright in the darkness of this burial place.

Like a lantern in a brave man's hand. Aye, like that.

Hornfel raised Stormblade high and even the shadow of Duncan's Tomb did not obscure its light.

The wind fell silent. Those standing by Tyorl's cairn lifted their heads a little as though, all at the same moment, they scented something in the silence.

Stanach heard Lavim catch his breath, a sharp sound of delighted surprise.

Hornfel grounded the gleaming blade on the largest stone of the cairn, a soldier's farewell. As the blade tip touched the stone, Stormblade's light seemed to grow momentarily brighter, shattering the darkness, just as Lavim's laughter, a gleeful whoop, shattered the silence.

"Of course! Of course!" the kender cried.

Kelida gasped. Stanach turned sharply, reaching for the kender to grab and silence him. Lavim, nimble and quick, ducked out of Stanach's reach and scrambled around Tyorl's cairn to Hornfel.

"I know where it is! I know where it is! Piper told me! He kind of suspected it all along, ever since you got your sword back. Me, I wanted to go get it right away, but he said no, he wasn't sure yet. It's been like an itch in his mind, he said. But he had to wait. Once he came here, he knew. He says he's been in the valley a few times before, but that was when he was alive and couldn't see things the way he does now that he's dead.

"You're never going to believe it! Hornfel—sir! I know where it is!"

Finn grabbed the old kender by the shoulders, lifting him right off his feet. "Damn, kender! Now what? Can't we have a moment's peace from you, even now?"

Hornfel, his eyes still on the Kingsword, whose light was dimming as he watched, motioned for the rangerlord to release Lavim. "What, Lavim? You know where what is?"

Lavim took a quick step away from Finn. He looked up at

Hornfel, his grin threatening to split his face. "Piper told me. I know where it is. I'd've told you sooner, but I didn't really know what he was talking about. He said that this business of being king regent wasn't for you. I said I wouldn't know about that, but you didn't really look much like a fellow who'd watch the store while the shopkeeper has his dinner. He said to tell you to bring Stormblade tonight, and he'd show me, because the Kingsword would know where it is. And I said, sure, I'd do that—"

Light as spider's feet, anticipation crawled along Stanach's spine. Isarn's last words whispered in his memory. "Lavim!" he shouted. "Out with it!"

Startled, Lavim jumped and turned wide eyes to Stanach. "I'm trying to tell Hornfel something really important here, young Stanach. Just once I'd like to get through something without being interrupted. Now," He turned back to Hornfel. "Where was I? Oh, right. I know where the Hammer of Kharas is."

Hornfel, his hand still on Stormblade's grip, stared at the kender with an aching mixture of disbelief and hope. "Where?" he whispered.

"Oh, not far from here at all." Lavim laughed. "Not very far at all.

"Of course, you'll have to send someone to get it. A few people probably 'cause you know that Kharas hid it real well. He made it invisible and guarded it with all kinds of traps and magic because he didn't want just anybody finding it. He wanted a real high king to find it. Someone like Duncan, you see. Someone like you."

"Where?" Hornfel whispered again.

Lavim smiled and pointed straight up.

Hornfel looked up at the sky. Stanach, following Hornfel's gaze, stared at the first faintly glittering stars and saw the red star that dwarves call an ember from the Forge.

No, he thought, oh, Lavim, what are you on about now?

Kelida, following Lavim's point exactly, gasped and touched Stanach's arm. Hauk grinned and nodded.

"Not the sky, Stanach." Kelida said, her voice shaking with wonder and sudden understanding. "The tomb."

Lavim nodded. "Right. Duncan's Tomb. Where else

would it be?"

Stanach looked at Hornfel, head bowed over the red-hearted Kingsword in his hand. He saw the High King of the Dwarves.

"Hornfel King," he whispered.

Hornfel raised his head, and Stanach dropped to his knee, suddenly moved to this rare gesture of homage. He spoke before he thought, but the words were heart-spoken none-the-less.

"Hornfel King, the Hammer is yours. I'll find it. I'll bring it back."

"Oh, yes!" Lavim cried, stepping quickly to Stanach's side. "It won't be hard at all. There's just a few little traps, some magic stuff and things like that. Piper knows all about it, and we'll be able to get in and out before you know it."

Stanach turned. "We?"

"You and me and Piper and—" Lavim looked at the rangers and Kelida. "And whoever else wants to come along. I figured everyone would because—well, what else are they going to do all by themselves here in Thorbardin while you and me and Piper are off getting the Hammer?

"You know how these things are, Stanach. It might take a day or two."

Full night settled on the Valley of the Thanes. Shadows became darkness. Stanach, sitting on the ground beside Tyorl's cairn, looked up at Kelida.

" 'A day or two,' he says." He crooked a wry smile. "Or says *Piper* says."

"Stanach, do you believe that?"

The dwarf shrugged. "There's no denying that Finn backs up his story of Piper guiding them through the defile. Lavim says that Piper guided Tyorl's crossbow when he killed the dragon." Stanach was silent for a long moment. "He was a fine shot, Tyorl. But—"

Kelida nodded. "It was dark. No one could have seen through that to aim so perfectly at the dragon's one vulnerable spot. It would be nice to think . . ."

Stanach sighed. It would be nice to think that Piper was, in some way, still with him. It would be nice to think—

DRAGONLANCE HEROES

Stanach drew back, scowling. "I'm going after the Hammer of Kharas on the word of a ghost-haunted kender?"

"We're going after the Hammer."

"We, eh?"

Kelida dropped to a seat beside him and did not answer the question. She ran a forefinger lightly along a cairn stone. After a moment she said, "I'll miss him."

"Aye, so will I."

Kelida turned suddenly, the color high in her cheeks. "Stanach, I said it in the Deep Warrens, I'll say it now: I go where Hauk goes. I go where you go. I will help you find the Hammer of Kharas."

Stanach looked up at the tomb suspended above the lake. The calm, icy waters feathered in a light breeze. Starlight softened the water's black surface to gray as it lapped gently against the shore.

Kelida covered his ruined hand gently with hers.

The dwarf rose and pulled her to her feet. "We'd best get back. I don't recall that Lavim ever gave Piper's flute to Hornfel. I've heard enough about what he's done with it, and there'll be no sleeping for me until it's safely in Hornfel's hands."

Kelida walked silently beside him as they left the Valley of the Thanes. When he paused at the gate into the mountain and looked back, Stanach saw the shadow of Duncan's Tomb, cast in Solinari's light, shrouding Tyorl's cairn.

The breeze became a low singing wind, and Stanach entered Thorbardin thinking of forests.

Tyorl's Song

The river wide flows through the forest.
Sunlight glistening at will,
Daystars around the edge
Of an image of Autumn.

Jeweled with woven patterns of ice,
Bare trees take on new beauty
Under a cold Winter's twilight.
Diamonds? Mere glass on a night such as this.

Alive with whispered promises,
New life is hidden in old thickets.
And young stir in their nests,
Turning a soft eye to Spring.

Rising with the dew burning from the leaves,
Walking through the heat of the midday sun,
A breeze dances through the glade
On a hot Summer's night.

Chorus:

Seasons of beauty,
A quiet land of peace
Under seclusion of the trees.
Find the beauty at your feet.

—Mark Varian

TALES OF GOTHIC HORROR BEYOND YOUR WILDEST SCREAMS!

Tapestry of Dark Souls
Elaine Bergstrom
The monks' hold over the Gathering Cloth, containing some of the vilest evils in Ravenloft, is slipping. The only hope is a strange youth, who will become either the monks' champion . . . or their doom.
ISBN 1-56076-571-2

Heart of Midnight
J. Robert King
Even before he'd drawn his first breath, Casimir had inherited his father's lycanthropic curse. Now the young werewolf must embrace his powers to ward off his own murder and gain revenge.
ISBN 1-56076-355-8

MORE TALES OF TERROR

Vampire of the Mists
Christie Golden
ISBN 1-56076-155-5

Dance of the Dead
Christie Golden
ISBN 1-56076-352-3

Knight of the Black Rose
James Lowder
ISBN 1-56076-156-3

Carnival of Fear
J. Robert King
ISBN 1-56076-628-X

Available now at book and hobby stores everywhere!

RAVENLOFT is a registered trademark owned by TSR, Inc. ©1994 TSR, Inc. All Rights Reserved.

FANTASY ADVENTURE

The long-awaited
sequel to the
Moonshae Trilogy
The
Druidhome
Trilogy

Douglas
Niles

Prophet of Moonshae   **Book One**
Danger stalks the island of Moonshae, where the people have
forsaken their goddess, the Earthmother. Only the faith and
courage of the daughter of the High King brings hope to the
endangered land.   ISBN 1-56076-319-1

The Coral Kingdom   **Book Two**
King Kendrick is held prisoner in the undersea city of the
sahuagin. His daughter must secure help from the elves of
Evermeet to save him during a confrontation in the dark
depths of the Sea of Moonshae.   ISBN 1-56076-332-9

The Druid Queen   **Book Three**
Threatened by an evil he cannot see, Tristan Kendrick rules
the Four Kingdoms while a sinister presence lurks within his
own family. At stake is the fate of the Moonshae Islands and
the unity of the Ffolk.   ISBN 1-56076-568-2

The Dark Horse Trilogy

By Mary H. Herbert

Follow the heroes of the Dark Horse Plains as they forge the destiny of their medieval world . . .

Valorian

Prequel to the best-selling *Dark Horse, Valorian* is the epic story of the sorcerer-hero who unites the horse clans against the tyrannical Tarnish Empire.
ISBN 1-56076-566-6

Dark Horse

Gabria, a young woman turned sorcerer-warrior, seeks revenge upon the vile sorcerer responsible for the massacre of her clan.
ISBN 0-88038-916-8

Lightning's Daughter

In the sequel to *Dark Horse*, Gabria and her people must conquer a magical creature bent on destroying the Dark Horse Plains.
ISBN 1-56076-078-8

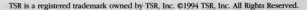

FANTASY ADVENTURE

The Dark Elf Trilogy
By R. A. Salvatore
The New York Times best-selling author

**Featuring Drizzt Do'Urden, hero of *The Legacy*,
Starless Night, and *The Icewind Dale Trilogy***

Homeland
Book One

Journey to Menzoberranzan, the subterranean
metropolis of the drow. Possessing a sense of
honor beyond the scope of his kinsmen, young
Drizzt must decide – can he continue to tolerate
an unscrupulous society?
ISBN 0-88038-905-2

Exile
Book Two

The tunnel-mazes of the Underdark
challenge all who tread there. Exiled from
Menzoberranzan, Drizzt battles for a new
home. Meanwhile, he must watch for signs of
pursuit – the drow are not a forgiving race!
ISBN 0-88038-920-6

Sojourn
Book Three

Drizzt emerges in the harsh light of Toril's
surface. The drow begins a sojourn through a
world entirely unlike his own and learns that
acceptance among the surface-dwellers does
not come easily.
ISBN 1-56076-047-8

On Sale Now

DragonLance® Saga

THE HISTORIC SAGA OF THE DWARVEN CLANS
Dwarven Nations Trilogy
Dan Parkinson

The Covenant of the Forge   **Volume One**
As the drums of Balladine thunder forth, calling humans to trade with the dwarves of Thorin, Grayfen, a human struck by the magic of the Graystone, infiltrates the dwarven stronghold, determined to annihilate the dwarves and steal their treasure.   ISBN 1-56076-558-5

Hammer and Axe   **Volume Two**
The dwarven clans unite against the threat of encroaching humans and create the fortress of Thorbardin. But old rivalries are not easily forgotten, and the resulting political intrigue brings about catastrophic change.   ISBN 1-56076-627-1

The Swordsheath Scroll   **Volume Three**
Despite the stubborn courage of the dwarves, the Wilderness War ends as a no-win. The Swordsheath Scroll is signed, and the dwarves join the elves of Qualinesti to build a symbol of peace among the races: Pax Tharkas.   ISBN 1-56076-686-7